WITHDRAWN

Phantom Limb

Books by Dennis Palumbo

The Daniel Rinaldi Mysteries
Mirror Image
Fever Dream
Night Terrors
Phantom Limb

Other Fiction
From Crime to Crime (short story collection)
City Wars

Nonfiction
Writing from the Inside Out

Phantom Limb

A Daniel Rinaldi Mystery

Dennis Palumbo

Poisoned Pen Press

Poisoned Pen Press
6962 E. First Ave., Ste. 103
Scottsdale, AZ 85251
www.poisonedpenpress.com
info@poisonedpenpress.com

Printed in the United States of America

To my parents,
With love—

Acknowledgments

The author thanks the following people for their continued help and support:

Ken Atchity, friend and literary manager;

Annette Rogers, my editor, as well as Robert Rosenwald and Barbara Peters, founders of Poisoned Pen Press, for their creative insights and ongoing encouragement;

Elizabeth Weld, Suzan Baroni, Tiffany White, Beth Deveny, and Pete Zrioka, also at Poisoned Pen, for their professionalism and enthusiasm;

And, as always, my long-suffering friends and colleagues, too numerous to mention, but with special appreciation to Hoyt Hilsman, Bobby Moresco, Norm Stephens, Richard Stayton, Rick Setlowe, Bob Masello, Garry Shandling, Jim Denova, Michael Harbadin, Chi-Li Wong, Claudia Sloan, Dave Congalton, Charlotte Alexander, Mark Evanier, Bob Corn-Revere, Lolita Sapriel, Mark Baker, Mark Schorr, Bill Shick, Thomas B. Sawyer, Fred Golan, Dick Lochte, Al Abramson, Bill O'Hanlon, Sandy Tolan, Stephen Jay Schwartz, and Dr. Robert Stolorow;

To Carey Rupert, for suggesting the shortest route for Dr. Rinaldi to get home;

And, most importantly, to my wife, Lynne, and son, Daniel. (And a special thanks to Daniel for his much-needed technical assistance and advice!)

"You don't need a weatherman to know which way the wind blows."

—Bob Dylan

Chapter One

The last time I saw Lisa Campbell, she was naked.

That was almost thirty years ago, when I was in junior high and she was the latest Hot Young Thing, smiling invitingly out at me—and thousands of other lonely guys—from the pages of *Playboy Magazine*. Barely nineteen, sprawled seductively across rumpled satin sheets. Every horny adolescent's fantasy. Perfect breasts, perfect ass, perfect teeth.

Now, as she stood in my office waiting room, cashmere sweater folded neatly over her arm, I had to admit that the years since had taken their toll. Her face—though still comely, fine-boned—was lined, leather-tanned. Framed by thick chestnut-brown hair, lightly streaked with silver. Strained, weary eyes burned behind fashionable wire-rimmed glasses.

She'd been standing at the waiting room's single window when I came out to greet her. Her still-shapely body turned away from me, she stared out at the cool light of early spring. Five floors up from Forbes Avenue, the view included the University of Pittsburgh's urban campus—its gabled buildings, chain stores and local hangouts—as well as the new green shoots on the venerable maples and oaks lining the sidewalks. Plus the familiar cacophony of car horns, downshifting semis, and shouting students crossing against the streetlight, hurrying to make their last classes of the afternoon.

At first, Lisa didn't seem to register me. Then, as if reluctant to pull herself from the sights and sounds beyond the window, she turned to face me.

I felt her shrewd, guarded gaze as we shook hands. Her undisguised appraisal of my looks, my clothes, my apparent social status. I returned the favor, taking in her designer-label blouse, slacks, and heels, her five-hundred-dollar haircut, the expensive diamond bracelet and matching wedding ring.

"Pleased to meet you, Mrs. Harland," I said. "I'm Daniel Rinaldi."

"Obviously." Her lips tightened. "And don't use my goddamn married name. Nobody else does. I'll always be Lisa Campbell."

I nodded stiffly, then led her into my office.

I knew her story, of course. At least the public version. Most people here in Pittsburgh and environs did, too. Especially in her hometown of Waterson, about a hundred miles east of the city. Her career journey, from small-town beauty contestant to *Playboy* Playmate to sexy film actress, had been a long, well-publicized one. Accompanied by the shrill carping of Waterson's outraged local press, excommunication from her church, and the painful yet predictable estrangement from her pious, deeply conservative family.

It didn't help that, once she'd moved to Hollywood, her acting career consisted mostly of roles in low-budget horror films, in which she was frequently naked, and invariably tortured and killed. She also developed a reputation as a reliably freaky party animal, clubbing every night with the rich and trendy, showing up late and disoriented for work, sleeping with the usual mix of celebrities and Eurotrash.

Until her very public second divorce, a protracted and ugly drug scandal, and a series of embarrassing box office flops pushed her out of the glare of the tabloid spotlight and—seemingly overnight—into the purgatory of semi-obscurity.

At least, that was how her story was told in a two-part feature the *Post-Gazette* ran on Lisa when, almost a decade ago, she abruptly returned to her hometown. "With her tail between her legs," as one self-satisfied neighbor had put it.

According to the paper, Lisa claimed she tried to reconcile with her family, but was flatly rejected. As broken in spirit as she was financially, Lisa had no choice but to seek work here in the city. After six weeks, she landed a job as a clerical assistant in the CEO's suite at Harland Industries, a Fortune 500 favorite. After six months, she landed the CEO himself.

Lisa Campbell and Charles P. Harland, thirty years her senior, were married in a private ceremony in Barbados. Accompanying the feature story was a series of photos of the happy couple, now back in Pittsburgh, relaxing in the expansive, manicured gardens of the billionaire's gated estate in tony Fox Chapel. A few people thought the marriage was romantic—a damaged, unhappy woman's dream come true. Most thought it was a scandal. Or else a cruel joke played on a deluded old man.

Regardless, in the years since, Lisa and Harland had become a fixture among the city's wealthy and powerful, hosting charity events, attending lavish premieres, jetting off to vacations in exotic locales. Blending in quite easily with the heirs of the Mellons, the Scaifes, and the Carnegies, until, apparently, some undisclosed illness landed Harland in a wheelchair.

Since this was hardly my crowd, everything I knew about Lisa and her life nowadays came from the occasional news item that caught my eye, or some piece of gossip excitedly shared with me by one of my more starstruck patients.

Which was why now, ushering the sharp-tongued, middle-aged woman into my office, it was difficult to match her name to that of the seductive young girl I recalled from the magazine. To be honest, the present-day Lisa Campbell looked like any number of proud, arch women in designer clothes who stride purposely through newly gentrified Shadyside, kids long since grown and flown, resigned to the inattention of their workaholic husbands, defined by their jewelry.

Lisa paused before taking a seat, giving my office the same kind of cool appraisal with which she'd favored me. The antique marble-top desk, cherry wood cabinets, my battered Tumi brief-case. Books jammed into wall shelves, psych journals piled in more or less tidy stacks in the corners. Another broad picture window, slightly opened to let in the late March breeze. The pale, diffused sunlight. The muffled sounds of the street life below.

Finally, sitting upright on the chair opposite mine, she composed herself into a picture of grim determination. Jaw set. Legs demurely crossed. Only her clear hazel eyes, blinking, betrayed any anxiety.

A long silence.

"I must admit," I said finally, "I was surprised when you called for an appointment. How do you know about me?"

"Don't be so fucking coy, okay, Doc? It's very unattractive in a man." Her gaze narrowed. "And I might as well warn you up front, I got a real mouth on me."

"Duly noted."

"The thing is, I know about you because *everyone* knows about you. The famous trauma shrink."

"I'm not a shrink. I'm a clinical psychologist."

"Either way, you must have one hell of a publicist."

"Sorry to disappoint you, but—"

"No shit? That *is* a surprise, Dr. Rinaldi. Given how often you've been on the news…"

"Not by choice, I assure you. Last couple years, it's mostly been a case of wrong place, wrong time."

She shrugged, unconvinced.

"Whatever. Besides, I had my people do the customary due diligence before choosing you. Well, my *husband's* people. So I know all about you."

I risked a smile. "Really?"

"Really."

She reached into the Louis Vuitton bag on her lap, withdrew a single piece of paper and peered down at it through the bottom half of her progressive lenses.

"Let's see. I know your father was a cop and an alcoholic, and that your mother died when you were very young. In your late teens, you became an amateur boxer, God knows why. Golden Gloves, Pan Am Games. Looks like you didn't set any records, though." She cleared her throat. "Then you went to Pitt, making it all the way through grad school. The first one in your family to even *go* to college. Though by the time you got your PhD in psychology, your father, poor bastard, had passed away, too. Cirrhosis of the liver."

She glanced sharply up at me then, obviously to gauge my reaction. Whether due to my clinical experience or some innate stubbornness on my part, I didn't give her any. Still, though my face was composed, I could feel the blood pounding in my ears.

"I know you were married," she went on reading from her notes, "and that you and your wife got mugged one night and she was shot. You *both* were, but she died and you didn't. So you kinda went around the bend. Survivor guilt and all that. Now you're a consultant with the Pittsburgh Police, treating victims of violent crime. Last couple years, your involvement in some high-profile cases landed you on the national news." She sniffed, looked back up at me. "My opinion, you're about ten minutes into your fifteen minutes of fame."

After which, she casually folded the paper in half, dropped it back in her bag. "I miss anything?"

I'd felt my chest tighten, the dull pang of a rising anger, as she'd calmly laid out my story like it was some anecdote at a dinner party. Then, forcing myself, I exhaled slowly. Giving myself time to carefully choose my words.

"No, Lisa. You pretty much got it right."

"My husband's people are very good. Hell, they're fucking bloodhounds. The final report ran to fifteen pages. But I just read you the highlights. None of the more...well...intimate details."

"I appreciate your discretion."

She snapped her bag closed. "Look, I don't give a shit what you do in your private life. But a woman in my position has to be careful. I have to know who the hell I'm dealing with."

"I can understand that."

"Good. By the way, they ever catch the prick who did it? Killed your wife?"

I shook my head. "Just some kid. Seemed coked out of his mind. Probably needed money for drugs."

"Christ, who doesn't at that age? Though I never had to shoot anyone to score. Usually a blow job worked just fine."

"I assume you're talking about your time in Hollywood. In the movie business."

"Assume what you want. Though you and I both know I could walk two blocks up Forbes Avenue, right now in the middle of the day, and carry out that exact same transaction. In some back alley, behind some bar. Cops know, everybody knows. The same holds true in my hometown. Sleepy little Waterson. Cheerleaders blowing jocks for a dime bag. It's American as apple pie."

I sat forward in my chair. Let my own eyes narrow. It didn't take a psychologist to know Lisa Campbell was in pain, and keeping me at a distance with hard banter. With attitude.

Yet here she was, in my office. Which meant she wanted something. Needed something. From me.

"Look, Lisa, obviously you're hurting, or in trouble, and I want to help. Has something happened to you?"

She placed a fist against her chest, over her heart.

"Happened?" As her face paled.

"Something bad? It doesn't have to be recent. Maybe something that happened when you were out west, or even earlier. In childhood…"

"Has something *happened* to me?" Voice rising. Shrill, choked. "*Has something happened?*"

Her hazel eyes had gone black, lasering into mine. A fierce, unbelieving, agonized look.

"Jesus, Lisa, I'm sorry if I—"

Then, with a slow, deep breath, she lowered her head. Let her fist drop to her lap, fingers still clenched.

"Lisa…?"

She just shook her head. I shut up.

Another thick, uncomfortable silence followed. Filled only by the rise and fall of the breeze sifting through the foliage beyond my window. The gentle rustling of leaves and branches. And nothing else. The street traffic below, for an odd, brief moment, suddenly hushed. Stilled. As though holding its breath.

"Okay, listen." Her eyes meeting mine again. Voice even, almost flat. "I've made all the financial arrangements. I have the means at home, in my desk. A bottle of pills." She glanced at her watch. "It's a little after four. These sessions are what?—forty-five, fifty minutes?"

"Fifty."

She considered this.

"All right then, Doc. Here's the deal: I plan to kill myself at seven o'clock tonight. Which means you have fifty minutes to talk me out of it."

Chapter Two

It took me a few seconds to fully comprehend Lisa's words, to convince myself I'd heard her correctly. When I did, I felt a flood of conflicting emotions.

Because what she'd said certainly surprised and alarmed me, challenged me in terms of how best to help her. But to be honest—and despite my best efforts—it also angered me.

And so, without a moment's thought, I blurted out, "Why wait till seven o'clock? Why don't you just die now?"

Lisa started. "What did you say?"

My only reply was to repeat the question, since I had no goddamn idea what I was doing. Other than stalling for time.

"I said, why don't you die now?"

She stared, at a loss. "Are you trying to be funny?"

"I don't think so."

I literally *did not know* what words were going to come out of my mouth, even as a vague, fairly ludicrous idea began forming in my mind.

"I just think, since you're planning to do it anyway later tonight, we might as well take advantage of the time we have now. Let's at least get *something* out of this session."

"I'm fucking *serious*, Doctor. Why the hell aren't *you*?"

Her own anger flamed, sheeting her face. I ignored her.

"Would you be willing to try something?" I asked.

"That depends." Though clearly still rankled, she seemed more curious than suspicious at this point.

Then, as reasonably as I could, I suggested that she lie down on the floor on her back.

"You're kidding, right?" Her voice grew an edge.

"Not at all."

She gave me a grim, openly hostile look.

"Are you afraid to try it?" Pushing her now.

"I'm not afraid of anything."

I folded my arms. "Then prove it."

We merely stared at each other for a long moment. Then, grunting from the effort, she got off the chair and somewhat stiffly lay on her back on the office carpet.

"Okay," I said. "You're dead."

She frowned up at me. "I'm dead? What the fuck—?"

I didn't answer, but instead took two chairs, a small lamp table, and the piles of psych journals from different corners of the room, arranging them in a vaguely rectangular pattern around her on the floor.

"Your coffin," I informed her, taking my seat again.

She let out a long breath. "This is such bull—"

I interrupted her. "Who's viewing you in the coffin?"

"I'm supposed to *answer* that? Christ, I *hated* this stuff in those acting classes I had to—"

"Humor me. Who's at your funeral?"

A long pause. "My family, of course. What's left of them."

"You mean your parents? Siblings?"

"I'm an only child. As for my parents…I guess you don't read the papers, do you, Doc? Or watch TV. Or go online."

"I know you're estranged."

"We don't speak, if that's what you mean. They slammed the door in my face when I came crawling back to Waterson. To beg their forgiveness, try to fix things with them. Turns out, their pastor ordered them to shun me. In this day and age. Shunned! Like a fucking leper."

I said nothing.

"I guess," she went on, "from their point of view I *am* a leper. Corrupted in mind and body. Damned."

She frowned. "Been that way for years. You know, back in my Hollywood days, when I started making money, I used to send them checks. They were always returned, torn into little pieces. Then, after I came back here and married old man Harland—the fifteenth-richest man in the state, by the way; you could look it up—I sent them a *humongous* check. I'm talking a shitload of money. Plus the nicest *mea culpa* letter I could write."

"What happened?"

"Both the check *and* my letter came back, torn to pieces." A short, bitter laugh. "Praise the Lord."

◇◇◇

Outside, the wind had risen, pushing harder against the trees. Reducing the familiar, almost comforting noise of street traffic to a thin, barely audible hum. I tried to remember if some early spring shower was in the forecast.

Lisa was rubbing her eyes, glasses riding up and down on her knuckles. Then she very deliberately adjusted them again.

I leaned forward slightly, looking down at her. "When you mentioned your family, viewing you in the coffin…"

"I was talking about my daughter Gail. She still lives back in L.A. with her husband, Tim. He's a wannabe-actor. Gay, too, but the stupid shit doesn't know it."

Another bitter laugh. Then, without my suggesting it, she closed her eyes. Her breathing slowed. She seemed to be consciously, gradually, allowing herself to "die."

Lisa wasn't an idiot. She'd quickly realized that I'd asked her to imagine lying in her coffin so that she could make real her suicidal ideation. It allowed her defensive armor to go down, her sharp wit to take a recess. In other words, "dying" gave her the freedom to express genuine, unfiltered feelings. A passive, unhurried way to…let go.

"What's your daughter doing?" I said at last. "Right now, at your funeral?"

"Crying. Those big sobs, like when she was little. Like she can't catch her breath."

"What about Tim?"

"Tim's looking down at me, not doing a fucking thing. But I know damned well what he's feeling."

"What's that?"

"Guilt. And it's about time. I had to *die* before he'd finally feel it, though. Ungrateful son of a bitch."

I saw the yearning on her face. And took a chance.

"You sure he's feeling guilty?"

A resigned sigh. "Probably not. Tim's probably *glad* I'm dead. Now he doesn't have to pretend anymore to give a shit about me, just to make sure my husband keeps paying their bills. For the new house, new car, the kids' private schools…"

She opened her eyes. "Yeah, he's glad I'm gone. Especially since he figures my husband will keep supporting them. Tim would throw a public hissy fit if the money stopped coming, and even *he's* smart enough to know Harland Industries couldn't tolerate it. All that bad publicity."

"But you clearly see that your daughter's grieving."

"Only because I *wanted* to. *She* doesn't give a damn about me, either. I don't believe those tears for a minute."

"You don't?"

"Hell, no. But I…Look, truth is, I want them both to be *sorry* for how they've treated me. But you know what? I bet they won't. I bet they'll just go on, relieved not to have to deal with me anymore. Well, fuck *both* of them."

Lisa folded her arms across her chest. A long sigh, as she stared now at the ceiling.

"Shit, I'll probably even *die* for nothing, too."

I took a measured pause.

"Lisa, when you talked about your family viewing your coffin, you didn't mention Charles Harland. Where's your husband in this scenario?"

She smirked. "Might as well ask, 'Where's Waldo?' I mean, you *know* the little bastard's in the picture somewhere, but…"

"Can you be more specific?"

"I'll be clear as crystal, Doc. I'm not interested in talking about my marriage. I already know what everybody thinks: I married the old guy for his money. Which I did. End of story."

"Got it."

For now, I thought.

◇◇◇

We spent the rest of the session this way, Lisa on her back on the floor, glancing over at me on my chair as we talked.

Despite some initial reluctance, she gave me a brief overview of her childhood history. Her father's physical and verbal abuse, interwoven with Old Testament rants about the sins of mankind and the imminent End of Days. Her mother's lifeless, submissive piety, devotion to church work, and profound, never-discussed depression. Lisa was only slightly more forthcoming about her own painful adolescence as a chubby outcast in conservative, blue-collar Waterson, Pennsylvania.

"Ever been to Waterson, Doc?"

"Afraid not."

"Even when I was a kid, it wasn't much of a town. Nothing but prudes and rubes. County Fair was the biggest event of the year. But, hell, it's even worse now. In *this* economy? Place is like Mayberry on life support."

I tried to interject, to ask some follow-up questions about her upbringing. But she cut me off.

"Forget all that therapy crap, Doc. Trust me, I've been through it all before, with a dozen therapists. Besides, we don't have the time." A grim smile. "In case you forgot, we got kind of a ticking clock going here, right?"

"Right."

In brisk, emotionless sentences, she sketched out the details of her arrival in Hollywood after leaving home at eighteen, her big acting break in a low-budget slasher film that turned into an unlikely hit, and her first marriage a year later to one of the movie's financial backers. A man twice her age, who turned out to be a drug addict, gambler, and both physically and sexually abusive.

"I'll skip the gory details," she said, "but he was into a lot of weird, kinky shit. One of his favorite things involved duct tape and a tennis ball. He wouldn't stop 'til I screamed."

Seeing the pained, sympathetic look that must have crossed my face, she let out a short laugh.

"Sorry if I shocked you, Doc."

I paused, carefully considering my next words.

"Actually, I'm okay with how I reacted. I mean, how would you feel if nothing you said impacted me at all?"

She smiled. "Surprised."

I have to admit, I was feeling a bit disoriented. Not that I hadn't dealt with suicidal patients before. But Lisa Campbell was different—sardonic, deliberately provocative. As though daring me to treat her, understand her.

No. There was something else. It occurred to me suddenly that perhaps my role in our dynamic was to *try* to help her, but *ultimately to fail.* Confirming her belief that she was somehow defective, permanently damaged. Beyond saving. Beyond hope.

However, before I could give this half-formed notion further thought, Lisa turned her face away from mine and went on with her narrative.

This time I merely listened, keeping in mind Martin Buber's sage advice: "People need to be heard, not answered."

After divorcing her sadistic husband, Lisa fell into what she described as "the usual drugs, sex, and rock 'n' roll" of high-octane Hollywood life.

"At first, I only slept with A-list actors. We'd go to these insane parties, girls like me. New starlets or whatever. We were all Grade-A pussy, believe me, and you just got put in the rotation. Horn-dogs like Beatty, Nicholson, Jagger—though Warren could be sweet. But it was all so fucked up….

"I remember, toward the end, waking up one morning next to *People Magazine*'s 'Sexiest Man Alive,'—at least for *that* year, you ought to see his sorry ass *now*—and we're both covered in white powder. And I'm thinking, what are we doing in the snow, are we in Aspen or someplace? Man, I never saw so much coke in my life. I was so out of it, I just lay there, naked, watching the sexiest man alive, on his hands and knees, scooping all the blow he could find into one of the hotel's laundry bags. So much for afterglow."

Her promising acting career had suffered as well. Given her youth and inexperience, it wasn't surprising that she let her agents put her in one lurid, pointless film after another.

"But at least I got to travel, see places all over the world. I remember, on this one shoot…"

Suddenly her voice faded, and she swiveled her head, away from my sight. Gaze drifting lazily to my office window.

"What are you thinking about now, Lisa? You seem to be going off somewhere…in your head.…"

She turned back. "You mean, dissociating?"

At my quizzical look, she smiled again. "Impressed? I played a psychiatric nurse once early in my career. Before she was gang-raped and strangled, I got to do a scene where she worked with a patient who had these dissociative episodes. See? Movies *can* be educational."

"Okay, nurse," I said. "When you 'dissociated,' where did you go? What were you thinking about?"

"Don't get all excited, it's not that sexy. I was thinking about the one good thing that came out of that first marriage. My daughter, Gail. A great kid, back when she *was* a kid. I used to take her on location with me. We used to—"

She stopped abruptly, blinking up at the ceiling.

"Yes?" I said quietly.

"Hey, I said forget all that therapy stuff, remember? It's not why I'm here. That was a long time ago. When Gail was a kid. When *I* was a kid. Now we're both…different. I'm just old. And she's a mean, entitled bitch with two kids of her own, stuck in L.A., married to a failed actor who works at Denny's and flirts with the busboys." She frowned. "The only thing those two are good for is spending my husband's money. Okay, maybe it's just chump change to *him*, but still it galls me."

Lisa reached up and removed her glasses, holding them in her hand on her stomach. Her voice was listless.

"Anyway, unless you've been living in a cave, you know the rest of the story. Stalled acting career. Short second marriage to a studio exec who was into kiddie porn. Now I was a single mother raising a rebellious teenager, dreaming of making movies again someday. Years of struggle, rejection. All that money I'd made… gone. Just gone. Then things *really* turned to shit."

By this point, she was blinking back tears.

"I got busted. Twice, for dealing and using. My drug addiction meant losing custody of Gail to my ex. No irony there, eh? In and out of rehab, all the time trying get my daughter back. Which I finally did."

"How?"

"Easy. Suddenly her father was engaged to some skank who wanted kids of her own, and didn't want a brat from somebody else's eggs messing up the Norman Rockwell family portrait."

"Is that when you retired from films?"

Lisa gave me another of those withering looks with which I was quickly becoming familiar.

"Is that what you call it when nobody returns your calls, or can find time for lunch, or pretends they don't recognize you on the street? Then, yeah, I fucking retired."

I was about to follow up with another question when I glanced at the table clock. Lisa's eyes followed mine.

"You're *shitting* me! Is that it?"

I nodded slowly. "I know, and I'm sorry. There's still so much we have to cover if I'm to help you. We never even got to the question of *why?* Why you want to end your life…"

"And whose fault is that? I said you had fifty minutes to talk me out of it, and you didn't."

"Well, then we have a problem." I looked at her as directly and intently as I could. "Because our time is up."

She regarded me skeptically.

"So suddenly you're a hard-ass? You're going to just let me go home and *do* it? Without even finding out why? Thanks a lot."

With that, she slowly got to her feet, straightening her clothes with great care.

"Wait a minute, Lisa."

No reply. Glasses back on, she made a point of looking away from me, toward the door.

I took a breath. Actually, since Lisa was my last patient for the day, my next hour was free. But I was still going on pure instinct, plus a belief that she and I had made a real connection. And that the conventional structure of treatment scheduling was crucial to working with her. To providing a firm though supportive foundation. So I suggested something else.

"Lisa," I asked gently, "would you like to come back tomorrow, same time, and die again?"

"Are you serious?"

"Absolutely."

She considered this for a long moment. "What the hell, why not?" Followed by a wry, mirthless chuckle.

Not exactly a ringing endorsement of our work together, but I'd take what I could get. I knew that what I'd done with Lisa was clinically outrageous, therapeutically questionable. Maybe even actionable. Yet as far as I could tell, she was no longer intent on killing herself.

At least, not today.

Still, as I walked her out through the empty waiting room, toward the hall door, I figured I'd call Lisa in a few hours to confirm tomorrow's appointment, and to assess again for suicidal ideation. But my clinical intuition—my gut—told me that my new patient was out of danger, at least for the foreseeable future.

My gut was wrong.

He was standing right there when I opened the door.

Big, taller than me. Filling the doorway. In a black jacket and jeans. Eyes hidden by dark glasses.

He had something in his hand. Raising it…

I thought I heard Lisa scream, though it could have been the soundless, panicked screech exploding from my brain as the thing in his hand came down.

And my head seemed to split open.

And then everything—my life, my world—was gone.

Chapter Three

An eternity or two passed. And then I heard the voice. Hard, gruff, commanding. With a smoker's rasp.

"Hey, looks like he's comin' around...."

A sudden nausea gripped me as I blinked, repeatedly, willing my eyes to open.

When they finally did, I found myself on the sofa in my office waiting room. Staring up into the ruddy, scowling face of Detective Sergeant Harry Polk.

"So, Rinaldi, you *are* alive...." He jerked a thumb over his shoulder, indicating a youngish EMT in hospital greens leaning in behind him. "Which means I owe Hornbeck here twenty bucks. I had you figgered for a goner."

I managed a faint smile. "Tough break, Harry."

Polk muttered something unintelligible and stood to his full height, rubbing the small of his back with both hands. As always, the veteran Pittsburgh PD detective looked aggrieved. Put upon. As though he always wished he were anywhere but here—no matter where "here" was.

I'd come to know Harry Polk pretty well, having first met him when I became involved in the Wingfield investigation some years back. Though he was uncomfortable with my being a psychologist, let alone a consultant to the Department, we had arrived over time at a kind of uneasy truce.

Polk was a burly, barrel-chested cop of the old school, with thinning hair and a drinker's bleary squint. Now, vainly trying to straighten the wrinkles from his ill-fitting gray suit, he gave me a last, dubious look before stepping back to let the EMT take his place at my side.

Lean and wiry, with a tuft of curly reddish-brown hair, Hornbeck unspooled his stethoscope and gave me a professional smile. Then he methodically checked my vitals, giving me another two or three minutes to come fully into consciousness.

Which may have been a mistake, because suddenly I was aware of the searing pain at the side of my skull. Aware, too, of the memory of the big man standing in the corridor outside my office when I opened the door.

Then I remembered something else. Lisa Campbell.

Gasping from the effort, I tried to get up on an elbow. Another mistake, as a second volley of nausea coursed through me. I struggled not to pass out.

Hornbeck raised his hand, as though to restrain me, but I batted it away.

"Harry! There was someone with me before. When I was attacked. A patient—"

"Yeah, we know, Doc. Lisa Campbell. Why the hell you think we're here?"

I looked past where Polk stood by the waiting room window, wearily shifting his weight from one foot to the other. Saw that the sky outside had grown dark, blue-black. Heard the whistling of an ominous wind as it threaded the trees below.

"Wait a minute. You *knew* Lisa had an appointment with me?"

"Her husband did. Charles Fuckin' Harland, for Christ's sake. So when she didn't come home by sundown, at least he knew the last place she'd been was your office."

"The last…?"

"Lisa's missin', Doc. Harland says he tried all her phone numbers, then called the Department." A wry look. "To be exact, he called the chief. *At home*. Precinct sent me over here. And what do I find? Your suite door open, and you lyin' on the floor here. Unconscious. That's when I got Dispatch to send an EMT."

I shook my head, trying to clear it. Mistake number three. Even that small a gesture sent a spike of pain down my neck.

"I wouldn't make any sudden moves." Hornbeck's voice was smooth, confident. "You got hit pretty hard, sir."

I slowly reached up, gingerly running my fingers over the damp, raised lump.

"It's a real goose egg, all right," Hornbeck went on. "It'll hurt like hell for a day or two, but you'll be okay."

Polk suddenly cleared his throat. "Thanks for givin' him the once-over, Hornbeck. Appreciate it."

The young EMT got the hint. Grinning, he shoved his coiled stethoscope in his coat pocket and made for the door.

"Gentlemen," was all he said as he went out.

Polk took a step toward me again, at the same time putting on a pair of thin latex evidence gloves.

"Your patient—Lisa Campbell—looks like she was your last for the day."

"That's right, Harry."

"So what happened?"

I hesitated. Normally, of course, I wouldn't disclose the name of someone who was in treatment with me. But since it was clear that Harry already knew her identity, the point was moot.

"I was seeing her out. When I opened the door to the hall, some guy was standing there. Had something in his hand. Must've been what he hit me with."

The sergeant nodded. Then, with a grunt, squatted and picked up a small leather pouch. I was still so out of it, I hadn't noticed it lying on the carpet a few feet away. Near the opened door.

Polk turned back to me, hefting it in the bowl of his thick, latex-gloved fingers. A small grin.

"Guy musta dropped it after he dropped *you*, Doc."

"What is it?"

"Your basic sap. Real classic. Lead-weighted, most likely. My old precinct captain used to hand 'em out to us, back in the day. Made suspects a helluva lot more cooperative. Not bad when it came to breakin' up bar fights, either." He gazed at it with something like affection. "Too *un*-PC for our modern Department now, o' course."

Wincing, I once again traced the lump in my skull.

"Trust me, it still gets the job done."

"Damn right. Ya see 'em around sometimes, even nowadays. Persuader-of-choice for hired muscle sent to collect for some loan shark. Good for knees, elbows. I mean, ya don't wanna kill the guy, ya just want him to pay up. Right?"

"If you say so. How long have I been out, anyway?"

"Three, four hours at least, given the time frame we're workin' from. Can you describe the guy?"

"Big. Leather jacket. Jeans. Dark glasses."

"In other words, pretty much like every other goddamn perp in the world."

"So I didn't get a good look at him before he clobbered me. My bad. Right now, I'm more worried about Lisa."

Just then, Polk's cell rang. He tugged it out of his jacket pocket, clicked it on.

"Yeah?…Uh-huh. Yeah, figgers…Okay, thanks, Jerry. Be right down."

He hung up, sighed heavily. As I awkwardly got to my feet.

"What's happening, Harry? Is it about Lisa?"

Sergeant Polk's face had turned the color of wet sand.

"Harland just got a call with the ransom demand. Like I knew goddamn well he would. Lisa Campbell's been kidnapped."

Chapter Four

After locking away my patient files, I followed Harry Polk out of my office just as three CSU techs were stepping from the elevator. All wearing blue jumpsuits and gloves, the lead guy carrying a large zippered case. His name tag read "Rizzo."

He and Polk exchanged greetings in the middle of the hallway, after which Harry handed over the sap. Rizzo slid it smoothly into a small plastic evidence bag.

Polk indicated the trio with a dismissive wave.

"Is this everybody?"

Rizzo shook his head. "Naw, we got another team in the building's parking garage. Workin' the lady's car."

One of the other techs whistled appreciatively. "I seen it, Sarge. Porsche Turbo Carrera. Silver, fully loaded. Sweet!"

Polk stifled him with an icy stare. "Just keep your mind on your job, okay? 'Cause in case you clowns haven't heard, this is high-profile shit. As in, our asses are on the line."

Rizzo sniffed. "Not for nothin', Harry, but our captain already read us the riot act. So don't you worry 'bout it."

Polk nodded glumly, obviously unconvinced, then headed down the hall toward the elevator. I was right on his heels, only glancing back to watch the three CSU techs entering my office suite. Soon, I knew, the door would be crisscrossed with crime scene tape.

I tried to get Polk to say more about Lisa Campbell as we

waited for the elevator. But he merely peeled the latex gloves from his hand and rolled them into a ball.

Then, turning, he made a point of showing me his fist as he squeezed the latex tight.

"See, Doc? Hand strength's comin' back."

"Glad to hear it."

Harry Polk had been wounded some months back, during the manhunt for that renegade shooter in the Jessup case, and his recuperation had been slower than his doctor had promised. At least that was the scuttlebutt coming out of the Old County Building, headquarters of the Pittsburgh PD.

Though I hadn't seen Harry since that time, Angela Villanova—my distant cousin, and the Department's community liaison officer—always kept me up-to-date with the latest news and gossip. This was in addition to her official role, which included referring certain crime victims to me for treatment. People who may have survived the crime itself—the carjacking, rape, home invasion—but who still suffered the psychological after-effects of the experience. Symptoms usually associated with post-traumatic stress disorder. Anxiety, depression, recurrent nightmares of the horrific event. As well as a pervasive dread about some future violence. A kind of ongoing, soul-deadening vigilance…

As Lisa Campbell had correctly pointed out, reading from her notes during our session, people like that are my specialty.

I rode in silence with Polk in the elevator down to street level. I knew it was my reputation with this type of patient that had drawn Lisa to me in the first place. Though I didn't know what personal trauma had brought her to my door, it had obviously triggered enough emotional pain to prompt thoughts of suicide. Serious thoughts, according to Lisa herself. She'd had a plan, the pills, even a deadline—seven p.m. Tonight.

I glanced at my watch. Two hours ago now, I thought.

When I'd walked her out of my office, I felt confident I'd bought myself—and Lisa—some time. That I'd managed to forestall, at least for one more day, her threat of suicide.

The awful irony was that now something new, perhaps far more emotionally and physically devastating, had happened. Something neither of us could have anticipated.

Now my concern wasn't about her possible suicide. It was my fear of what might happen to her at the hands of her kidnapper.

Lisa was the wife of one of the state's richest, most powerful men. Regardless of the size of the ransom, abducting her in broad daylight was a risky, audacious act. By someone who was either foolish or desperate, perhaps both. Or else coldly, dangerously bold.

From my years of consulting with the police, I'd learned at least one thing about such kidnappings.

They rarely ended well.

Polk and I stepped through the double doors of my building's front entrance and out onto the sidewalk. The night had deepened, laced with a cool, assertive wind. Tree branches sawed each other overhead, and some loose pages from today's *Pitt News* skipped along the pavement.

A few passersby—mostly students in Panthers sweatshirts and shiny windbreakers—gave us wary, suspicious glances as we crossed to where Polk's unmarked sedan waited at the curb. The CSU van was parked behind it, in a red zone, while a black-and-white unit had its nose lodged between the two vehicles. A lone patrolman stood out in the middle of Forbes Avenue, directing traffic around the scene.

Leaning against the trunk of Polk's car, tie fluttering in the wind, was a twenty-something man in a smart suit, making notes on an iPad. He was about my height, with a shrewd, narrow face and close-cropped black hair.

"Hey, Banks!" Polk's tone had more than its standard gruff authority. "Come and meet Dan Rinaldi. That guy I been tellin' ya about."

The plainclothes cop pocketed his iPad and sauntered over. His handshake was firm, though perhaps a bit more forceful than it had to be.

"So you're the famous Dr. Rinaldi." His grin was broad, assured. "Heard a lot about you from Sergeant Polk. Funny, you don't *look* like a pain in the ass."

I shrugged. "First impressions can be deceiving."

Polk laughed. "Doc, this here's Jerry Banks. Detective, second grade. My new partner."

I must have stiffened involuntarily, for Banks gave a short chuckle. "It's just temporary, Doctor. While Detective Lowrey's on leave. Family issues, from what I hear."

"That's right," I said. "Eleanor took some personal time."

I glanced over at Polk, who was giving me a significant though unreadable look. He knew that my relationship with his former partner had become intimate this past winter, during the harrowing weeks of the Jessup case. Though whether he knew *how* intimate, or how quickly—and why—it had ended, I couldn't guess. God knows I wasn't about to discuss it with him.

"Yeah," Polk was saying, absently, "Lowrey took six months off. Just long enough for me to break in Banks here, turn him into a real cop. And then he moves on, makes some other precinct sergeant look good."

Banks' grin remained intact. "Sorry, Sarge. I know it's not fair. But, hell, what is?"

"Enough bullshit, Detective. First off, did you talk to the parking valet?"

"Yeah. Didn't get much. He says Lisa Campbell pulled into the lot at 3:45 this afternoon. His valet ticket has the time stamp. He also admitted that she gave him a twenty-buck tip to park her Porsche in *two* spaces on the top floor, to make sure no other cars dinged it. Or scratched the paint."

"Fascinatin'. What about the canvass of the area? I know it's early yet, but anything turn up?"

"You mean, like eyewitnesses? Somebody who saw the perp dragging the lady to his car? Who maybe got the license plate? Something like that?"

"Now that ya mention it, Detective, somethin' like that would be just swell."

Banks spread his hands. "What can I say? I got a pair of uniforms going door to door. Asking street vendors, store clerks, the usual drill. Nobody's seen anything. Nobody heard screams, or a car peeling off. Zip."

"Well, they couldn'ta just vanished." Polk turned to me. "Is there a back way out of the building?"

I nodded. "Emergency exit door, leads to an alley. He could have taken Lisa out that way. The alley's narrow, but I think you could just fit a car in. Maybe he had one waiting. Maybe with a driver, too."

Polk considered this. "Okay, Banks, when CSU gets done up in Rinaldi's office, have 'em do that alley. Prints on the exit door, tire tracks. The works. And call in some more uniforms. Canvass a wider area, at least five blocks in every direction. Somebody musta seen a car, maybe drivin' too fast, or goin' the wrong way down a one-way street. Who the hell knows, we could get lucky."

Banks shook his head. "All due respect, Sarge, I believe we make our own luck in life."

"Ya do, eh, Detective? Thanks for the tip. Now how 'bout goin' upstairs and seein' how CSU is doin'?"

With a quick mock-salute to his superior, Detective Jerry Banks strode across the pavement and went into the building.

Watching him go, I said, "This kid for real, Harry?"

He grunted unhappily. "His *uncle* is. Jerry Banks is the assistant chief's nephew."

"So that explains it."

"Not all of it. City budget's tight, Department's stretched thin. So either way, you end up with mooks like Jerry Banks. Two years in Parks and Rec, one in Vice, and suddenly he's kicked up to junior detective. Fuckin' Jimmy Olsen with attitude."

He took out a pack of Camels unfiltered, tapped it against the side of his hand. Oddly unhurried, given the circumstances.

I didn't hide my impatience. "Jesus, Harry, are you gonna tell me anything more about what's going on? About Lisa?"

"Nope."

Turning his back to the brisk wind, he carefully lit a Camel. Took a few deep, grateful puffs.

"Even though we just met," I said, "Lisa Campbell is still my patient. She came to me for help."

"Yeah, well, I don't think needin' therapy's her biggest problem right now."

"C'mon, Harry. *Talk* to me." I turned, got in his face. "Because this whole thing doesn't make sense."

"What do ya mean?"

"I mean, why kidnap someone right outside her therapist's door? In a busy office building, in the middle of the day. Why not wait in the nice, dark parking garage 'til she was getting in or out of her car?"

"I don't know. When we catch the prick, I'll ask him."

"And another thing: how the hell did the kidnapper *do* it? How did he get Lisa away after assaulting me? Did he knock her out, as he did me? If so, then what? Drag her unconscious body down the hall? Use a fireman's carry to take her down the elevator and out the emergency exit? Because if he did, he took a real risk of being seen."

"Okay, so he didn't knock her out. Probably threatened her with a gun. Stuck it in her ribs, told her to keep her mouth shut. Then he walks her down the hall, down the elevator, out the exit door. And she doesn't scream or call for help or nothin' 'cause she's terrified."

"But that's my point. If he had a gun, why not use it on me? He could've used it instead of the sap to hit me. Hell, he could've just *shot* me with it."

"Maybe he didn't wanna risk the noise." Polk took another long pull on his cigarette. "How the fuck do *I* know? Maybe he's some kinda humanitarian and didn't wanna kill nobody if he didn't have to. Or maybe he figgered, hey, if things go wrong and I get caught, who needs a murder beef added to kidnappin'?"

"Which might be a good sign." I thought about it. "Perhaps you're right, Harry, and this guy *doesn't* want to hurt Lisa. Doesn't want to kill *anybody*. Just wants money. What did the kidnapper say on the phone to Harland?"

"Even if I knew, Rinaldi, I sure as shit wouldn't tell ya."

"Why not?"

He exhaled slowly, acrid smoke blowing back in his eyes.

"Man, I gotta get the hell outta this wind."

Without another word, Polk opened the driver's side door and slid heavily behind the wheel. Cigarette dangling from his lips, he slammed the door shut.

Glowering, I went around to the passenger side and got in. Then, snatching the cigarette from his mouth, I tossed it out my side window.

He gaped, unbelieving. "What the fuck—?"

I stared at him. "Is this the part where you tell me to keep my nose out of it? To just go home and wait 'til I'm called to give my statement?"

To my surprise, Harry Polk started to laugh. A thick, hoarse drinker's laugh.

"Not this time, Doc. Thing is, *I'm* the one's been put on the bench. Me and Banks are just supposed to supervise the crime scene. Do the scut work on this thing."

"What? I don't get it."

"Then let me explain it…so even a PhD can understand. See, all of a sudden, this case is way above my pay grade. But not yours."

Before I could even try to make sense of his words, Polk's cell rang. He picked up.

"Yeah, Lieutenant, he's right here. But he's havin' a hard time understandin' the facts o' life."

Polk said "Uh-huh" a few more times, then handed his cell to me. "Lieutenant Biegler wants to speak to you."

I stifled a groan. Lieutenant Stu Biegler was Polk's boss at Robbery/Homicide. A thin-skinned, officious jerk, at least as far as I was concerned. From our many heated encounters in recent years—primarily due to his objection to my involvement in some prominent cases—it was clear he was no fan of mine, either.

"Rinaldi?" Though nearly forty, Stu Biegler had the reedy, almost petulant voice of someone much younger.

"What's going on, Lieutenant? I assume that, like everyone else, you know Lisa Campbell had an appointment with me this afternoon."

"Of course I do. I also know she was snatched while she was with you. Right under your nose."

I felt my cheeks flush. "Look, Biegler—"

"No, *you* look. Lisa Campbell is married to Charles Harland. *The* Charles Harland."

"Yeah, I know."

"Then you also know he's scary rich and deeply connected. Hangs out with the mayor, the governor. Very influential. *Very* political. A real king-maker, you get me?"

"Loud and clear."

And I did. Last summer, when the city's district attorney, Leland Sinclair, ran his abortive campaign for governor, it was no secret that Harland had been one of his major contributors.

"So you know the kind of problem we're dealing with," Biegler went on. "A VIP who's just found out his wife's been kidnapped, and that the last person to see her alive was you."

"I said I understand, but—"

"You don't understand squat! You're not seeing the big picture here. Harland is a powerful man with powerful friends. *And he's not happy.* Which means trouble for me, the chief, the district attorney. Hell, the fucking *mayor*. For anyone Harland decides to blame if something happens to his wife."

"Including me, I take it."

"*Especially* you. Not that I give a shit."

"Of course not. It's your *own* hide you're trying to save. Same with everybody above you on the political food chain."

Suddenly, a car horn sounded to my right. I turned and saw a sleek Cadillac limo, windows blackened, pull up right next to Polk's sedan. Its clean lines glinting in the reflected light from the streetlamps above, the limo idled smoothly in the middle of the street.

Polk leaned across the seat, speaking loudly into the cell in my hand. "Limo's here, Lieutenant."

I gave him a puzzled look.

"You've been summoned, Doc." He grinned. "Have fun."

"Like hell I am."

"Suit yourself, it's a free country. But if you really wanna know what's goin' on, you oughta go for the ride."

Before I could reply, Biegler's agitated voice came from the cell speaker.

"Sergeant Polk? What's happening? Give me Rinaldi again."

"I'm right here, Stu," I said evenly into the phone.

"Look, Rinaldi, all Harland wants to do is talk to you. Ask you about his wife."

"He can ask, but I can't tell him. My session with Lisa Campbell is confidential."

An exasperated sigh. "Okay, whatever. That's between you and him. But you're supposed to care about people, right? So give the old guy a break. His wife's been kidnapped, for God's sake. Harland's probably falling apart. Worried sick."

Like Biegler would care. *Nice try*, I thought. Knowing full well what was coming next.

"Besides," he went on, voice hardening, "you don't want your taxes audited every year for the rest of your life, do you? Or to get a ticket every time you drive your damn car? Or have trouble getting your clinical license renewed?"

A pointed, deliberate pause.

"One thing's for certain, Stu," I said finally. "Harland sure has *you* scared."

"Okay, Rinaldi. Let me put it another way. Get in that fucking limo right now or I'll have Sergeant Polk arrest you. Throw your ass in jail."

"On what charge?"

"Obstruction. Withholding information in a major felony. Accessory after the fact. Believe me, I'll think of something. It's the kind of thing I'm really good at."

I believed him. At least about that last part.

I sighed, tossing the cell to Polk. If this was what I had to do to find out about Lisa, then I had no choice. Besides, I thought, maybe I could be of some help. Though, at the moment, I didn't see how.

Gripping the door handle, I smiled at Polk.

"Tell Biegler to relax. Message received. I'm off to see the Wizard."

Chapter Five

To my surprise, I had a fellow passenger in the spacious rear of the limo. He was pouring himself a drink when I opened the door. Wild Turkey on the rocks.

"What's your pleasure, Dr. Rinaldi?"

He indicated the well-stocked mahogany liquor cabinet to his right as I slid onto the plush leather couch. Though we sat next to each other, the wide space between us felt like a chasm. Which, I suspected, was the point.

"I'm Arthur Drake." He replaced the whiskey bottle and reached to shake hands. "Charles Harland's personal counsel."

The lawyer favored me with a brief smile. I guessed he was in his sixties, though fit-looking in his Brooks Brothers suit. Nearly bald, except for the scallops of trimmed gray hair above his ears. Clear blue eyes. Manicured nails. Rolex watch. The very model of the well-bred, Ivy League-educated WASP.

He seemed to read my thoughts.

"And, yes, Doctor, I'm aware that I look every inch the corporate attorney that someone like Charles Harland would employ. Though actually, the other partners in my firm do all of Mr. Harland's legal work for Harland Industries and its various subsidiaries. My role is of a more personal nature. I've been with Charles Harland for almost twenty years, and I like to think he views me more as a trusted advisor. A confidant."

"Is that why you've been sent to escort me?"

"Among other reasons. Given the delicate nature of the present situation, Mr. Harland would like to keep the circle of those involved as small and contained as possible. I'm sure you understand."

He took a healthy sip of his drink. Then he pointed the glass at me, jiggling the ice.

"Sure I can't fix you something?"

"Thanks, no."

Drake swallowed the rest of his drink and spoke into a speaker just over his head.

"Okay, Trevor. Let's go."

I heard the driver shift into gear, and felt the limo start to move. While Drake carefully poured himself another whiskey, I took my first real opportunity to check out my ride.

With seating for eight, the white-paneled, softly lit cabin was the size of your average den. Including the brushed white carpet, wall speakers, recessed TV, and computer monitors. All separated from the driver up front by an opaque screen.

A soft though insistent ringing broke the silence.

"Excuse me, Doctor." Drake took out his cell.

He bent and read a text, face tightening. Then he began texting a reply. A long one.

While he did, I glanced out my smoked window. We were driving out of Oakland, headed northeast toward Fox Chapel Borough. The gleaming, light-dotted spires of contemporary Pittsburgh rose against the black night. An urban silhouette now devoid of its storied steel mills and soot-coated buildings. The arch of sky no longer darkened by factory smoke. Its industrial past a dim memory, the Steel City in recent years had reinvented itself as a pioneer in finance, state-of-the-art medical research, and cutting-edge technology.

Yet alongside its modern silver and glass towers, and newly gentrified shopping areas, there are still vibrant echoes of its immigrant-forged past. The ethnic neighborhoods, cobblestone streets, muscular red-bricked buildings. So though the children of former steel workers have long since traded their parents' blue collars for white ones, Pittsburgh remains—often uneasily—forever situated between the present and the past.

Watching the blur of lights pass by my window, their reflection mingling with my own in the shadowed glass, I was reminded that I too had a foot in both worlds. The son of an Italian-American beat cop and an Irish homemaker who died when I was three, I worked as a teenager in the old produce yards on the Strip. Traveled to amateur bouts in every small town in the tri-state area with my hard-drinking, bitter father, who coached me from the corner. Carry to this day the psychic scars from his unrelenting criticism, if not the physical ones from the beatings I both took and gave in the ring.

But then, as had Pittsburgh itself, I underwent a transformation. College, grad school. A professional career. A passionate though difficult marriage that ended in tragedy. Living a life in the years since that I suspected my father wouldn't even recognize, let alone understand. And of which I often wondered if he'd approve.

I was pulled from my reverie by the sound of Arthur Drake wryly chuckling. When I turned, he was still peering intently at his cell phone. Then, sighing, he pocketed it once more.

"There are times when being considered indispensible is more of a burden than a compliment."

"Was that Charles Harland?" I asked.

"No. Mike Payton. Mr. Harland's head of security. A very proud, formidable man. Ex-Navy SEAL. Highly decorated. So you can imagine what this situation is doing to him." A tense smile. "It might also interest you to know that Mike compiled a fairly extensive dossier on you, at Lisa's request. Did she happen to mention that during your session?"

"I'm not at liberty to mention what she mentioned."

"Of course not. Foolish of me."

He went back to swirling the remains of his drink, its rich amber hue thinned by the melting ice.

"Poor Lisa. She's under the impression that she and Mike Payton have a personal relationship. A close friendship. Not surprising, since he's at the residence almost daily, conferring with Mr. Harland on various security matters. He often shares meals with them…as do I, of course. In addition, Mike accompanies the couple whenever they travel.

"Apparently, last week Lisa asked him to do a background check on you, before calling to make an appointment. She also asked Mike to keep her request confidential. Just between the two of them. She told him she didn't want her husband to know that she was seeking therapy."

"I guess Payton didn't turn out to be much of a friend."

"He's been with Mr. Harland for many years, almost as long as I. Though he's no doubt fond of Lisa, his primary loyalty is to his employer. He came to us at once after he'd delivered his report to her. Gave us a copy."

"You said 'us.'"

"Mr. Harland and I happened to be discussing another matter when Mike came in to the study. Charles had no problem with my being privy to what Mike had to say."

I considered this. "That's how come Harland knew his wife had made an appointment with me. Where and when. Mike Payton told him."

Another thought occurred to me, which had me instinctively touching the tender lump on my head.

"You know, that makes Payton a viable suspect in Lisa's kidnapping. *He* could've been the big guy waiting for us outside my office door."

"Mike Payton?" Drake gave a blue-blood version of a snort. "Involved in the kidnapping? Ridiculous."

"Maybe. But what does he look like?"

"I won't even dignify that with an answer. Besides, you can get a look at him yourself when we arrive at the residence."

Drake took another long swallow of his drink, rolled the glass between his elegant fingers.

"Lord, this is exactly the kind of thing I'd expect from Lisa. Kidnapped, for pity's sake. How dramatic."

"What do you mean?"

He grew thoughtful. "I don't know what your impression of Lisa Campbell was, Doctor. And I understand you can't tell me anyway. But I've known her since she and Charles married, and I've always found her…well, let's just say Lisa's personality has always seemed very extreme. Histrionic, if I may use your profession's jargon. Perhaps because she was once an actress."

He looked at me over the rim of his glass. Gaze suddenly stern, almost fierce.

"I will say this: She has not been a comfort to Charles Harland. Not from the earliest days of their marriage. For those of us close to him, it hasn't been an easy thing to witness."

I was taken aback by the raw intensity in his voice. As he himself seemed to be. He reddened, eyes averted.

I said, "Is there some reason you're sharing all this with me? Given that we've known each other for about five minutes, and you're Harland's longtime personal attorney, I'm surprised at your candor. About both your employer *and* his wife."

"A reasonable observation. And normally I pride myself on my discretion. But these are not ordinary circumstances. Mr. Harland loves his wife, my own misgivings to the contrary, and I suppose I want to enlist your sympathy for his situation. Your understanding. So that you don't get the wrong impression when you meet him."

"And what impression would that be?"

A pause. "How much do you know about Harland Industries?"

"What most people do, I guess. Family business that Charles Harland inherited from his father. Manufacturing, mostly. Made a fortune during World War II and afterwards."

"That's right. The company developed and built armaments, in partnership with Pittsburgh's steel industry. Though by the time Charles took over the reins, the company had begun to diversify. A prudent move, too, given that the city's industrial base was disappearing. Under Charles' leadership, particularly in the past twenty years, Harland Industries has morphed into a major supplier of high-end electronics and innovative software. Enhanced by some important mergers with foreign firms. The city's economic foundation has changed, obviously, and Mr. Harland made sure his business changed with it.

"Quite remarkable, in my view, given his advanced years. Many businessmen his age have grown hidebound and intransient in their thinking. Dinosaurs oblivious to the changing environment. Which is why most of them are extinct."

"But not Charles Harland."

There was more than a trace of pride in his voice. "I'm pleased to say that Harland Industries has never been more profitable, nor more relevant in terms of meeting the demands of a globalized marketplace."

"Nice talking point. You trying to get me to invest?"

Another cool, placid smile.

"I'm trying to impress upon you that Charles Harland is not a rich, doddering fool who was tricked into marrying some gold-digging failed actress thirty years his junior. He has a sharp, calculating mind. He's also a man of strong likes and dislikes. Of unbending judgment."

"Sounds like *you* are, too, Mr. Drake. At least where Lisa Campbell is concerned."

"As I say, my opinion of her is irrelevant. I merely want you to know that Lisa means a great deal to Mr. Harland, and that you shouldn't misunderstand if he comes across as brusque or unfeeling. Or somewhat condescending."

"In other words, that just happens to be who he is, whether or not his wife's been kidnapped."

He didn't comment. Instead, he finished the rest of his drink and turned toward his window, feigned looking out at the sweep of the night stars as we rounded a tree-crowned hill.

I sat back in my seat. By this point, I, too, wanted a stiff drink. But I also wanted to keep a clear head for whatever lay in store tonight.

Suddenly, face still in profile, Drake spoke.

"I *am* curious about something, Dr. Rinaldi. Something in Mike's report on you. I wonder, may I ask a personal question?"

"You can try."

He swiveled back to face me. "It's about Troy David Dowd. According to Mike, *he's* the reason you started working with the police. That was a good many years ago, correct?"

I nodded carefully. Dubbed "the Handyman" by the media, Dowd was a serial killer who tortured his victims with screwdrivers, pliers, and other tools. Though he was eventually captured and convicted, he's been sitting on Death Row ever since, his attorney managing to win appeal after appeal.

Dowd would snatch people outside of roadside diners or highway rest stops in isolated rural areas throughout the state. Only two of his intended victims managed to escape. One of these, a single mother of three, was so devastated by her ordeal that she was sent to me for treatment. It was my work with her that led to my signing on as a consultant to Pittsburgh PD.

"What about Dowd?" I asked Drake.

"Like everyone else at the time, I followed that case quite closely. In fact, I know his lawyer. Well, just socially. From Bar Association events, my club, that kind of thing. Good man."

"I don't know too many people who'd agree with you."

He gave a wry laugh. "Probably not. Anyway, I wondered if you'd ever met him. Dowd, I mean. The Handyman."

I shook my head. "No. No interest."

"Do you know what ever happened to that other victim who escaped? The twelve-year-old boy?"

"Well, he'd be almost twenty by now. And his name was never released to the press. I can only hope he's okay."

"Yes. Of course." Another pause. "Though, as someone once said, 'It's not the despair that kills you, it's the hope.'"

A pained, almost grief-stricken look crossed his face. Shadowed his eyes. Then, just as abruptly, vanished.

At the same time, a voice crackled from the speaker overhead. Trevor, the driver.

"We're at the gate, Mr. Drake. I'll take us in."

Chapter Six

Painted with a coat of lunar light, the grounds surrounding Charles Harland's immense home had a well-maintained, European grandeur. Rows of perfectly trimmed hedges. Tasteful stone fountains. Oval ponds whose waters rippled in the blustery night. Nature brought to heel by armies of landscape engineers, gardeners, and groundskeepers. And, of course, money.

I'd read somewhere that the residence itself was originally built by some wealthy land developer in the nineteenth century, and its opulence was apparent as we rolled up the circular drive to the front entrance. Evenly spaced lawn lights outlined the mansion's gabled turrets and elegant carved cornices.

Somehow our driver Trevor managed to slip out from behind the wheel and open the rear passenger door before I could. Tall, black, and indifferent in his chauffer's uniform, he didn't meet my eye as I climbed out into a cool, steady night wind.

Arthur Drake had already gotten out on his side and, as I went around to join him, I saw another man coming toward us from the white-columned front porch. Face grim as he approached.

He was shorter than I, with trimmed, salt-and-pepper hair. Well-muscled under his nondescript jacket and tie. A two-way radio clipped to his belt.

Drake began the introductions.

"Dr. Rinaldi, this is Mike Payton, our—"

That's as far as he got before Payton, with one smooth, easy motion, grabbed my elbow and spun me around. Slamming me gut-first against the trunk of the car.

"Hey, what the—?!"

The impact pushed the air out of my lungs. At the same time, I felt thin plastic restraints pulled tightly around my wrists behind my back.

"Mike!" Drake shouted. "What are you doing—?"

Payton's hands had already begun snaking under my suit jacket. Up and under my armpits.

"You bother to frisk the son of a bitch, Arthur? Let me take a wild guess—no, you didn't."

"Because I would never have thought it necessary. Moreover, I prefer to leave the Dirty Harry tactics to you."

Payton growled. "I'm Mr. Harland's head of security. And I don't know this guy. The only thing I know about the Doc here is that he let the boss' wife get grabbed. So why take chances?"

He finished running his hands up and down my pants legs and rose to his full height, pushing his jaw next to my face.

"I'm right, aren't I, pal? Lisa got herself kidnapped on *your* watch…?"

"Why don't you untie my wrists and we can discuss it."

A dark laugh. "Right. Listen, Doc, you don't want to give me an excuse to kick your ass."

Drake spoke up again. "Mike, for God's sake, stop this! Release Dr. Rinaldi at once. Mr. Harland is anxious to meet with him."

By now, enough breath had returned to my body to fuel a rising anger. The rough treatment I'd received had started my head wound throbbing again. During the long drive here, it had thankfully quieted to a dull ache.

Meanwhile, Mike Payton was undoing the plastic constraints. When I turned around again, he was calmly coiling them and putting them in his pants pocket.

Then, surprisingly, he held out his hand.

"Mike Payton. Nothing personal. Okay?"

"Fuck you. Totally personal. Okay?"

A childish retort, I knew. A knee-jerk response to being man-handled by this macho idiot. In lieu of slugging him.

On the other hand, at least one thing was clear. The guy who hit me outside my office was a good head taller than Mike Payton. Leaner, too. Though this didn't necessarily rule out Payton as a suspect. If he *were* behind the kidnapping, the taller man might be his accomplice. As I'd learned from my work with the police, the crime was rarely a one-man job.

Then, rubbing my chafed wrists, I glanced over at Trevor. Amazingly, our driver had stayed where he was while Payton frisked me. Perhaps in case his help was needed in subduing me. Or maybe just because he found it entertaining. God knows, there were no clues in his smooth, stoic expression.

Drake cleared his throat. "Okay, Mike. Now that you and Dr. Rinaldi have exchanged pleasantries, is there any news about Lisa? Has the kidnapper contacted Charles again?"

"No. There was just the one call, to Mr. Harland's business line. He was working in the study, alone, when it came in."

Drake sighed. "I should have been there. Unfortunately, I was in town for dinner with my ex-wife and the kids. They were both home from college for spring break."

"Hey, you get to have a life, too." Payton tried on a grin. It didn't take. "Anyway, the guy said he had Lisa and wanted five million dollars in bearer bonds for her safe return."

I stirred. "What are bearer bonds?"

"Negotiable currency," Drake said, "that has the dubious benefit of being both transferable and anonymous."

"Kind of like travelers' checks on steroids," Payton added.

"But how do we know if Lisa's even alive?" I said. "Did the guy put her on the phone with Harland?"

"No," Payton replied. "But he said he'd call again with more instructions. Then he warned Mr. Harland not to contact the police. After that, the guy hung up and Mr. Harland called me into the study. At first, he wanted to obey the kidnapper's warning. Luckily, though, the boss listened to reason and I got him to call Chief Logan. Get the cops involved from the get-go."

Drake shook his head. "Poor Charles. He must be beside himself with worry."

The security man shrugged. "Hey, you know the boss. When in doubt, take action. He made a call to the president of his bank in Harrisburg. Pulled him out of some fancy dinner party. An armored van will be delivering the bearer bonds any time now."

With that, Payton turned and headed toward the broad steps leading to the front entrance. Drake and I followed. Behind us, Trevor had finally returned to the driver's seat and was pulling the limo into a garage just off the circular drive.

I also noticed four other vehicles parked there, two of which were easily recognizable under the blazing fluorescents as unmarked sedans. Over the years, I'd spent enough time in cars like those to understand what they meant.

Official "unofficial" vehicles. Either cops or the Feds.

Or both.

As it turned out, I would be greeted by one of each. Though I'm not sure "greeted" is exactly the right word.

After entering the house, Payton had led Drake and me across a high-ceilinged foyer, our footsteps clicking on the polished marble. Various art objects and wall hangings were arrayed on either side, individually lit, their museum-like display obviously meant to both impress and intimidate.

Drake paused at the foyer's other end, looked around.

"Where are the servants?" he asked Payton.

"Daytime help have all been sent home. I asked the three live-in staff to stay put in the service wing. I figured the best way to keep this thing contained is to limit the number of people involved. A lot better, too, security-wise."

The lawyer nodded, then gestured for us to keep moving. Again, Payton took the lead.

After passing through two more spacious, similarly appointed rooms, we followed him down a long hallway to a set of wooden double-doors. He opened them without knocking.

We entered a large, well-lit study. Aggressively male. Oak-paneled. Stuffed leather chairs and sectional couch. Brass fixtures. Huge mahogany desk. Pool table.

An unaccountable breath of wind made me turn. Along the entire length of one side of the room was a floor-to-ceiling window, intersected by opened glass sliding doors that led onto a broad, pine-planked porch. Dimly lit by hidden sconces, girded by an ornate wrought-iron railing, its deck extended to the edge of a vast stand of ancient, night-shrouded trees.

But then my gaze was drawn back to the room's remaining three walls. Hanging on each of them, handsomely framed and mounted, were lobby posters of some of Lisa Campbell's old movies. In pristine condition, the garish, full-color posters featured lurid images of a scantily clad, provocatively posed Lisa. Her back arched, full breasts half-exposed. Most depicted her with her hand over her mouth, screaming, as some knife-wielding rapist or bloody-fanged alien monster advanced on her.

I glanced back in surprise at Drake, who merely smiled.

"Mr. Harland enjoys seeing the looks on visitors' faces when they see the posters. Like the look on yours, for example."

This brought a short laugh from Mike Payton.

"Yeah, the boss likes to tweak politicians and other ass-kissers who come around wanting a handout. I have to admit, it's fun watching them try not to stare at the pictures."

By then, I'd crossed the room to take a second look at Harland's massive desk. An array of digital equipment surrounded the elaborate cordless phone console on the leather blotter.

Payton joined me there. Pointed.

"The Feds set that up. For when the kidnapper calls again. It's got a wireless patch into their com lab on the South Side."

"To trace the call. Get a fix on the location."

"Right. Their tech guy was manning it, but said he had to run out to his car to get something. Be right back."

"Speaking of which," Drake said, "has Donna returned? Or at least called in?"

"Nope. Nobody's seen her since this morning, when she drove off on some errand. I've tried her cell. Even called her sister in Penn Hills. Nobody's heard from her."

Drake clucked his tongue. "Of all times…"

"Who's Donna?" Hearing the irritation in my own voice. I realized I was getting tired of playing catch-up.

"Donna Swanson," Payton answered. "Mr. Harland's live-in nurse. Been with him since his former wife died, years ago."

He scooped up a file folder on the far end of the blotter.

"The cop in charge here said her disappearance might be connected to the kidnapping, though the boss thinks that's just crazy. I happen to agree. Donna's devoted to Mr. Harland. But the cop asked to see her personnel file anyway. Then he detailed some uniforms to go out looking for her."

He flipped open the folder, bent it toward me. Along with the standard forms, there was a photo of Donna Swanson. Fifty-three, according to the file, though her careworn Nordic face made her look older. Sullen dark eyes contrasted with her faded blond hair, worn pulled up in a tight bun.

Drake stroked his chin. "At least on this point we can agree, Mike. The thought that Donna might be involved somehow in all this is ludicrous."

"Maybe," I said. "But if not, her being missing right now is a hell of a coincidence."

Just then, a young man in a bulky sweater and jeans came in through the same doors we'd used. He wore severe, tortoiseshell glasses and carried a small briefcase.

"There you are." Payton waited till the young man strolled over to the digital console on Harland's desk. "Where'd you have to go, Radio Shack?"

"Old memory card was fried. I knew I had another one in the trunk. Couldn't find the damned thing."

The kid casually swung the briefcase onto the desk and snapped it open. Payton turned to Drake and myself.

"Mr. Drake, Dr. Rinaldi. This is Barney. FBI tech."

Barney barely acknowledged the lawyer and me, except for dutifully flashing his Bureau ID badge. Then he pulled on some surgical gloves and started working on the console.

Suddenly, I heard another set of footsteps. Two people had entered from an adjoining room, both of whom I recognized. Lieutenant Stu Biegler was the first of the pair to reach me.

"Glad you could make it, Rinaldi." Planting his feet, arms folded. "I was starting to wonder."

Biegler's face was unlined and callow, giving a disquieting impression of youth rather than experience. Model-thin, with small, suspicious eyes, he practically radiated ambition.

"It's not as though I had much choice, Lieutenant. Besides, I'm worried about Lisa."

"We *all* are. That's why Chief Logan wanted me to handle this personally. Keep things on a need-to-know basis. Which is also why I tried to talk Mr. Harland out of bringing you into this. But he insisted. Wanted to meet you." A crooked smile. "Though I don't think it's gonna be a pleasant conversation."

"Who knows, Lieutenant? I might still make myself useful."

"That's what I was afraid of," said the other newcomer, stepping up to shake hands. Her grip was firm, no-nonsense.

Agent Gloria Reese, FBI. A slender, pretty brunette with wary eyes and a placid manner, she had been part of a Bureau team working with Pittsburgh PD this past winter on the Jessup case.

"Nice to see you again, Agent Reese. Surprising, but nice. I didn't know kidnapping was a federal crime."

She lifted short, unpainted fingernails through her bangs.

"It isn't, Dr. Rinaldi. Unless the victim's been taken across state lines. Regardless, Mr. Harland called the governor personally, and had him request that a senior FBI officer be present, if only in an advisory capacity." A nod at Biegler. "In cooperation with local police, of course."

"Senior officer?"

"I'm *Special Agent* Reese now. Deputy section chief for the tri-state area."

"Where's Neal Alcott?"

"Quantico. A new Bureau research project. The director feels his field experience will be invaluable."

Total bullshit. Alcott had been the point man for the Bureau during the Jessup investigation, for which he hadn't exactly won any laurels. I remembered that he'd been called back to Quantico after the case was over, but I'd figured it was to get a lecture and a slap on the wrist. Not anything permanent.

Biegler suddenly stepped between us, eyes darkening.

"Look, you two can catch up later. We're in the middle of a goddamn shit-storm here."

"More like the lull *before* the storm, Lieutenant," Gloria said. "Before the next one, anyway."

Biegler scowled, but she ignored it. Giving me a quick, collegial smile, she turned to consult with Barney the tech guy.

"Let's try to keep our composure, okay, Lieutenant?"

Arthur Drake spoke forcefully, striding over to where a gleaming, brass-railed wet bar stood against the wall. He peered avidly at the array of bottles. "Besides, at this point, all we can do is wait."

"For what?" I said.

"For the next phone call."

It was a new voice, coming from the opened doorway to a second adjoining room. Accompanied by the low squeak of wheelchair tires turning on the hardwood.

Arthur Drake froze where he stood, fingers half-closed around the neck of a whiskey bottle.

His boss, Charles Harland, was wheeled into the room.

Chapter Seven

Harland looked to be at least eighty, his frail body swallowed up by his incongruous Armani suit. The hair framing his pale, sunken face was a threadbare carpet of gray wisps. His thin hands were gnarled, age-spotted, gripping the rails of his wheelchair as though welded there.

It was only his eyes—sharp, cunning—that were vibrantly, arrogantly alive. As Harland looked intently from one of us to the other, his eyes seemed paradoxically dark and incandescent. Like miniature black holes, drawing everything and everyone into the pull of their urgent, insistent command.

Unlike the small, hooded eyes of the fair-haired man behind him, pushing the wheelchair. Maybe late fifties. Equally well-dressed, though much more casually. Tall and languid, his neck was encircled by a thin gold chain with a pendant hanging at its lower end, though I could only see its vague impression where it was tucked in under his designer-label sweater.

The man brought the chair to a stop, then stood impassively as Charles Harland's gaze settled on me.

"You're *him*, I assume." Harland signaled that he be brought further into the room. The man behind him complied.

"That's right, Charles." Drake quickly answered for me. "Dr. Daniel Rinaldi. The psychologist."

I left Biegler and Agent Reese to meet Harland in the middle of the room. Offered my hand, but he ignored it.

"You're the person Mike told us about." Harland's voice was clear and strong, despite a slight quaver. "The therapist my wife saw this afternoon. Without my knowledge. *Or* permission. I understand you also consult with the police."

This time, before I could respond, Biegler spoke up.

"Only occasionally, sir. Dealing with crime victims who need professional help. He has no role in our investigations." He cut me a disdainful look. "As I mentioned earlier, I see no reason why he should be involved in this present situation."

With some effort, Harland sat up straighter in his chair, squinting coldly at Biegler.

"Rinaldi's here because I requested it, Lieutenant. As you well know. And for a very *good* reason. He was the last person to be with my Lisa before some vile creature abducted her."

Harland peered at me again. "I presume you've given a detailed description of the kidnapper to the police."

"To Sergeant Polk, at the scene. Though I couldn't tell him much. It all happened pretty quickly."

"So I've been informed by Lieutenant Biegler here."

"That's right," Biegler said. "I conferred earlier with my people still there. Dr. Rinaldi was found unconscious in his office waiting room. Apparently assaulted by the same man who took your wife."

"Too bad you couldn't have done more to stop him," said the man behind Harland. Though his words were challenging, they had curiously little bite. "Maybe prevented it from happening."

I stared at him. "And *you* are…?"

"My son," the old man said brusquely. "James Harland."

Apparently it was the custom in this household for people to answer questions addressed to other people. However, I didn't see much value at the moment in pointing this out.

"I'm also vice-president of Harland Industries," James added evenly. "Though, as my father implied, my only *real* title is that of Charles Harland's son. It's also my only real job. Which is why I'm pushing this damned chair in Donna's absence."

Then the younger Harland left his father's wheelchair and joined Arthur Drake at the wet bar.

"I'll have whatever you're having." He gave the lawyer a thin smile. "But make it a double."

"Don't listen to him, Arthur," Harland said flatly. "Unlike you, James can't hold his liquor. Never could."

James Harland looked over at me. "My childhood in a nutshell, Doctor. My father's unending disappointment with his only son. Only *surviving* son, that is."

Drake shook his head. "Jimmy, please...not now."

"What do you mean? He's a psychologist, right? I'm sure he'd be interested in our family history."

By now, I was aware of the subtle though unmistakable slur in his voice. He'd already had a few.

"Besides," James went on, "all Rinaldi's heard about us so far came from Lisa. And God knows what that bitch said. I just wanna go on the record, too."

With a quick, knowing glance at his boss, Mike Payton walked over to the wet bar. But spoke only to Drake.

"Mr. Harland's right, Arthur. Junior's had enough. Time like this, we can't get distracted. We have to stay focused."

But James kept his eyes on the family lawyer, who'd quietly returned his whiskey bottle to its place on the shelf.

"Dammit, Arthur, pour me a fucking drink. I'm not a child."

"Then stop acting like one." Drake stepped away from the bar and went to Charles Harland's side. "This is a crisis, Jimmy, and your father needs us. *All* of us."

The old man looked up at him, offering a wan smile. "Thank you, Arthur. I can always rely on you."

"Yeah," James said, to no one in particular. "Arthur's a good dog. Such a good, good boy."

A tense, uncomfortable silence settled on the room. Only to be broken, to my surprise, by Agent Gloria Reese.

"People, please. I appreciate that this is a difficult time for everyone. And I know how emotions can get churned up under extreme stress. But the only thing that matters right now is doing what's best for Lisa. Concentrating on that."

Another long silence followed her words. During which she swept the room with her eyes, as if searching for confirmation from those assembled. Barney, adjusting his digital equipment. The Harlands, Senior and Junior, avoiding each other's stares. Mike Payton exchanging guarded looks with Arthur Drake. Biegler, arms still folded. And me.

Finally, Charles Harland stirred in his chair.

"Agent Reese is correct. All that matters is getting my Lisa back. Nothing else." A glance at James. "*Nothing.*"

"Understood, sir," Biegler added importantly. "And to do that, we gotta—"

Gloria interrupted him. "Excuse me, Stu. If I may…?"

Biegler's jaw tightened, but he merely watched as the FBI agent crossed the room and sat on an arm of the couch, looking kindly down at Charles Harland. The movement, as well as her demeanor, seemed to catch him off guard.

"Mr. Harland, can you tell us exactly what the kidnapper said to you on the phone?"

He glowered up at her. "I already *told* you what he said. That he had my Lisa, and that she was unharmed. But if I wanted her to stay that way, I'd have to give him five million dollars in negotiable bearer bonds. When he got the money, and was safely away, he'd release my wife."

"Anything else?"

"Yes. I wasn't to contact the authorities. And that he'd call again with the time and place of delivery."

Harland glared at his head of security.

"Perhaps unwisely, I allowed Mike to persuade me to call Chief Logan. As well as the governor, to ask for the Bureau's assistance. I can only hope Lisa doesn't pay the price for that decision. If she does, I promise she won't be the *only* one."

I have to give Payton credit. He stood, unflinching, for the duration of his boss' less-than-subtle reprimand.

After which Gloria said, hurriedly, "You did the correct thing in calling law enforcement, Mr. Harland. Both Pittsburgh PD and the Bureau have a great deal of experience dealing with crimes like these. Believe me, it's never a good idea for people to attempt to deal with kidnappers on their own. It's simply too dangerous."

In reply, Harland waved a shaky hand in dismissal and again twisted in his wheelchair. This time, I was on the receiving end of his hard, disapproving squint.

"Perhaps, Doctor, now would be a good time to—"

He didn't get to finish the thought. All of a sudden, the two-way radio on Payton's belt crackled to life. At a nod from his boss, he hurried out of the room, smoothly unhooking the radio as he went.

"Hey!" Biegler called after him. "Wait a minute…!"

He and Gloria Reese exchanged disgruntled looks. It wasn't hard to guess why. This was supposed to be *their* case, their operation. Yet Harland and his head of security were acting as though they were in charge.

I'll never know whether either of them was going to risk challenging the old man about it. In less than a minute, Mike Payton had returned.

"That was Breck, on guard duty tonight at the front gate. The armored truck from the bank has arrived with the bearer bonds. I told them to bring it up to the front of the house. Wait for our instructions."

Biegler frowned. "I assume this Breck guy and the truck driver are armed. Just in case."

"Yes. Trevor, too. He's joining them. The perp'd have to be crazy to make an end run move on the truck."

"So we're back where we started." James gnawed pensively at a fingernail. "Waiting for this bastard to call."

Arthur Drake looked longingly at the wet bar. "Yes. I'm afraid so."

What threatened to be another tense, awkward silence was immediately dispelled by Charles Harland. Tapping his knuckles imperiously on his wheelchair arm, he called to his son.

"James, since we have no choice but to wait, I'd like to be taken to the library. Dr. Rinaldi will accompany us."

As though tugged by an invisible wire, James reluctantly roused himself and shuffled sullenly toward his father. Meanwhile, the old man was smiling at my puzzled look.

"As I was about to say, Doctor, before Mike received his call, I believe that now would be a good time for you and me to have a private conversation."

"If you're hoping to discuss Lisa's therapy session with me, that isn't going to happen."

"Don't worry, Dr. Rinaldi. I will instruct James to leave us once we're safely behind closed doors. We'll have all the privacy we need."

"I don't think you're hearing me…"

"Despite my years, my hearing is perfectly fine. I can also assure you that I'm unaccustomed to losing when it comes to difficult negotiations. Sooner or later, we'll arrive at a mutually satisfying arrangement."

"Look, Mr. Harland—"

Suddenly, I caught sight of Gloria Reese, now standing just beyond the old man. Her face had turned ashen, and she was staring with alarm at something over my shoulder.

"Barney!" she cried. "Freeze! Don't move!"

I whirled, as did everyone else in the room, all eyes falling on the young FBI tech. Stunned by Gloria's panicked tone, he'd frozen where he stood behind the huge desk. Like a human statue, Barney kept his hands locked in position, unmoving, inches above the complex equipment on the blotter.

Then, shifting only his eyes, he allowed himself to glance down at his left arm.

We all did.

There, as though some live thing, an ominous red dot was slowly moving up the sleeve of his sweater. Instantly, his face went as white as Gloria's, and beads of sweat appeared on his brow. Slick, glistening.

Payton was the first to find his voice.

"It's a laser point. Some kind of guided weapon is trained on him. Everybody stay where you are. Nobody fucking move!"

"He's right," Gloria said. "Nobody move!"

Nobody did, except for Biegler. I noticed he'd crouched behind the pool table. His service weapon was in his hand.

Gauging the angle, I looked past Biegler and saw that the thin, almost translucent laser beam was streaming into the room from outside. Through the opened sliding glass doors. Its origin somewhere beyond the varnished porch. In the darkness.

Payton must have seen the same thing I had.

"Guy's outside," he said. "In the trees."

Arthur Drake forced out the words. "But it's so far…"

"High-caliber sniper rifle. Laser-guided. If it's got a Reticle system, it's accurate up to a mile. Maybe more."

"Oh God…" James Harland's stricken voice was a gasp.

I turned back to check on Barney. By now, the glowing red dot had settled in the middle of his forehead.

As though having guessed the dot's location, Barney gave out a low, sickly moan. But still he did not move a muscle.

Except for his eyes, blinking rapidly, frantically.

Gloria kept her own voice measured, authoritative.

"Everybody stay calm. Just don't—"

Abruptly, the red dot started moving again. Mesmerized, we watched it meander down the sweat-drenched front of Barney's sweater. Finally settling on the chrome top of the recording equipment. On the desk, next to the phone console.

Suddenly, the sharp, booming crack of a gunshot pierced the silence. Along with Barney's anguished screams as he fell backward, the equipment in front of him exploding. Shards of metal, wire, and plastic flying.

Now we were all shouting, ducking under chairs and behind tables. Scrambling for cover. Except for Payton, who took hold of Harland's wheelchair and pushed it into the nearest corner, facing the wall. Bending, he shielded the old man with his body.

At the same time, I rolled under the pool table, near where Biegler crouched. Waiting for the next shot.

It never came.

Ten seconds ticked by. Nothing.

Then I spotted Gloria, across the room, huddled behind the massive couch. Her eyes didn't meet mine. Gun drawn, her gaze was riveted on the opened glass doors.

Another ten seconds of silence.

Steeling myself, I crawled from my hiding place and went around the corner of the desk, where I found Barney. He lay cowering on the floor, covered in dust and slivers of metal, clutching his arm. Blood oozed from between his fingers.

I quickly checked him over. He was hurt, but would be okay. I took a handkerchief from my jacket pocket and pressed it against his wound. The relieved murmurs of the others in the room assured me that nobody else had been injured.

Meanwhile, the thunderous sound of the gunshot had long since faded, leaving only entrails of smoke curling up from the tangle of twisted metal and burnt wire.

Until another sound—common, familiar—took its place.

Mundane, but terrifying.

The desk phone, undamaged.

Ringing.

Chapter Eight

"Get off me and answer the goddamn phone!" Charles Harland shoved away his head of security with a surprising ferocity. "But first, turn me around."

Mike Payton stood to his full height, turned the old man's wheelchair so that it was facing into the room, then hurried to pick up the phone.

Behind the desk with Barney, I was close enough to hear a muffled voice coming from the phone, telling Payton to put it on speaker. He did.

"Good evening." The voice on the other end was metallic, otherworldly. The caller was obviously using some kind of voice-distortion device. Though it still sounded male.

"As you can all see," the voice went on, "the Feds won't be tracing this call now." A pause. "Though I trust the kid hasn't been hurt too badly."

Barney gave me an astonished look, which probably mirrored my own. Putting my arm around his waist, I helped him carefully to his feet.

By now, Biegler and Gloria had also come out from cover. As had Arthur Drake and James Harland, though the latter stood in a far corner, back pressed against the wall.

The laser light had returned, its glowing scarlet point tracing a wandering path up and over the room's furniture, and along the hardwood floor.

"I told my associate merely to disable the equipment," the

voice continued, "but sometimes ricocheting bullets have a mind of their own. Sorry, Barney."

At this, Barney's gaze changed from surprise to alarm. I didn't blame him. How could the kidnapper know his name?

I could tell from their faces that the same question had occurred to Biegler and Gloria. Joining Payton at the front of the desk, both still had their guns drawn, at the ready.

"You called in the authorities, Mr. Harland." The voice had an almost reproachful tone. "After I expressly told you not to. A grave miscalculation on your part. For those keeping score, let's call it Strike One."

I glanced over at Harland, whose eyes burned like embers.

"Listen, you cowardly piece of shit, do you really have my Lisa? Is she alive?"

"Yes to both questions. As I'll let her tell you herself."

There was a sharp, tearing sound. Probably duct tape. And a woman's startled yelp.

Then her voice. Choked, terrified, but defiant.

"Charles! You gotta help me! Do what this motherfucker says or he's going to kill me! He already—"

"Lisa!" Despite his frailty, Harland looked as though he might jump out of his chair. "Are you all right? What did he—?"

"That's enough, Lisa," said her captor. "They only needed what's called 'proof of life.' You just provided it."

"Fuck you! I hope you burn in hell, you cocksucking—"

A gruff, mirthless laugh. "Don't get so excited, you'll hurt yourself. Stop squirming."

"Then untie me, you slimy prick. I—"

Suddenly, her words slurred into an enraged, muffled gasp. Her captor had obviously—and roughly—reapplied the tape.

"Don't worry, Harland," he said. "She's okay. But, Christ, your wife's got a mouth like a two-dollar whore. I don't know how the hell you put up with it."

"I swear, if you hurt her…"

"Well, that's up to you, Charlie. You don't mind if I call you 'Charlie,' do you? Now that we're getting acquainted. You can call me...oh, I don't know...call me 'Julian.' I've always liked that name. Has a classical sound to it."

Gloria leaned in toward the phone's speaker. "Since you're so interested in being sociable, *Julian*, how about getting your guy to stow his weapon? It's making everybody nervous."

"A reasonable request, Agent Reese. Let me see."

The speaker went silent. Perhaps so that "Julian" could contact his partner, the sniper in the trees.

I must have guessed right, because the laser light abruptly winked off. Though the phone speaker remained silent.

"Is he *gone*?" James whispered. A half-minute had gone by. "Why doesn't he *say* something?"

Biegler blurted out, "More important, how the hell does he know who we are?"

Gloria let her gun hand drop to her side. "It's apparent he can see us, somehow. *Hear* us, too."

"From those trees? I don't care how good his sniper is, how powerful the sight. I don't believe it."

"Besides," I pointed out, "he seems to know our positions in the room. Including Mr. Harland's, over at the wall. Nobody out in the trees could see all those angles."

Payton grimaced. "Nobody has to. This Julian—whoever the hell he is—has been watching and listening to us the whole time from *inside* the room."

"What?" Drake exclaimed. "But how—?"

Payton pointed up at each of the two interior wall corners, at their junction with the ceiling. Small, insect-eyed video cameras hugged the shadows. Lenses glinting dully.

"The security cameras," he said. "With microphones. All over the residence, in every room. Including this one."

Drake looked unconvinced. "But aren't they all controlled by the central security station, off-site?"

"They *should* be, given what we pay the security company." Payton shrugged. "But nowadays, a good hacker can 'bot' any video system remotely. This guy could be watching us from a van out on the street, or from a hundred miles away. Which means—"

James Harland stepped forward, sighing heavily. "Which means, we're all on a reality show from hell."

"Very clever, James." That same metallic voice, coming from the phone speaker, as the laser point flickered on again. Flitting around the room like a predatory firefly, alighting on a chair or table, then drifting along a wall. But always in motion.

"I discussed Agent Reese's request with my associate," Julian said, "and we decided to maintain the tactical advantage of keeping you all in his crosshairs. Sorry."

Gloria glanced at me, her voice low. "Jesus, this isn't a kidnapping, it's a paramilitary op."

I nodded. Whatever the hell it was, it was clearly well-planned and well-executed. By people with specialized knowledge and training.

Julian spoke again, sharply. "Okay, Charlie, let's get things moving. Has your bank delivered the bearer bonds?"

Harland's thin lips tightened. I could tell that being spoken to like this was more than an affront to him. It was actually disorienting. In its way, inconceivable.

Finally, the old man found the words.

"Yes. The money's in an armored truck. Outside."

"Good. I want the bonds delivered in a plain, zippered suitcase. I'll tell you the time and place. I don't care who the courier is, as long as it's a civilian."

"What do you mean?"

"I mean, no cops or Feds make the delivery. You already disappointed me by calling them in. But this is as far as their involvement goes. The drop-off will take place where I'll have a clear vantage point in all directions. If I see so much as an off-the-rack sport coat or an eight-dollar haircut, your wife dies."

Julian's tone hardened. "And trust me, I'll make sure it isn't quick. Truth is, I don't like her attitude. Not one bit. So it isn't going to be a bullet in the brain. You understand? I can go through a whole round before hitting something vital. Could take her hours to die. Maybe a whole day, if I do it correctly. Am I making myself clear, Charlie?"

Harland slowly nodded.

"I can see that you're nodding, Charlie. So I'll take that as a yes."

Suddenly, Mike Payton growled something under his breath and reached inside his jacket. Pulling out an automatic pistol, he aimed it at one of the ceiling cameras.

Drake called out. "Payton, no—!"

The red laser point swept across the room in seconds, pinning itself on Payton's shirt front. He froze, staring down at it with a mix of frustration and rage.

And then, exhaling quietly, he lowered his gun.

Julian spoke evenly.

"I appreciate how difficult this is for you, Mr. Payton. For a man of your background and experience, your impotence must be especially galling. Even humiliating. But if you don't holster your weapon immediately, my associate will put a good-sized hole through your heart."

Swallowing hard, Payton did as he was told. Then very deliberately looked off, the planes of his face tight.

After which, the laser point dropped away from his chest and continued its lazy, circuitous journey around the room.

"Now, Charlie," said Julian, "where were we? Ah, yes. I need you to choose who is going to make the delivery. Other than yourself, of course. Regrettably, the drop-off point is not wheelchair-accessible."

Harland hesitated only a moment, then peered intently at his son.

James showed his palms. "Me? No fucking way. I'm not getting my ass killed for that slut. Sorry, Dad. No can do."

Payton gave him a disgusted look. Then, almost eagerly, the security man turned to his boss. As though grateful at last for an opportunity to act. To *do* something.

"I'm the logical choice, Mr. Harland. I'll go."

Julian's voice rose sharply. "No, you won't, Mr. Payton. Under the circumstances, I'm not prepared to consider you a civilian. You're sitting this one out."

For some reason, I wasn't surprised when Arthur Drake spoke up next. Calmly and resolutely.

"*I'll* go, Charles."

"No." Harland's jaw set. "I won't allow it. It's too dangerous, and I simply can't spare you."

His son stared at him. "Gee, thanks, Dad."

Harland studiously ignored him. Then, as though finally regaining his sense of his own authority, he looked up and directed his words to one of the security cameras.

"I choose Mr. Payton. He is my head of security, charged with the protection of myself and my family. He will go."

"Maybe he would, Charlie…*if* you were calling the shots. But you're not. *I am.* So I guess that means *I* get to choose."

Another brief silence. Followed by the red laser point, moving silkily along the edge of the desk. Drawing a half-dozen pair of eyes as it sought its next target.

Me.

I watched the glowing dot travel up my right arm, until I couldn't see it anymore. But from the concerned look on Gloria's face, staring at me, I knew where it had stopped.

"Looks like you're it, Dr. Rinaldi," Julian said. "*You'll* make the delivery."

I wanted to respond, but my mouth had gone dry. My heart pounding hard and fast in my ears. I imagined I could feel that insistent red dot burning into my forehead, like the sun's rays focused through a magnifying glass to a single incendiary point.

Gloria gave me a commiserating look.

"You don't have to do this, Daniel."

"Yes, he does," Julian snapped. "*If* he wants to see Lisa Campbell alive again. And remember—no cops, no Feds, no choppers. Just Dr. Rinaldi and the money. Otherwise, Lisa won't be the only one who ends up dead tonight." A brief pause. "You feeling me, Doctor?"

I knew, since he could see me, that all I had to do was nod. So I did.

Chapter Nine

I parked on a side street off Perrysville Avenue, climbed out of the late-model SUV and looked up through a tangled skein of trees at the Allegheny Observatory. Perched at the highest point of Riverview Park's steep, dense woodlands, outlined by pale exterior lights, the neoclassical basilica's towering Ionic pillars and three massive domes dominated the hilly landscape.

It was almost midnight, sky so black and clear it shone. Wind cold enough to burn my cheeks. As instructed by Julian, I'd driven alone here to the park, just north of the city, in one of Harland's company-owned vehicles. A large zippered suitcase containing five million dollars in bearer bonds had been belted into the passenger seat beside me.

After selecting me from among those in Harland's study, Julian had outlined a set of instructions for the delivery of the ransom. Any deviation from the plan would result in Lisa's death. Then he told us all to stay exactly where we were for ten minutes, and warned against anyone using his or her cell, or trying in any way to leave the room. To guarantee our compliance, his "associate" would keep his weapon trained on us until the brief time was up. As if to emphasize the point, the laser dot began once more to roam the room.

After these final words, the phone went dead.

Then began one of the longest, most agonizing ten minutes of my life. Most of which was spent in a strained, uneasy silence, during which nobody moved. Except for Gloria. Keeping her gun drawn, she'd gone to sit with Barney, who remained behind the desk, clasping his wounded arm.

Alternately embarrassed or angry, Mike Payton kept glancing over at his boss, whose face was curiously unreadable. Biegler was quietly seething. Arthur Drake looked morose and older suddenly than his years, while James Harland sat with his shoulders slumped, frightened eyes scanning the floor.

I also took a seat, and found myself drawn as if hypnotized to the wandering movement of the laser point. Not the most tranquil way to spend ten long, tortuous minutes, granted. But for some reason, it helped focus my concentration. Gave my conscious mind something to do, other than to surrender to panic or despair.

Until, finally, I saw the red dot disappear. Our signal that the time was up.

As if to confirm this, Arthur Drake glanced at his Rolex. Then nodded to Harland.

But Mike Payton's eyes were on me.

"You ready to do this, Rinaldi?"

"Hell, no."

He almost smiled. "Then you better get going."

Gloria Reese rose and walked me to the door, urging me to be careful. I think I thanked her, though by then all that concerned me was remembering Julian's instructions.

Lisa's life was at stake.

As was mine.

◇◇◇

Now, after locking the car, I carried the heavy suitcase back to Perrysville Avenue, searching with a flashlight along its endless bank of trees for a marked trailhead. For some reason, Julian hadn't specified the marking. He'd just assured me I'd know it when I saw it.

He was right, though I almost passed by the dirt path that wound up into the wooded hills. The trail was marked by a coarse wooden stave buried in the earth. Something hung from a nail atop it, glinting dully in the frozen light of the moon.

A pair of glasses. Cracked, smudged.

Lisa Campbell's glasses. The pair she'd worn in my office earlier today. A million years ago.

I drew in a breath, laced with bitter cold.

I stood there, unmoving, at the trailhead. I told myself it was to give my eyes a few more moments to adjust to the dark, but the truth was, I needed to calm my nerves. Looking at the trail curving up into the deep gloom of gnarled trees and coiled branches, I kept imagining a laser dot appearing suddenly on my arm, my chest. Crawling remorselessly up to my forehead.

Gathering myself at last, I tightened my grip on the suitcase handle and took my first step onto the trail. My breathing quick and shallow, I wound my way up the steep, broken earth, flashlight beam bouncing before me, ducking under thin-fingered branches and stepping over exposed roots. Every few minutes I peered up through the patchwork of foliage to the majestic domes of the observatory, using them as a kind of reference point.

Though the building itself was not my destination. Julian told me only that I was to ascend the marked trail until it split into two separate paths.

I was to take the one to my left.

Despite the cold, I could feel sweat beading my forehead. Feel the stiffness in my fingers from their death-grip on the suitcase handle, as though someone might wrest it from me. Feel the pounding in my temples from the raised lump on my head.

It was entirely possible, I realized for the hundredth time since leaving Harland's house over an hour ago, that I wouldn't survive this night.

Then, also for the hundredth time, I pushed that thought from my mind.

And kept walking, stumbling more than once on the slippery, unforgiving trail. Up and up, one foot after the other, moonlight showing through the foliage like shards of porcelain.

Until, gasping, head throbbing, I came to where the trail broke off into two smaller paths.

I was about to take the one on my left when my cell phone vibrated in my pocket.

I froze, mouth going dry. Julian? The police? Some news, some change in plans?

With my free hand, I plucked my cell from my pocket and read the display. And, despite myself, almost laughed aloud.

It was Noah.

◇◇◇

I ignored it, and watched the display until it indicated that a voicemail message had been left. Naturally, Noah had marked it "Urgent." He usually did.

Noah Frye was a paranoid schizophrenic, his grotesque delusions kept barely in check by psychotropic meds and the devotion of his girlfriend Charlene. I'd known him since my days at a private psychiatric clinic years before, when I was an intern therapist and he was a patient. Now we were friends.

Which was why I also knew what he was calling about. With everything that had happened since Lisa Campbell's appointment with me this afternoon, I'd totally forgotten my original plans for tonight.

As I stood now at the fork in the trail, holding a suitcase worth five million dollars, the absurd triviality of those plans came crashing in on me. Instead of exchanging a ransom demand for a woman's life, I was supposed to be having drinks with Noah and Charlene at the saloon where they both worked. Deciding on a wedding gift for a mutual friend.

I could just see Noah now, his bear-like frame in stained overalls, pacing back and forth behind the bar. Hair unruly, sweat-matted. That familiar lunatic's glint in his eyes. Wondering where the hell I was. Perhaps constructing elaborate, delusional fantasies about what might have happened to me.

Maybe I'd been in a car accident. Or been murdered by one of my patients. Or brainwashed by rogue Russian spies. For Noah, it was an entirely reasonable possibility that I'd been abducted by aliens.

That image made me smile. Tightening my grip on the suitcase, I headed for the narrow path on my left, wishing that something as fanciful as alien abductions did occur. As opposed to the murders, sexual abuse, and myriad other real-life horrors that afflicted human beings in this hard, uncertain world.

Like kidnapping. And what usually happens afterwards.

Steeling myself against the cold, the darkness, and my own unyielding fears, I plunged forward along the steep dirt path, deeper into the haunted night.

Chapter Ten

I hadn't gone a hundred feet up the path when I saw the large, shambling utility shack. The wood-framed, tin-roofed building was right where Julian had said it would be. Perched at a precarious angle at the crest of a hill, its rough-hewn walls were shrouded in darkness. Enveloped by low-hanging branches and scalloped by deep shadows, it stood as forlorn and isolated as an outpost on the moon.

Instinctively crouching, I made my way slowly toward the only visible entrance, a narrow plywood door. Moving closer, I saw that it was unlocked and swayed slightly, rusty hinges creaking, in the steady wind.

A distant, muffled sound made me stop, still bent low, and look up to my right. Up to where the observatory could be seen through a lattice of branches. I had to squint to make him out, but my ears hadn't been deceiving me. Stepping resolutely in and out of the basilica's faint exterior lights was a solitary figure in a bulky jacket and brimmed hat. A security guard, slowly making his way around the building's perimeter.

I froze for a moment, wondering if he could see me. But he never ceased his steady, rhythmic march along the side of the building, soon disappearing from view as he rounded a corner.

Some part of me wanted to call out to him. Solicit his help. But I kept silent, remembering Julian's warning that he had a clear view of the trail and surrounding areas. *And that any deviation from his instructions meant Lisa's death.*

Drawing a couple deep breaths, I hastened across the final dozen yards to the shack's entrance and pulled open the door. Its thin plywood slats rattled mournfully in my hand.

I shone my flashlight beam into the cold darkness of the interior. One large, rectangular room, it was divided by mottled aluminum shelving into smaller compartments. Dirt and dust clung to every visible surface, ash-gray webs hung from exposed ceiling beams. Shadows draped the worn hand tools hooked to the walls, the splintered rakes and shovels bundled in the bleak corners. The chilled air itself seemed old, congealed. A choking, tangible thing.

Fighting a rising panic, I crept slowly, carefully, across the room, sending my flashlight beam warily into each segregated area I passed. Nothing but more dust, old tools. Wicker bundles of dead grass. An upside-down wheelbarrel, caked with rust.

Finally, as the shadows dispersed before my light at the far end of the room, an unseen barrier emerged as though from a dream. Spanning the width of the rear wall from floor to ceiling like a hanging curtain, was a thick, oily tarp. Oddly unnerved, I played my flashlight across its creased, opaque expanse. Deliberately. Reluctantly.

Until the beam revealed what looked like a bulge. Like something was pushed up against the tarp from the other side.

Heart thumping, I took another step—

When I heard a sudden rush of movement behind me.

I whirled, bringing my flashlight up, but it was too late.

The man was big. Tall. All in black.

Maybe the same man I'd seen at my office. Maybe—

He threw his arms around me and brought us both crashing to the uneven wood floor. I was on the bottom, pinned under two hundred eighty pounds of solid muscle. My back buckled in agony. My teeth rattled in my skull. Pain exploded in my ribs.

I tried to peer up at him, get a look at his face. But he'd already rolled off me and grabbed for the suitcase that had flown from my hand. I'd also lost the flashlight, whose beam plumed uselessly up against the unrelenting darkness.

I was still on my back, gasping for breath, when I heard my assailant head for the door. Then, to my surprise, I heard a second set of footsteps. Hurrying *into* the room.

Head clouded, back aching, I forced myself to turn over, scramble up to my knees. Then I grabbed up the flashlight.

I trained its beam in the direction of the shack's open doorway, just in time to see my attacker swing the heavy suitcase at the newcomer. It caught him on the jaw, hard, and he went down like a collapsing sail.

Then, without a backwards glance, my assailant slipped through the opened doorway to be swallowed up by the night.

Gulping mouthfuls of midnight-cold air, I crawled gingerly across the floor to where the second man lay. Before I even shone the light on his face, I could hear the slow, labored rasp of his breathing.

I let out a grateful breath of my own. He was alive.

Getting up on my haunches, I played the light on his face. At first, I almost didn't recognize him in the security guard's pea-green jacket and standard-issue hat.

But this was no security guard.

It was Jerry Banks. The assistant chief's nephew.

Harry Polk's new partner.

◇◇◇

With an abrupt, shallow moan, Banks tried to raise his head. There was an ugly bruise sprouting on his jaw, and I realized he'd have to be evaluated for a concussion. But other than that, he appeared to be unharmed.

I, too, seemed to be okay, except for the fact that every part of me was bruised. Including, I must admit, my ego. This was the second time that hulking son of a bitch took me down. I swore to Christ, there wouldn't be a third.

Not the most mature, psychologically healthy response to what had happened, but there it was. Sue me.

I'd already detached the two-way from Banks' belt and was about to call for back-up and an ambulance when another figure filled the doorway.

Lieutenant Stu Biegler.

He looked winded, spent. Shoes scuffed, the bottom of his overcoat mud-spattered.

"The perp got away." Struggling to catch his breath. "I gave chase, but I lost him in the damn trees…"

I angrily tossed aside the two-way and jerked my thumb at Jerry Banks, who was finally rousing himself.

"This *your* idea, Biegler?" By now, I'd climbed to my feet. "The kidnapper said no cops. Just me alone. You could've gotten both of us killed. Me *and* Banks."

Biegler shrugged. "It was a calculated risk. I figured that Julian—or whoever was watching—wouldn't take notice of a lone security guard up at the observatory. Hundred yards away."

"Well, you figured wrong. Besides, why the hell didn't you tell *me* about your little plan?"

"Need-to-know basis, Rinaldi. The cornerstone of any successful covert operation. And *you*—as far as I'm concerned— didn't need to know. Hell, if you had, you coulda blown the whole thing."

"I think we can safely consider it blown. Big-time." I bent and helped Banks get woozily to his feet. Though my gaze never left Biegler's. "I bet you didn't inform Gloria Reese about your master plan, either. Because she didn't 'need to know,' right?"

"Agent Reese is merely acting in an advisory capacity. I saw no reason to enlist the Bureau's cooperation."

"Right. You're a real piece of work, Biegler. Now we don't have either Lisa Campbell *or* the ransom. I can't wait to watch you tell Charles Harland all about it."

Biegler pursed his lips, but said nothing. His silence told me he'd already begun dreading that conversation.

I turned to Jerry Banks.

"Was Sergeant Polk okay with you doing this?"

"No, sir. He said I'd either fuck it up or get my ass killed. Either way, he looks bad. So *he* offered to do it."

"Sounds like Harry."

"Doesn't matter. *I* said no." Biegler had his hands on his hips, looking about the shack. "I wanted Polk to stay put, supervising things at the crime scene. Besides, the docs just took him off the injured list. Old fart like Polk gotta take things easy. Oughta be retired by now, anyway."

Yeah, I thought. *Like that'll happen anytime soon.*

Rubbing his hands together, Biegler stepped over to Banks. "You okay, Detective?"

"Never better, sir."

"Just in case, I'll have the EMT look you over. I already called for an ambulance and CSU. Now let's all get outta here, before we compromise this new crime scene any worse."

I stared at him.

"Before we *what*—? Are you crazy, Biegler? Do you realize what happened here? Lisa Campbell is still being held. And now that Julian has the money, what reason does he have for keeping her alive? He can just—"

The words died in my throat. Because through the fog of my physical discomfort and anger at Biegler, I suddenly remembered the tarp. And the bulge pushing from the other side.

I quickly turned and made my way through the room to the back wall. To where the immense tarp hung like a shroud.

I could sense Biegler and Banks coming up behind me, but I didn't bother to wait. I bent and lifted the bottom of the tarp, and slipped underneath.

And almost tripped over the large canvas bag on the floor. Wedged between the back wall and the hanging tarp, it was the size and shape of a body bag.

As I knew it would be.

I couldn't breathe. Unmindful of the ache in my ribs, I knelt and began clawing at the rough canvas with my fingers. Then, kneeling beside me, Banks held up a pen knife.

I nodded, and he carefully slit the bag along its seams. Then I hurriedly peeled back the thick, ropey layers.

It was a body. A woman.

Dead. From the bloody pulp where the back of her head used to be, her killer had used at least one high-caliber bullet.

By now, Biegler had crouched on my other side. He'd brought the flashlight. Played it now across the woman's still, lifeless features. The staring eyes. The streaks of loose blonde hair.

It was then that I realized it wasn't Lisa Campbell.

Though my gratitude for that fact faded almost as quickly as it had arisen.

Banks whispered, "Who is it?"

I paused before answering. My voice heavy, flat.

"Her name's Donna Swanson. I recognize her from her photo. She was Charles Harland's personal nurse."

Biegler grunted. "The one who's been missing since this morning."

Sighing, I lifted a loose flap of canvas and lay it across her face. As I did so, something fell out of the fold of fabric. Something small and metallic. Glinting in the beam of the flash.

A miniature recorder. Digital. LED button blinking.

"Nobody touch it." Biegler withdrew a silk handkerchief from his breast pocket. "In case there're prints."

I stared at the device. "There won't be."

He ignored me. Wrapping a forefinger in the white silk, he carefully pressed the glowing, pulsating button.

It was Julian's voice. Again, distorted. Unrecognizable. Even so, I could detect impatience. Malice.

"I said no cops or Feds, remember? So Ms. Swanson's unfortunate demise is squarely on you. Let's call this latest error Strike Two. *Three* strikes and Lisa Campbell dies a slow, agonizing death. I'm sure you don't want that to happen. Though the price for her safe return has gone up. Another five million dollars in bearer bonds. I'll get in touch soon with my new instructions."

An ominous beat of silence.

"And this time, don't get creative. Just do as you're told. Or else, when you find what's left of Lisa Campbell, you'll see how creative *I* can be."

The message ended.

Chapter Eleven

"I think I have some Vicodin." Gloria Reese was rummaging through her small shoulder bag. "Couple pills left over from when I sprained my wrist one time."

I leaned over and peered into the bag.

"You wouldn't happen to have a morphine drip in there?"

"Don't be such a baby. As I recall, you got a lot more banged up last winter. The Jessup case."

"And I've got the scars to prove it."

Finally, she fished out a medicine bottle and tossed it to me. Two lone pills, visible behind a label that indicated the prescription had long since expired. I popped one in my mouth anyway and swallowed.

Gloria gave me a wry look. "You know, 'til I met you, I didn't know being a shrink was so dangerous. I mean, to life and limb."

"Normally it isn't."

"So what's the deal with you, anyway?"

"Just lucky, I guess."

I winced as I shifted position on the edge of the massive oval tub. Gloria sat at an angle from me on a similarly oversized marble bench with ornately carved legs.

We were back in the Harland residence, in an enormous master bathroom, all gleaming Moroccan tiles and mural-sized mirrors. Illuminated by evenly spaced wall sconces that glowed with the bright, insistent light of miniature suns.

At just past three a.m., after the discovery of Donna Swanson's body, Biegler, Banks, and I had waited outside the utility shack until we heard the muffled sound of car doors slamming far down the hill on Perrysville Avenue. Fifteen minutes later, a pair of uniformed cops trudged along the narrow trail toward us, followed by a winded, glowering Harry Polk.

Biegler was still debriefing the sergeant on the night's events when we heard more vehicles screeching to a halt at the curbside below. Again, some minutes later, these new arrivals—CSU techs laden with equipment and a dour, balding pathologist from the ME's office—were making their way up the tree-shadowed path to the shack.

Polk and Banks soon found themselves once more in charge of a crime scene, after which Biegler and I headed back down to the street in an awkward silence. By then, an EMT had parked at the crowded curb and was clambering from behind the wheel.

The EMT gave me a questioning look, but I waved him off, so he turned to Biegler, who gave him directions up the winding path and instructed him to examine Jerry Banks. Then the lieutenant got into his unmarked, I got back in Harland's SUV, and we each pulled out into the street.

I took a breath. Still shaken, physically and emotionally, from my experience in that hellish shack, I was looking forward to the solitude of the drive back to Harland's place.

I hadn't gotten halfway down Perrysville Avenue when I saw a KDKA-TV news van slowly coming from the opposite direction. Soon, I knew, to be followed by others. Reporters. Helicopters.

And so it begins, I thought. No surprise there. The discovery of a dead body—a murder victim, no less—at the famed Allegheny Observatory was big news, and the local media would no doubt hype it for all it was worth.

When I got back to the Harland residence, the first person to meet me at the front door was Gloria Reese, furious at having been left in the dark about Biegler's little operation. After I warned her that the lieutenant was probably right behind me, she grabbed my arm and marched me across the foyer to a garlanded, winding staircase.

On the second floor, we found an immense master bedroom. Like the study, it boasted imposing furniture, as well as a king bed, full bar, and in-home theater screen. A high-end man cave.

"His, I assume," I said.

Gloria nodded. "Lisa's bedroom is down the hall. Bigger, if that's possible."

On the far side of the room was the adjoining bathroom. She quickly pulled me inside, shut the door, and demanded that I tell her everything. I did.

Now, as I rose unsteadily from the edge of the tub, I saw Gloria glancing in awe at the bathroom's size and elaborate fixtures, as though registering them for the first time.

"Jesus, this bathroom is bigger than my whole apartment. Nicer, too."

"Like they say, it's good to be king."

I went to the twin standing sinks and splashed cold water on my face. The eyes that stared back from the facing mirror were red-rimmed, shot through with fatigue, hollowed by latent stress. But I was afraid to close them, lest the image of Donna Swanson, the back of her head a bloodied pulp, should rise up in my mind. Should etch itself there.

When I shut off the tap, I heard voices wafting up from the floor below. The front foyer. I could just make out Biegler's. Mike Payton. Arthur Drake.

Behind me, Gloria had gotten to her feet as well.

"Better go back down and join the others." She straightened her jacket. "Julian could call again at any minute."

I smiled. "Thanks for playing nurse."

"No problem. Besides, it gave me an excuse to be away from Biegler for a few minutes. *And* the Addams Family."

"Yeah, the Harlands are a strange bunch. I include their lawyer and head of security."

I opened the door and we stepped back into Charles Harland's bedroom. By now, the voices below had faded.

"I guess everyone's back in the study."

She shook her head. "No, not anymore. They've set up a situation room in the library. More interior."

"Good idea. Away from any windows. And snipers in trees."

"Plus I don't have to stare at all those movie posters of Lisa Campbell. She had a helluva rack, at least in those days. Reminds me of my ex."

"Beg your pardon?"

She gave a curt laugh. "One of the things we used to fight about. He wanted me to get breast implants. Claimed he'd be more turned on by me. I said, sure, when you grow a bigger dick. As you can tell, it was a real love match."

"Your ex sounds like a jerk."

"He was. Still is, I guess. Though, in his defense, we got married way too young. And it wasn't easy having an FBI agent for a wife. The hours sucked, and I had to travel a lot. Especially early in my career. Then, when I *was* home, we'd just fight and—"

She reddened. "Wow, why am I telling you all this? We barely know each other. I'm sorry."

I shrugged. "I'm a therapist. Occupational hazard. Besides, wait'll you get my bill."

Gloria smiled, and for a brief moment that studied wariness faded from her eyes. Then, just as quickly, she drew her slender shoulders back and nodded toward the hallway.

"C'mon, we better get down there before Biegler has a fit."

We made our way across the carpeted landing to the top of the stairs. Then I stopped, hand on the railing.

"Tell me something. Any idea who might be behind all this?"

"Well, it's Biegler's show, but I assume he's having his people run discreet background checks on Lisa's family, friends, and associates. You'd be surprised how often a kidnapping is the work of someone close to the victim. Someone who knows the vic's lifestyle, habits—"

"And her schedule. I'm still trying to figure out how these guys knew she'd be at my office. And when."

"Best and easiest guess, they followed her from home. It's

Occam's Razor—the simplest theory is usually the correct one. Though I don't know why they didn't snatch her in the parking garage. Fewer people around. Easier to get her into their own car and get away."

"Same question I had for Sergeant Polk."

She started to go down the steps, but I hesitated. Took out my cell.

"Tell Biegler I'll be there in a minute. I just realized I never checked my voicemail for messages. I have a patient in crisis, and he might have called me earlier tonight."

A flicker of doubt crossed her face, but she said nothing. Just gave me another smile—a much more guarded one this time—and hurried down the stairs.

I hated lying to her—especially since she and I both knew I'd done so—but I wanted to be alone. Once she was out of sight, I pocketed my cell and continued down the hall. I soon found what I was looking for.

Gloria had been right. Lisa's bedroom appeared even larger than her husband's. Though the furnishings were definitely more tasteful, softer in tone yet not overtly feminine. Unlike her husband's masculine retreat, whose obvious overcompensation was more dispiriting than impressive.

Not that I gave this other than a passing thought. Of more interest to me was the antique rolltop desk in a far corner.

As quickly but carefully as I could, I went through each drawer, checked each upper compartment. I even looked for any hidden latches, inlaid sliding panels. Nothing.

Then, to be on the safe side, I went over to her elaborate vanity table and repeated the same steps I'd taken with the desk. I did a similarly thorough examination of the lamp tables on either side of her four-poster bed.

Finally, I went through the medicine cabinet in her own opulent private bath. Again, nothing.

I returned to the bedroom. Lisa had told me in our therapy session that she had a bottle of pills at home in her desk. The method by which she intended to take her own life.

I'd found plenty of pills, in many of the places I looked, but not what I'd expected. Aspirin, vitamins, antacid tablets.

There was a bottle of prescription sleeping pills, too, but it contained only three tablets. Not lethal enough to kill her.

I stood, puzzled, in the middle of the room. Maybe she'd meant some other desk in the house. The library, perhaps, or the old man's study. Or else maybe she had her own office somewhere in the residence.

Still, I doubted she'd risk leaving the pills anywhere more public and accessible than her own bedroom. Plus she'd been so emphatic. "I have the means, a bottle of pills, in my desk…"

Had she been lying? Was her threat of suicide a ruse of some kind? If so, it was a very convincing one. Then again, she *was* an actress…

Which brought me back to my questions about the kidnapping. How her assailant knew where she'd be and when she'd be there. How he'd gotten her out of my office building unnoticed.

What if he *hadn't* had to knock her out or threaten her with a gun? What if she'd gone along with him willingly?

I reached up and touched the still-tender lump on my head. Could it be true? Had Lisa Campbell staged her own kidnapping? She told me herself she'd married Charles Harland for his money. Maybe she'd had enough of the querulous, demanding old man, but had grown accustomed to all that money.

I considered this. If she did manage to pull off the scam, she'd have what she'd perhaps wanted all along. Millions of dollars of Charles Harland's money without the inconvenience of being married to him.

Money and freedom. Two powerful motives, rolled into one.

Then, unsurprisingly, I felt a twinge of guilt. I wasn't used to impugning a patient, let alone suspecting him or her of possible criminal acts. Especially one I'd known so briefly.

Plus, I'd found myself liking her a great deal, even after only one session. So, despite my doubts about the kidnapping, I wasn't comfortable with my suspicions about her. And yet—

"Hey! What the fuck are you doing in here?"

I turned to find James Harland, holding a drink, leaning against the opened bedroom door. With his free hand, he absently fingered the gold chain under the V of his dress shirt.

"Gotcha!" he said. And started to laugh.

Chapter Twelve

"Christ, I *hate* shrinks. Ever since I got sent to one after my brother croaked. I swear, the guy was some kinda perv. Maybe *you* are, too, eh, Doc? Pretty damn freaky finding you in Lisa's bedroom, that's all I'm sayin'…"

For some reason, I didn't take the bait.

"I understand everybody's re-grouped in the library."

"Yeah. They sent me up here to fetch you. Far as my old man's concerned, I'm just some lame-ass errand boy."

James was keeping pace with me as we headed down the stairs, though he hewed close to the railing to steady himself. Apparently his father had relented and let him loose on the bar. The glass in his hand was nearly empty, and the telltale slur in his voice I'd noted earlier had gotten worse.

Once we'd descended to the foyer, he led me through a different door, and down a different hallway, to the library.

"Been some changes since you were gone, Doc. Barney got sent off to the hospital, and some new tech nerd's taken his place. And the grounds are practically crawling with cops."

"Really? I'm surprised your father went along with that."

"Me, too. But Biegler, Payton, and Drake ganged up on him. Finally wore the old bastard down, I guess."

By now, we'd arrived at the entrance to the library. With a sardonic nod, James Harland ushered me inside.

As I'd expected, the library was another cavern of a room, with rows of bookshelves lining the walls. Hundreds of old, seemingly untouched volumes upright and close together, as though soldiers at attention.

As I set foot on the polished hardwood floor, I saw Barney's replacement, a young Indian in black jacket and jeans, whose Bureau ID badge hung from his neck on a lanyard. He was bent over an ornate, antique writing desk, setting up new recording equipment similar to that which had been destroyed by the sniper's bullet. Next to it was the library's phone console, a duplicate to the one in the study.

James left my side and pointed theatrically up above his head. I followed his gaze and saw two video cameras jutting out from opposing corners of the ceiling. Or what was left of them. Each camera had been dismantled, lenses detached from their casings, wires hanging in a jumble. Someone had made damned sure that Julian wouldn't have eyes and ears in *this* room.

"That was me." Mike Payton, as though sensing my thoughts, gave me a grave smile. "Just to even the odds a bit."

He strode across the room to greet me. Gloria Reese, dark hair now pulled back into a ponytail, joined us.

They led me past a dual row of matching library tables to a suite of leather wing chairs, one of which practically engulfed Arthur Drake. His own inevitable whiskey glass sat on a small table beside him. Lieutenant Biegler, his back to the room, stood with his cell phone glued to his ear.

Meanwhile, James had found another wing chair, and was desultorily sprawled across its wide arms. Perhaps to drive home the point, he yawned.

Though, to be fair, everyone—with the exception of the studiously busy new FBI tech—looked spent. Wrung out. Exhausted by the night's events.

Everyone but Charles Harland, whose knotted fingers clutched the rails of his wheelchair. Eyes hard, black, shining.

"Well?" His withering gaze settled on Biegler, who'd just pocketed his cell.

"That was Banks, one of my detectives on-scene. CSU is still there, though the ME's man okayed removing the body. And the

Department's media flack just showed up to handle the press. They're arriving in droves."

Payton grunted. "I'll bet. A murder victim found at the observatory is roadkill for those vultures."

"Poor Donna's death will be all over the morning news." Drake sighed heavily. "Let's pray to God her murder isn't linked to Charles—*or* to Lisa's kidnapping."

"I doubt it will be," Biegler said. "Probably all that'll come out is the fact she was Mr. Harland's personal nurse. Which will be withheld until her next of kin is notified."

"That'd be her sister in Penn Hills," Payton said. "Donna's only living relative."

"I'll have Sergeant Polk do the notification. Even after that, no reason we can't sit on it. At least for a while."

"What good will *that* do?" Harland practically spat out the words. "If you're worried the news of Lisa's kidnapping will leak, you never should've brought in half the goddamn force. Christ, I was a fool to give my consent...."

I turned to Biegler. "Yes, James mentioned something about a bunch of cops showing up."

"Chief Logan okayed my detailing a dozen uniforms to scour the woods out back. Looking for spent shells, anything that might've been left behind by the sniper."

Harland was still grumbling. "A dozen Neanderthals, from a police department notorious for leaks. I don't know why the hell I let Logan talk me into it."

Drake climbed out of his chair and approached Harland and peered frankly at his employer.

"Because, Charles," he said, "you know that any clues pointing to the kidnapper's identity helps the police find Lisa. Yes, there's a chance of a leak, but I sincerely believe it's worth the risk. Otherwise, we're at Julian's mercy."

The old man's jaw tightened as he considered his attorney's words. Finally, he offered a curt nod, then swiveled in his chair to glare again at Biegler.

"All right. But tell those men outside I'll give ten thousand dollars to the first one who finds something that leads to the kidnapper."

"With all due respect, sir, that's not how we do things."

"But it's how *I* do things, Lieutenant. It's how I get things done."

Biegler was still weighing his response when the new tech guy suddenly spoke up. For the first time, I realized.

"All set here, Agent Reese."

"Good, Raj. Thanks."

I glanced at my watch. Almost four a.m.

"Sounds like you're all assuming Julian will make contact again tonight," I said. "Or in the morning."

"You've got a point." Gloria rubbed her temples. "The prick could decide to make us sweat for a day. Or two."

James shrugged. "If he hasn't killed her already…"

His father stiffened in his chair, but said nothing.

"*He won't.*" Payton stared evenly at James. "Not when he can get another five million for her."

Gloria nodded. "And he has to demonstrate proof of life again to get it. If nothing else, the new ransom demand means he has to keep Lisa alive."

"For now," Biegler added.

I said nothing, keeping my suspicions about Lisa's possible involvement in her own kidnapping to myself. It's not as though I had any proof, anyway.

Then, abruptly, Gloria aimed a steady gaze at me.

"One other thing. After tonight's disaster, I don't think Julian's going to trust our using Dr. Rinaldi again to deliver the ransom."

I bristled. "Hold on, we don't know that."

I was surprised at the defensive tone in my voice. Perhaps it was foolish, but I felt blindsided by her comment. Vaguely betrayed.

"I'm just thinking of your safety," she went on hurriedly. "You were lucky to have escaped with your life back there."

"I agree with Agent Reese." Biegler took a step toward me. "Which means there's no reason for you to stay involved."

Harland spoke up again. Even more sharply.

"Wait a goddamn minute! What if *I* want him here? Rinaldi

and I still have things to discuss. About my wife. Things I have a right to know—"

"Charles. *Please*." Drake leaned down, now eye-to-eye with the old man. "Forget about Dr. Rinaldi. We've all agreed that the most important thing is getting Lisa back safely. Trust me, there'll be time for discussions—for recriminations—later."

At once, a thick, guttural sound issued from Harland's throat. Gripping the wheels of his chair, he angrily pushed himself back, away from Drake. His cadaverous head swiveling from the lawyer to Biegler to Gloria.

"You tricky, conniving *bastards!* You think I don't know what you're doing? You're trying to *manage* me. You figure you'll just handle the sick old man while *you* deal with the crisis…!"

Drake sighed. "Charles, if you'll just listen to—"

"No! *You* listen to *me*! Despite my wishes, more police are on the premises. Despite my wishes, you want Rinaldi gone. But Lisa is *my* wife, this is *my* house, and all of you—*all* of you— better get that through your heads."

He raised a shaking forefinger.

"Drake. Payton. My 'loving' son James…In case you forgot, you greedy, self-serving shits, *you work for me!* Which means you do whatever the hell *I* say! *When* I say it! As for *you*, Biegler— *and* Agent Reese—I make two phone calls and your pathetic little careers are effectively *over*. Do I make myself clear? To *all* you sons of bitches? *Do I?* Or do I *have* to—"

Suddenly, the old man began to sputter, his words slurring. Unintelligible. Coming in short, staccato gasps—.

As though wired to the same trigger, Payton and Drake raced from either side of the room to their employer's chair. The lawyer got there first, just as Harland's thin body began to jerk spasmodically.

By the time I joined them, Harland's head had slumped to one side. Tongue lolling, skin gone deathly white.

Drake gingerly put his fingers to the old man's throat, feeling for a pulse.

As the color drained from his own lean, patrician face…

Chapter Thirteen

"Sounds like gunfire."

Mike Payton indicated the flag on its pole high above us, snapping in the hard, incessant wind. It was just past first light, a pale spring dawn bringing little warmth in its wake.

He took a final puff on the cigar stub he'd been working over for the past ten minutes and tossed it to the ground.

"Brings back a lot of memories, that sound. All bad."

I regarded him. "Drake mentioned the SEALS."

"Usual story. Too many tours. Too many firefights. Too much goddamn sand, 'til you end up fried, freaked, and fucked. That's if you don't come home in a box."

The security man and I stood in an alcove just outside the entrance to Pittsburgh Memorial. The only other person in sight was a Goth kid—another smoker exiled to the elements—leaning against a mailbox some fifty yards away, near the entrance to the hospital's open-air parking lot.

"So that's when you went to work for Charles Harland?" I asked. "After the service?"

"Nah. For a couple years I worked for a private security firm. Starr Sentinel, Inc. Top-of-the-line personal protection for VIPs. Arab sheiks, CEOs, movie stars. I was part of an elite team in the field. Mostly ex-military. Or ex-cops."

"Why'd you leave?"

"Going solo made more sense. A bigger paycheck, sure, but what I really wanted was to do things my way. Plus most of the firm's clients were first-class assholes."

"And Charles Harland?"

He gave me a careful smile. "Not as bad as some, believe me. You just have to know how to deal with guys like him."

Payton stirred, suddenly uncomfortable. As though he'd said too much. Then he made a point of staring off at the sky.

"Man, I suck at waiting," he added abruptly. After which, he lapsed into silence.

Three floors above us, Charles Harland was in intensive care. After being brought here by police ambulance, he'd been listed as a John Doe, condition critical, and immediately placed in a secured section of the ICU. His own private doctor had already been summoned, and was waiting to receive his patient when the old man's unconscious body was wheeled in.

Sectional curtains drawn, a plainclothes cop assigned by Biegler inconspicuously lounging nearby, the doctor and two nurses—sworn to secrecy—attended to the stricken man.

All this in an effort to keep the news of Harland's sudden stroke from the ravenous maw of the media. The only person from the house allowed in the ward unit was James, who'd demanded to ride in the ambulance with his father.

I thought about this now, as Payton restlessly fiddled with his watch. To my jaundiced eye, it was obvious that James was playing the "worried son" to the hilt. Yet what did I know? My years as a therapist—as well as one-half of a difficult father/son dynamic myself—taught me that love can sometimes hide, unbidden and unspoken, in the fissures of the most fractured, the most damaged of relationships. In plain truth, what had transpired between Harland and his son, or what residue of feeling—if any—remained behind, was a mystery to me.

Just as Mike Payton's motives were hard to fathom. No sooner had the ambulance left the Harland compound than he and I were on its tail, following in his Lexus. For some reason, the taciturn head of security had insisted I accompany him.

Meanwhile, Biegler, Gloria Reese, and Arthur Drake had stayed behind at the residence. As I'd assumed, Drake had power of attorney in all of Harland's affairs. If in fact the kidnappers *did* call again to relay the next set of instructions, Drake was authorized to speak on Harland's behalf. More to the point, he was empowered to secure any additional funds required to obtain Lisa's release.

Drake had also promised Payton, before we'd left the residence, that he'd call the security man as soon as the kidnappers made contact again. If and when that occurred.

So far, Payton's cell had been ominously silent.

"Look, Rinaldi..."

I'd been watching the Goth kid casually walk across the near-empty lot when Payton spoke up suddenly. I turned to see that he'd unbuttoned his jacket, and put one foot on the guardrail fronting the alcove.

Without looking at me, he said, "See, the reason I asked you to come down here with me...Well, truth is, I wanted a few minutes alone so I could apologize."

"For what?"

"For when you first showed up at the house. Frisking you like that. I shouldn't have gone all hard-ass on you. I'm sorry about that."

"You just overreacted. Happens to the best of us."

"Bullshit. I'm still alive because I *never* overreacted. Not over there. Not once. But this thing...Lisa getting kidnapped..." A pause. "I've been with Charles Harland for a long time. And it's my job to protect his interests, business *and* personal. That includes making sure his family is safe."

"So you take your responsibilities seriously. That doesn't mean the kidnapping is your fault."

He considered this. "Guess we'll just have to agree to disagree, Doc."

I watched his jaw set, his profile all flat planes and strong lines against the brightening bask of the sun. I saw what Lisa's kidnapping was doing to him. His pride, his sense of mission. His duty.

At the same time, I remembered that she'd sought his help in doing research on me, asking also that he keep her request confidential. Which he hadn't. After delivering his report to her, he'd gone directly to Harland and shown him a copy, plus informed him about where and when Lisa was meeting with me.

Perhaps Payton was now having second thoughts about what he'd done. Arthur Drake was in Harland's office when he handed over the copy of the report. What if Payton now suspected that Drake had something to do with the kidnapping? Or even Harland himself, unlikely as that seemed.

I knew one thing for sure. Mike Payton was feeling guilty. Responsible, for whatever reason, for what had happened to Lisa.

His foot still planted on the guardrail, he turned at last to face me. Pulled tentatively on his lower lip. "You know, Doc, it's important to remember that this thing could still go our way. We could still get Lisa back."

Frankly, I didn't know which one of us he was trying to reassure. But he needed support, so I gave it to him.

"I agree. In fact, I'm counting on it. I think not hearing yet from Julian is a positive sign."

"Me, too. I don't see that guy missing out on the chance to get five million bucks richer."

He managed another half-smile.

"Besides, I remember something my old unit commander once said. 'Never give up, never give in, never give out.'" He sniffed. "'Course, the next day, he got hit with mortar fire. Split the poor bastard in half, right down the middle."

And he let me see the unleavened pain behind that smile.

By seven a.m., I was in a cab weaving through thickening early-morning traffic toward the Liberty Bridge. And home.

Arthur Drake still hadn't called, so Payton had gone back up to the ICU to consult with Harland's doctor. Meanwhile, since it was a Friday—a regular workday—I had patients to see.

At first, given my concern about Lisa's welfare, I'd considered cancelling the day's appointments. Though there was little I could do at the hospital, and Biegler had made it clear before I left the residence with Payton that I was *not* to return. He smugly pointed out that if, as Gloria had suggested, Julian wouldn't trust using me again as a courier, then what little value I added to the investigation had ended.

As the cab lumbered up the ramp to the bridge, I lay my head back against the torn leather seat. I needed about a gallon of coffee, as well as a shave and shower. Barring some worse-than-usual traffic on the other side of the river, I'd have plenty of time for all three.

After the long climb up to Mt. Washington, I directed the cabbie along Grandview Avenue, my street, 'til we came to my wood-and-brick framed house. The yellow porch light was unlit, reminding me that I hadn't been home since yesterday morning.

To my surprise, my green, reconditioned '69 Mustang was parked out front. Since I'd been driven by limo from my office to the Harland residence, Polk must've ordered some uniforms to bring my car up here to my place.

I paid the cabbie, opened the front door, and stepped into the curtained living room. Tossing my keys on the rolltop desk, I went into the sun-spackled kitchen and put on the coffee.

While it dripped into the carafe, I pulled open the sliding glass doors and stepped onto my rear deck. The wind had fanned out any threads of clouds, and the arch of blue sky seemed to go on forever. Below me, the city's famed Three Rivers met at the Point, their combined surfaces wrinkled by that same steadfast wind, throwing up shards of twinkling sunlight.

I shaved and showered, relishing the familiar sting of steaming hot water on my sore muscles. I knew I'd be feeling the painful aftereffects of my struggle with the big man in the utility shack. Especially since I'd barely recovered in these past months from the bruised ribs and whiplash I'd suffered during the Jessup case.

Standing naked in front of the mirror, I saw the sorrowful tread-marks of these recent exertions. Once again, I had to remind myself that I wasn't the strapping young amateur boxer I used to be. And that this fortyish body—despite the occasional hour I spent working the heavy bag in my basement gym—was never going to repair itself as quickly and easily as it once did.

After gulping down two mugs of black coffee, I dressed, locked up the house again, and climbed behind the wheel of my car. Though it had gotten pretty banged up itself this past winter, the Mustang's chassis had proved to be as durable as mine.

As I revved the engine, an Earl Klugh track that had been playing in the deck when I last shut off the car flowed smoothly from the speakers. I was about to turn it off when I hesitated. Instead, I pulled out of my driveway and onto Grandview, content to let the guitarist's graceful harmonics soothe me as I drove. Calm me somewhat as my thoughts kept returning to Lisa, and what—despite my doubts—she might be going through.

Before leaving Harland's house, I'd discreetly asked Gloria Reese for her cell number. I wanted to be able to check in during the day between patient sessions to see if Julian had called, or to find out if there'd been any progress on the case. Not the most proactive of moves, given how involved I'd been the night before, but the only one available to me.

I frowned to myself. As worried as I was about Lisa, I was reminded of what Biegler often said about me: I'm a civilian, not a cop. Despite having been drawn into a number of investigations in the past, my real—and only—job was tending to the psychological needs of my patients.

Which I fully intended to do. The lieutenant had informed me that CSU had already finished scouring my office, as well as the hall just outside the door. Meanwhile, Lisa's car had been towed from the parking garage to the police impound, to be more thoroughly examined by lab techs.

When I commented on the unusually fast turnaround at the crime scene, he explained that the area involved was relatively small. And that there was little likelihood of discovering any real evidence. What he *didn't* say—and what I suspected—was that the sooner any signs of a police presence vanished, the better.

Less chance of drawing the attention of any curious media types. Though whether this order came down from Chief Logan or Charles Harland was anybody's guess.

By the time I turned onto Forbes Avenue, the Oakland traffic had predictably slowed, impeded even further by blithely jaywalking Pitt students. The sun had risen enough to coat my windshield with a bright morning glare, and the grating bleat of car horns and downshifting semis drowned out my speakers.

I let out a long, slow breath. After the horrors of that endless night, I felt suddenly, inexorably propelled into the sights and sounds of everyday life. The hustle, the noise. Busy commuters. People with shopping bags. Starbucks. For a moment, I couldn't tell which experience felt more surreal.

Finally, forcing my head clear, I arrived at my building. Biegler had been right. When I pulled into the parking garage, I noticed there wasn't even a black-and-white unit at the curb, which meant that the second, expanded canvass of the area had concluded as well.

I went up the elevator to my office. As expected, the crime scene tape was gone, too. I was grateful, since it wasn't the kind of thing I wanted my first patient of the day—due in twenty minutes—to find at the entrance.

But what of the office itself? I unlocked the door and stepped inside. Other than a few pieces of furniture moved slightly out of position, and some sprinkles of leftover fingerprint dust, the suite appeared completely unchanged.

Eerily, disturbingly unchanged.

As though Lisa's kidnapping hadn't even occurred.

As though, in fact, nothing had happened at all.

Chapter Fourteen

Noah Frye placed a draft Iron City in front of me.

"Like the man said, beer is proof that God loves us and wants us to be happy."

I lifted the glass to my lips. "Which man was that?"

He placed his elbows on the bar, flannel sleeves rolled halfway up his beefy forearms.

"Benjamin Franklin. And I'll thank you to take that surprised look off your face. I may be crazy, but I happen to know lots o' shit. Most of it's pretty useless, but still…"

A grin split his broad, bearded face. But I could tell from his slow, careful movements as he tended bar that his meds had been either changed or decreased. Though his eyes, while lacking their usual excited glint, still shone with intelligence.

It was sometime after seven, an hour or so since I'd seen my last therapy patient out the door. Then, as I often did, I'd driven across town to my favorite saloon on Second Avenue. Called Noah's Ark, it was a refurbished coal barge permanently moored at the edge of the Monongahela River. Bought by a retired businessman who named the place after him, it provided Noah and his long-suffering girlfriend, Charlene Hines, both employment and, in the rear, living quarters.

The owner had done a good job converting the place, while retaining evidence of its nautical origins. Despite the brass-trimmed bar, café tables, and a small stage where jazz musicians performed nightly, tar paper hung from the ceiling. Portholes looked out on the shimmering, wind-creased waters. And there remained a faint though unmistakable riverfront smell.

Sipping my beer, I noticed there were only a few other customers in the place. A quiet couple at a corner table. Secretaries sharing cocktails after work. Dusk still lingering outside, it was much too early for the serious drinkers and rabid jazz fans who normally crowded the intimate bar.

"Hey, Danny!"

I looked across the room. Bent over a table, wiping it with a cloth, was Charlene. Almost as big as Noah, her smiling face was framed with frizzy red hair. She waved the cloth at me.

"Don't go anywhere. I got someone I want you to meet. My brother's in town. Be here any minute."

"Look forward to it."

When I turned back to the bar, I found Noah glaring at me.

"She's too nice to say so, but me and Charlene are really pissed about you standin' us up last night. We ended up pickin' out Dr. Mendors' wedding present ourselves. Though you're still on the hook for a third of the price."

"Sorry I couldn't make it, man. Something came up."

"Right. Spare me your usual bullshit about some patient in crisis. I just hope you were out gettin' your pole greased."

"I wish." I offered my glass for a refill. With a grunt, he lumbered down the bar to the massive keg.

Dr. Nancy Mendors was an old friend of mine from Ten Oaks, the private psychiatric clinic where we both met Noah. In the years since his discharge as a patient, Nancy had privately—and somewhat covertly—prescribed and monitored his meds. She'd also been instrumental in getting Noah his job at the bar.

Though I ultimately left Ten Oaks to go into private practice, Nancy stayed on, eventually becoming clinic director.

What nobody knew was that, prior to this, she and I had had a brief affair. I'd been devastated for months by the loss of my wife, and she from a bitter divorce, and so we'd more or less fallen into each other's arms.

This was many years ago, and we'd each moved on, our contact since then fairly casual. Until she told me last year of her engagement to a pediatric surgeon. In fact, it was to select a group gift for their upcoming wedding that Noah, Charlene, and I had planned to meet last night. Instead…

I was still mulling this when Noah returned with my refill. On his way back, he'd casually picked up the TV remote and clicked on the wide-screen hanging above the bar. As expected, the local CNN affiliate was still leading with the discovery of a body at Allegheny Observatory.

According to the news anchor, the murdered woman had just been identified as fifty-six-year-old Donna Swanson, apparently the victim of a gunshot. A registered nurse, Ms. Swanson had lived and worked for many years at the home of Charles Harland, attending to the well-known Pittsburgh businessman. The police were unwilling to divulge any further details of the homicide, claiming that the investigation was in its early stages.

The report went on to say that Mr. Harland himself was unavailable for comment. However, Arthur Drake, an attorney and family spokesman, had just released a statement.

I stared intently at the screen as the station cut to a live shot of Drake, standing at the gated entrance of the Harland compound, facing camera lights and upraised mikes.

"On behalf of Charles Harland and his family, I want to convey how shocked and saddened we are at the news of Donna Swanson's death. The fact that she was the victim of a brutal murder makes her loss even more painful, more incomprehensible. Ms. Swanson was a beloved employee, and will be greatly missed."

By now, Noah had become as riveted by the news report as I was. Then, when it ended, he gave me a wry look. "Given the kinda shit you usually get mixed up in, I'm surprised you didn't find the body."

I offered him a brief smile and said nothing.

"The observatory, eh?" Noah scratched his unruly hair. "I used to get stoned up there all the time. Damned shame."

I must admit, I was relieved when Noah sidled down the

bar to serve another customer. I wanted a few moments alone, to drink my beer and collect my thoughts. I'd checked in with Gloria Reese at the Harland residence every few hours during the day, but was always told the same thing: no call from Julian. No contact of any kind from the kidnappers. And the search of the grounds had turned up nothing.

We'd spoken one last time before I left the office. Gloria told me that Charles Harland's condition was still listed as critical. She also informed me that she was leaving the residence for a short while to check in at the FBI building downtown. Then, after filing her report and getting updated on other active cases, she'd head back to the house.

I stared now at the half-finished beer in my hand, going over the day's work in my mind.

In the wake of last night's events, it had been hard at first to stay focused on my patients. But soon enough I became absorbed in their stories, in helping them address long-held, shaming beliefs. This was often true among crime victims. Even those who'd survived an armed assault. A robbery. Rape.

With many of these victims, their horrific experience prompted deep feelings of vulnerability, helplessness. With others, lacerating self-recrimination. The belief that what happened to them was their own fault. They'd been careless, cowardly. Maybe, some thought, they *deserved* what happened to them. Maybe they'd been *asking* for it...

I pushed the beer glass across the counter and signaled for Noah. I wanted something stronger. As he came sauntering toward me, I heard Charlene suddenly and excitedly cry out.

"There he is! My little bro!"

I turned on my stool and saw a handsome, thick-shouldered man in his mid-thirties push through the door. V-necked sweater and jeans, under a military jacket. Close-cropped, reddish-brown hair. The same color as his sister's.

But there the resemblance to Charlene ended. Unlike her open, spirited features, his own face was pinched. Haunted. His returning smile to hers an effort.

She seemed unmindful of this as she hurried across the floor and swept him up in a hug. He almost toppled in her embrace, which had them both laughing. Perhaps a bit too much.

Instinctively, I thought of something Mike Payton had said about returning vets. Fried, freaked, and fucked.

I slid from my seat to shake the man's hand. Charlene had released him by now, and was brushing tears from her eyes.

"Dr. Dan Rinaldi, this is my baby brother, Skip Hines."

His handshake was strong and sure. As was his gaze.

"Funny name, eh? Since I don't do much skippin' nowadays."

Charlene's brother had only one leg.

◇◇◇

Skip and I sat alone at a table near the back of the bar. Charlene had made a point of seating us there, then bringing her brother a schooner of Iron City and me a Jack Daniels, and *then* very deliberately backing away.

Grinning, Skip shook his head. He sat at a slight angle, to give his prosthetic leg more room under the table. "Subtle, eh, Doc? She thinks I need to talk to someone about what happened over there. Someone like you."

"Well, if this was a setup, I'm as surprised as you." I raised my glass. "Cheers."

We touched glasses. Then I watched him take a couple huge gulps of beer. Like a man dying of thirst.

"As you probably guessed, I'm a vet. Afghanistan. A week before my tour is up, I trip over an IED. I don't even feel it. Just hear a boom, then I wake up in a field hospital. Minus my left leg. One fucked-up Marine."

"I'm sorry. Truly."

"Luck of the draw. That's what they say, right?"

He took another long pull, draining the large glass. Called out for Charlene to bring over a pitcher.

I thought then of someone else I knew who'd lost a leg. Angie Villanova's husband, Sonny, a former construction worker whose right leg had been crushed in a job site accident. An angry, complaining bigot even before his forced retirement, he'd only grown more bitter with time.

I could tell that Skip had already begun suppressing his own anger and grief. Masking the trauma of his war wound with sardonic humor. Military-style bravado.

And, I was beginning to suspect, alcohol.

Charlene weaved her way through a maze of tables and placed a full pitcher of beer before Skip. Then gave me a broad wink.

"That takes care of *him*, Danny. What'll *you* have?"

I didn't miss the anxiety in her voice. Neither did Skip.

"We're fine, Char. *I'm* fine. I'm just missin' a leg, not my marbles. Not yet, anyway." His short laugh seemed as inauthentic as her wink.

"Hey, bro, if *you're* fine, *I'm* fine. Now quit bothering me, I got actual paying customers to wait on."

After she'd left, Skip poured himself another beer. "Poor Charlene. The brother she remembers was a big jock in high school. Varsity football *and* baseball. I was popular, too. She used to tease me about it. Called me a 'chick magnet.' Whatever. Anyway, that was a long time ago…Things change."

A measured beat of silence.

"Look, Skip," I said carefully, "I *am* a psychologist, but as far as I'm concerned, I'm off the clock. We can talk about anything you want or nothing at all."

"I appreciate that, Doc…"

"Please. Dan. Or Danny."

He nodded, then took a long pull.

"Thing is…Danny…There's nothin' to talk about. Shit happens. I got disability pay, sooner or later I'll find the right job. I'll be fine. I'm fine *already*, like I said. Okay?"

"Okay."

He raised his glass again, then stopped. "Well, there *is* this one thing…I mean, I'd heard about it before, but it's still pretty weird…"

He leaned in closer. "See, the damned thing itches. My leg, I mean…the one I lost…"

"It's pretty common. The feeling—"

"That it's still *there*, I know. Drives me crazy, especially at night. In bed. I'm half-asleep, and all of a sudden I'm tryin' to scratch it. Scratch empty air…"

"It's called a phantom limb. Think of it as the body's nervous system short-circuiting. Reacting as if the leg were still attached. Sending signals to your brain."

"Well, whatever it's called, I wish my brain would get with the program. The leg's gone. Sucker's in pieces in the Afghan desert somewhere. End of story."

"I don't know about that, Skip. I'd say your story's far from over."

He raised the schooner to his lips again.

"Your mouth to God's ears, Danny."

Just then, my cell rang. Gloria Reese.

"Sorry, Skip. I have to take this."

He waved a hand, and I picked up.

"Any news?"

Her voice was breathless. Urgent. "Julian just called and left instructions for handing over the next ransom."

"That's great, Gloria. That means—"

"Yes, Lisa's still alive. He put her on the phone. But she doesn't sound too good."

"Jesus…"

"Danny, listen. I was wrong. Julian still wants you to make the drop. In fact, he insisted on it. Says it *has* to be you."

I paused. Long enough for Skip to notice and give me a quizzical look.

Finally, I said, "Okay. I'm on my way."

Now there was a pause on her end. When she spoke again, her voice was more like a whisper. Strained, hushed. "Look, Danny, you know you don't have to do this. You're under no obligation to—"

"Yeah, I know. I'll be there as fast as I can."

I clicked off before she could reply. Then got to my feet. "Look, Skip, I—"

He shrugged. "Sounds like you got places to go, people to see. Totally cool. I'll catch ya later."

I extended my hand. "Great meeting you, though."

"Back atcha, Danny."

Thirty seconds later, I was outside, without having said good-bye to Noah or Charlene. For all I knew, Julian had put a time clock on his new delivery instructions. Which meant that every moment counted.

Though not yet nine, a deep darkness flowed down, the kind that froze your heart. And, once more, that insistent March wind, whistling. Making knife-edged divots on the black waters of the Monongahela. Across the river, the glistening, fast-growing urban skyline, silhouetted against prehistoric hills.

My Mustang was parked at the curb about half a block east on Second, in front of a recently shuttered store. I quickened my pace to get there.

I almost made it.

Suddenly, stepping from the shadows of the storefront, a man blocked my path. Big. Black jacket and jeans. Face hidden by the brim of a cap. But I knew who it was.

The man who'd stood at my office door.

Except this time he had a gun.

And he wasn't alone.

His arm was around her shoulders, clutching her slight body close. The ugly automatic at her throat. Gloria Reese. Cell phone still in hand.

Trembling. Eyes edged with tears.

"I'm sorry, Danny," she said haltingly. "So sorry…"

I stared at the big man. Though his face was in shadow, I could just make out his easy, assured grin.

Chapter Fifteen

"Turn around, Doc. Slowly. Or the bitch dies."

The big man's voice was crisp, his words clipped and uncompromising. As he buried the gun barrel deeper into the flesh of Gloria's throat.

For a moment, I hesitated. Risked a glance around. The sidewalk was empty. Silent. No help was coming.

I gazed again at Gloria. Her breathing had slowed, and the fear had left her eyes. Replaced with a glint of defiance.

"I said, turn around, asshole."

He knew what he was doing. From the moment he'd stepped in front of me, holding Gloria hard against his side, he'd kept a measured distance between us. A safe distance.

I had no choice but to turn around. As soon as my back was to him, I heard a metallic rattle. He spoke to Gloria. "Put these on him."

Suddenly, I felt hands pulling my arms behind my back. It was Gloria, handcuffing my wrists behind me. Her lips at my ear.

"I am so goddamn sorry about this, Danny."

I stiffened. Instinctively closed my hands into fists.

The big man said, "I'd let her finish, Doc. I have the gun pointed at her pretty little head."

I felt the snap of the cuffs, then started to turn back.

"Did I say turn around again? Shit."

I froze where I stood. And heard a sharp gasp of pain behind me. The big man had obviously grabbed Gloria again.

"The gun's back at her throat, Doc. So don't do nothin' stupid or she starts gushin' blood like a geyser. Got it?"

I nodded.

"Good. Now start walkin'…"

I did, the back of my neck prickling. Feeling the presence of our captor and Gloria right on my heels.

Two blocks from Noah's Ark, a nondescript van stood with its rear doors open. As we approached, I could make out the faint glow of an interior ceiling light.

"Get in," said the big man. "Slowly."

I climbed up on the fender and stepped inside, wobbling slightly. With my hands behind my back, my balance was off. Once inside the empty, windowless compartment, I finally turned around. Just in time to see the big man shove Gloria roughly inside. She fell to the ribbed canvas floor.

As he started to close the van doors, I shouted out. "What the hell's going on?"

He paused, that same easy smile creasing his face.

"Boss wants to talk to you." He aimed his gaze at Gloria. "As for *you*, honey…Gosh, I'll think o' *somethin'*…" He gave a short laugh, then slammed the doors shut.

Immediately, Gloria went to the doors and tried them. "Locked, of course," she said.

She came back and found a place on the van floor, next to where I'd awkwardly managed to sit. She glanced behind my back.

"He kept the keys to my cuffs." A long, deep exhalation of breath. "Shit, I'm so mad at myself I want to scream."

"Don't blame yourself, Gloria. He had a gun on you."

Suddenly, I heard the sound of a motor starting up. Then felt the van sway, lurch forward. We were moving. She acknowledged this with a nod. Pulling her knees up to her chest, she hugged them. Eyes narrowed with frustration.

"What happened, anyway?" I asked.

She wouldn't look at me. "Prick must've followed me when I left Harland's place tonight. Pulled into the Federal Building garage right after I did. I'd just parked, and was locking the door, when suddenly I felt a gun pressed against the back of my neck. I mean, damn! Caught flat-footed like some stupid rookie."

"It happens, Gloria. You were probably preoccupied with the Harland case, and…"

"Save it, will you? I screwed up." She looked off. "I tried to struggle, to scream, but he clamps this big hand over my mouth. Digs the gun harder into my skull. Then he drags me over to his vehicle—this van—and makes me get in. Orders me to tell him where you are. Me and my smart mouth, I said, the Doc's done shrinking heads for the day. He could be anywhere. For which I get slapped in the face. Hard. Creep's strong as a bull."

As if for emphasis, she rubbed her cheek.

"Then how *did* you know where I was?"

She turned to face me. "You have to understand, Danny. He had the gun at my head. I…I *had* to keep doing what he said. I just thought, sooner or later he'd be distracted. Make a mistake. Then I'd get a chance at him."

"He doesn't strike me as that kind of guy."

A rueful frown. "Tell me. Anyway, the only thing I could think of was to check your file. The Bureau has a detailed one on you, and I was able to access the data from my cell. Friends, family, known places you frequent."

"Like Noah's Ark."

"Neal Alcott had flagged it, so I figured there was a decent chance you'd be there."

"Good ol' Neal. Then what happened?"

"He pulls out into the street. But first, using my own handcuffs, he hooks me to the inside passenger door grip. So there was no way I could get to him as he drove. And if I tried to jump out, I'd be dragged along the street outside the van."

"Jesus, he *is* good."

She tilted her head. "Do you have to keep saying that? I feel bad enough already."

Gloria hugged her knees tighter. "You know the rest. He pulls me into the doorway of that empty store. Says he'd kill me if I didn't do exactly what he said. And he…I looked into his eyes and knew he meant it. That he *wanted* to do it."

"I have no doubt."

"With his gun at my throat, he made me call your cell and tell you that Julian had contacted the house again. And that he wanted you to deliver the ransom. Like before."

I sighed. "He knew I'd come…"

"That's why I feel so terrible, Danny. So did I. Remember, I saw what you were like last winter. The Jessup thing. Some kind of hero complex." A wan smile. "You really ought to see someone about it."

"Yeah, I get that a lot."

I shifted position, trying to ease the growing pain shooting up my arms. Soon, I knew, they'd go numb.

"Listen, Gloria. Did this guy *say* anything the whole time you were together? Something that might tell us who he is. Or what's going on?"

She shook her head. "No, nothing. He just gave orders. Though I sure wish I knew who his boss is." She'd no sooner said this than I felt the van begin to slow down. The tires below us bumping on gravel.

"I have a feeling we're about to find out."

Chapter Sixteen

Moments after the van came to a stop, the doors opened just enough for the big man to throw what looked like a couple of rags in the compartment. Then he locked us in again.

Gloria quickly snatched them up, showed me what they were. Two cloth hoods. Black. Eyeless.

Our captor's sharp voice came through the doors. "Listen up, slut…put one of the hoods on the Doc. Then the other on you."

Gloria and I exchanged guarded looks. Then, reluctantly, she pulled the hood over my head. The cloth weave was just porous enough for breathing, but I was swathed in total darkness. Then I heard a rustle of movement beside me. Gloria putting the other hood over her own head.

"Okay," she called out, her tone strained.

I realized again the effort it was taking to keep herself together. To stay resolved. Focused. And if the relentless pounding in my temples was any indication, the same was true for me.

Once more the doors opened, all the way this time. I could tell by the squeak of the hinges, the inrush of air.

"All right." The big man's voice. "Time to get out."

Suddenly the van floor shifted beneath us, bounced. The weight of a man, maybe two, climbing inside.

Good guess. A huge pair of hands grabbed my shoulders, pulling me up, guiding me toward the van doors. Gloria's slight gasp told me a second pair of hands had done the same with her. Stepping carefully on the rear fender, I got out. The hands at my back tightened their grip.

The big man spoke again.

"Just so we're clear, Doc, I got hold of the bitch and my buddy's got you. And I still got my gun. Maybe I'm pointin' it at *your* head, maybe at *hers*. Either way, you both better stay cool or things'll go really bad, really fast. Got it?"

"Got it." My words a dry murmur, muffled by the hood.

"Okay, then. Let's go."

I felt a shove at my back and started walking, my guy's fingers welded to my shoulders. From the sound of their breathing, I could tell that Gloria and the big man were right beside us.

I tried to get a sense of my surroundings. The floor beneath my feet felt like concrete. And the air was icy cold. But there wasn't a trace of wind. The van had been driven inside some kind of structure. Garage, maybe.

No, it was too big. Spacious. The way our footsteps echoed, the length of our march. I could also make out the smell of oil or engine grease. Machinery, perhaps. Equipment? Cars being serviced? Were we in a some huge auto repair place? Or, more likely, a chop shop?

Regardless, I didn't hear any other voices as we crossed the cavernous room. No sounds of workmen. Or tools being used. Maybe the place was deserted, abandoned.

I was aware the whole time of Gloria's measured breathing beside me. Like me, she'd decided not to struggle or make some kind of move. Hooded, outgunned, we didn't stand any kind of a chance with these guys. Not at the moment.

Suddenly, the hands gripping my shoulders pulled me back with a jerk. The scrape of shoes on concrete next to me ceased as well.

"This is where we stop," the big man said. "Thanks for walking yourselves here. We *coulda* knocked you out back at the van, but then me and my buddy woulda had to carry your sorry asses all this way. And, fuck, neither one of us is gettin' any younger."

The guy behind me snorted.

I tensed, waiting for the blow that was coming.

It never came.

Instead, a huge paw of a hand clamped around my mouth. Even through the hood's fabric I could tell that the hand had something in it. A sponge, or thick cloth.

And the smell. The fumes. Chloroform.

I struggled, impotent, my hands still cuffed behind me. But all my movements did was make the hand press harder, as a kind of panic seized me. I gasped, choked. Even as I inhaled the fumes, I could make out the sounds of Gloria's equally panicked struggle. Her strangled cries.

Then I felt myself spinning, free-falling in a deep, gaping darkness. And stopped hearing anything at all....

When I came to, groggy from the effects of the chloroform, I found myself sitting up in a wooden chair. My arms were still held behind me, the hard slats of the chair-back between them and my cuffed wrists. While unconscious, I'd been un-cuffed, then re-cuffed to the chair.

The hood had been removed.

Blinking myself into full wakefulness, I looked around me. The first thing I saw was Gloria Reese, similarly bound to a chair with electrical tape. Still unconscious, her head lolled to one side, ponytail draped over a shoulder.

Jesus, I thought, *she looks so young.*

"Hey, you're awake."

I swiveled my head around. The voice belonged to a grungy, long-haired man. Late twenties, maybe. Standard-issue denim jacket and jeans. Medium build, but with large, rough-hewn hands. Obviously the ones that had guided me here.

Wherever that was.

He was sitting on one end of a long couch, playing a video game on his cell. I could tell by the cheery rings and beeps.

As soon as our eyes locked, he got to his feet, stretched, and hurried out of the room. Giving me my first chance to survey the place.

It was a big room, walls hung with black crepe. No windows, a single opened doorway leading out. The one Long-Hair had used. The couch, some stuffed chairs. The only illumination came from twin floor lamps, on either side of the room.

But it was what stood in a far corner, barely discernible in the dim light, that caught my eye. A tripod with a video camera atop. Plus a rack of lights, unlit, upended like a broom in a closet. And a fold-out bed.

Finally, I glanced down at the floor. It was covered from wall to wall with thick padding, the kind furniture movers use. Old, spotted with stains, bunched at the corners.

Just then, I heard Gloria stir. When I turned, I saw her doing neck circles, trying to relieve the kinks.

"You okay?" I said.

She nodded. "Just glad not to be wearing that damned hood."

I watched her rouse herself into full consciousness. After which, she rolled her shoulders. More kinks.

I almost envied her. After being held behind my back so long, my arms had pretty much gone numb. And my shoulders weren't much better.

"How about you?" she said. "*You* okay?"

"I'll live."

Another voice made me snap my head around.

"That remains to be seen, Dr. Rinaldi."

A man stood in the open doorway. Tall, gaunt. Grotesquely thin. Balding, no more than forty, though his features were hard to make out in the dim light. He wore a white shirt and tie but no jacket. Both the shirt and his trousers hung loosely, in folds, as though his limbs were made of sticks.

He stepped into the room, eyes roaming to find Gloria. "I see you're both awake. Excellent."

She glared at him, defiant. "You know I'm an FBI agent, right, dirtbag?"

The man turned to me, smiling. One guy to another.

"Reminds me of Nancy Drew, this one. Small and pretty and plucky. Very plucky."

Gloria pulled against the tape binding her. "Let me loose, asshole, and I'll show you how plucky I can be."

"Relax, Agent Reese. You'll live longer." He shrugged. "Though that, too, remains to be seen."

I'd had enough of this prick's attitude.

"Who the fuck are you?"

He casually pulled up a chair and sat facing Gloria and me.

At this distance, I could see his face more clearly. The narrow jaw. Pencil-thin mustache. Sleepy, cunning eyes.

"Well, since you asked nicely, my name is—"

"I know damned well what your name is." Gloria's voice was like ice. She gave me a sidelong glance. "Meet Raymond Sykes. AKA "Splinter" Sykes. The Bureau's had a line on him for years. But we've never had enough solid evidence to get him."

Sykes grunted. "And what is this 'line' you have on me?"

"Upper-class kid gone bad. Ambitious but smart. You don't challenge the East Coast families or the Russians. Limit your operation to the tri-state area. Big-fish-small-pond type."

"What kind of operation?" I asked.

"Drugs. Porn. Human trafficking."

Sykes laughed, shaking his head.

"*Barely* human, Agent Reese. Young, poor, female. Street people, mostly. Looking for a better life. Which I provide."

I stirred. "About the porn. Is that what you 'provide' in this room? I notice the camera, the lights."

"I prefer to think of what happens in this room as an experiment in human relations. Mutually consenting adults exploring the boundaries of their sexuality."

"Except I'd bet most of the females aren't adults. Or consenting."

"You're mixing apples with oranges, Doctor. This room has nothing to do with what Agent Reese calls 'trafficking.' That's a whole separate enterprise, conducted elsewhere. This room is for paying customers only."

"Which paying customers?"

"The rich kind."

"Right," Gloria said sharply. "In *this* shitty room?"

I stared at Sykes. "We *are* in some kind of warehouse or auto shop, right? Unused, abandoned…"

"Something like that. Very out-of-the-way. In fact, in a particularly dicey neighborhood. Scares *me* at times."

"That's just it," I said. "If the area's so bad—"

"But that's the point, Doctor. Some of our most prominent citizens do their slumming here. They go totally 'ghetto,' away from their fancy friends and colleagues, and do as much blow and booze as they want. Then, in this very room, get their gold-plated rocks off. And we offer a full range of services. Fantasy role-play. BDSM. SST. Trannies. Whatever the customer wants."

"And it's all on video."

"For viewing later, if they wish. I assure you, there are no hidden cameras in here. Just the one video camera. My valued customers know full well that they're being filmed."

Gloria scowled. "But I bet you keep a copy."

"Only for my own protection. Blackmail is a fool's game. Too much personal interaction with the victims. The threats, the pleading, the one-in-a-hundred guilt-ridden husband who might call in the police. Trust me, it's not worth the grief."

"Look, Sykes," I said, "as much as I'm enjoying this little journey though the criminal mind, I'd like to know why you brought us here."

"Yes," Gloria added. "If you wanted to know how much the Bureau had on you, you could've had your muscle just bring *me* in. To threaten me, torture me, whatever. But why Dr. Rinaldi? He has no connection to you."

Sykes slowly clasped his hands behind his head.

"Well, well, Agent Reese. Quite the ego, eh? The only reason I had *you* grabbed was so that you'd lead us to Rinaldi. You're just the side dish in this meal, young lady. The Doc here's the entrée."

Despite acting like the villain in a James Bond movie, he was clearly growing impatient. Voice gone hard, flat.

"Okay, Sykes," I said suddenly. "If I'm the one you wanted to see, why not let Agent Reese go? There were no windows in the van. We were hooded 'til we were brought here. She can't know where we are. Which means she can't tell anyone anything."

"True. But that doesn't mean she can't serve a purpose."

Sykes turned his head toward the open door.

"Griffin! Your presence is required."

Within moments, the big man from before strode into the room. Same black jacket and jeans, same towering build. But no dark glasses or cap this time. Nothing to shield his cold, empty stare.

Chapter Seventeen

Griffin stood beside his boss, arms folded across his chest. His unzipped jacket flared at his sides, like fins.

Sykes said, "I have a few questions for you, Dr. Rinaldi, and Griffin is here to provide the proper motivation. He got his training in Iraq, you know. Same as I did."

I smiled at Sykes. "Somehow I can't see you lugging an M-16 and picking sand out of your teeth."

"Neither could I. So I gave orders to the stupid bastards who did. I jumped straight up the ranks to first lieutenant, courtesy of Harvard and a relative on the Joint Chiefs. I *was* there, I assure you. But let's say I was combat-adjacent."

I considered this. "An Ivy League degree, plus nepotism. Explains both the pompous vocabulary *and* sense of entitlement."

Without a word, Griffin stepped in front of me and raised his fist. But Sykes held up his palm.

"No. I want him conscious. For the moment."

The big man didn't budge. Then, reluctantly, he nodded. And took his place once more behind his boss.

Sykes sat forward in his chair, bony hands on bony knees. Regarded me intently. "But enough about me, Doctor. I'm more interested in *you*—and your therapy session with Lisa Campbell."

"Why don't you ask *her*?—since your pal Griffin here is the one who snatched her."

"Unfortunately, she's indisposed at the moment."

Gloria stirred. "You mean, dead?"

"I mean what I said, Agent Reese." His gaze was still locked on mine. "So I'll ask again: what did you and Lisa discuss in your session?"

"I'll tell you the same thing I told Charles Harland. It's confidential."

He leaned back, clucked his tongue. "I was afraid you'd make things difficult, Doctor."

Steeling myself, I spoke with a bravado I didn't feel. "Is this where you have Griffin unhinge my jaw? Add another lump or two to my skull?"

"Good Lord, no, Doctor. You're of no use to me if you can't talk. Now Agent Reese, on the other hand…"

My heart stopped as he glanced up at Griffin. The big man answered with a smile and walked over to where Gloria sat.

I found my voice. "Sykes…"

I stared in horror at the sight of Griffin standing in front of Gloria's chair. With his height and bulk, he looked like a giant looming over her small, compact body.

Sykes cleared his throat. "I wonder if you feel more like talking now, Doctor?"

Cold sweat sheened my brow. My arms long numb, cuffed to my chair, I felt disembodied. Restrained, yet oddly weightless. Helpless.

I could only watch as Griffin withdrew a large, serrated knife from a sheath on his belt. Still smiling, he bent closer to Gloria and lay the flat of the blade against her cheek. She managed to raise her chin, but her eyes were flecked with fear. Then, closing them tight, she called to me.

"Don't tell him anything, Danny! Sykes is gonna kill us anyway."

"Not necessarily," Sykes replied casually. "As Dr. Rinaldi pointed out, neither of you know where you are."

"But we've seen your face. Yours and Griffin's."

"So? It'll be your word against ours. And we happen to have an airtight alibi for tonight. In fact, as we speak, Mr. Griffin and

I are having dinner with business associates at Rocco's. If you ever stop in, try the clams casino."

Sykes swiveled in his chair, once more facing me.

"Now, Doctor, despite your professional ethics, I doubt you'll let Agent Reese suffer agonizing pain and disfigurement."

Before I could respond, Griffin leaned in over Gloria, his leather jacket pressed hard against her face. The chair-back's thin wooden slats creaked as he reached around her, using the knife to saw off a length of her ponytail. Then, straightening again, he showed her the lock of her hair in his fist. And slowly shoved it in the pocket of his jeans. A souvenir.

Gloria glowered up at him. "My hair'll grow back, asshole."

The big man smiled. "But not your eye."

Suddenly he thrust the knife at her face. She gasped, as the blade's tip stopped less than an inch from her eyeball.

"Sykes!" I shouted.

Gloria had begun to hyperventilate, quivering.

"Dammit, Sykes!" I said again. "Call him off!"

The gaunt man shrugged. "I hope I can. Though I *did* promise him some entertainment after we'd conducted our business."

His knife still at Gloria's panicked face, Griffin idly appraised her. "Not much meat on her bones, Sykes. But broads all got the same plumbing. I'll make it work."

Not if I could help it.

"Wait, Sykes! I'll tell you whatever I can. Just don't let him hurt her."

Under the circumstances, I didn't see much point in keeping my session with Lisa confidential. She was either hurt or dead. Or else, if she *had* orchestrated her own kidnapping, there was a good chance that much of what she told me was a lie. Especially her suicidal plans.

Regardless, Gloria was the one in danger now, and—so far—unharmed. I had to do what I could to keep it that way.

"A wise choice, Doctor." Sykes rubbed his aquiline nose. "Besides, I'm not interested in Lisa's rotten childhood or any of that therapy nonsense. I just need to know one thing: what did she tell you about the Four Horsemen?"

"What?"

"Did Lisa mention the Four Horsemen? It's a simple question."

That vague feeling of unreality swept over me again. Taking a deep breath, I tried to collect my thoughts. Center myself.

"I don't understand, Sykes. You mean, the Four Horsemen of the Apocalypse? Hunger, war…whatever the hell they are…?"

He sighed. "War, Famine, Pestilence, and Death. My God, Rinaldi, for a man of your advanced education, your ignorance is appalling. Anyway, that's not what I'm referring to…and you damn well know it."

"I *don't!* I swear, I don't know what you're talking about."

"He's full of shit, Sykes." Griffin lay his knife blade against the front of Gloria's blouse. "Let me take a nipple. That'll get him talkin'."

"No—!" I bucked in my chair. Uselessly.

Griffin turned the knife and calmly sliced off a shirt button. Gloria sat frozen, unable to move. Mouth open in a silent scream. Using the tip of the blade, Griffin spread her blouse open, revealing a wisp of her bra.

"Okay, bitch," he said. "Left or right tit?"

Sykes leaned in closer to me. "The situation is getting out of hand, Dr. Rinaldi. I'd answer my question."

"Goddamnit, I *would*—if I knew what the fuck you're talking about. But please don't—"

As though deeply disappointed, Sykes shook his head. Then he turned to look at Gloria. "I'm sorry, Agent Reese…"

Griffin's eyes glistened with anticipation as he slipped the knife blade under the front of her bra. Slit the thin, gauzy fabric with one smooth motion—

"Boss!"

It was the long-haired thug from before. He stood at the open doorway, breathless. Red-faced.

Sykes whirled in his seat. "What?"

"Boss, we got a problem! Big motherfuckin' problem!"

Now Griffin was looking up, knife in hand. Gaze riveted on Raymond Sykes, who'd risen to his feet.

"What fresh hell is this—?"

"I *mean* it, boss!" Long-Hair could barely get the words out. "You gotta come! *Now*, man!"

Sykes hesitated, lips pursed. Then turned to Griffin. "Okay, leave them. We'll pick up where we left off later."

Griffin's jaw tightened, his bitter disappointment evident in the way he sullenly sheathed his knife. Meanwhile, Sykes took one last moment to look down at me.

"Besides, a little extra time spent contemplating what Griffin is going to do to Agent Reese might jog your memory. If not... well, then, we'll *have* to kill you. *Both* of you."

With a nod at Griffin, Sykes followed Long-Hair out of the room. For a moment, the big man stood motionless, like a mountain. Staring avidly down at Gloria.

"You just sit tight, bitch. When I get back, I'll have you bleedin' outta every hole you got. That's a promise."

Then he too strode through the door.

Gloria's chin had lowered to her chest. She was so still, I wasn't sure she was breathing.

"Gloria?" I kept my voice low. "Are you all right?"

Instead of answering, she suddenly sat up straight. Pushing off with her toes, she heaved herself backward. The chair tipped over, the wooden slats cracking beneath her on the floor. Twisting her shoulders, she rolled away from the broken chair, hands still bound behind her with electrical tape.

Then, exhaling, she tucked her body into a fetal position, tight enough to slip her taped hands under her, up along her knees and calves, and finally over her shoes. Now her hands were in front of her.

Only then did she glance up at me. Then she awkwardly got to her feet. And, head bent forward, opened her mouth. A snub-nosed key dropped into her bound hands.

"The key to my handcuffs," she said. "It was in the breast pocket of Griffin's jacket. When he leaned in against me, I grabbed it with my teeth. Held it inside my cheek."

"Very impressive, Agent Reese."

A faint, weary smile. "Small but mighty."

Gloria stepped behind me, using the key to unlock the cuffs. When I stood, arms finally free at my sides, I was momentarily light-headed. Then steadied myself, heartened by the sensation of blood rushing to my lifeless limbs. The tingle of feeling returning to my hands and fingers.

I took the opened cuffs from Gloria, and, using the saw-toothed inner edge of one, gnawed through the tape wrapped around her wrists. In moments, her hands were free as well.

As soon as they were, she re-did the buttons that remained on her blouse. Then closed and buttoned her jacket as well.

"Perv." She whispered the single word to herself.

I said nothing, giving her a brief moment alone with her thoughts. Then I indicated the open door.

"If you don't mind, I'd rather not wait to say good-bye."

"Works for me."

I tossed her the handcuffs. Hooking them onto her belt, she followed me out.

◇◇◇

"We have to look for Lisa." We were moving quickly and quietly down a dimly lit hallway. "There's a good chance she's in here somewhere."

"And *I* say we get out of here and call in the cavalry. Bring the wrath of God down on this shit-hole."

"Maybe we could do both."

I paused at the end of the hall, which was intersected by corridors going in either direction. I glanced down each in turn, but saw nothing. No one. Empty shadows.

Gloria tugged at my elbow. Showed me her cell phone.

"I just noticed, my cell's disabled. They took out the memory card. How about yours?"

I quickly checked. "Mine's dead, too. They must've done it while we were unconscious. Just in case."

"All the more reason to get outside the building. Find a way to call for help."

I shook my head. "Not without Lisa."

"Dammit, Rinaldi, that's not how the Bureau works. There's procedure. I'm part of a team."

"*I'm* not. Deal with it."

She tried staring disapprovingly at me, but it didn't have much heat. Then, sighing, she spread her hands in surrender.

I picked one of the side corridors and crept down its darkened length, Gloria at my heels, until we came to another opened door. We both carefully peered inside. It was a similar room to the one in which we'd been held. Windowless, black crepe on the walls. Camera. The only addition was an old theatrical trunk, half swallowed in shadow.

"Must be where they keep the whips and chains," she said.

Gloria was smiling, but I could detect a tinge of hysteria in her voice. The impact of what Griffin had done—and promised to do—was still with her. Unlike what happens in the movies, people don't suffer traumatic events like that and then blithely move on to the next "scene." Stalwart, untroubled. Gloria Reese was a brave young woman, but she was also human.

As am I. I realized it was possible, even likely, that images from our experience in that blackened room would haunt my dreams for some time. Especially the part about being bound.

Helpless. Unable to prevent some horrific thing from happening. Like Gloria's possible torture and sexual violation, or—as had occurred years ago—my poor wife Barbara's senseless murder...

I pushed these thoughts from my mind and led us back down the corridor in the opposite direction. We did encounter one more door, but it was locked. We kept going.

All the while, heart pounding, I kept glancing behind me. Ever since we'd made our escape, I'd been wondering where Sykes and his men were. As anxious as I was to find Lisa, I was also worried about running into *them*.

"You know," Gloria said, "maybe Sykes isn't keeping Lisa here. Maybe she's under guard somewhere else. With Julian."

"Unless Sykes *is* Julian. Which seems likely. Griffin is his man, and he's the one who grabbed Lisa at my office."

"I know. But something tells me we're not seeing the whole picture yet."

"I have the same feeling."

A sturdy sliding door stood at the end of the hallway. To my surprise, it was unlocked. Gripping the handle, I slid it all the way open. We stepped into a cavernous, concrete-floored building the size of an airplane hangar. Fluorescent lights buzzed from the ceiling, revealing hulking machinery pushed against the walls. Old, long unused. Coated with dust. Draped in shadow.

As we started across the yawning expanse, our footsteps echoing, I inhaled cold, still air. The smell of oil.

"This was the place they first brought us." Gloria hugged herself against the chill.

Even in the poor light, I could make out the industrial printing presses. The massive rollers. I also noted the faded posters on the walls. Bundles of brochures and flyers thrown haphazardly into corners. Old samples, maybe.

"An abandoned printing company." I glanced about me. "Large-scale jobs. Probably couldn't keep it going anymore."

She nodded. "So Sykes took possession. Unofficially. Turned the adjacent offices into rooms like the one we were in. About as far below the radar as his fancy customers could want."

By now, we'd reached the other side of the work area. A huge pair of doors-on-wheels served as the entrance to this end of the immense structure.

"This was where we were driven in." Gloria frowned. "But where the hell's the van? No other cars, either. Looks like they've all left. Sykes, Griffin and that other guy. With the long hair."

I regarded her. "Which makes me think you're right about Lisa. They've got her stashed somewhere else."

"*If* she's still alive…"

It took a few minutes, but we finally found an unlocked service door. Stepping out into a cold, wind-whipped night, we crossed a broad gravel lot to the nearest street corner.

"Where are we?" She squinted in the feeble light of an overhead lamp a dozen yards away.

As my own eyes adjusted to the flooding darkness, I looked around, trying to get my bearings. For a dozen blocks in every direction there was nothing but garbage-strewn vacant lots, abandoned cars, and low-roofed, dilapidated buildings. The whole blasted landscape eerily illuminated by fires blazing from a scattering of trash cans.

Squinting, I could now see that there were people huddled around the fires. Homeless. In twos and threes, warming their hands at the flames. Wrapped in old blankets.

Finally, from the slope of the streets and the shining sliver of the Allegheny River visible to the east, I figured out where we were. Somewhere in the Hill District. Predominantly black and achingly poor, it was what playwright August Wilson once called "an amalgam of the unwanted." Having been born here, he knew what he was talking about.

Suddenly I thought of Eleanor Lowrey. She, too, had been born and raised in the Hill. And, like Wilson, she'd worked her way up and out of grinding poverty and the ravages of unfettered street violence to build a meaningful life.

The image of her in my mind brought me up short. It was crazy—*absurd*—given what Gloria Reese and I had just gone through. What we were *still* going through. But for a moment, I found myself wondering where Eleanor was. How she was doing. When, if ever, I'd see her again…

A shout from Gloria abruptly shook these thoughts loose.

"Danny! A phone!"

I turned to find her walking briskly toward a pay phone attached to a pole about thirty yards away. I hurried to catch up. When I did, I found her standing in front of the chipped, graffiti-covered phone. Its receiver cord severed. Useless.

"Dammit!" She pounded the top of the phone with her fist.

Just then, the street was swept by the twin headlights of an approaching car. Gloria and I both turned at the same time.

It was an old Ford Torino wagon, tailpipe scraping the asphalt as it lumbered slowly toward the corner. Though the streets were empty, the driver paused at the stop sign.

Gloria gave me a quick smile, then bolted toward the car. I followed.

Before the car started moving again, Gloria ran up to the driver's side window and flashed her Bureau ID badge. By the time I came to stand behind her, the driver had slowly rolled down his window.

It was a teenager, black, about sixteen or seventeen. He wore the uniform of a fast food chain. He also wore glasses and a pained, resigned expression.

"Shit, man, am I gettin' jacked?"

I felt bad. He seemed like a nice kid, coming home from working the late shift. Life was probably tough enough for him, without two crazy white people commandeering his car.

Which was exactly what Gloria told him we were going to do.

Chapter Eighteen

The first thing the Feds did—only minutes after Gloria and I stumbled into the FBI's downtown office—was split us up. Two apparently senior colleagues, both older males, flanked Agent Reese as they hurried down the lobby corridor of the Federal Building, all talking at once. In the urgent mix of voices, I could make out Gloria detailing the location of the abandoned printing facility. She also identified our captors, Raymond Sykes and his men, explaining their obvious involvement in Lisa Campbell's kidnapping.

At the same time, one of the senior agents was barking into his cell, demanding to be connected to Lieutenant Stu Biegler. I knew that, following jurisdictional protocols, the Bureau would have to give Pittsburgh PD first crack at the possible whereabouts of the kidnappers.

The trio of agents had no sooner disappeared around the corner than I was placed in a cramped, windowless interview room, where I gave my statement about the night's events into a tape recorder. The blond, callow junior agent sitting opposite me—a kid named Riggs—could barely keep his eyes open. Not that I blamed him. It was after four a.m., and the vending machine coffee he'd brought in for us was weak as broth.

An hour before, Gloria Reese had driven the borrowed Torino out of the Hill District, its terrified owner now relegated to the passenger seat. I'd climbed into the back and stayed pretty much quiet during the drive downtown. The tight, compact streets of the sleeping urban core, cradled between the V-shaped embrace of the Allegheny and Monongahela rivers, were whipped by a cold, bitter wind. The night as black and empty as I'd ever seen it. As though even the city's ghosts had fled.

When we'd finally pulled up to the curb in front of the Federal Building, Gloria turned in her seat to offer her hand to the kid. He merely stared at her through his smudged glasses, by now more aggrieved than anxious.

Before we got out of his car, I reached over the seat-back and gave him a twenty from my wallet.

"Gas money," I said.

Now he was staring at *me*. Maybe he felt insulted or condescended to. And maybe he was right. Nevertheless, he took the cash. Then he slid back behind the wheel, put his car in gear, and headed down the deserted, night-shrouded streets. Returning once more to the Hill, his home. A few miles—and an entire world—away.

I kept seeing the kid's face in my mind the whole time I was giving my statement. Now, having finished answering Agent Riggs' questions to his satisfaction, I watched mutely as he made some hurried notes on a pad. Then he rose to his feet, tucked the tape recorder under his arm, and went to the door.

"You stay right here, okay, Doc?"

Stifling a yawn, Riggs strode out of the room, closing the door behind him. Leaving me alone with my thoughts and the cooling Styrofoam cup of watery coffee.

I could guess what was happening in whatever room they were questioning Gloria Reese. As I had, she was describing the night's events. But given Charles Harland's considerable juice— and the political consequences if his wife's kidnapping turned tragic—I knew it wouldn't be into a tape recorder manned by some junior agent on night duty. She'd be making her report to those two superior agents I saw, who'd perhaps even be joined by phone or Skype to someone at Quantico.

In her quiet, calm voice, Gloria would detail how she'd been forced to lure me out of Noah's Ark, and how we'd been taken to an abandoned printing facility in the Hill District. She'd inform her superiors that Ray "Splinter" Sykes and two accomplices—one called Griffin, the other unidentified by name—had questioned me about my therapy session with Lisa Campbell. And that before they could get what they wanted from me, Sykes and his men left to deal with some urgent problem. After which, we had made our escape.

That would be it. The extent of her report. Unless I misread Gloria Reese, I suspected she'd leave out the part about Griffin terrorizing her. Using the knife to open her blouse, cut through her bra.

I reluctantly sipped the thin, tasteless coffee. Gloria was young, female and newly promoted to Special Agent. If she revealed the facts of her ordeal, the threatened sexual violation and mutilation, she'd be instantly taken off the case and ordered to begin treatment with a Bureau shrink, removed for a good while from the field, and assigned to a desk. Dropped a significant number of rungs down the hierarchical ladder, from which it wouldn't be easy to climb up again.

I'd seen similar things happen to officers and detectives in the Pittsburgh PD. And while I understood why Gloria would cover up the facts to safeguard her career, I worried that—like other law enforcement personnel—she'd underestimate the after-effects of her traumatic experience. Suppressing her feelings, keeping silent about what had happened to her. Unless, at some future time, I could persuade her to get help from someone. Some independent clinician, not on the FBI payroll. But not me. I was a witness, an unwitting participant in her terrifying experience, which made me a part of the very thing she'd need to relive, process, and integrate. Her waking nightmare had included me.

Another hour passed. Then Agent Riggs stuck his head into the room.

"They want to see you, Doc."

I got up and followed him down to the end of the lobby corridor, around the corner, and into a paneled conference room.

Standard issue FBI. Long metal table, fabric-backed chairs. Bottled water and a burbling coffee carafe on a side table. Rectangular windows whose shades blocked the dawn sun.

Riggs pointed me to a chair, grunted distractedly, and went out the double-doors, closing them behind him.

Lieutenant Biegler, scowling, eyes creased with fatigue, sat opposite me. Next to him was Gloria Reese, narrow shoulders slumped. Jacket still buttoned all the way to the top. Two seats away, sitting on a corner of the table, was one of the senior agents who'd whisked Gloria away when we'd first arrived.

I'd seen the type before. Close-cropped salt-and-pepper hair. Taciturn features. Suspicious eyes. Trim, golfer's body beneath the ubiquitous blue suit. He offered me a thin smile.

"My name is Anthony Wilson. Section chief. Agent Reese and I have just teleconferenced with the director, who's conferring with the governor as we speak. Obviously, both are quite concerned about the direction this investigation has taken."

"Hasn't been a day at the beach for me, either."

Bristling, Biegler leaned forward and pointed a forefinger at me across the table.

"Stuff it, Rinaldi. This is the part where *you* shut up and the people in charge do the talking."

I looked from one man to the other.

"And which of you would *that* be?"

Wilson let his smile widen. "This is Pittsburgh PD's case, Doctor. As it has been from the start. The Bureau is only acting in an advisory capacity."

"So people keep saying. Okay, then. What do you advise?"

"I'd advise you to cooperate with this investigation. By which I mean, tell us everything you can remember about what happened tonight."

"I already gave my statement. It's on tape, witnessed by one of your guys. Looks like he escaped from a boy band."

"Lieutenant Biegler and I have just listened to your statement. We believe you left something out."

"Look, shouldn't your troops and the cops be hauling ass to that printing plant? Maybe Sykes and his men came back. Even if they didn't, there's bound to be evidence or—"

"Not your concern, Rinaldi." Biegler sniffed. "Besides, we got a SWAT team on the way there now. Plus some of my people working the kidnapping. Agent Reese gave us the location. If those pricks *are* there, we'll nail 'em. And hopefully find Harland's wife in one piece."

Agent Wilson adjusted his position on the table. Gave me a cool, assured look. He seemed pretty invested in conveying the impression of unflappable composure, of grace under pressure. I also guessed he wanted to separate himself, intellectually and stylistically, from Stu Biegler's tiresome posturing.

"Speaking of Charles Harland," I said, "how is he?"

"Still in ICU," the lieutenant replied grimly. "And still critical. Docs say it could go either way."

"What about the kidnappers? Any more calls?"

"None so far. I just checked in with Sergeant Polk there at the house. He said that Mike Payton and Harland's son James have returned home, too. Not much they can do at the hospital." A brief, sarcastic laugh. "Any other questions? I wouldn't want you to feel left out."

"Appreciate that. What about Arthur Drake?"

"Polk says the lawyer's just had another five million in bearer bonds delivered to the residence. So it'll be ready when they get the new ransom demand."

"*If* the call ever comes. After tonight…"

"Yes." Wilson slid smoothly off the table edge. Then, hands in his pockets, he peered at me. "About tonight. And what you neglected to mention when you gave your statement…"

"What are you talking about?"

"You said that when you were being questioned by Sykes, he asked you something about the Four Horsemen. Mind telling us what that means?"

"I would if I could. No idea."

"This was in reference to what Lisa Campbell might have disclosed during your therapy session, correct?"

"Sykes wanted to know if she'd mentioned the Four Horsemen. And I told him I couldn't reveal what Lisa and I discussed in therapy. Not that I'm going to tell *you*, either. Though even if I did, I can assure you it would have no bearing on the case. It was just personal material, relating to issues in her life."

This time, Biegler rose halfway out of his chair. Clenched fists on the table bracing him up.

"And we're supposed to just take your *word* for that?"

"You don't have much choice."

"Don't I?" His lean face darkened. "Goddamnit, Rinaldi! I don't give a shit about you and your confidentiality. Answer the man's question—*now!*—or I'll have a judge revoke privilege so fast your head'll spin!"

Now I was on my feet, too. Anger crowding my chest.

"You *do* that, Biegler! Call every judge in town. But I'm telling you, I don't know what the hell Sykes was talking about. The Four Horsemen could be a fucking *Vegas act*, for all I know!"

Gloria looked up at me. "Calm down, Danny..."

Easier said than done. Adrenaline was pulsing through me, as though my suppressed reaction to the long night's events had finally broken through. Flooding me. Until, by sheer effort of will, I forced myself to take a deep, cleansing breath.

Meanwhile, Agent Wilson was staring pointedly at Biegler. "That goes for you, too, Lieutenant."

Still flushed, Biegler managed a curt nod. Then, before he could take his seat again, Agent Riggs pushed open the doors.

"Sorry to interrupt, sir, but I think you should go up to your office. You and Lieutenant Biegler."

"What is it?" Wilson asked.

"There's something you better see."

Minutes later, we were all crowded into Anthony Wilson's spacious office, intently watching the flat-screen TV monitor on the wall. The KDKA morning news.

It was a live remote image, obviously taken from the station's chopper. At first, all I could make out through a veil of rising smoke was a blur of flashing lights, the outlines of a half-dozen vehicles. People scrambling, gesturing. And at the center of the chaotic scene a sprawling, gaping structure. Hunched, blasted. Flecked with angry, spitting flames.

Then I registered the graphic at the bottom of the screen: "Explosion and fire in the Hill District!"

As the chopper circled the fiercely burning building, a reporter's breathless voice provided the details:

"According to first responders on-scene, an explosion just twenty minutes ago ripped apart this abandoned printing factory in the Hill. Eyewitnesses nearby said they saw and heard a giant fireball erupt from the building, which was instantly engulfed in flames. Obviously, the fire is still out of control, so all police can do at the moment is keep onlookers away from the danger area, as firefighters begin battling the blaze."

The reporter went on to say that the Fire Department captain at the scene had no information as to whether the building had been occupied, and that no search for survivors could begin until the fire was extinguished.

At which point, Lieutenant Biegler slumped against a file cabinet, arms crossed.

"Shit, they're not gonna find anyone. Sykes probably came back to the place, saw that Rinaldi and Reese were gone, and figured he'd better cut his losses. Torched the place."

Wilson considered this. "The eyewitnesses said there was an explosion. According to our intel, Sykes and Griffin are ex-military. They could've used C-4. A lot more bang for your buck than using some fire accelerant. And quicker."

Gloria turned to her boss. "Which also means we probably won't find much useable forensics in the ashes."

"Instant demolition." Wilson used the remote to lower the TV audio. "Incinerating those cameras you saw, whatever evidence there might've been—"

"You mean, like info about his VIP clients? Maybe even the videos of them having sex. Probably on discs, or a flash-drive. Sykes mentioned keeping copies, for his own protection. His insurance against exposure."

"Though I don't think he'd keep them there," I said. "Sykes strikes me as having enough smarts to stash his 'insurance policies' in a separate location. Just in case he had to get out of there in a hurry. In fact, he and Griffin might've pre-set the explosives months ago. This way, if they suspected the cops were coming, all they'd have to do is pull the trigger."

The room fell silent as we all turned once again to the image on the screen. Fire hoses shooting arcs of water into the maw of flames. Blackened sections of the building collapsing, folding in on themselves. Gray-blue smoke billowing, outlined against the dull haze of the morning sun.

"Well," Wilson said at last, turning from the screen to look at Biegler. "We'll know more when your CSU team examines the scene. The Bureau can supplement your techs if you think it might speed things up, Lieutenant. I can also offer you the use of our forensics labs."

"Thanks." Biegler's eyes were wary. "But my gut says we're not gonna find much. Place looks totally trashed."

For once, I found myself agreeing with Biegler. If Wilson was right—and I believed he was—Sykes had used explosives to create a quick, ravenous fireball. A blast that would scour the premises, like bones stripped clean.

Agent Wilson let out a low, reflective sigh, then went to stand behind his desk. His features looking suddenly pallid, weary. Which he tried to conceal by drawing himself to his full height as he faced Gloria Reese and Agent Riggs.

"Okay. Agent Reese, you have an hour to go home, get cleaned up, and get back down here. I'll want you to go over everything that's happened since you were first assigned to the Harland residence. A sequence-of-events time line. Then I want you to brief the next shift when they arrive at eight. We need to be available to Pittsburgh PD if and when Chief Logan and Lieutenant Biegler request our assistance."

"Yes, sir." Her voice a whisper, threaded with fatigue.

Wilson then turned to the younger agent.

"And you, Riggs, coordinate all the intel between the Harland residence, Pittsburgh PD techs on scene at the fire, and whatever current evidence Lieutenant Biegler's people have with regard to the kidnapping itself. That okay with you, Stu?"

Biegler seemed a bit taken aback at being called by his first name, but he managed one of his patented officious nods. Then, as if to reassert his authority, he turned to me.

"As for *you*, Rinaldi. Stay available. In case Sykes—or Julian, or whatever the hell he calls himself—makes contact. It's possible he'll still want you to deliver the new ransom."

"Right. Unless, after tonight, he knows we know who he is, and is willing to settle for the money he's already got. A guy can go a long way on five million dollars."

Wilson grew thoughtful. "I'm inclined to agree with you, Doctor. Even with the full resources of the FBI and Pittsburgh PD on his tail, he could be hard to catch. God knows he's been able to evade federal prosecution for years, despite the fact we've long known about his criminal activities. Like you say, he's a smart guy. If he does decide to disappear, I suspect he'll be damned good at it."

"In other words," Gloria said, "he could be out of the state in a couple of hours. Or out of the country. And there's no way he'd take Lisa with him."

"That's for damn sure." Biegler idly scratched his chin. "Which means she's probably dead."

Chapter Nineteen

It was mid-morning by the time I got home.

I'd exchanged brief good-bye nods with Gloria Reese, who was clearly glad that Wilson had told her to go clean up and change before returning to work. After which, I was subjected to another round of questions from both the FBI agent and Biegler, until each was satisfied I'd told them all I knew. Then Wilson assigned another rookie G-man the task of driving me down to Noah's Ark, where my Mustang was parked.

Though the sunlit air was still cool, the wind had finally subsided, and it felt good to be behind the wheel. The only stop I made on my way across town was to get a new battery and memory card for my cell. Then I drove through sparse Sunday morning traffic to the Liberty Bridge, and up to Mt. Washington.

As soon as I entered my house, I pulled open the living room curtains, ignoring the dust motes swirling in the sun's pallid rays. Instead, my eyes were drawn to the answering machine on the rolltop desk. Message light blinking.

Thankfully, none of the messages were important. Angie Villanova inviting me to dinner next Sunday. Johnny Mannella, my cousin and accountant, calling again with questions about my tax return. And Noah, with the news that he was reconsidering the merits of our friendship. *Right*, I thought.

Next I checked my office voicemail. Nothing crucial there, either. A patient wanting to re-schedule an appointment. And an invitation to speak at an upcoming clinical conference.

I let out a sigh of relief, then went down the hall to the bathroom. Like Gloria, I was grateful for the chance to shower and change. I also craved some real coffee. So, hair still damp, dressed in a Pitt t-shirt and sweats, I padded into the kitchen to make some.

Finally, steaming mug in hand, I went into the living room, collapsed on the leather sofa, and clicked on the TV news.

As I'd expected, the printing factory fire was still the lead story. Apparently the blaze had been put down, and firefighters were already moving through the structure's smoking remains, looking for survivors. Or bodies. So far, according to the anchorman reporting, neither had been found.

I swallowed a mouthful of coffee, savoring the pungent flavor. The responders on scene weren't going to find any bodies. Nor much else, other than mounds of hot ash and a scattering of blackened debris. Sykes was long gone, taking knowledge of Lisa Campbell's whereabouts—and fate—with him.

I sat up on the sofa, suddenly restless, finished my coffee in a single gulp, staring down into the empty mug. Where the hell *was* Lisa, anyway? And why hadn't her kidnappers called with the second ransom demand?

I was still mulling this when the anchorman turned to a story about Donna Swanson's ongoing murder investigation, with breaking news about a related aspect to the case. A spokesman for Pittsburgh Memorial had just confirmed rumors that Charles Harland had been admitted the night before. He remained in ICU, recovering from an apparent stroke. There was speculation that the murder of Ms. Swanson, his longtime personal nurse, might have triggered the crippling event. The famous industrialist, married to former starlet and local celebrity Lisa Campbell, had been known to be in poor health for some time.

Here they cut to old footage of the well-known couple in happier times, hosting a gala charity ball in town. Though by now confined to a wheelchair, Harland seemed vigorous and ebullient as he joined his glamorous wife in greeting their guests. Switching back to the studio, the news anchor said it was assumed that Lisa was at her husband's bedside, though family spokesman Arthur Drake was unavailable for comment.

I clicked off the TV. So Harland's hospitalization had finally leaked, which made me wonder how long Lisa's disappearance could be kept under wraps. Not much longer, I suspected.

Exhausted, yet too wired to sleep, I thought about pulling on the training gloves and taking my frustration out on the heavy bag. I had a sort of makeshift gym in my basement, a low-ceilinged room cluttered with boxes and old tools, as well as some ancient workout equipment. The hanging bag, barbells, a weathered weight bench.

But the moment I envisioned heading for the basement stairs, I was aware of the lingering numbness in my arms, the dull ache in my ribs. Not to mention the goose egg decorating my skull. As the EMT had predicted, though some of the swelling had gone down, it still hurt like hell.

Great, I thought. *Inaction wedded to self-pity.* So much for that "hero complex" everybody always tagged me with. Especially Eleanor Lowrey. Christ, if she could see me now…

Without thinking, I got to my feet and went over to the landline phone and dialed her cell. Heard her outgoing message. So I tried her home number. Another outgoing message.

After all this time, I wasn't sure what exactly I wanted to say to her. Especially since I'd just be leaving a message on her machine. A short, one-way conversation, spoken into empty air. At a loss, I said only that I'd been thinking about her, and that I hoped she was okay. Then I hung up.

The moment I did so, I was sure my message had merely come across as foolish, or needy, or presumptuous. If not all three.

I knew she was on leave, dealing with some family issues. Her brother's addiction. Helping her mother tend to his kids.

But she'd made it clear that she was also on leave from me. From us. As for how long the break would last, I didn't know. Neither did she. Especially since she'd confessed when we ended that she still had feelings for her former lover, a woman she'd been with years before.

But I still had to know how she was doing. If she needed anything. Help, support. If she needed *me*...

So I decided to ask the one person who might know. That is, assuming he'd even tell me.

◇◇◇

"This is Sergeant Polk."

"Harry? Dan Rinaldi. You still at the residence?"

"Where the hell else would I be? In the library. Me and Raj, the FBI tech. Million laughs, that guy."

I could just make out another voice, nearby. Then Polk's hasty reply. "Jesus, Raj. I was fuckin' with ya."

Back to me: "Everybody's so goddamn sensitive nowadays."

I let that pass.

"What about the others, Harry?"

"The gang's all here."

A deliberate pause. Then I heard the slow trudge of his footsteps as Polk carried his cell somewhere. Probably out to the hallway or into a side room, away from the others.

In moments, he spoke again. "I was gettin' the stink-eye from Arthur Drake, so I figured I better go someplace private."

"How's he holding up?"

"Nervous as hell, but keepin' it together. Can't say the same thing for Harland's son James. He came back from the hospital with Payton and headed right for the bar. Guy's blotto. Like he's ready to pass out, lucky bastard. I wish to Christ *I* could. I'm sick o' these rich pricks."

"I feel your pain. Listen, I called to ask you something."

"About the case? Forget it, Doc. Besides, didn't Biegler tell you to take a hike?"

"Yes and no. I'm still on call in case the kidnappers want me to deliver the ransom."

"Ya mean, 'cause it worked out so good last time?"

"Look, Harry, I wanted to know about Eleanor. How she is."

"Lowrey? How the fuck should I know?"

"C'mon, you've been partners a long time. There's no way you two haven't talked. Even with her on leave."

"Once or twice, yeah. Not that it's any o' your goddamn business. But she sounds fine. Got her hands full with her no-good brother's kids, plus her mother's health is gettin' worse. But she's handlin' it."

"Is that just your opinion, or did she say so?"

"Lowrey's got more balls than either of us. If she says she's okay, she's okay." A sour grunt. "All I know is, her leave can't end too soon. That kid, Jerry Banks, just got released from the hospital. Which means I gotta keep workin' with that mook till Lowrey gets back."

Suddenly, there was a metallic click on his end. Another call coming in.

"Probably Biegler," Polk said. "Gotta go."

He hung up before I could say another word.

◇◇◇

My next call was to Noah. It was too early for the bar to be open, but I figured he'd probably be cleaning up from the night before. Restocking the booze before the lunch-time drinkers trickled in.

I was right. Though he didn't pick up the bar's landline till the tenth ring. Being Noah's friend requires patience.

"Noah, it's Danny. How are you?"

"I'm feelin' all kinds o' weird, is how I am. Maybe I oughta talk to Dr. Mendors about upping my meds. Again."

"Maybe. You sounded upset on your message."

"No shit? I'm pretty pissed at you right now, Danny. I mean, first you stand me and Charlene up the other night. If I was the suspicious type, I'd think it was so you could bail on your third of Doc Nancy's wedding gift. Then *last* night you leave without even sayin' good-bye."

"You're right, man. I'm sorry."

"Sorry, my ass. If this is the kinda friend you're gonna be, I'll have to ask you to take care of your bar tab. Ya know, I read in *Psychology Today* that money issues can really screw up a relationship. I should send you the link to the article."

I was glad he couldn't see my smile of relief. I'd heard enough jocular lucidity in his voice to know he was maintaining. Though

I made a mental note to get in touch with Nancy Mendors and make sure he was still on the right medication cocktail.

"On the positive side," he went on, "Charlene's brother Skip really liked you. Guess there's no accounting for taste. Anyway, he asked us to give him your number. So you guys could hang out. I figured, why not?"

"Okay with me."

Then Noah said he had to go. Making sure I heard the aggrieved tone in his voice.

"Glad you and Skip hit it off. But I'm still mad at you."

"But you'll get over it, right?"

"'Course I'll get over it. What the hell's *wrong* with you?"

He slammed down the phone.

Like I said. Patience.

I checked all the news channels one more time, but there were just follow-up stories to the Hill District fire and the Swanson murder investigation. Though the Fire Department spokeswoman did announce that, thankfully, there had been no bodies discovered in the print factory's ruins, and that the cause of the blast was still being determined.

Tossing the remote onto the couch, I climbed wearily to my feet and stretched. It was frustrating. I was clearly in need of sleep, but couldn't stop the buzzing in my mind. I knew that if I went to bed, I'd simply lie there, looking up at the ceiling.

I was still debating this with myself when my phone rang. It was Charlene's brother, Skip Hines.

"Hey, Skip. Noah told me you might call—"

He interrupted me, voice choked by agitation. "I'm in trouble, Doc. I mean, Danny…"

"What kind of trouble?"

"You gotta help me, man. Or else I'm screwed. You gotta get here right away."

"Okay, okay. Try to stay calm. Where are you?"

Chapter Twenty

The big outlet store was at the back end of the Monroeville Mall, right off Route 22. The parking lot was crowded with Sunday shoppers, and I had to pull into a spot a fair distance from the entrance. As I approached the broad glass doors, I noticed a squad car parked at the curb, light flashing.

Inside the sprawling structure, and beyond the maze of aisles whose display shelves seemed to tower over bustling customers pushing their carts, I spotted a sign that read: "Employees Only." My destination.

I pushed through the swinging metal doors and hurried down a corridor to the manager's office, where I found Skip Hines sitting in the airless, cluttered room. Head down, prosthetic leg jutting at an awkward angle. On either side of him stood two grim-faced men. One was short, round and bald, his brow dotted with sweat and his tie askew. The other—older, taller, and broad-chested—was a uniformed cop.

Skip's eyes snapped up, found mine.

"Thanks so much for comin', man. This whole thing is my fuck-up, but—"

The cop grumbled. "I'd keep my mouth shut, Hines. You're lucky I haven't run you in already."

The shorter man looked over at the cop.

"I'm still thinking I ought to press charges, Officer."

Then, stepping forward, he put out his hand to shake mine. "My name's Larraby. I'm the store manager. Your friend here got into an argument with one of my salesclerks and ended up taking a swing at him. I had to give my employee the rest of the day off—*with pay*—to keep him from making a federal case out of it."

I introduced myself and gave Larraby my most sincere, solicitous smile.

"I appreciate your letting me come and help straighten this out, Mr. Larraby. You're obviously a reasonable man."

"Don't thank *me*, Doctor. Thank Officer Parker here."

I turned to the uniform. "Let me guess. You'd like to wrap this thing up without all the paperwork, right?"

Parker gave me a wry smile. "Not only that, Doc. When Mr. Hines said he knew you, and that you could vouch for him, I figgered, what the hell, why not? I mean, you're sorta on the job and everything. Right?"

"I'm a consultant with the Department, yes."

"Besides, it'll get me some primo brownie points when I tell the wife I met you. She's seen you on the news a bunch o' times, thinks you look very distinguished. I told her it was just the beard, but—"

Skip stirred, reaching for the handle of a file cabinet next to him. Pulled himself to his feet.

"C'mon, guys. How many times do I gotta say I'm sorry? I lost my temper with that clerk and acted like an asshole. I admit it. I'll even call the guy and apologize if that'll help."

The store manager scratched his chin, pondering.

"Look, Mr. Larraby," I said, "Skip Hines is a veteran who lost his leg in combat. None of the rest of us in this room can imagine what he's been going through since then. The stress, the frustration. I'm hoping you'll cut him a break here."

The uniform nodded. "I agree with the Doc, Mr. Larraby. Guy's a wounded vet, for Christ's sake."

Larraby spread his hands. "Okay, you both can stop waving the flag. Just make sure Mr. Hines stays away from my store from now on. I don't need the grief…from him *or* my employees."

Skip offered him a crooked grin. "Thanks, man."

But Larraby had turned away, shaking his head in disgust. Meanwhile, the cop took out a notepad and handed it to me.

"How 'bout an autograph, Doc? For the wife."

◇◇◇

"Thanks again for havin' my six back there, Danny. Hell, maybe you shoulda been a lawyer instead of a shrink."

"Word of advice, Skip. Don't thank a guy and insult him at the same time."

He smiled, and took another healthy bite of his burger.

We were having lunch at a crowded diner on the other side of the mall. Skip was on his second beer.

"Anyway," he went on, "I know it musta been a surprise when I called you. I mean, we hardly know each other. But I couldn't call Charlene. I…I was too ashamed to tell her what I did. She worries enough about me already."

"I get it. And I'm glad I could help. Just don't make a habit of duking it out with store clerks."

I'd finished my meal and was nursing a beer myself. Though it was a bit early in the day for me.

"Never again." Skip raised a palm. "Honest. Thing is, the clerk was a real smart-ass, but…Anyway, I'll keep my cool from now on."

"Good idea." I leaned forward. "Look, at the risk of sounding like a therapist, I think you should consider seeing someone. A professional, who can help you deal with your feelings. About the war, your injury, whatever. If not, there are also plenty of support groups, and—"

"You mean, like anger management class?"

"Something like that. Or any place where you can get together with other vets. People going through the same things you are. Let me give you some referrals. Just hang on to the phone numbers 'til you think you might want to look into it. Couldn't hurt to think about it, right?"

"Right."

He studied the rim of his beer glass as I wrote out a few numbers on the back of one of my business cards. When I handed it to him, he stuffed it in his shirt pocket without giving it a moment's glance. I regarded him coolly.

He frowned. "Hey, I said I'd think about it. Okay?"

A measured beat of silence followed. I watched as Skip occasionally stared up at other people in the diner—couples, working men, white-collar types. Civilians, comfortable in a world which I suspected now felt quite alien to Skip. Hard to navigate. As though, after years in the Middle East, it was America that had become a foreign country.

His lunch finished, Skip ordered a third beer. At one point, he shifted in his seat, and had to twist his torso to accommodate his prosthetic leg.

He noticed my noticing.

"I tell myself every day that I'm finally used to it." He sighed. "But I'm not. And I still feel the damn thing at night. I'm lying in bed, the fake one's leanin' against the wall across the room, and I can feel my leg. Sometimes it's cold, sometimes it itches. Like it's still there. Crazy, eh?"

I shook my head. "Not at all. Even if you're consciously getting used to it, as you say, your brain's neurons aren't. But they will. I can't say when, but it'll happen."

He nodded, unconvinced. Then, as if eager to change the subject, he talked about his efforts to find a job. And his plan to enroll in a junior college, though—as he jokingly admitted—he worried about being the oldest student on campus.

Even as I assured him that this wouldn't be the case, my thoughts were elsewhere. Skip's feeling that his missing leg was still there—his phantom limb—struck a chord. I remembered how I reacted when my father died. How for so many years after, it still was hard for me to believe he was gone. That he wasn't sitting at home in his favorite chair, getting drunk, casting a jaundiced eye on everything I said and did. Wistful yet bitter about his years as a cop. Mourning the loss of his sainted wife.

Then I thought about the weeks and months following Barbara's murder. Though our marriage had been a difficult one, her death tore my world apart. For the longest time, I couldn't accept what had happened to her. Even now, all these years later, I have to sometimes remind myself that the person she was is no longer on this Earth.

Yet, like with my father, a felt sense of her lingers. Perhaps this is true for everyone. That those with whom we're most intimately connected persist, not only in memory, but almost like missing parts of ourselves. Like phantom limbs, we feel their presence, even though they're gone forever….

I finished my beer and looked over at Skip, who was regarding me with an amused expression.

"Sorry," I said. "I was just thinking."

"No problem. I plan on takin' that up someday myself. And lunch is on me, by the way. Least I can do."

I protested, but he wouldn't budge. Then, as we parted out on the street, he gripped my hand hard.

"Please don't tell Charlene about this, okay? I'll never hear the end of it."

I gave him my word, and we each headed off to where our cars were parked. Though I kept glancing back over my shoulder, watching as he hobbled down the rows of parked cars. The proud, determined angle of his head. The speed of his awkward gait.

Which reminded me of something Noah once said. That no matter who someone was, no matter what his or her circumstances, "life kicks the shit outta people." He'd said this without rancor, or self-pity, or easy pessimism. He'd merely reported it as a simple fact. The humane wisdom of a paranoid schizophrenic.

I'd found my car and had just slid behind the wheel when my cell phone rang. I picked up.

"Dr. Rinaldi? Arthur Drake here."

"Where are you calling from?"

"The residence, of course. I'm in my office."

"How did you get my cell number?"

A wry chuckle. "Mike Payton gave Charles a copy of his dossier on you, remember? I have it on the desk in front of me. Of course, all your numbers are there."

Of course, I thought. "How can I help you, Mr. Drake?"

"Frankly, I need to see you. I was hoping you could come to the house now. If it's convenient."

"I don't know if Lieutenant Biegler would be so wild about that idea. Or Sergeant Polk, for that matter."

His tone sharpened. "I'm a civilian, Doctor. As are you. If I invite you here as my personal guest, there's nothing the police can do to stop it. We're not interfering in the ongoing investigation. We're just going to have a drink."

I paused. Something was definitely up with the lawyer, but I'd be damned if I knew what it was.

"And you'd like me to come by now?"

"As I said, only if it's convenient."

To my ear, his words betrayed a certain urgency, despite the courtesy of his speech. He almost sounded…frightened.

I looked at the phone in my hand. For the second time today, someone was reaching out to me, asking for my assistance. Both relative strangers. Each from worlds as disparate from one another's as could be imagined.

At least I *liked* Skip Hines. Whereas my opinion of Arthur Drake was a lot more mixed.

So I'm not exactly sure why I agreed to meet him.

But I did.

Chapter Twenty-one

Compared to his employer's, Arthur Drake's office was of a modest size, though tastefully decorated. The requisite shelves laden with law books, memorabilia from two different Ivy League schools, a bag of golf clubs in the corner. Framed photos of the lawyer's wife and two grown daughters. Some award plaques on the walls from various charities and legal organizations.

The one discordant note was the disabled video camera hanging from a ceiling corner. As in the library, the casing had been opened. Wiring exposed, dangling.

Drake followed my gaze.

"I asked the FBI tech to take care of the security camera in here, too. And the microphone. After what's happened, I don't want to take any chances. Privacy is very important to me."

He indicated a stuffed leather chair opposite his neat, orderly desk. I took a seat. Then he closed the office door and turned the lock.

"*Very* important," he repeated as he returned to sit in the plush armchair behind his desk. Notable among the squared stack of files and gold-plated pen holder on the blotter was a bottle of Wild Turkey and two glasses. One was filled with the rich amber liquid. He raised the empty glass to me.

"Join me?"

"Why not?"

We each took a long swallow of the whiskey. Then, leaning back in his chair, he regarded me carefully.

"I'm taking a chance talking to you. Especially here in the house. But I don't dare leave, in case the kidnappers call."

I nodded. "I saw the armored truck parked out front. The additional bearer bonds, I assume."

"Correct. Another five million."

"I also noticed a few more cops on the grounds and in the house. In fact, the front door was answered by a uniform. Was this additional police presence Biegler's idea?"

"After he'd cleared it with Chief Logan, yes. Now that Charles is out of commission, Logan and Biegler are seemingly emboldened to act with a freer hand. Let's hope their decision doesn't come back to haunt them."

"You mean, in case it spooks Julian."

A thin smile. "I understand from the lieutenant that the kidnapper's real name is Raymond Sykes."

"News travels fast."

"Surely you can understand why. The police wanted to know if Mr. Harland or anyone in the family had any connection to this Sykes. Obviously, the idea is ridiculous. Charles and Lisa are public figures. The perfect targets for a kidnapping. And once someone had access to the security cameras inside the residence—eyes and ears on their personal lives, as it were—it would be easy to orchestrate an abduction."

"Makes sense. Though I still don't know why I'm here. Or why Sergeant Polk allowed it. I assume he's remained on duty in the library…?"

"Yes. But I told him I needed to speak to you privately, as a psychologist. A personal matter."

"Is that true?"

His easy smile faded. "What do you think?"

"I think you're scared. Maybe you know something about Lisa's kidnapping. Or maybe it's something closer to home. Involving the family."

"You're very perceptive, Doctor."

He threw back the rest of his drink and poured another.

"I do have something to tell you, but I must first insist that you treat it with the same discretion as you would if I *were* your patient. Are you willing to do that?"

I shrugged. "Sure. As long as you don't reveal your plans to injure or murder someone. Then I have to amble down the hall and alert Sergeant Polk."

Drake chuckled dryly. "The Tarasoff Law. Of course. Your duty to warn. However, I assure you that's not something you'll have to worry about."

Again, the amusement quickly melted from his face. He seemed to be steeling himself for what he had to say.

"As you may know, James was not Mr. Harland's only son. Charles and his first wife had another child, Charles Junior. Though everyone called him Chuck. He was born three years after Jimmy came along."

He paused, glass in hand, and peered out the office window at the broad expanse of manicured lawn stretching to the bank of trees beyond.

"Chuck was the proverbial apple of his father's eye. He grew into a fine young man. Model student, good at sports. Handsome, too. But the thing everyone loved about him was his character. It's rare to find a gifted young person who's also kind. Considerate."

"Did you know him?"

"I knew both boys, though they were practically grown men by the time we met. Jimmy had already graduated college, and Chuck was a senior. That's when it happened."

"What happened?"

"Chuck began to change. I mean, his personality. Almost overnight he became surly, foul-mouthed. He broke up with his fiancée and started hitting the clubs. Gambling, whoring, doing drugs. The kinds of things that…well, to be candid…that Jimmy had always done."

"What do you mean?"

"Since his teens, Jimmy had been in and out of trouble with the law. Drugs. Petty crimes. Associating with undesirables.

Low-life types. Though even the wealthy young people he partied with, men and women from prominent families, were of dubious character. Black sheep, if you will. Which made Charles furious, as you can imagine. It certainly broke his mother's heart."

I had a sense of where this was going.

"Did the family believe that James had introduced Chuck to this lifestyle? The club scene, the drugs and women?"

"It wasn't a belief on our part. Jimmy *bragged* about it. He loved seeing the brother to whom he'd been unfavorably compared all his life brought low. The Golden Boy. His father's pride and joy. Now just another out-of-control trust fund kid, as embarrassing to the family as Jimmy. If not more so."

By then I'd remembered what James had said to me after he'd found me in Lisa's bedroom. That following his brother's death, he'd been sent to a psychiatrist.

"I know that Chuck died," I said carefully. "How?"

"An overdose. The police found him in an alley behind a club in Shadyside. The autopsy revealed that Chuck had enough meth and coke in his system to—" Drake lowered his glass to the desk. "It was…tragic. Obscene, really."

"I don't remember hearing about it. Or seeing anything about it on the news."

"That's one of the advantages of wealth and power, Doctor. Charles was able to cover up the true cause of Chuck's death. They created the story that he'd been killed by a hit-and-run driver who's unfortunately never been found."

I let a silent moment settle between us.

"Now I understand Harland's antipathy toward James," I said at last. "The insulting way they speak to each other."

Drake slowly nodded. "Charles has never forgiven Jimmy. And never will. But Jimmy suffers, too. He's confided in me over the years how guilty he feels about Chuck's death. I believe that's why he drinks so heavily. Which only disgusts his father more. No wonder Jimmy's so embittered. So…lost. Can you imagine? Despised by one's own father…"

Once more, the lawyer peered out the window.

"As far as I'm concerned, Jimmy's paid enough for what he did. Emotionally, I mean. *He's* a victim, too."

Another long pause. Eyes still averted, Drake spoke again, voice as soft as breath.

"I *love* Jimmy, Doctor. I've loved him for years, despite his flaws. His drinking. His insolence."

I nodded, though I knew he didn't see it. His gaze still fixed on the opulent stand of trees. The wind had picked up again, its fingers combing through the full, leafy branches.

"It cost me my marriage," he went on. "And my daughters look at me now like I'm a stranger. Someone they don't recognize anymore. We still have dinner occasionally, but…"

"I'm sorry, Arthur. Really. Does James know how you feel?"

A bitter laugh. "Oh, yes. I made the mistake of…I tried to touch him once. To stroke his face, that's all. And he…he rebuffed me. Has nothing but contempt for me now. But I still care for him. I'm the only one who does."

"Yes, I got that impression."

He took a breath. "The way everyone treats him…It's terrible. Unfair. Mike Payton shares Mr. Harland's disgust. As did poor Donna Swanson, Charles' nurse. She *hated* Jimmy, probably for the pain he's always caused his father."

Drake turned back to face me, his eyes moist. He dabbed them with the knuckle of a finger.

I kept my voice even. "I also got the impression that James doesn't care much for Lisa Campbell…."

The lawyer sniffed. "Obviously not. The age difference, for one thing. It infuriates him. He thinks it's ludicrous. Plus, Jimmy sees her as an interloper. Only after his father's money."

"Which could mean a lot less leftover for James when Daddy dies. Is Lisa now the primary beneficiary of Harland's estate? As the family lawyer, I assume you would execute any new will— whatever revisions were made after Charles and Lisa married."

"You know I'm not at liberty to discuss that."

"Right." I leaned forward in my chair. "One more question. You still haven't told me what you're afraid of."

He very deliberately folded his hands in front of him.

"I have no proof of this, you understand. But I'm convinced that Mike Payton is behind Lisa's kidnapping."

"Based on what?"

"As I say, nothing concrete. Of course, he appears to be very upset about it. *Over*reacting, in my opinion. And I know he's always seemed friendly to Lisa since she married Charles. But he *is* the head of security for Harland Industries. And the Harland family. He's the one who contracted with the security company that installed all the cameras in the house. So he'd certainly be able to help whoever hacked into the system. Maybe even did it himself."

"Anything else?"

"Don't forget, at Lisa's request he prepared the dossier on you. He knew she was going to see you. She'd probably even told him when. No matter who this Raymond Sykes is, I think it's possible that Payton was behind this all along. That Sykes and his thugs work for *him*."

"But why would Payton do this?"

"Why would anyone, Doctor? The money. Believe me, I've seen it before. A person spends years around all that wealth, and suddenly wants some of it for himself. Even feels entitled to it, after all his hard work and dedication. His sacrifice."

I thought this over. "I don't know, Drake. Seems pretty flimsy to me."

"And to me. I'm a lawyer, after all. I know circumstantial evidence when I hear it. That's why I haven't shared my concerns with the police."

"So why share them with me?"

"In case something happens to me, I…well, I want someone to take my theory to the proper authorities."

"But why *me*?"

"I'm pretty perceptive myself, Doctor, and my instincts tell me you can be trusted. Certainly more than anyone else in this house. Even Jimmy. Even given the way I feel about him…"

He managed a rueful grin. "Funny. A man my age, lusting after a rebel. A bad boy…"

"James is hardly a boy. Not anymore."

"Oh, there you're wrong, Doctor. In all the ways that matter, Jimmy's stayed a very young man…Impulsive, unashamed of his appetites, unwilling to conform to being what his father wants him to be…"

I was struck by the wistfulness in his voice. The unmet yearning. The sober desperation of unrequited love.

Drake himself seemed aware of it, and quickly looked down.

Suddenly there was a pounding at the door. And a harsh voice, bellowing. Harry Polk.

"Drake! It's Sergeant Polk. Open the damn door!"

The lawyer climbed out from behind his desk and unlocked the office door. Polk, face flushed, stood on the threshold.

"That prick Julian finally called. He's on the line in the library. It's go time!"

Chapter Twenty-two

Again, the caller identified himself as Julian. And again, his voice was electronically altered. Robotic, without inflection. As if coming from the other side of the moon.

"I'm afraid I'm at a loss. Someone's disabled the security apparatus, so I can't tell who I'm speaking to."

"Makes us even, scumbag," Polk growled.

Drake shot him a shocked, warning look. His expression said it all: We can't afford to antagonize Julian. Not at this stage.

I caught Polk's eye, giving him a slightly more collegial version of the same look. He scowled, but got the message. All these hours waiting around in this house hadn't done much for his attitude. Nor his professional composure.

Drake, Polk, Payton, Raj, and I were all huddled around the library desk, listening to Julian on speakerphone.

"Under the circumstances, I don't have time for our usual pleasantries. So I'll get straight to the point. I have Lisa. And I assume you have the additional five million dollars. In bearer bonds, of course."

Drake spoke firmly. "This is Arthur Drake. I have the funds, yes. But we need proof that Lisa's still alive."

"Naturally."

This time, the woman's voice on the speaker was strained, weak. It was Lisa, unquestionably. I recognized her immediately. But the vehemence she'd shown previously, the defiant outrage, was gone. She sounded compliant, defeated.

"Please…give this bastard whatever he wants…*Please*… He's gonna *kill* me…"

"Lisa! Mrs. Harland!" Drake leaned in toward the phone console. "Are you all right? Are you hurt?"

There was a muffled sound of movement, a faint, anguished cry. Then a heavy silence. Until Julian spoke once more.

"She's alive, as you all heard. But she's not doing very well. This whole ordeal has been a terrible strain."

"Prick." Payton whispered under his breath. Hands clenched into fists at his sides.

"Look, I have the money," Drake went on, hurriedly. "What are the instructions? How do we make the transfer?"

"That depends. Who's making the delivery? Again, no cops or Feds…or else Lisa dies."

"We understand. That's why I'll deliver the ransom myself. Just please do not harm Mrs. Harland."

"You'll get instructions. But first, is Dr. Rinaldi there?"

"Yes," I said. "Right here."

"Good. Because part of the deal involves you, Doc. You have to accompany Drake to the delivery point."

"What?" Polk squinted at the speaker. "No goddamn way."

"In case it's slipped your mind, people, I'm still in charge here. And I say Rinaldi comes with the lawyer. The Doc and I have some unfinished business."

There it was. The proof that Sykes was the man on the other end of the call. Our "unfinished business" had to refer to his question to me about the Four Horsemen. The one he was pressing me to answer when he'd been called out of the room.

Before I could reply, however, Mike Payton put himself between me and the phone console. Face grim.

"Listen, Rinaldi. Don't do it. It's got to be a trap of some kind. Right, Sergeant?"

Polk shrugged. "That's the way I read it."

"Except we don't have a choice," I said.

"He's right, you don't." That eerie, unseen voice. Tinny.

Remorseless. "And I'm losing what little patience I have left, gentlemen. You have one minute to decide. Tick-tock."

I didn't hesitate.

"If I come with Drake, do you guarantee Lisa's safety?"

"Let's put it this way, Doc. I guarantee her a slow, excruciating death if you *don't*."

Jaw furiously working, Sergeant Polk stepped a few feet away from the table, indicating that the rest of us should do the same. He spoke in an urgent whisper, bloodshot eyes flitting between Arthur Drake and me.

"This is bullshit. I can't let either o' you do this. Not without clearin' it with Biegler. Maybe even Chief Logan."

Drake drew himself up. "Don't be absurd, Sergeant. You think Julian's going to wait while we call them?"

"Not a chance." Payton frowned. "Sounds like he wants to wrap this thing up as fast as he can."

"I agree," I said.

Nobody spoke for a moment. Then Raj gave Polk a tentative tap on the shoulder.

"Sir, we could put a wire on Mr. Drake and the doctor. Or a GPS tracer on the car they use."

"And risk Lisa's life?" Drake's eyes narrowed. "You saw what happened the last time we tried some funny business."

Payton nodded. "Again, I'm with Drake on this one."

The unearthly metallic voice crackled from the speaker behind us. "Time's up, folks. What's the verdict?"

Before anyone else could respond, I turned around.

"We'll do it. Drake and I will bring the cash. Now tell us where and when."

It was dusk by the time we'd covered the first two hundred miles. Drake and I were in his own car, a Lexus, and the lawyer was behind the wheel. I sat next to him, the black suitcase filled with stacks of bearer bonds on the floor at my feet.

Julian's instructions had been simple. Drake and I were to set his car's odometer to zero, and, leaving from the front gate of Harland's residence, drive exactly two hundred thirty-three miles east on the turnpike. At which point we'd find an access road heading north, barred by a wooden gate. There we were to park and await further instructions.

No sooner had Julian hung up than Polk was on his cell to his boss. I could only imagine Biegler's response as Harry explained the situation, but I had no interest in lingering to hear it. My sense was that every second counted if we were to find Lisa Campbell alive. From his stricken look, it seemed that Arthur Drake shared my conviction.

The lawyer and I spoke only a few words during the long drive. Shared anxiety about whatever real or imagined dangers lay ahead, no doubt. But I also wondered if it was something else. After his frank disclosures to me in his office, Drake seemed suddenly diffident. Uncomfortable. As though perhaps he regretted having taken me into his confidence.

The sun had dipped lower, purpling the sky. The wind had risen, too, more sharply as we left the city further and further behind. We were now heading into the verdant woods and rolling hills of rural Pennsylvania. Past weary towns shorn of their former industries, and family farms lost to foreclosure or agribusiness. Past old railroad tracks and unused covered bridges and exhausted coal mines. Past the vestiges of a small-town way of life made irrelevant by the globalized economy.

We were about twenty miles from our first designated stop when Drake abruptly opened his window. The wind coming out of the thickening dusk roared briskly into the car, as though summoned. The whistling, insistent gust was cool and slightly damp against my skin. The promise of a spring rain.

I saw a smile slowly form on the lawyer's lips.

"Whenever I feel a strong wind, I think of Elvira." He glanced over at me. "Our old nanny when I was a child. She used to say the sound of the wind was the wail of lost souls, the dead flying around the world looking for a way into heaven."

"Wow. That's the kind of thing that would've given me nightmares as a kid."

"Rest assured, it did. For years. Until the horrors of the real world took its place. The illusions. The false promises."

I realized then that I'd been wrong. His silence these past two hours hadn't been due to shame about what he'd revealed to me. More likely, something about the deadly nature of what we were doing, its life-and-death consequences, had triggered a cascade of memories. Sober reflections on his life, his choice of profession. Of his friends and lovers.

As I'd learned in my therapy practice, the old saw—that in the face of impending danger or death, your life flashed before your eyes—was frequently true. Certainly enough of my patients had related their experience of it at times of great stress or fear to convince me. Especially those victimized by violence, or the threat of violence.

I studied Drake's profile, backlit against the setting sun. He'd turned to focus again on the road, hands tight on the wheel. Driving with increased intensity. And with good reason. A quick glance at the odometer told me we'd almost arrived at our first stopping point.

My throat grew dry. For both the lawyer and myself, there was a real possibility we'd soon be joining those unhappy souls crying in the wind.

◇◇◇

At mile two hundred thirty-three, a weathered wooden gate appeared on the left side of the highway. Not an off-ramp, but a dirt access road, as Julian had described. Drake slowed and pulled the car onto the wide gravel strip in front of the gate. Then he cut the ignition.

"Now what?" His hands still clamped to the wheel.

"We'll find out soon enough."

I peered out through the windshield. Nothing but fields, dotted with leafy oaks. In the far distance, a sluggish creek shone dully in the moonlight.

Not ten minutes passed before Drake's cell rang. Exchanging a quick, nervous look with me, he picked up.

"Get out of the car. Both of you. Open the gate. Walk a hundred yards up the access road."

I could hear the same digitally altered voice through the cell's speaker. Then, before Drake could reply, the call ended.

I let out a long breath, then reached for the suitcase in front of me.

"Ready when you are," I said, giving Drake what I hoped was a mildly encouraging smile. I don't think it worked.

We did as instructed. The gate was unlocked, and swung open freely on its hinges. The access road on the other side was primarily dirt, flecked with gravel, and rose to a slight elevation in the near distance. An easy hundred-yard walk.

My grip tight on the suitcase handle, I took the lead as we started along the road under a clear, star-strewn sky—clouds having long since scattered by the ardent sweep of the wind.

As we trudged along in silence, I couldn't help but think of the last time I carried such a suitcase climbing up the path to the Allegheny Observatory. And how that night had ended.

I pushed those thoughts from my mind and kept walking. I glanced behind me once, to find Drake swiveling his head from side to side searching the barren fields whose few shrubs and tall shoots were white-tipped with moonglow. Peering anxiously, compulsively, into the open darkness.

"There's nothing," he whispered. "No one. I don't see anything out there."

I met his gaze, but didn't reply. Then faced front again.

By my mental reckoning, we'd walked about a hundred yards. I stopped, took a look around myself. Nothing.

Drake came to stand beside me. "Think that's a hundred yards?" he asked.

"Close enough." I put down the suitcase.

Swallowing hard, Drake pulled out his cell. Stared at it.

"Come on, why don't you ring? *Ring*, dammit!"

Silence. Not a sound. Nothing but the whirr of the wind, bending the branches of distant trees.

Suddenly, off to the right about twenty-five yards, a light flared in the fields. Bobbing as it came toward us. The familiar lift and drop of a flashlight in hand. Someone was coming.

I tensed. Hands instinctively balling into fists. Pure muscle memory, from all those years ago…

The man was getting closer. Then abruptly stopped, not more than ten feet away from the side of the road.

"Nice night, eh?"

I recognized his voice, even before he took another couple steps and I could make out his hard, chiseled features.

It was the big man. Griffin. The same jacket, same jeans. He aimed the blinding light directly at us. Flare-bright, silhouetting us against the darkness.

"I wouldn't try nothin' if I were you, Rinaldi. Guess what I got in my other hand?"

I didn't have to guess. The ugly gun barrel, nose pointed at me, glinted in the pale moonlight.

"Now," he said smoothly, "it'd make my life a lot easier if I just whacked you two fucks right now. Then all I'd have to do is pick up the suitcase and be on my way. But Sykes wants to see you. *Especially* you, Doc."

The gun swung in a steady, gut-high arc, back and forth between Drake and me.

"So let's get going. Straight up this same road, about another hundred yards. You two in front, me in back. And all the time itchin' to blow your fuckin' heads off. Which I'll gladly do, if either o' you losers tries anything. Everybody on board with the plan?"

I mutely nodded, and saw Drake do the same.

Griffin spit into the grass at his feet. "Okay, then. Let's hit it. And, Doc…Don't forget the suitcase."

Chapter Twenty-three

We must have walked another hundred yards or so before we saw it. Parked off to the side of the access road, wheel-deep in tall grass. The same van in which Gloria Reese and I had been held, its headlights shining bright as miniature suns.

At Griffin's urging, Drake and I left the road and stumbled across the uneven field toward the van. As we approached, I squinted against the bright lights, trying to make out who was sitting in the passenger seat. But all I saw was the outline of a slender man, and the faint orange glow of a cigarette tip.

"Okay." Griffin's voice cut through the rustling of wind. "That's close enough."

Drake and I stopped about a dozen feet from the front of the van, bathed in the harsh glare of its headlights. Taking a breath, I risked a glance over at the lawyer, whose hands trembled at his sides. His lean face painted a ghostly pallor.

Griffin stepped from behind us and took a position just to the side of the van's front grille. Backlit, he seemed somehow even taller and more formidable. His gun pointed steadily at a spot between where Drake and I stood. So that a flick of the wrist could put a bullet into either one of us.

Just then, to my surprise, Drake boldly called out.

"Is Lisa in the van? I demand to see her."

Griffin laughed. "You don't get to demand *shit*, douche bag. Besides, your part in this is pretty much over."

He indicated me with his gun. "Sykes wants to talk to the Doc here. After he sees the money."

I tightened my grip on the suitcase handle and took a step toward Griffin. But Drake crossed in front of me, and began walking briskly toward the big man. As though fueled by a long-suppressed outrage, a panicked belief in his moneyed omnipotence.

"Enough of this! You have your damned money. Now where is Lisa? I'm not leaving without her!"

"You're right," Griffin said easily. "You're not."

He raised his gun and shot Arthur Drake in the head. The lawyer staggered once, then fell backwards onto the tall grass.

"Drake! No!" I cried out. Stunned, I scrambled over to him, crouching by his side. "Jesus…"

A single bullet hole was centered in his forehead, blood oozing thick and darkly red. He'd died instantly.

In the obscene brightness of the headlights, every line and plane of his contorted features met my eyes. His countenance a blanched mask, registering equal parts surprise and indignation.

"Griffin…" My words a strangled gasp. "Why'd you..?"

Bent over Drake, I heard the big man striding toward me. My hand still unaccountably gripping the suitcase, I rose quickly from my haunches, pivoted, and slammed the heavy bag at Griffin with all my strength.

Instinctively shielding himself with his forearm, the impact of the blow discharged his gun. Blinded by the sudden muzzle flash, he roared in anger, stumbling backward. Out of the bright glow of the van's lights, and into total darkness.

Foolishly, unthinkingly, I threw down the suitcase and headed after him, blood pulsing in my temples. Eyes scanning the grass and dirt around me for his gun. Assuming he'd dropped it when startled by the muzzle flash—

Then I remembered the second man, the one in the van. Sykes himself, probably. I halted, gasping, and turned toward the still-blazing headlights. Half expecting to see Sykes climbing out of the passenger seat, raising his own gun…

Heavy footfalls brought me around again. It was Griffin, stepping once more into the light. Powerful frame almost shaking with rage. Eyes tear-streaked, squinting with pain.

I froze where I stood. Somehow, the ugly revolver was still in his grasp. Its barrel rising to point at me.

"Fuck Sykes!" He steadied the gun with both hands. "I'm *smokin'* your ass!"

I was a dead man, and I knew it.

Suddenly, a sharp, staccato blast of the van's horn sounded. Harsh, demanding.

Momentarily startled, Griffin turned toward the van. The flaring, unremitting lights.

It was all the chance I needed. His attention diverted, I took off, running at full speed toward the darkness of the fields beyond. Toward the clutch of shadowy trees outlined against the low hills, the cold spray of stars.

I hadn't gone a dozen yards before I heard the shot. Felt the breath of the bullet's path as it narrowly missed my ear. Griffin, obviously unmindful of Sykes' warning with the car horn, was chasing after me. Firing as he ran.

Two more shots echoed. Then silence. He was re-loading. Given a man of his skill, he was probably doing so on the run.

I pushed myself to go faster, almost stumbling on an upraised root. But the image of Griffin in pursuit, his murderous single-mindedness, was enough to spur me on. I was literally running for my life.

I'd just reached the first tree, an ancient oak, when a bullet buried itself in the bark inches from my head. Heart pounding in my chest, I moved further into the trees.

Within moments, I was plunged into a spiny cluster of low-hanging branches and thick foliage that concealed what little moonlight there was. Hearing nothing but the sound of my own labored breathing, seeing nothing but shadows and obscure shapes looming before me, I pressed on. Twigs snapping underfoot, pushing my way past an endless tangle of leaves and gnarled branches. Waiting every moment for the telltale signs of

Griffin closing the distance between us, listening for the whistle of that fatal bullet.

Finally I reached a dense cluster of trees, and positioned myself on the other side of the largest one, back pressed against the rough bark. Willing myself to stay calm, quiet.

Behind me, not a hundred feet away, the sound of movement among the low weeds and tuffs of grass. Slow, heavy footsteps.

Steeling myself, I peered around the curve of the tree trunk and saw the beam of Griffin's flashlight, sweeping the untracked brush and exposed roots in his path. He was getting closer. Revolver gripped in his other hand, upraised. Straight-armed, he followed the arc of his light as it scythed across the gloom.

Panic rose in my chest. I knew I couldn't stay where I was, hidden behind the tree. But if I tried to run, I'd be pinned in that oscillating, unforgiving light.

Griffin kept moving, a remorseless juggernaut. Closer and closer. I could now hear his deep, resonant breathing. Steady, unhurried. The practiced hunter on the trail of his prey.

Get a grip! Words echoing soundlessly in my mind. Scolding. *You can't stay here, you have to move! You have to—*

Instinctively, I took a step back. And felt my foot sink into the rich dirt beneath me. Startled, I quickly righted myself, then got to my haunches.

I'd stepped into some kind of depression in the ground. A scalloped pocket of sunken earth, perhaps four feet deep.

I didn't hesitate, sliding as far down into the dark crevice as I could. Huddled amidst twigs and sodden leaves and caked, loamy dirt.

Moments later, I spotted Griffin's flashlight beam poking restlessly along the upper edge of my hiding place. Then it flitted on past, taking up again its steady arc, illuminating a nearby low-hanging branch or knotty tree trunk.

I held my breath. Listening for the measured tread of Griffin's advancing footsteps.

At the same time, I kept replaying the image of Drake's death. The awful suddenness with which his life had been snuffed out.

Less than five hours ago, we'd been sitting in the tidy comfort of his office, having drinks. Discussing the conflicts plaguing the dignified lawyer, his unrequited love for James Harland, his suspicions about Mike Payton.

And now he was gone, at the hands of a ruthless killer. Body lying in a nameless field in the middle of nowhere.

I closed my eyes, willing myself to come back to the present. To stay focused on that same killer, now bearing down on me. But was he? I'd been straining to catch the telltale snap of a twig, the crunch of a boot on dry leaves. Yet I wasn't hearing anything.

Then, as quickly as it had appeared, that piercing beam of light winked out. Now all I saw was the familiar ink-black blanket of night. All I heard was a rustle of movement, the sound of Griffin turning, heading back the way he'd come.

Still not daring to breathe, I waited another couple minutes, until I was sure he was gone. Searching elsewhere.

At last, I felt safe enough to risk using my cell phone. I pulled it from my pocket and clicked it on. No signal. Probably not a cell tower for a hundred miles in any direction.

But there was no use staying where I was. Better to keep moving, since I doubted Griffin would stop looking for me. He might even have gone back to the van to enlist Sykes' help.

I took a couple of deep breaths, tinged with the smell of wet dirt and old moss. It was time to move. To climb out of this earthen womb and—

Suddenly, the ground shifted under my feet. Fell away. Gasping, I grabbed for some roots protruding from the dirt wall.

Too late. I was falling, legs churning empty air. Tumbling down a deep, widening hole in the earth…

The impact was jarring, but I didn't lose consciousness. The wind knocked out of me, I was momentarily light-headed. Disoriented. Then, carefully reaching with outstretched fingers, I felt cold, moist dirt. Below and on either side of me.

I took a couple swallows of dank, musty air. Then, limbs still unreliably shaky, I craned my neck to look above me. Given the darkness, it was hard to judge accurately, but I guessed I'd fallen about fifteen feet through what appeared to be a sinkhole. I must have been hiding from Griffin in an indentation at the mouth of the hole. Then, when I tried to climb out, the shifting of my weight sent me plummeting.

But plummeting where? Brushing dirt and leaves from my face, I swiveled on my heels, trying to get my bearings.

It didn't take long. I'd no sooner turned than I saw a squared edging of light. It outlined what looked to be a small door of some kind, slightly ajar, and not twenty feet away.

Breathing more easily now, I collected my thoughts. I seemed to have fallen into some kind of access tunnel. Maybe, behind me, it once led to a larger tunnel. Perhaps a mine shaft, long abandoned since the collapse of the mining industry.

But then what was in front of me, at the end of that narrow tunnel? On the other side of that slightly open door?

Whatever it was, I'd have to find out. If only because there was no getting out of here by climbing back up the slippery, loosely packed earthen walls of the sinkhole.

Resigned, I began crawling slowly down the short length of tunnel. Even on my hands and knees, the low ceiling of dirt and rotting leaves brushed the top of my head.

I quickly reached the small door, then bent close against the rough wood, listening for any sounds from within. Nothing.

As quietly as I could, I took hold of the exposed edge of the door and pulled it toward me. Once it was fully open, I could see the source of the light. A high-wattage bare bulb, encased in a metal cage, suspended from a wooden ceiling beam.

I blinked, eyes adjusting to the sudden brightness. The room was small, some kind of cellar, with walls of damp earth reinforced by upright, weathered two-by-fours.

Sitting on an old crate beneath the hanging bulb, his arms crossed, was a bald, stocky man in jeans and a t-shirt. Of indeterminate age, his exposed arms and neck were covered with tattoos. Horned skulls, flaming swords, swastikas. An upsidedown cross, dripping blood.

But then my gaze was drawn by what lay beside the sleeping man. Huddled in a fetal position on the rough dirt floor.

Her hands and feet were bound with thick, oily rope. Mouth cruelly banded with duct tape. Wearing the same trendy designer clothes—now torn and mud-spattered—as the last time I'd seen her.

Eyes closed, but breathing.

Unconscious, but alive.

Lisa Campbell.

Chapter Twenty-four

I crossed the tiny room in a couple of strides. Awakened by the rush of movement, the tattooed man roused himself enough to clamber to his feet. About half a second too late.

The roundhouse he threw was so telegraphed I had no trouble ducking under it. Then I clipped him with my forearm, snapping his head back. For good measure, I grabbed his shoulders with both hands and slammed his head against one of the standing two-by-fours. He collapsed in a heap.

I stood with feet apart, breathing hard. While my old pugilistic instincts had served me, my no-longer-young body protested. My forearm stung from the blow, and my legs felt wobbly. Still aching from my tumble down the sinkhole, my back was threatening to seize up.

All of which I barely registered. My only thought at the moment concerned the unconscious woman on the floor. Thankfully, and somewhat surprisingly, alive.

I crouched by Lisa's side and carefully removed the duct tape from her mouth. She stirred, but didn't open her eyes. As I leaned in closer, I noted the bruises on her cheeks and chin. Her lips were cracked, bone-white.

I could also smell the ketones on her breath. Lisa was dehydrated. We'd have to get some water into her, and soon.

I'd untied her hands and was struggling with the ropes binding her ankles when she came to. Finally, I freed her legs and scrambled back up, so that our eyes could meet.

Blinking in the harsh light from above, I saw recognition slowly dawn.

"Doctor?…Jesus, Rinaldi, is that you?…"

Her voice feeble, a hollow croak.

"It's me, Lisa. Are you okay?"

"Define your terms."

She tried to stretch her limbs where she lay, and winced in pain. Let her head droop back to the ground.

"You're safe now, Lisa." I gently pushed her hair back from her forehead. Exposing another ugly bruise.

"Safe?" Her dry lips curled. "I've had the shit kicked outta me and I'm in a hole in the ground. I don't *feel* safe…."

I slipped my arm under her head.

"We've got to get moving, understand? Before Sykes and Griffin show up. They're probably heading here now…."

She lolled, limp as a rag doll. "I'm fine where I am, Doc. My arms and legs don't work anyway…"

"They will, soon enough. Now here, let me help you…"

Putting my hands under her armpits, I more or less hauled her to her feet. She was obviously still dazed, exhausted. Stumbling on rubbery legs.

"You remind me of a punch-drunk fighter," I said.

"You should see the other guy…"

I smiled, encouraged by her attempt at banter. As though she were summoning from her deepest core the old, resilient Lisa. Good thing, too. Given the trauma of her ordeal, that sly, rueful humor could be a powerful ally in her recovery.

Straightening, I put my arm around her waist, even as I felt her taking most of her weight on her own legs.

"Looks like you're able to stand."

"Theoretically."

I glanced around the small, cold cellar. "How did they bring you here? That tunnel?"

She shook her head, then pointed up at something in the shadows. Attached by a kind of peg-and-pulley system to the ceiling. An aluminum ladder.

I risked letting go of her and reached my hand up, grasping the ladder by the bottom rung. When I pulled it down, its length extended to about a foot off the cellar floor.

"What's up top?" I asked her.

"Trapdoor. The way out."

I glanced up again. Now I could see the trapdoor, its outlines blurred by the hanging bulb's relentless glare.

"Let me go up first," I said. "Just in case."

"My fucking hero."

The old Lisa was coming back, all right.

I took hold of the ladder and quickly climbed up to the trapdoor. When I pushed, it opened easily, with the merest squeak of its hinges. Poking my head through, I found myself looking at a much larger room. Bare-bricked walls, two broad shuttered windows. Fluorescents hanging from the waffled tin ceiling.

But it was what filled the room that caught my attention. A long metal table, on which were arrayed a half-dozen monitor screens. Now blackened, I had no doubt they'd once been connected wirelessly to the security cameras in the Harland residence. As was the phone, in its cradle next to some kind of communications console. Probably the device used to digitally alter the speaker's voice. There were also two computers, one of whose screens displayed a map of Western Pennsylvania.

I climbed the rest of the way up and stood on the hardwood floor. This was the room from which Julian—Raymond Sykes—contacted the residence, making his ransom demands. All these hundreds of miles away.

Not exactly convenient to that abandoned print factory in the Hill District. But then again, Sykes had said that his human trafficking operation was located elsewhere, too.

I considered this. Sykes may just be a big fish in a small pond, as Gloria Reese had put it, but he was a fish who knew how to diversify. Regardless, it couldn't be easy for him to keep tabs on everything himself. Which got me wondering how exactly he did it.

"Hey!" Lisa's voice, calling from below. I could hear her footsteps slowly ascending the ladder. "You wanna lend me a hand, Doc? Before Tattoo Man wakes up?"

"Sorry. Just checking things over." I bent and extended my hand, helping to hoist her up into the room.

"I wonder what this place is," I said.

She let out a breath. "Abandoned ranger station, I think. Or maybe some field office from when the mines were working."

"How do you know?"

"I saw it from the outside. It has some old-fashioned antennas and stuff on the roof. I remember things like that from when I was a kid. Back in the Stone Age, God help me."

"But when did you see it?"

"When I escaped. Or *tried* to, anyway." She sighed. "Christ, I see I'm gonna have to get you up to speed."

"You sure are. But not now. Now we get some help."

I went over to the table and snatched up the cordless phone. Tried, but failed, to get a dial tone.

I turned the phone over. A tangle of unhooked wires.

"They took the guts out of it. Probably did this every time they left here. In case you got free and came up the ladder. So you couldn't use the phone to call for help."

Besides, I thought, once they had the second ransom money, there'd be only one reason to come back here. To kill Lisa.

Meanwhile, she'd crossed the room to peer over my shoulder at the disabled phone. "Son of a bitch. Now what—?"

I put my finger to my lips. I'd just heard the tattooed man stirring down below. Quickly, I went back and closed the trapdoor. As I'd hoped, it had a bolt lock. I slid it home.

"That'll keep him for a while. But we still have the others to worry about. Sykes, Griffin."

She nodded soberly. "Two scary bastards…"

This time, her tone lacked its usual sturdy humor. She looked genuinely afraid. Perhaps recalling a painful memory, some recent terrifying encounter with her captors.

Then, just as quickly, she seemed to shake it off. Survival instincts trumping everything. Even fear.

I gripped her hand and led us to the sole exit door. On the way, I noticed a portable refrigerator in a corner. I stooped and opened it, happy to find what I'd been hoping to.

"Here." I offered her a bottled water, then put another two bottles in my jacket pockets. "You need to hydrate. Drink that whole bottle."

"Yes, sir." She took a long, grateful swallow from the bottle. "But just 'cause you rescued me, that doesn't mean you get to boss me around."

"Point taken. Now keep drinking."

Frowning theatrically, she managed to finish the bottle before following me through the door.

We stepped out into a cold, clear night, undergirded by a ceaseless wind. I took a quick look at our surroundings. The building was fronted by a compact clearing, studded with gravel. A makeshift parking area, served by a fire road that meandered into the hills to our right. To our left was the expanse of trees through which I'd fled, pursued by Griffin. I could only hope he was still in there, trampling the underbrush, pushing his way past stubborn foliage.

It was a false hope. Two lights suddenly flared at the edge of the trees. Flashlight beams, bobbing. Two men, walking steadily out of the grove.

Griffin and someone else. Sykes, maybe. Or that long-haired guy from the printing factory. It was too dark to see at this distance, and I wasn't going to stick around to find out.

"Come on!" I whispered, pulling Lisa again by the hand. She didn't resist. Instead, she pushed herself to keep up with me.

At a good run, I led us past the trees and toward the east, the rounded shoulders of the nearby hills. As long as we hewed to the shadowed awning thrown by the bank of trees, I figured we had a chance of reaching the foothills unseen. If we strayed too far from its protective shroud, we'd risk being silhouetted against the moon's light, brighter now in the cloudless sky.

The wind rose and fell around us as we ran, as though the night itself was breathing. Co-mingling with our own labored exhalations, Lisa and I now both gasping. Legs weakening, as we stumbled over exposed roots, tufts of brush, unseen divots in the black earth.

The whole time expecting to hear gunfire erupt behind us, feel the stinging heat of a bullet tearing through my flesh.

Any moment now, any moment…

◇◇◇

We'd just reached the first stone-pitted slope, a knoll rising like a set of stairs to the hills, when Lisa abruptly stopped, her grasp pulling me back. I whirled, as angry as I was puzzled. But before I could speak, she pointed back the way we'd come. All the way back, to the old brick building.

"Look! They're going inside."

She was right. The two men were crunching across the gravel to the entrance, their flashlights lowered.

Lisa struggled to catch her breath. "Maybe they think we're still there. Maybe they never saw us running away."

"Whatever, it buys us time. But we have to keep moving."

Allowing ourselves to resume at a slower pace, we headed up the mild incline of craggy boulders, hillocks of grass and dirt. Soon enough, though, we were climbing a steeper, unbroken path of shrubs and thick brush, using handholds for balance. It was hard, slow going, and I didn't like how exposed we were without the grove's shadow to cloak our movements.

Moreover, Lisa's fear had been replaced by a growing irritation. With the steep hill, the wind, her aching feet.

And with me.

"Great escape plan, MacGyver. We're either gonna die of exposure or get eaten by mountain lions."

"I doubt it. And didn't you call me your hero back there?"

"That was then, this is now. Besides, shouldn't you have arranged for a goddamn helicopter or something to pick us up? A crapload of Marines? The Boy Scouts?"

"It's not like I had a plan. So cut me some slack, okay?"

"Sure. I guess I can look at this as some kinda bonding exercise." A deliberate beat. "But I'm sure as shit not *paying* for this session!"

I managed a quiet laugh. By now, we'd reached an elevated cleft in the hill. A broad stretch of rock, like a stone table without legs. Beyond lay another, steeper mound. A somber, treeless shape whose rounded hump was glazed by moonlight.

Lisa stood gasping at my shoulder.

"Fuck it. This is as far as I go, Rinaldi."

I nodded, aware that our pursuers could have long since left the old building and might even be heading this way. Swiveling slowly left and right, I searched for someplace safe to hide.

And found it.

"Nice." Lisa took a seat on a small boulder. "I love what you've done with the place."

I found another rock opposite her and gratefully sat down myself. We were in a cave, hewn out of a rockface adjoining the crest to which we'd climbed. At my urging, we'd crawled to the very back, far enough from the mouth to avoid detection.

The downside, of course, was that except for a sliver of moon glinting off a huge rock halfway between us and the cave opening, we were in total darkness.

At least, I thought, we were out of the wind.

"Maybe it's a good thing you can't see my face," Lisa was saying, "'cause I'm staring daggers at you."

"Yeah, I'm sorry to miss that."

A heavy, not unwelcome silence settled between us. Broken only by the rhythmic sound of our twinned breathing, slowing at last to a normal pace. And growing quieter.

Finally, Lisa spoke.

"How long do you think we should stay here? I mean, when do we go and try to find some help?"

"It's not safe to move now. Not with those men out there. Especially since I don't even know where we are. I figure if we wait here till daylight, at least maybe we can get our bearings. For all we know, there could be a town right over the hill."

Another silence.

"Okay." She took a breath. "If we're stuck here all night, I guess there's time to tell you my story. The *whole* story…"

Chapter Twenty-five

It was strange, listening to Lisa talk as we sat opposite each other in the dark. Unlike in a therapy session, I didn't have visual cues to guide me in my responses. Nor did she get to see what was on my face. My reactions, my own body language.

If anything, I was reminded of my childhood years in the Church. The hallowed darkness of the confessional, speaking my youthful sins into the hushed stillness, unable to see the priest's expression behind his little screen. To see empathy, or sorrow. Or, as I feared, disgust.

Now, as an adult, I've come to realize I merely replaced my faith in one institution with faith in another. Both burdened with dogma, with rigorous rules of behavior. Both susceptible to doubt. Heresy. Renunciation.

But, at the moment, Lisa was neither patient nor penitent. I don't know how to describe what was transpiring in that absurd cave, other than words being spoken by one unseen person for the benefit of another, equally unseen. Like two ghosts, talking.

"It all started with me and Mike Payton," she began. "The company's head of security."

"What started?"

"Our affair." A beat. "Bet you didn't see *that* one coming, did you, Doc?"

"No, I didn't."

"Well, believe me, neither did I. Now don't get me wrong. Marriage to Charles Harland was a fucking nightmare from Day One. Hell, the Bataan Death March was probably more fun. On the plus side, he was rich, which I really, really liked. But he's a cold bastard. Cold and cruel. Know what I mean?"

"I was around him long enough to get a sense of that, yes."

"Anyway, after a few years of wedded shit, we were spending more and more time apart. Christ knows, that creepy house of his is big enough to stay happily lost in. Of course, we continued doing all those public functions together—the charity balls, museum fundraisers, that crap. Plus every year, our big-ass anniversary gala. The most important event on Pittsburgh's social calendar. Every VIP in the state, from the governor on down, shows up to kiss Charles' ring. Which they *have* to do, if they want his financial support come election time.

"And there I am, the former sex symbol, older now but still hot enough to drive all his geezer friends and enemies nuts with envy. Imagining all the great sex he's getting, even at his age. All the tricks I must've learned as a Hollywood starlet, the tabloid party girl. One step up from being a high-priced whore."

She paused, voice thickening.

"You should see the look on the old man's face every year at that event. It's the only goddamn time I ever see him happy. When the truth is…"

She grew quiet, and I heard the first trickle of a soft rain. A steady, melancholy misting, barely audible as it reached my ears from the shadowed mouth of the cave.

"The truth is," she went on, "there wasn't anything like that going on between us. Hadn't been since the earliest days of our marriage. We've slept in separate bedrooms for years. Then, after his first stroke—"

"Was that what put him in the wheelchair? I don't think the exact nature of his illness has ever been made public."

"It hasn't. He and Arthur Drake made damned sure of that. Although Charles was still sharp as a tack after his recovery, they were afraid it would hurt the Harland Industries brand if word got out about a stroke. Instead, they floated the idea that it was some sort of muscular degeneration. Genetic or some bullshit. In other words, 'Don't you worry, Mr. and Ms. Investor, the mighty Harland financial brain is still A-OK.' And the funny thing is, it was...."

I could feel her hand sweeping the air in front of me.

"Hey, Doc, you got another one of those water bottles? I always get a dry throat doing monologues. Not that I had that many in the crappy scripts I got stuck with. Mostly I just had to scream a lot."

I pulled a bottle out of my jacket pocket and managed to find her grasping fingers in the dark. Then I heard her twist it open and take a long drink.

As she did, I simply listened to the rain and kept quiet. Whether or not it was the right call, I'd decided not to tell her yet about her husband's latest stroke and hospitalization. Nor did I feel it appropriate to inform her of Arthur Drake's murder. Lisa had just survived a grueling, horrific ordeal, and my instincts told me that letting her tell her story, in her own way, was perhaps the most therapeutic thing I could do for her. At least here, in this godforsaken place.

She spoke again, her voice now stronger.

"Thanks, Rinaldi. Hit the spot. Anyway, after the stroke, Charles and I barely touched each other. Not even a kiss, unless there was a camera around, or an audience of big-shots..."

Lisa sighed. "Which is the other weird thing. I think the old man still loves me. Really. No matter what anybody says. Even that tight-ass Drake has sworn to me that Charles told him so. But I also know something else. That the Lisa Campbell he loves is the one on those old movie posters in his office. The Hollywood sex bomb. All tits and no brains. Someone I haven't been for a long time."

"When did the affair with Payton start?"

"About a year ago. Funny, too, 'cause I knew that at first Mike was suspicious about my marrying the old man. Had me pegged as a gold-digger, pure and simple. But as we got to know each other, he kinda mellowed. Actually talked to me like I was a person. Though I can't say the same for Drake, or Charles' nurse, Donna Swanson. Neither of 'em ever came around, really, but at least they had the courtesy to be passive-aggressive about it. Unlike James, who was totally upfront. Openly hostile. But, Christ, if I were him, I'd feel the same way."

"What do you mean?"

"James really *hated* his father. Everything he was, and everything he did. And believe me, the feeling was mutual."

"Because Charles blamed James for what happened to his other son, Chuck. The overdose."

"Charles said more than once that the wrong son died. To James' face, in front of company. Can you fuckin' *believe* it?"

She took another deep swallow from the water bottle.

"Even Mike Payton, who has no love for James, thought the way the old man treated his son was really shitty. That was one of the things we used to talk about…"

She paused, as though lost in the memory.

"Anyway, the point is, I hadn't been laid in, like, forever. And I may be older, but I'm not dead. So…"

"You and Mike started seeing each other."

"I was about to say we started fucking like rabbits behind my husband's back, but I like how you put it better. But it wasn't just the sex, Danny. We *liked* each other. Still do. Me and Mike were together for months, 'til we both realized how crazy it was. What'd happen if Charles ever found out…"

"So you ended it?"

"Yeah. Truth is, I think Mike couldn't deal with the guilt. Underneath all that G.I. Joe, take-no-prisoners crap, he's a real, honest-to-God good boy. Total straight arrow."

"It was hard, wasn't it, Lisa? Giving him up?"

She nodded. "At first. I mean, I knew damn well it was for the best, but…Yeah, it was hard. Then, about a month ago, just when it was starting to get easier…"

She hesitated. I heard her twisting the empty plastic bottle in her hands.

"What happened a month ago, Lisa?"

"One night, after dinner, James finds me in the study. Charles had already gone up to bed, so James suggests I join him for a nightcap. Real casual and friendly. Which is pretty strange, since he's never been exactly chummy before this. But I figure, why not? I was about to get hammered anyway…"

A short laugh. "I know what you're thinking, Doc."

"I didn't say anything."

"You don't have to. But trust me, nobody could live with Charles Harland without being tanked most of the time. Anyway, James mixes the drinks at the wet bar, hands me one. We toast, I take a healthy swig, and then everything goes black."

"He drugged you?"

"Yep. The next thing I know, I'm in the backseat of a cab driving through these winding, empty streets. Though I'm still woozy as hell, and can't tell where we are."

She paused again. I leaned in closer, though I knew she couldn't see it.

"When we get where we're goin'—some shitty, rundown building—James has to practically lift me outta the cab. I mean, I am fucking *out* of it. Then he brings me in to meet this weird guy with a mustache. Raymond Sykes. Real skinny, this guy. Like a toothpick. And the place itself—all the rooms and hallways are dark, gloomy. And then we go to this one room, no windows or anything. Padded floor. Then I…I pass out again, I don't know for how long. But when I come around, I'm on this narrow bed… totally bare-assed. Not a stitch. There are lights, really bright lights, shining in my face…

"And then I see James, and he's naked, too. And he's not alone. He's with three other guys, and *they're* all naked. And wearing these masks—like ski masks, I guess. And then James starts telling me who these guys are. I'm so drugged-out I can barely register their names, but I can tell James really wants me to know. Like he's getting off on it. 'Cause one guy's a big state senator, one's president of a worldwide bank. I think the third ran a huge multinational corporation. Strange thing was, I thought

I remembered one of the names. Some high-roller who always shows up at the anniversary gala. Fawns over Charles...*and* me. At the time, I figured I was just fucked up from the spiked drink. He *couldn't* be one of the men behind the masks. But now..."

Another long silence. I waited, the only sounds the rasp of her quickening breath, the gentle insistence of the rain.

"And then James pulls a mask over his own face, and says to me, 'See, Lisa, you're gonna entertain three of the city's most prominent citizens. *Four*, if you count me...'"

I sat up, straining to see her face in the darkness.

"The Four Horsemen. James Harland and these other three."

"Yeah, that's what he said they called themselves. They come down to this canker sore of a building in the Hill District—this old factory—and do drugs and girls. Hookers, mostly. Coke whores. The skankier, the better. 'Going ghetto,' James called it. 'Course he told me all this afterwards. After—"

I heard a sharp intake of breath.

"Take your time, Lisa. Or you can keep the details to yourself, if you want."

"Oh, don't worry. They'll keep. What happened in that room, every horrible, unbelievable thing, is burned right into the old memory banks. Whether I like it or not. I'll be thinking about it, replaying it all in my head, on my deathbed.

"But you're in luck, Doc. I can't even describe what those four monsters did to me. I don't have the words. It went on for hours. Sometimes they took turns, sometimes it was all at once. They...used things, too. Things that hurt. It made what my first husband used to do to me seem like patty-cake.

"What they did...what they made me do...I mean, I always figured I was tough, but...Christ, I can't even talk about it."

"That's all right, Lisa. Unfortunately, I have a pretty good imagination. I can guess."

"No," she said simply. "You can't."

◇◇◇

My eyes more accustomed to the dark, I could now make out

enough of Lisa's features to see the tears streaking her cheeks. The way they glistened wetly in the hushed gloom of the cave.

"I...I don't remember much of what happened afterwards. Maybe I passed out again. Anyway, when I come to, I'm in the library at the residence. With no idea how or when I'd gotten there. It was daylight. Late morning. Me and James were both totally dressed, and there was an elegant coffee service on the table between us. I guess one of the maids had brought it in. Anyway, the thing that struck me the most—that scared the shit outta me—was this look on James' face. This creepy, satisfied smile..."

I took a guess. "That's when he told you about the video."

"Yeah. Though I don't know how the hell *you* know about it."

"I was once in that same room where you were assaulted, Lisa. I saw the lights, the camera."

She nodded. "James told me that everything that happened the night before had been shot. Put on video. But in a special way. I didn't understand all of it, but apparently he had some stoner friend of his, some computer geek, run the camera and download the video into an encrypted file. I mean, it was all techno-babble to me. But he said the file couldn't be copied, or even opened by someone who didn't know the key code."

"Which only James had, I assume."

"Yeah. He said it had something to do with algorithms, or random numbers, or some shit. The important thing was that nobody, not even Sykes, could download it or duplicate it. And that the file was on a flash-drive, hidden where nobody could find it. Jesus, you should've seen his face. He was all excited, like a teenager with some secret porno stash. Really freaked me the fuck out."

I thought then about how Arthur Drake had described James. Implying, almost wistfully, that he was still a boy, with a boy's appetites. A defiant adolescent in an adult's body.

"What did he say he wanted to do with it? Sell it?" I paused. "Or, more likely, blackmail you?"

She shook her head. "Much worse than that. He said he planned to hang on to it until the next anniversary gala, which takes place in a month. He's going to show the video on a big screen at the event. So that Charles, and hundreds of the old man's VIP guests, could see his famous trophy wife gang-raped by four guys in ski masks. See her naked. Tortured and humiliated."

"My God, Lisa…"

"Then, after that, he said he'd probably upload it to YouTube. Why should his father's high and mighty friends be the only ones to see it? Why not share it with the whole world?"

I merely stared in her direction, at a loss.

She lowered her chin. "I knew then that my life was over. I mean, I *did* feel a twinge of pity for my husband—I'm not *that* much of a bitch. But what I mostly felt was panic. For me. Because it would be the end of everything. Once Charles saw that video, the marriage would be over, of course. And believe me, he'd see to it that I was left without a pot to piss in. But that's not what horrified me. It was the publicity, the scandal. All that shit, like before. All stirred up again. And if James *did* decide afterwards to put it up on YouTube…Christ, then *everyone* would see it. My poor parents, my daughter, everyone. The damned thing would go viral, and…"

Her voice trailed off.

"I can't imagine how you must've felt, Lisa."

"It was so…what's that word?…*Surreal.* James tells me what he's going to do, calmly sipping his coffee. Then he adds that it'd be best if we avoided having any contact in the future. Then the bastard gets up and leaves. Just like that."

She cleared her throat. "That's when I began thinking about killing myself. I mean, why not? Who'd care, anyway? My loving husband Charles? Hell, no. Not once he'd seen the video, and been mortified in front of all his so-called friends."

"What about your daughter, back in Los Angeles? Didn't you consider the effect your suicide would have on her?"

"I told you already, Gail doesn't care whether I live or die. Neither does her greedy shit of a husband. Guess she shares her mother's great taste in men, eh? All those two care about is making sure I send them money. Like my twat's an ATM machine."

"And their kids? Your grandchildren?"

"Never met 'em. Never will. So you see, when you crunch the numbers, suicide was my best option. At least I thought so."

"That's not exactly true, Lisa. Some part of you fought that urge. Or else you wouldn't have sought me out. Wouldn't have been so desperate for someone to help you figure out a reason to keep living."

She hesitated, letting me see the consternation on her face. Slowly rubbed her temples.

"I guess you're right. Maybe. But I don't really understand it. There I was, making plans, gathering together my stash of pills. While at the same time, I'm asking Mike Payton to do research on you. Make sure you were as good as your rep."

"But that's what *I* don't understand, Lisa. Why didn't you tell me all this at our first session?"

"It took me the whole time to decide if I could trust you."

Beyond us, outside the mouth of the cave, the rain had strengthened. Not only could we hear its increasing intensity, but a subtle dampness now clung to the air, even as far back as we were in the pocket of the rockface.

"Okay, Lisa," I said carefully. "Can you tell me what happened after our session? When Griffin showed up?"

"When the door opened, and this big goon was standing there, I just started screaming. And then, after he knocked you out, he grabbed me and put his hand over my mouth. I thought he was gonna *kill* me, or worse. But instead, he tells me that his boss had sent him. Raymond Sykes, from that night at the old factory. Sykes wanted me to know that *he* had the video now. That he'd gotten the flash-drive away from James. Griffin said Sykes didn't give a shit about embarrassing me or Harland in public. He didn't know how to open the damned file anyway. He just wanted money. Lots of it. And if I got it for him, he'd give me the flash-drive."

"But how could he have gotten it from James? Unless he'd threatened him in some way. Forced him to hand it over…"

"Yeah, probably. Though I wasn't thinking real clearly at the moment. Not with the big guy's hand on my arm. It felt like he was going to tear it off. I knew that if I didn't come with him, he *would* go ahead and kill me. Besides, the thought that I could get that horrible video back…I didn't care what it was going to cost, it'd be worth it…"

"So you went willingly with Griffin."

"Yeah. We were just two people walking down the hall. Then we went down the service stairs to the parking garage…"

I paused. "So that's how it happened. I wondered …"

I saw her face tighten in the dimness.

"Wait a minute! You son of a bitch, *you thought I staged my own kidnapping…?*"

"Well, it *had* occurred to me. I couldn't find those pills you mentioned, for one thing."

A gruff laugh. "You never did a lot of drugs, did you, Doc? You just gotta know where to hide your stash. Bottom desk drawer on the left, taped to the underside. We've got two live-in maids I call the Snoop Sisters. I had to be careful, since I know they go through my shit all the time."

Then she leaned forward and punched me hard on my arm. "*That's* for thinking I arranged everything myself. Some pal you turned out to be, Rinaldi. What an asshole."

"I *am* sorry, Lisa. For what it's worth."

"You should be. Anyway—not that you deserve to hear the rest of it—once Griffin walked me to my car and had me unlock it, he chloroformed me. When I woke up, I was bound and gagged, on the ground in that cellar. With the tattooed man watching over me. Except for when I was brought up to the room, when Sykes called the residence. Making his ransom demands."

"He needed you there to put you on the phone. He had to demonstrate proof of life for your husband."

"Yeah. It was weird, too. Watching you and all the others in Charles' study. Sykes was able to see into every room in the house on those monitor screens."

Then I remembered something else.

"You said you tried to escape once. What happened?"

"It was the night before this. I'd spent all day loosening the ropes around my wrists. All I had to do was wait. I saw my chance when the tattooed guy went up the ladder to take a leak. Dumb-shit left the trapdoor open. I freed my hands, untied my legs and went up to the room. Nobody was there, and Tattoo was still in the adjoining bathroom. So I bolted out the door into the woods. And suddenly realized I didn't know where the hell I was, or how to get out of there. Sort of like the same plan *you* had, Rinaldi."

"I told you, I didn't have a plan. Things just happened."

"Whatever. Anyway, Tattoo must've discovered I was gone and called his boss. Meanwhile, I spend hours wandering around the damn fields and trees until I collapse in some ditch. Finally Sykes, along with Griffin and Tattoo, find me. After they drag me back to the cellar, Griffin slaps the shit outta me, then they tie and gag me again. That's it. Not exactly *The Great Escape*, but then I didn't have Steve McQueen helping me out."

"It was still a brave thing to do."

"For all the good it did me."

I gave her story some thought. It explained what had made Sykes and his men leave the printing factory so quickly. After the tattooed man had found Lisa missing, he'd panicked and called his boss there. Interrupting our interrogation.

Then Lisa abruptly spoke again.

"Now I have a question for *you*, Doc. Though I don't know if you can even answer it."

"What?"

"It's about this Griffin ape grabbing me outside your office. How the hell did he know where I'd be? The only one who knew I was considering seeing you was—"

She stopped, eyes going wide. "Goddamnit! It was Mike! My God, I can't believe it. Not *him*…Not when we'd been so…"

Her voice fell, softening. Layered with hurt and betrayal.

"He must've told Charles that I'd asked him to check up on you. And after I made him *promise* to keep it secret…"

"I'm afraid that's not all, Lisa. He gave your husband a copy of the dossier he'd prepared on me. And Arthur Drake was in the room when he gave it to him."

"Drake? Figures. Charles' expensive scut-monkey. His only confidante. That pompous, Ivy League shit."

Something about the vehemence in her voice made me suddenly protective of Drake. Of his memory. His sacrifice. So, taking a long breath, I made myself say the words.

"Listen, Lisa...I think you should know. When Sykes called the house earlier today, demanding the additional ransom, Drake insisted on being the one to deliver it. Then, once we met up with Griffin, Drake refused to hand over the money until he knew you were safe. Unharmed. It cost him his life."

"Wh-what...?"

"Griffin shot him. Killed him on the spot, with no more thought than he would have swatting a fly. If Sykes hadn't suddenly distracted him, I'd be dead, too."

"Arthur Drake is...he *died* for me...? Shit, now I have to feel guilty about *him*, too. Another black mark in the book of my stupid, selfish life."

She grew quiet again.

"I *am* sorry to hear about him, Doc. I mean it. Or at least as much as I mean anything."

"I don't know, Lisa. I get the sense that you feel things deeply. Very deeply. And that you always have. Underneath."

She snorted. "*Way* underneath."

Her defenses were up again. Not that I blamed her. Not after the events of the past three days. And the new realization that Mike Payton, her former lover, had broken his promise. Had chosen loyalty to Charles Harland over loyalty to her. So I said nothing more.

We both sat, vague outlines in the sepulchral dimness, listening to the sad song of the rain.

Chapter Twenty-six

It didn't take long before Lisa dozed off. Emotionally and physically spent, she slumped against the cave wall, head lolling. I slipped out of my jacket and lay it across her like a blanket, hoping it might help ease the chill. Then I sat back, folded my arms, and watched her sleep.

Until, soon after that, I drifted off myself.

When I woke suddenly, just after sunrise, I was still sitting with my arms crossed. Every joint in my body felt stiff, every muscle ached. It was as if every one of my forty-plus years wanted to be heard from. And acknowledged.

Since Lisa was still asleep, I rose as quietly as I could and stretched. Then I made my way carefully along the cave wall to the entrance, the small opening now suffused with a clear dawn light. The rain had stopped. At the mouth of the cave, I looked cautiously out at the sun-spackled morning, the hills webbed with rivulets of rainwater, the trees crowned with glistening, dappled leaves.

Craning my neck around, I tried to catch some sign of our pursuers from the night before. Griffin, or the tattooed man. Or Sykes himself. But I saw nothing. No men prowling the fields and the edges of the grove. Nor the van, which I half-expected to see parked on the gravel in front of their hideout.

I knew this didn't mean that Sykes and his men were definitely gone. They could, of course, still be in the area. Yet some part of me was convinced they'd left. With the second suitcase of money in hand, and Lisa and me on the run, they'd probably decided to just take off with the cash. Get as far away as possible, before Lisa and I managed to contact the authorities. After which an army of cops and Federal agents would be swarming over the place, looking for *them*.

I heard a slow cadence of footsteps behind me. It was Lisa, coming to join me at the cave opening. In the light, I saw the toll the past three days and nights of terror had taken. Her clothes were torn, streaked with dirt and blood. Her face and arms bruised, crisscrossed with scrapes, raised welts. Her hair was disheveled. Eyes haunted, crusted with fatigue.

She offered me an unconvincingly brave smile.

"Present and accounted for, sir."

I took hold of her shoulders. "How are you doing?"

"If that's code for 'Jesus, you look like shit,' let me just say, you could use a makeover yourself, Doc."

Over her protests, I left Lisa tucked safely in the rear of the cave, with instructions not to move until I returned. Then I spent the next hour scrambling over rocks, slogging along damp gullies, and trudging up steep ridges, seeking the best vantage point. Or at least a good enough one.

Luckily, I came upon an outcropping with an expansive view of the surrounding area. Squinting against the sun's glare in the east, I spotted a thin sliver of highway. About three miles away, it ran past a cluster of shops, gas stations, and fast-food joints—what passes for modern civilization in most parts of the country nowadays.

That said, I was never so happy to see the Golden Arches in my life.

◇◇◇

By noon, Lisa and I had reached the small town's main street. I used a gas station pay phone to call the local cops, then bought us some sandwiches at a mom-and-pop diner while we waited for them. Though her captors had fed her intermittently, she seemed undernourished and still quite dehydrated. I knew I wouldn't feel confident about her condition until a doctor had checked her out.

When the town uniforms arrived, I quickly filled them in about Lisa's kidnapping and Arthur Drake's murder. I also gave them a description of Sykes and his men.

At first, the two cops were skeptical, but came around when I showed them my Pittsburgh PD credentials. The Department had given me a wallet ID when I signed on as a consultant. It also didn't hurt that both Lisa and I looked like we'd been in a war.

When I offered them a rough idea of where Sykes had been keeping Lisa a prisoner, one of the cops announced that he knew the place. As it turned out, Lisa had guessed correctly. The old building had once been a field office for a mining company.

The cop then called for backup and went barreling toward the hills. Meanwhile, his partner borrowed the diner owner's pickup to drive Lisa and me to the county station. Once there, I called first the Pittsburgh PD, then the FBI.

To say that both law enforcement agencies were relieved to learn that Lisa was alive and free would be the understatement of the year. Especially elated was Lieutenant Biegler, to whom I'd asked to be patched through. It was obvious he couldn't wait to hang up with me and call Chief Logan with the good news.

Unfortunately, Lisa adamantly refused to be examined at the local hospital. So I got on the phone with Special Agent Wilson at the Federal Building downtown, asking that he arrange for a helicopter to fly us home. After which, Lisa could be taken to Pittsburgh Memorial, where, still unbeknownst to her, her husband Charles was being treated in the ICU.

◇◇◇

Wilson came through. After a short though bumpy flight, we were met at the airport by a Federal unmarked, then driven straight to the hospital. Pittsburgh PD was there waiting for us, as well as a rep from Victims' Services. She had nondescript but fresh clothes for Lisa and me, so we could shower and change after our respective medical examinations.

Lisa went first. A stoic uniformed officer at my side, I sat in the ward lobby while she was in with the doctor on call. Taking out my cell, I used the time to call my Monday patients to cancel their appointments. I had enough experience with the Department—and the FBI—to know that given the high-profile nature of the case, they'd both probably want to have me available throughout the day tomorrow for questioning.

I'd just left a message for the last patient when the physician who'd examined Lisa came in. He was young, handsome, arrogant. He said that Lisa was in surprisingly good shape, and could be allowed to speak briefly with the authorities.

Then he crooked a finger at me. "Okay, Dr. Rinaldi. You're next."

◇◇◇

Though Lisa had been transferred to a spacious private room—ironically, in a wing of the hospital donated by her husband—it was still pretty crowded in there.

In addition to myself—showered and changed into jeans and a sweatshirt (both too big), and sporting bandages to cover various cuts and abrasions—Lieutenant Biegler, Harry Polk, Mike Payton, and Agents Anthony Wilson and Gloria Reese all stood in a semi-circle around Lisa's bed.

She herself had multiple bandages on her arms and face. She'd also been given an IV drip, probably to combat the dehydration. It wouldn't have surprised me if a strong pain reliever had been added to the mix.

Her face was pale, pinched, as would be expected after what she'd been through. However, before I entered the room, I was told that she'd just been informed of her husband's condition and that he was here, in this same hospital. Despite her long-soured feelings about him, it had to be a shock. Another one, I thought, in a recent string of them.

I'd no sooner pushed through the door and been guardedly greeted by the others than Biegler's cell rang. While he took the call, Gloria Reese and I exchanged somewhat awkward looks.

I realized then that we hadn't had a moment to talk since our own abduction two nights before.

Biegler hung up and turned to Agent Wilson. As though what he had to report wouldn't concern the rest of us. God, he could be a condescending prick.

"That was the state police. They've searched the old mining office. Say it looks like some kind of makeshift control room. They're also combing the surrounding area. So far they found two bodies. One has been identified as Arthur Drake, shot in the head and left in a grassy field. The other deceased male was found in the cellar of the mining office. Also shot in the head. Guy was covered in tattoos. Real 'Aryan Nation' stuff. According to his driver's license, his name's Fred Gilroy."

Lisa looked up at him. "That was the creep who kept an eye on me in the cellar. When the others were gone."

"Griffin probably killed him, too," I said. "Payback for letting Lisa escape."

"Or else simply one less loose end to deal with," Gloria offered. "One less guy to cut in on the ransom money."

I nodded. "Yeah. I'm betting that long-haired guy from the print factory doesn't have much of a shelf life, either. Now that Sykes has the cash."

Wilson spoke to Biegler. "Did the state forensics people find anything in Julian's control room? Prints? Hair or fibers?"

"They just got there, so it's too soon to get a detailed report. But prints, yeah. Plenty." He referred to a notepad on which he'd hastily scribbled during his phone call. "But forget this 'Julian' bullshit. Might as well call him Ray Sykes. His prints are all over the room. Others, too. All in the system. Max Griffin, that Gilroy stiff, and somebody called Tommy Ames. Griffin and Sykes are known associates. Go way back."

"Believe me, Lieutenant, the Bureau knows all about Raymond Sykes. Max Griffin, too. The two met in the service. Served together in Afghanistan. Sykes led the outfit, and Griffin was their best marksman. Expert sniper."

"Probably the guy out in the trees with the laser scope."

Wilson deigned to nod. "Probably, yes."

Gloria looked over at me. "If Gilroy is the one with the tats, then the long-haired perp we encountered the other night must be Tommy Ames."

Biegler grunted. "Who cares? According to their jackets, Ames and Gilroy are just a couple of bottom-feeders. Local talent that Sykes must've brought in to help with the job."

He flipped the notebook closed. "But what we need is a line on Sykes and Griffin. Maybe we'll know more when the state techs make a full report."

"Which will hopefully be expedited." Wilson cleared his throat. "I spoke to the director right before I got here. In consultation with the governor, it's been decided to send a Bureau forensics team to the crime site. To pitch in."

Biegler stiffened. "We could also send the Department's CSU techs out there. Not our jurisdiction, but…"

"No need." Wilson smiled. "Our team's already en route. It's not about stepping on anybody's toes, Stu. It's about bringing these perps to justice. We all want the same thing."

Like hell, I thought. I'd heard the Bureau was still upset that it was Pittsburgh PD who bagged the killer last winter in the Jessup case. So they sure as hell weren't going to let the Department garner even more accolades by bringing in Lisa Campbell's kidnappers. Since her case didn't fall under the FBI's jurisdiction, they'd been called in by the powers-that-be merely to advise. How sweet would it be, then, to actually make the collar themselves?

A quick glance in Harry Polk's direction confirmed that I wasn't alone in my thinking. Standing just behind Wilson, Polk was clearly scowling at the imperturbable agent. And he didn't seem to care who saw it, either. Forbidden to smoke in the hospital, Harry had just popped another stick of gum in his mouth. And was chewing furiously.

Seemingly unconcerned with the rising tension in the room, Agent Wilson stepped closer to Lisa's bedside. Smiled coolly down at her.

"Now, Mrs. Harland…"

"Call me Lisa." She eyed him warily.

"Very well. Lisa. The doctors say we can only talk for a few minutes, so I wonder if you can just tell us a little bit about what happened? There'll be plenty of time to take a more detailed statement when you're feeling better."

Once again, I was reminded that Lisa Campbell had been an actress. Without a trace of guile, she told Wilson that she'd come to therapy with me to deal with her growing depression. And that she was terrified when the man we now know as Max Griffin appeared outside my office. After knocking me out, Griffin put a gun to her ribs. Threatened to kill her unless she went with him quietly. Once at her car, he chloroformed her. When she awoke, she found herself in a dank dirt cellar, tied up and gagged.

She did make one escape attempt, she explained, but only got as far as the woods. Soon her captors found her and dragged her back to the cellar, where she was beaten and then once more restrained and gagged with duct tape.

I watched her performance in silence. Lisa not only lied about Griffin threatening her with a gun. She'd also left out her affair with Mike Payton, the gang-rape at the old printing factory, the encrypted file containing the video of her assault, and the Four Horsemen. Further, she neglected to mention what James told her he planned to do with the video. How he intended to screen it before Charles Harland and his fancy guests at next month's anniversary gala.

Of course, I understood her reluctance to share all these humiliating details with the authorities. Nor would I share them. As far as I was concerned, I remained Lisa's therapist of record, which meant I was bound by doctor-patient confidentiality.

By this point, Biegler had joined Wilson at Lisa's bedside.

"I can tell what an ordeal this has been for you, Lisa, but I do have some follow-up questions."

I stepped forward. "They'll have to wait, Lieutenant. Lisa's said enough for now. She needs her rest."

Agent Wilson stared at me. "*I'm* not through questioning her, either, Doctor."

"Actually, Agent Wilson, you are. As Lisa's therapist, I insist on it."

As if on cue, Lisa's pale hand went to her bandaged brow. Fingers trembling. "Yes...please...I *am* really tired."

"The Doc's right."

It was Mike Payton, speaking firmly from the other side of the bed. He gazed down at Lisa with concern. "She's told you enough. Hell, we *know* who the perps are. You two should be out there trying to find them, not hassling the victim."

Biegler's face darkened. "We *are* looking for them! We've put out a nationwide alert. Sykes and his guys are in the wind, so it won't be easy. But we'll get it done."

"Indeed," said Wilson, "the Bureau's coordinating with every local precinct in the tri-state area. Within an hour, we'll have suspect profiles and case intel sent to every FBI field office and every police department in the country."

"That's right," Biegler added. "We'll *find* the bastards. Sooner or later. Count on it!"

I wasn't about to. After the second ransom was received, the plan had obviously been to kill whoever delivered it. And then kill Lisa. Though their victim had survived, the kidnappers still had their ten million in bearer bonds. Their identities now known, the smartest thing to do was disappear.

I pointed this out.

"Given Sykes' brains and resources, not to mention the money, I bet he and Griffin are onboard some overseas flight as we speak. Probably to a country that doesn't have an extradition treaty with the U.S."

Gloria nodded. "Sounds right to me. I'm just glad Lisa's safe. For which we all owe Dr. Rinaldi our thanks."

"It was just dumb luck," I said. "I only wish Arthur Drake had made it back as well."

For once, neither Biegler nor Wilson had anything to say.

Then, unexpectedly, Mike Payton turned to me. "That reminds me. I've been wondering why you even went along with Drake to make the drop. On the phone, Julian—I mean

Sykes—said he had some unfinished business with you. What was *that* all about?"

"When Agent Reese and I were his captives, Sykes had some questions about my session with Lisa. I tried to tell him—"

"Yeah, yeah." Biegler frowned. "You and your precious confidentiality. Try learning another tune, will ya, Rinaldi?"

I ignored him. "The point is, Sykes and I were interrupted when he was told about Lisa's escape. He and his men had to run off to deal with it. I guess he figured we never got to finish our conversation."

Which was why, I realized, he'd insisted I accompany Drake with the second ransom delivery. Sykes wanted to press me again about what Lisa may have revealed about the Four Horsemen. No wonder. If the other three men were as high-profile as James Harland—and from what Lisa told me, it sounded like they were—then having their identities exposed would be bad for Sykes' business, if not his health. These were prominent, powerful men who might go to any lengths to protect themselves. Sykes not only provided them with sex and drugs, and whatever thrills they got from "going ghetto," he also promised anonymity. He *had* to find out if Lisa had told me any names. And if so, he couldn't risk making dangerous enemies in the hope that I'd keep what I knew confidential. To be absolutely sure, he'd have to kill me.

Which was also why he stopped Griffin when the big man, after shooting Drake, was about to put a bullet in *my* head, too. Why Sykes frantically blew the van's horn. He wanted me alive long enough to tell him what he needed to know. After that, I could be safely dispatched. The final loose end severed.

"I don't know why you went along with Arthur," Lisa was saying now, "but I'm glad you did. You saved my life."

I just shrugged. But Biegler's response was more pointed.

"We're all glad things turned out okay, Mrs. Harland, but, as civilians, neither Dr. Rinaldi nor Arthur Drake should have been permitted to deliver that ransom without official sanction. It was too dangerous, as Mr. Drake found out to his sorrow." His stern glare targeted Harry Polk. "Something that Sergeant Polk and I will discuss at another time. For now, there's work to do."

Harry stared back at him, stone-faced.

"I agree with Lieutenant Biegler." Wilson stirred. "We have forensics to gather, leads to run down. Suspects to apprehend."

"Sir," Gloria said, "I'll get the word out to airport security, bus and cab companies. Highway Patrol, too. Though Sykes has probably already ditched the van."

"Probably. There's a lot to coordinate, but this is not the time and place to discuss it." A forced smile at me. "Besides, according to her therapist, we need to let Lisa rest. But make sure you clear your schedule, Doctor. We'll be wanting to take your complete statement."

"Only after he gives one to *us*," Biegler said sharply. "Complete and detailed."

I met his gaze. "Now *there's* something to look forward to." He didn't reply. Instead, he turned back to Harry Polk.

"Harry, I'll need you to make the next-of-kin notification to Drake's family. Whoever they are."

Payton spoke up. "He has an ex and two grown daughters. I have their info on file. Numbers, addresses."

"Good. That'll speed things up."

With that, the quartet of law enforcement personnel started filing out of the room, Mike Payton on their heels.

I didn't follow. Having caught a beseeching look from Lisa, I stayed behind.

Chapter Twenty-seven

After the door closed, Lisa awkwardly pulled herself up on her elbows. Puzzled, I leaned over the bed rails.

"Hey, what are you doing? You're supposed to rest."

"I will. But we gotta talk first—and fast. Before that know-it-all doctor comes back. He's pretty, but a total douche."

"Well, you seem to be feeling better. A minute ago, you looked like you were about to pass out."

"I just wanted Thing One and Thing Two to leave me alone with you, Doc."

"By now, I think you should call me Dan. Or Danny."

"Okay, whatever. But take that therapeutic tone out of your voice. I don't need to talk about my feelings. I need your help in getting my hands on that fucking video."

"*My* help?"

"Look, I know you're saying to yourself, 'Shit, I saved the bitch's life and now she wants something *else* from me?' But you're the only one I can trust with this."

"First of all, I'm not thinking that. I'm your therapist, and I'll help you any way I can. But as everyone keeps reminding me, I'm not the police."

"Which is why you're the perfect man for the job. The fewer people who know about that video, the better. The problem is, I don't know where the flash-drive is. Or even who really has it. Sykes or James?"

I pulled a chair up next to the bed and sat.

"You know, I was wondering…What if Griffin was lying when he said that Sykes had it, and that all his boss wanted was money? What if it was only a ploy to get you to cooperate? To go with him without a struggle to your car."

"Exactly what I was thinking. Especially since nobody—not Sykes, not Griffin—*nobody* even mentioned the video again once they had me prisoner in the cellar."

I considered this. "Of course, Sykes would *know* about the video. He was there when it was shot. So maybe, when he gets the idea to kidnap you, he decides to pretend he's somehow gotten it away from James. So he can use the promise of its return to persuade you to go with Griffin."

Lisa nodded. "It's the only thing that makes sense. I can't see that slime-bag James just handing it over to him."

"Nor can I. Unless, like we said before, Sykes made threats on his life. Forced him to hand it over."

"Yeah, I guess that's true."

Lisa eased herself back against her pillow. I could tell she was tiring quickly. For real, this time.

"On the other hand," I went on, "I can't believe Sykes would risk threatening James Harland, one of his best customers, with bodily harm. Not when James is a conduit to some of the city's most powerful and influential men. No, Lisa. I don't think Sykes ever had the flash-drive. It was just a ruse."

"So James still has it? Hidden somewhere?"

"I think so. I could be wrong, but…"

She covered her face with her hands. From the way her shoulders slumped, I could see that another wave of fatigue had washed over her. And another wave of despair.

"Aw, screw it. I'm finished. There's nothing to stop James from showing that video at the anniversary party. I can't even prove he has it. He'd just deny it."

Lowering her hands, she gave me a weary smile.

"Hell, maybe me and Charles will both get lucky. He'll die here in the hospital, and I'll get to go home and swallow my pills. Then neither one of us'll be around for the premiere of

James' little S&M masterpiece. He can show it to whoever the fuck he wants."

I smiled back. "You can't take yourself out yet, Lisa. You promised me a follow-up session, remember? It's on the books."

To my surprise, she gently brought her palm up to my face.

"Give it a rest, will ya? I mean, you're a nice guy, and I owe you for getting me away from those evil pricks in the woods. But all you did was delay the inevitable. Once people see that video, I...Understand? Just the thought of it..."

Her eyes bored into mine.

"I can't live with that. *I can't.* So I won't."

Letting her hand drop to the bed sheets, she turned her face to the pillow. Voice muffled, tear-choked.

"Now, please leave me alone...Please? Just...go..."

I didn't budge.

"I'm still your therapist, goddamnit. So like it or not, Lisa, I'm not leaving until we have a contract. Until you promise me you won't try anything—pills, whatever—promise that you won't try to hurt yourself without calling me first."

She closed her eyes tight.

"If I promise, will you leave me the fuck alone?"

"It's the only way I *will* leave you alone."

"I could always fire your ass. Get another therapist."

"True. Though I can't think of any of my colleagues who'd put up with your shit. So looks like you're stuck with me."

A long beat of silence.

"I hate you, you know."

"I'm devastated. Now, do we have a contract or not?"

"Yeah, sure. What the hell?...I promise to call you. But just to give you a heads-up. I'm *not* promising I won't still do it." A measured pause. "I'm fucking serious...Danny."

"I know you are, Lisa."

And I did.

When I left Lisa's room, I found Mike Payton waiting for me at the end of the hallway. For the first time since I'd arrived at the hospital, I took note of his unshaven face and bloodshot eyes. It was obvious he'd had as little sleep as I had.

He seemed to read my thoughts. As I approached, he gave me a wan smile and said, "We also serve who only stand and wait."

"The Harlands are lucky to have you, Mike. No joke."

He shook his head. "It should've been *me* out at that drop site with Drake. Not you."

Now that I knew about his affair with Lisa, Payton's guilt about what had happened to her made more sense. As did his frustration at having played no part in rescuing her. He also probably regretted giving Harland a copy of that dossier he'd prepared on me. After promising Lisa he'd keep her request for it a secret. The painful consequences of divided loyalties.

I leaned my back against the wall next to him. Both of us oblivious to the doctors and nurses bustling up and down the hallway. Finally, I turned and regarded his haggard profile.

"Lisa's life was at stake," I said. "Sykes said it had to be me, or else. We *had* to play by the kidnappers' rules."

"Yeah, well maybe we shouldn't have. Drake's dead anyway, and the bad guys are in the wind. With ten million bucks of Harland's money. I figure *that's* on me, too."

I didn't reply. Merely watched as the security man pulled at his lower lip. A tic I was becoming familiar with.

"Look, Mike, if you stayed behind to see Lisa, I hope you'll reconsider. She was half-asleep when I left her."

"Then maybe I'll hold off on telling her."

"Telling her what?"

"I just went up to see Mr. Harland and they told me he was awake and talking. Asking where his wife was."

"Does he know she's been brought back safely?"

"According to the doctor, he doesn't even remember she'd been kidnapped. He's barely lucid. Just keeps calling out for Lisa. Wanting to know where she is."

"Sounds like they could both use some more time to rest. Recover. Why don't we give it to them?"

"Good idea. The docs'll probably agree."

He turned, held out his hand. "Thanks again for bringing her home, Rinaldi."

We shook hands, then he strode down the hallway toward the elevator. Presumably heading up to see his boss again.

The veteran military man, without a war to fight. Except for the one in his own mind.

Thankfully, the new hospital wing boasted an equally new coffee shop. I was halfway out the building's front entrance when I remembered that my car was still parked at the Harland residence. Which meant I'd have to take a cab there. But not before throwing back a couple cups of strong black coffee. By this point, it was obvious that fatigue was starting to affect my short-term memory. My ability to focus.

I'd gotten a refill from the girl behind the counter, and was on my way back to my corner table, when Gloria Reese came in. Lifting my cup in greeting, I motioned for her to join me. After getting her own large coffee, she did just that.

"First, the good news," she said, without preamble.

"Always happy to hear good news."

"Agent Gloria Reese is still on the case. The brass figures I've been in from the start, so I have firsthand knowledge of the facts. The bad news is, I definitely lost some points by getting abducted by Griffin. Taken by gunpoint to Sykes' spooky sex chamber. During my debriefing, there was a lot of veiled comments about my size, my gender. Pretty much what I expected."

I watched her gingerly sip the steaming coffee. Holding the cup with both hands.

"I'm sorry to hear that, Gloria. But at least you're still in the field."

"Yeah. I was worried they'd have me riding a desk for the next three months."

"Me, too. Though would you mind answering a question?"

Gloria took a quick, guarded look around the room. Then, voice lowered: "You want to know if I told them *everything* that happened at the print factory. With Max Griffin and his knife. What he did…or was about to do…"

"Well?"

"In a word, no. And for a very simple reason—which, as a psychologist, you should already know. Because I'm not crazy. The last thing I'd do is give those condescending jerks an excuse to put me on psych leave. Believe me, no agent's career ever survives that. No matter what they tell you."

"Okay, so you're not crazy. But you still had a traumatic experience. I ought to know, I was there. Hell, it was pretty traumatic for *me*, even though I didn't go through anything like what you endured."

"Meaning what? I should see a shrink?"

"Meaning, you should get some help. From someone outside the Bureau. I can give you some names."

"Thanks but no thanks. Small but mighty, remember?"

She gave me a wink. I sipped my coffee.

I also thought about Charlene's brother Skip. Only the day before, I'd suggested to him that *he* seek counseling. At least he'd been willing to let me write down some names and numbers. Although I doubted whether he'd ever look at them again.

Which suddenly made me feel like some kind of cliché. The psychologist who hears about a friend or colleague's troubles and automatically suggests therapy. As if by rote. As though it was the only option available to help ease someone's pain, help them make sense of their conflicted feelings.

Yet, for so many people, it *is* the right choice. As a therapist—as well as a patient—I see the proof of it every day. The right clinical treatment can offer solace, perspective. It provides tools to help navigate an inner world of confusion or torment. Sometimes it even saves lives.

It sure as hell saved mine.

Gloria must have seen the slightly abashed look on my face. Reached out her hand to touch my wrist.

"Hey, I appreciate the advice. But it's just not for me. No offense, okay?"

"None taken."

As if by mutual though unspoken agreement, the conversation turned to the kidnapping case.

"I just heard they found the van," Gloria was saying. "The one you and I were in the night Griffin grabbed us."

"It was also parked in that field where Drake and I went to deliver the second ransom. I think Sykes was behind the wheel, but I can't be sure. The lights were so bright, all I could see was a skinny guy smoking a cigarette."

"Frankly, I don't know if we'll ever get our hands on him and Griffin." Gloria tasted more of her coffee. "They have a big head-start and lots of money. Like you said back there, by now they could be anywhere."

"Besides, after the explosion at the factory, I guess Sykes is out of the VIP sex-club business. Probably finished with his human trafficking operation, too. But I doubt he's crying about it. Ten million dollars makes a helluva golden parachute."

"He may be in the wind, but that doesn't mean his operation can't keep going. Run by trusted lieutenants, with whom he can communicate from anywhere in the world. That's why the Bureau is keeping tabs on all his known associates, particularly those connected to the trafficking. Phone taps, email tracking. In case Sykes tries to get in touch with them, or they with him."

"But why risk it? Why not just enjoy his retirement?"

"Look, Sykes may be on a beach somewhere, drinking piña coladas, but that doesn't mean the people in his organization want to shut down the money train. In fact, it wouldn't surprise me if there's some kind of coup—one of the lieutenants taking over the whole thing. Permanently. With Sykes a wanted man, afraid we'd grab him the minute he showed his face, it wouldn't be that hard to do. Crime is like any other business. When the boss vacates, *somebody* has to take over the corner office."

Gloria gave me a puzzled look.

"By the way, did you ever figure out what Sykes was talking about when he asked you about the Four Horsemen?"

"No, I didn't." The second time I'd lied to her. But I had no choice, if I was to preserve Lisa Campbell's confidentiality. "That's why I'm glad he was called away. Before things got—"

"Tell me about it." With a slight shiver, she downed the rest of her coffee. Peered at the empty cup. "About that night. I assume you know that whether or not Sykes heard what he wanted to hear, you and I were dead meat. There's no doubt that was his intention all along."

"It did occur to me, yes. By killing us, his identity as Lisa's kidnapper would have remained unknown. But after we escaped, all bets were off. Now law enforcement knew who he was. That's why the scorched earth policy. Why Griffin shot Arthur Drake. And why, if they'd caught and questioned me again, he'd have killed *me*. No reason not to. What's another murder?"

I paused. "Though I'm sure the plan from the beginning involved killing Lisa. Right after they got the ransom money. Remember, she'd seen their faces. Both Sykes and Griffin. There was no way they would've let her live."

Gloria shifted in her seat.

"Time to go?" I asked.

"Yeah, back to work. On the Sykes case, as well as a few other ongoing investigations. See, a lot of air's gone out of the balloon now that Lisa's back safely. Or should I say, now that Charles Harland's *wife* is back safely. Politically, that's been the most important thing from the start. Now it's just a question of mopping up. Getting the bad guys who snatched her: a much lower-priority situation."

This somewhat surprised me. I frowned at her.

"Come on. You're making it sound like the case is over."

She shrugged. "For all practical purposes, it is."

After Gloria left, I sat in silence, nursing my now-cooling coffee. To my mind, there were still too many things we didn't know. Too many questions that needed answers.

For starters, how was Donna Swanson, Harland's longtime personal nurse, involved? Had she been covertly working with or for Ray Sykes? Helping him arrange the kidnapping by keeping an eye on Lisa? Her movements, her scheduled appointments? If so, then Arthur Drake's suspicions about Mike Payton were unfounded. It was possible that *she*, not Payton, told Sykes about where and when Lisa was planning to come to my office.

Which could also be a possible explanation for her murder. Perhaps her death wasn't—as Sykes suggested on that tape he left behind—merely a callous warning to the cops against trying another trick like the one they'd attempted at the observatory. Perhaps, as far as Sykes was concerned, Donna Swanson had served her purpose. That she'd become just another loose end to be cut.

Something else bothered me. What was the extent of the relationship between James Harland and Sykes? Was it merely a business arrangement? Money changing hands so that James and his high-roller friends could use Sykes' place in the Hill District for clandestine sex-and-drugs parties?

In other words, did Sykes come up with the idea to kidnap Lisa Campbell, his best client's stepmother, on his own? Or had James suggested it? Even helped plan it?

I was still puzzling over these and other things as I walked out of the coffee shop. For a second time, I headed across the lobby toward the front entrance. I hoped to find a cab outside at the curb. If not, I'd have to call for one.

However, before leaving, I decided to go up to Lisa's room again, to see how she was doing. As I approached her door, her doctor was coming out. We exchanged polite smiles.

"How is she?" I asked.

"Sleeping. Best thing for her now. But she'll be fine."

He made a point of looking at his watch. I made a point of ignoring it.

"How about Charles Harland? Can I speak to *his* doctor?"

"I just conferred with Dr. Horowitz. It looks like Mr. Harland will recover, though with impaired motor functions and speech. He'll certainly require physical therapy."

"But what's his prognosis?"

He scowled, impatient. Apparently a very busy young man.

"Let's put it this way. Neither Horowitz nor I think he can survive another stroke. Now if you'll excuse me…"

There were no cabs outside the hospital entrance, so I went back inside the lobby and called for one. I'd no sooner hung up than my cell rang.

"Rinaldi? Lieutenant Biegler. I'll need you to come down to the precinct house and give a full statement."

"What about the Feds? I know Agent Wilson wants a statement from me, too. And I like him better. Not by much, but still…"

"Cut the shit and get your ass down here. *I* want your statement first. Remember, you're a consultant with Pittsburgh PD, not the FBI."

"Normally you're not too happy about that."

"I'm still not, Rinaldi. If it was up to me—"

"Yeah, yeah. Maybe *you* ought to try learning another tune, Lieutenant."

A frigid silence.

"Just get down here," he said at last. *"Now."*

I saw the cab pull to the curb and went out to meet it. The sun had dipped in the sky, and a pale pink dusk spread to the mountains. Though the wind was still calm, the temp had started to drop, making me wish I had my jacket, which, at the moment, was in a plastic bag along with the rest of my dirty, blood-stained clothes in a lab downtown, waiting to be examined by Pittsburgh PD's forensics techs.

As I opened the cab's rear passenger door another vehicle rolled past. A sleek town car, whose driver I recognized. Trevor, from the Harland house.

I also recognized his passenger, slouching in the spacious backseat. Eyes half-lidded, he looked either bored or drunk. And was probably both.

James Harland. No doubt having been told that his father had awakened. After which, he must have decided—for the sake of appearances, if nothing else—that he ought to come visit the old man. Ask pertinent questions of the doctors.

As the car passed by, I felt the anger rise in my throat. As well as a gnawing frustration. Because there was no way to prove he'd done the horrific things Lisa had described. And no way to stop him from doing the one final thing he planned to do.

I stood there, frozen. Adrenaline pumping. Wanting nothing so much as to chase after him. Pull him out of that fancy car and beat him to a pulp.

But, of course, I didn't. Couldn't.

If I did, I'd get nothing for my pains but an assault charge. And a lawsuit. And a felony conviction, which, among other things, would cost me my clinical license.

The entire scenario ran through my mind in a millisecond. The righteous anger, the desire to take action, the sober assessment of that action's likely consequences.

So I simply got into the cab. Put my head back against the seat cushion. Closed my eyes.

And gave the cabbie directions to the Harland house.

Chapter Twenty-eight

When I finally got home, it was close to nine p.m.

After picking up my Mustang at the Harlands', I'd driven back into town for my meeting with Biegler. He and Harry Polk took turns grilling me as I gave as complete a statement as I could about the past three days' events.

Not that I didn't leave a good deal out of it. Gloria's sadistic treatment at the hands of Max Griffin, for one thing. I figured it was up to her to disclose as much about that experience as she chose. It hardly seemed relevant, anyway.

I also deleted the same things from my statement that Lisa Campbell had deleted from hers. About her affair with Mike Payton, what had happened to her at Sykes' place, and the video of the assault. While I realized that some—but certainly not all—of these facts might have been helpful to the investigation, I had no intention of violating Lisa's trust.

Nevertheless, the interview was pretty grueling, made more so by Biegler's obvious distaste for me. Not that Harry Polk did much to disguise his own jaundiced view of both me *and* his boss.

Now, in my kitchen, as I poured myself a beer and looked out at the rolling blackness beyond the rear deck, I was stunned to find I was too wired to sleep. I'd imagined, as I drove up to Mt. Washington through sparse Sunday night traffic, that I'd barely make it home before falling, still clothed, into bed.

Instead, I felt that familiar jangly energy, that animal restlessness I used to feel after going ten rounds in the ring. A teenager whose only desire was to please a father who couldn't be pleased, I'd get so pumped for a fight that, long after it ended, I still felt the after-effects of that intensity. Like an electrical current coursing through my veins.

Until, on the drive home from the local VFW hall or Police Athletic League gym, my father's bitter disappointment drained the energy from my limbs. Win or lose, he'd point out all the mistakes I'd made, the easy punches I'd missed, the foolish ways I'd left myself unguarded. Yet nothing that had happened that night in the ring left as many marks, as many scars, as those long, painful car rides back to my motherless house.

I finished my beer in two long swallows. How many times, I wondered, would I replay those memories of my father? Of those hard years as an amateur boxer? Of my own feeble attempts to wrest real conversations out of those prolonged, alcohol-fueled silences that defined my father's last years?

Dutifully putting the empty beer bottle in the recycling bin, I padded into the bathroom and stripped off the borrowed clothes. I'd make sure to have them washed and returned to Victims' Services in a couple days. Decent clothes for those who needed them were in short supply, though the same couldn't be said for the crime victims themselves.

It felt good to shower in my own home, just as it felt good to be wearing my own clothes again. As I went back into the kitchen for another beer, it occurred to me that I wanted something stronger. And that I didn't want to drink it alone.

Maybe it was the accumulated stress of the past days' horrors. Maybe it was fatigue-induced sentimentality. Maybe I just felt sorry for myself.

Regardless of my motives, I found myself picking up the phone in the front room and dialing Eleanor Lowrey's number. First home, then her cell. Again, I got her voicemail. This time, however, I had the presence of mind not to leave some foolish, stilted message. Some nakedly obvious and intimate words that begged a response. A warm, reassuring reply.

This time, I just hung up without saying a thing.

◇◇◇

I'd gone out on the rear deck for a minute to get a sense of the temperature, then came back inside and pulled on a jacket. In less than an hour, the night had grown much cooler. And the sleepless wind had once more roused itself.

Before leaving the house, I clicked on the local TV news. As I'd expected, the lead story concerned the murder of Arthur Drake, prominent attorney and personal advisor to Charles Harland. After replaying the video clip of Drake speaking on behalf of the Harland family two days before, expressing its grief over the murder of Donna Swanson, the station cut back to the polished anchorman. His look into the camera was grim.

"Authorities refuse to comment on the jarring coincidence that billionaire industrialist Charles Harland's personal nurse, and then his longtime lawyer and family spokesman, were both brutally murdered in the span of three days. When questioned by reporters as to whether these two murders were related, Chief Logan would say only that the investigation of each crime was ongoing. He added that no connection between the two victims, other than their both having been in Charles Harland's employ, had yet been found. Nor had any motive for either of the murders been discovered. Naturally, we'll keep you informed as more details become known in this bizarre case…"

I shut off the TV. Not surprisingly, the fact that Drake's death was in connection to a ransom delivery on behalf of Lisa Campbell, Harland's wife, was kept secret. Perhaps the police were unwilling, at this point, to reveal too much information about their investigation of Drake's death. Or the manhunt for his killer, Max Griffin, and his boss, Raymond Sykes. Maybe they felt that the less their suspects knew about what the Department was doing, the better. Moreover, why risk creating a public panic about the possibility that two killers were at large, perhaps still in the tri-state area?

Another thought crossed my mind. It was also possible that pressure from James Harland had been brought to bear on the police. Forcing them to keep the details of the investigation from the public as a way to avoid possible scandal, further intrusions into the family's affairs by the media. With Arthur Drake dead, and Charles Harland incapacitated, I presumed the reins of the Harland empire were in James' hands. At least ostensibly. His, and, more likely, the company's board of directors. With investor confidence as fragile as it was nowadays, Harland Industries would be eager to put a firewall of privacy between itself and a curious, fickle public. Not to mention a ravenous, unrelenting press.

There was no way to know. But between the Department's own reluctance and the political influence of the Harland empire, it was entirely possible that Lisa Campbell could be kidnapped, held in a dirt-walled cellar for three days, and then returned safely—without the world ever knowing it happened.

◇◇◇

I was hugging the curve of the Liberty Bridge off-ramp when my cell rang. Rolling up the Mustang's window against the noise of the wind, I switched on the dashboard's hands-free app.

"Danny? Sam Weiss. You awake?"

"I better be. I'm driving down to Noah Frye's place."

"Cool. Tell the crazy bastard I said hello."

Sam Weiss was a feature writer for the *Pittsburgh Post-Gazette*, but was known mostly for his best-selling book about Troy David Dowd, the Handyman. We'd met years ago, when he was doing research on the serial killer, and had become friends. That connection grew deeper when, not long after that, I treated his younger sister, the victim of a vicious sexual assault. The last I'd heard, she was a grad student at Columbia, and doing quite well. Thankfully, it *does* go like that sometimes.

With the proceeds from the book, as well as money he got from Hollywood for the rights to the as-yet-unmade film, Sam was able to buy a home in Squirrel Hill. Although he's the same age as I, and married with two kids, his boundless energy and shaggy-haired appearance always made him seem much younger.

"Look, Danny," he said, "there's something I want to run by you. I have a contact at Pittsburgh Memorial, keeping an eye on what's happening with Charles Harland. Whether he's getting better or worse. Anything you know that I ought to know?"

"Why ask *me*, Sam?"

"Because my guy also says he saw *you* there today. At the hospital."

"He recognized me?"

Sam chuckled. "Price o' fame, Danny boy. I warned you that all that 'expert commentary' stuff you did on CNN would come back to bite you in the ass. On the plus side, it must be fun having all those groupies…"

"Yeah, that's a real perk, all right."

"Seriously, man, what's the story with old man Harland? My guy says the family's keeping a lid on his prognosis."

"If they are, isn't it their business?"

"What were we just talking about, Danny? The Harlands are public figures. Just like you—only, brand-wise, you're sorta minor league. Limited demographic reach. But *they're* at the top of the celebrity food chain. Which makes them fair game. Especially since the old man married an ex-movie star."

"Remind me again why we're friends…?"

"Bite me. But I gotta ask, man. What were you doing at the hospital? Is Harland your patient? Or his wife, Lisa Campbell?"

"Jesus, Sam. You know I can't comment."

"Yeah, I know. But like I said, I had to ask."

I'd just turned onto Second Avenue, and slowed my speed as I drove along the riverside. The Monongahela's black waters shone like obsidian under the moon's unblinking gaze.

"Tell me, Sam, are you going to keep digging into the story about Harland's stroke?"

"Damn right. *If* my guy can get something concrete from one of the docs in ICU. They're tough nuts to crack."

I pulled into a curbside spot about half a block from Noah's Ark and killed the engine.

"Can I ask you one more question, Danny?"

"No way I can stop you, I guess."

"Is it true that Lisa Campbell has taken a room there at the hospital? Just to be near her ailing husband? That's another thing my guy picked up on. As an expert on human relationships, what do you think this says about the state of their marriage?"

"I wouldn't know, Sam. And wouldn't tell you if I did."

"Yeah, I figured that, too. Can't blame a guy for trying, though. Keeps things interesting."

"Why do you care about the Harlands, anyway? This kind of stuff isn't your beat. Don't you have any major crimes or political scandals you should be investigating?"

"If I did, I would. But it's been a slow news week in the Steel City, Danny. I'm stuck with table scraps."

I smiled to myself. Though Sam didn't know it, he was actually nosing around the edges of a *huge* story. Kidnapping, murder, family secrets. A story big enough to fill the pages of another true-crime book.

"Well, I hope things pick up, Sam."

"Me, too. The royalties from the Dowd book have dwindled down to nothing. And every three months, there's another rumor about cutbacks and layoffs here at the paper. If something juicy doesn't happen soon…"

Sam sighed heavily into the phone. "Aw, what the hell, life goes on, right? Speaking of which, why don't we grab a lunch? I haven't seen you in a while, and I could sure go for some 'old school' grub. How about Primanti Brothers on the Strip? One o'clock tomorrow?"

Truth was, it sounded good. A nice break from the almost unbearable stress I'd been under. Besides, since I'd cancelled my clients for the day, the only thing on my calendar was a meeting with the Feds. To repeat the same detailed statement I'd given to Lieutenant Biegler. With the same deletions.

"Okay, Sam. One o'clock. See you then."

I got out of my car and headed up the block to Noah's place. And felt myself actually breathe, perhaps for the first time since crouching beside Arthur Drake's lifeless body. It would be a relief to see an old friend like Sam, though I knew he'd probably pump me again for information about the Harlands.

I was wrong. Because what I *didn't* know was that I wasn't going to make it to that lunch tomorrow.

Noah's Ark boasted a pretty good crowd for a Sunday night. Most of the tables were filled, and there were only a few empty stools at the bar. As I took one, I caught sight of Charlene, laden with a tray of dishes, bustling out of the kitchen.

I called across the room for Noah, who was leaning against the back wall, eyes closed in wordless rapture. Engrossed in the sounds being laid down by the classic jazz trio up on the dais. Piano, upright bass, and drums. Doing a tasty cover of Herbie Hancock's "The In Crowd."

The musicians finished to a listless round of applause from their distracted audience. Then Noah, shaking his head sadly, went back behind the bar and made his way up to where I sat. His meaty forearms hit the polished counter with a moist thud.

"Philistines." His raised eyebrows conveyed a sweeping indictment of the paying customers all around us. "They wouldn't know great music if it came up and shook hands with 'em. All these morons come here to do is drink and spend money."

"Isn't that a good thing?"

He gave me an exaggerated frown. "Only for payin' the bills, Danny boy. What *I'm* tryin' to do is provide something for their sorry-ass souls. If any of 'em still got one. I'm a man with a mission, as you well know."

I asked for a Jack Daniels, straight, which he somewhat glumly poured. Another patron, three stools over—middle-aged, balding, and sporting an unfortunate soul patch—tried to get Noah's attention, but he ignored him.

"You understand what I'm talkin' about, don'tcha, Danny?"

"I think so. But let's face it, I'm not that cool myself."

"That's 'cause you think small. To paraphrase the Bible, 'Act as if you have cool, and cool will be given unto you.'"

I laughed. "Man, you're full of quotes lately."

"He's full of *somethin'*, all right…"

This was from the guy with the soul patch. When Noah turned, the unsmiling man held up his empty beer mug.

"Hey, what the fuck—?!" Noah headed down the bar toward him. "Was I talkin' to *you*, asshole?"

The guy stiffened. I tensed, watching the two of them closely. The customer was already half in the bag. Unfortunately for him, he was also half Noah's size.

"Noah!" I called out. He stopped in his tracks, head swiveling at the sound of my voice. "Cut the crap and give the guy another beer. On *me*, okay?"

Noah's big shoulders rose and fell, to the accompaniment of a massive sigh. He somberly nodded. Grabbing up the frightened customer's mug, he refilled it at the tap. Then slammed it back down on the bar.

"Appreciate your business," he mumbled. "Come again."

Then he lumbered back up to my end of the bar.

"Sorry, Danny. Just havin' a bad night."

Out of the corner of my eye, I saw Soul Patch finish his beer in two great gulps and hurry away from the bar. Looked like he left a nice tip, too. But my focus was on Noah.

"You get in touch with Nancy Mendors about your meds? You might need to make some changes."

"Yeah, maybe. I *am* feelin' a little wigged-out. I mean, even more than usual."

"Okay. If you don't mind, I'll give Nancy a call. But maybe you could close up the place a bit earlier tonight."

"I'll take that under advisement, Herr Doctor."

Then he offered me that familiar, pained grin. Below a pair of eyes burning with intensity. Holding either barely contained madness or profound knowledge of the Infinite. Or both.

Noah left abruptly to serve other customers, giving me some privacy for my call to Nancy. I got her service, and left a message detailing my concerns about Noah's behavior. Luckily, she always welcomed my input. Noah was as much her friend as her patient, and we both worried about him.

Though neither one of us fretted more than Charlene, who was suddenly standing next to me. Order pad in her pocket, she'd taken a quick break from waiting tables.

"I hope you were just talking to Dr. Mendors on the phone, Danny. Noah's got me a little worried."

"Me, too. But he's not delusional. Anyway, I left a message on Nancy's machine. She'll take care of it."

"I know. Thank God for that woman." Charlene blew a long stray curl of sweaty hair from her forehead. "And I could also say the same for you. I really appreciate your bailing Skip out of the mess at that store yesterday. And, yes, he finally broke down and told me about it."

"Glad I could help. I like your brother a lot."

"He feels the same way about you. Just this morning, he called and said, 'Bugs, that Rinaldi guy's all right.'"

"Bugs?"

"For Bugs Bunny. My nickname when we were kids. I had these two buck teeth that made me look like a rabbit. At least, that's what *he* said. You know what shits little brothers are."

"Not from my own experience, but I've heard."

Charlene sighed. "Just don't tell Noah about it. Or else he'll be calling me 'Bugs' the rest of my natural life."

I sipped my drink. "Nicknames *do* have a way of sticking."

"Funny. That's what happened to Skip. Everybody always called him that growing up, and he liked it fine. So he kept it. Not that I blame him. Not with the *real* name my parents saddled him with."

"Yeah? What was it?"

"Julian. Now what kinda name is *that* for a kid?"

Chapter Twenty-nine

Harry Polk was not the kind of guy who liked unexpected visitors knocking on his door. Especially at midnight.

I'd been doing just that for almost a minute before his apartment door finally opened a crack, and I was favored with one bleary, suspicious eye. As well as a glimpse of a threadbare robe, thrown over a baggy pair of boxer shorts.

"Rinaldi? What the fuck are ya doin' here? Ya got any idea what time it is?"

I glanced at my watch. "I know exactly. But I had to talk to you, Harry. It's important."

"Well, guess what? They got this newfangled thing now called the telephone. Has little numbers on it and everything."

"I figured, if I called, you'd just hang up."

"Good guess."

He started to close the door, but I pushed back against it with the palm of my hand. "Come on, Harry. It's important. About the Lisa Campbell kidnapping. I think I may know who's behind it."

"Yeah? Me, too. Prick named Ray Sykes."

"Unless he's working with or for somebody else. A guy who calls himself Skip Hines. Though his real name is Julian."

He blinked, brow darkening. "Are you shittin' me? Julian?…"

Polk stopped pushing back against me, and let the door open a few inches wider.

"How the hell do you know this?"

"Long story. Now are you gonna let me in or not?"

"Fuck that, Rinaldi. We ain't that close. Besides, talkin' to you always makes me thirsty. Gimme five minutes."

He slammed the door shut, leaving me alone in the quiet, dimly lit hallway. Harry Polk was still living in the forlorn Wilkinsburg apartment complex he'd moved into after his marriage ended. The majority of the tenants were elderly, or, like Harry, recently divorced. Yet most of the latter soon moved to better, more congenial accommodations. Providing, if only to themselves, external confirmation that they'd moved on with their lives.

But not Harry. After he and Maddie split, he took what few possessions he had and burrowed into this place like a wounded animal. And showed little sign of making a change any time soon.

As I waited for him, I thought about the call I'd made to Gloria Reese on the drive here from Noah's place. Though I'd tried her cell, she was at home in her South Side loft when she picked up. I remembered her mentioning once that it was the only asset she'd received from *her* divorce. Anyway, unlike Harry, she was still awake, and had just brewed herself a cup of chamomile tea to help her wind down. So she could finally sleep.

After checking to see how she was holding up, and getting her usual stiff-upper-lip reply, I asked her two questions: did she have access to the FBI's database from her home computer? And, if so, would she be willing to do me a favor? Naturally enough, she said it depended on what the favor was.

I told her.

Now, rocking back and forth on my heels, I felt a growing impatience. Harry's five minutes had clearly come and gone. I was just about to pound on his door again when it opened. The sergeant was wearing a faded Penquins sweatshirt over wrinkled pants and his customary Florsheim shoes.

"This better be worth it, Rinaldi. I need my beauty sleep."

"You get no argument from me, Harry. Where to?"

"Where do ya think?"

◇◇◇

The Spent Cartridge was an old cop bar uncomfortably wedged between two downtown high-rises, its wood-framed facade and buzzing neon signs a stark reminder of the blue-collar past now being gradually supplanted by the city's gentrification.

The place was just getting its second wind, so to speak, in that the precinct shift change brought with it a wave of off-duty uniforms and plainclothes dicks. Luckily, Polk and I had found seats in a corner booth before the bar filled to standing-room-only capacity.

Nursing an Iron City, Harry sat staring at me across the booth table. By agreement on the drive here, I wasn't to talk about the case until he'd been—in his words—properly lubed.

At last, contemplating my own whiskey glass, I recounted my conversation with Charlene.

"After she told me her brother's given name was Julian, I tried to probe some more, but without arousing her suspicions. Mostly because Charlene's a friend of mine. Besides, this thing about Skip's real name could just be a wild coincidence."

"Ya don't really believe that, do ya?"

"Honestly, no. Especially when she told me a little more about his life. Turns out, after a stint in the Marines, he went to work in high-level security. A company called Starr Sentinel, which happens to be the same firm that Mike Payton used to work for. Before going solo and hooking up with the Harlands."

"Payton and this Julian Hines both worked for Starr?"

"Right. And when I casually asked if her brother ever mentioned this other guy I knew—Mike Payton—she said yes. That Skip had talked about him more than once, and seemed to like the guy. He and Payton were on the same tactical team at Starr. Doing security work for CEOs, celebrities. That kinda thing."

Polk distractedly took a swallow of beer.

"So what happened to Julian? I mean, did he quit the job when Payton did?"

I shook my head. "According to Charlene, he stayed on a couple more months. But she says he always found civilian life difficult to manage. Confusing. So he re-enlisted and was sent back to Afghanistan, where he lost a leg in combat."

"Jesus." Polk massaged the dark stubble on his chin. "So you think this lady's brother is the same Julian who called the Harland house? Who ran the whole show?"

"Either he ran it or worked in partnership with Sykes. Think about it, Harry. Julian Hines is a former Marine, and the kidnapping felt like some kind of paramilitary op from the very beginning. Remember, we know about Sykes' background in the military. Griffin's, too. Maybe the three of them planned the whole thing together. Like a military maneuver."

"Maybe. Anything else?"

"I think that Julian—just like Mike Payton—had to know a lot about home security, having worked for Starr. In fact, the security system at the Harland house—the cameras, the off-site monitoring, everything—had all been installed and maintained by Starr Sentinel. It was the company Payton recommended to Charles Harland when he first came to work for the old man. Probably because he felt familiar with the company and its technology."

"How do you know all this?"

"I put in a call to Agent Gloria Reese before I showed up at your door. She could access a lot of it because Payton had, at the FBI's insistence, sent them a copy of the personnel data from the Harland files—which included Payton's own employment history, as well as the contract that Charles Harland, at Mike's suggestion, had signed with Starr Sentinel."

"Then maybe we should be lookin' at Mike Payton."

"Funny, because Arthur Drake had his own suspicions about Payton. He told me before he died that he believed Payton was behind Lisa's kidnapping. But I don't see it, Harry. For one thing, Payton was in Harland's office with the rest of us when the first ransom call came in. Just as he was in the library, in plain sight, when Julian called with his second demand."

What I didn't tell Harry was the *real* reason I ruled out any involvement on Payton's part. Namely, that he was still in love with Lisa. At least it looked that way to me.

"I don't care that he was there when the calls came in," Polk was saying. "Doesn't mean Payton couldn't be in on it. A silent partner, or whatever. It's worth checkin' into, that's for damn sure."

"I think the same thing's true about Julian Hines. Of course, I didn't give Charlene the slightest clue that I had any suspicions about her brother. She just thought we were talking about his past because I was interested."

"In other words, since everyone knows what a nosy, head-shrinkin' bastard you are, she didn't suspect a thing."

"Well, I guess that's another way to look at it."

He threw back the rest of his beer. "You talk to anyone else about this? Other than Reese?"

"No. And all I asked her to do was look up stuff about Mike Payton. I told her I was curious about his military background and employment history before coming to work for Harland."

"She didn't ask why?"

"Sure she did. I told her it was personal."

Polk considered this. "So she'd assume you couldn't talk about it. Which suggested that Payton had approached you about wantin' therapy. So if she *did* ask you, you couldn't say squat. Nice move, Doc. Sneaky, but nice."

"The point is, Harry, *you're* the one I've come to about Julian Hines. I sure as hell don't want to alert Biegler or Agent Wilson. In case I'm way off base, I don't want to cause Skip—or Charlene, for that matter—any additional grief."

"But even if you're right, Rinaldi, what's the motive?"

"Behind the kidnapping? What else? The money. Skip's been floundering since he got shipped home. God knows, a lot of returning vets go through that. Especially those who've been seriously injured. Though many still end up doing well, as long as they're given proper medical and psychological support."

"But not this Skip character?"

"Not based on my two interactions with him. I don't think he's sought treatment anywhere. My impression is of a guy who's wired tight as a drum. With nothing to show for his two tours of duty but a missing leg and a heart full of anger and resentment. Meanwhile, people like the Harlands live like kings."

Polk nodded soberly. Then gestured to a passing waitress for a refill. She swept up his mug and hurried away.

"Remember, too," I went on, "the Harland fortune came from building armaments. War machines. For a wounded vet like Skip, the painful irony of that must seem intolerable. How fitting, then, to grab some of that blood-stained cash for himself?"

The waitress returned with the full mug and vanished again into the crowd. Polk took a long pull, then wiped his lips with the back of his hand.

"Nice theory, Rinaldi. Except you left out the proof. Got any, or are you just flappin' your gums?"

"Isn't that where *you* come in, Sergeant? Not that I'm just dumping all this in your lap. Maybe I can do some more digging myself, and—"

"Watch it, Doc. I know you get a lotta leeway from the brass 'cause you're sorta on the job. But remember, you're just supposed to consult. So, okay, you consulted. Now leave it be."

"But you're going to follow up, aren't you? Discreetly, I mean. Like I say, I want to shield Charlene—*and* her brother—from unnecessary pain or embarrassment."

In answer, Polk merely sipped his beer. I swear I could almost see the gears slowly grinding in his skull.

Finally, he leaned back in his seat.

"This Julian thing is a real lead, no doubt about it. So I'll look into it. But at least we agree about one thing. I don't wanna shake Biegler's tree 'til I have somethin' solid. And I sure ain't gonna let the Feds in on it."

He let out a ponderous sigh.

"The pisser is, to do this right, I gotta go solo. If anybody gets wind o' this at the precinct, I'll have Biegler so far up my ass I'll be eatin' for both of us."

"What about Jerry Banks? Your new partner?"

"Let me see. He's young, green, and I don't trust him. That about cover it?"

"In other words, he's no Eleanor Lowrey."

"Few of 'em are, Doc. 'Course, I don't gotta tell *you* that. Though I think I remember warnin' you not to go there. One o' you was bound to get fucked. And I don't mean in the *good* way."

I bristled at that, but stayed cool. "Can we stay on task here, Sergeant? If you're not even letting your new partner in on this, how do you expect to work it?"

He gave me a wink. "Same way I do everythin', Doc. Hang onto my balls and jump in."

After another round, I was ready to leave. But Harry wanted to stay behind, having run into an old buddy from his former precinct. He said he'd get a ride home with him. Before leaving the bar, though, I got Harry's promise to keep me updated on anything he uncovered about Skip.

Driving now through mid-town's shadowed concrete canyons, in that eerie middle-of-the-night hush, I kept replaying my conversation with Polk. I knew I'd done the right thing bringing him my suspicions about Skip Hines, but still felt badly about it. As though I'd betrayed both Charlene *and* her brother, and had started something going that, regardless of outcome, would cause unwanted trouble and pain. The last thing Skip needed was to be considered a suspect in a series of capital crimes. And the last thing Charlene needed was to know that *I'd* been the one who put her brother's face in the picture.

On the other hand, I thought, there were simply too many connections between Skip Hines and some other facets of the case to ignore. Especially since his real name was Julian. Maybe I was rationalizing to ease my guilty conscience, but I still had a hard time believing that it was just a coincidence.

I'd reached Fifth, and was heading into Oakland, but instead of going directly home, I decided to swing by my office to get some patient files I'd been meaning to review. Since I was still too wired to sleep, at least I could work.

I turned onto Forbes Avenue and found a curbside parking spot in front of my building. I knew the parking garage would be closed at this time of night. Besides, I'd only need a couple minutes to go up to my office and retrieve what I needed.

I got out of the car, buttoning my jacket against the brisk wind, and looked around. The sidewalk was completely deserted, as were the streets. The only thing to catch my eye was the ceaseless activity of the traffic lights, dutifully going from green to yellow to red and back again. Directing a flow of cars that wasn't there.

Flipping through my keys, I found the exterior one and let myself into the darkened lobby. Then I took the elevator up to the fifth floor, stepping out into a similarly dimly lit corridor. Padding down the carpeted hallway, I felt familiar prickles on my skin. Spooked, as I often was, by the unnerving silence of an empty, after-hours office building.

When I reached my door, I took out the key that opened my suite. I was about to slide it into the lock...

At the touch of the key, the door sighed open.

It was already unlocked.

Which meant somebody had been inside my office. Or might still be there now. Waiting...

The breath caught in my throat, as I stood, unmoving. I tried to think. I knew I hadn't forgotten to lock it at day's end on Friday. Despite the stress of recent events. I even remembered making a point of doing so.

Pocketing my keys, I told myself that the smart thing to do was to back away from the doorway as quietly as possible and call the police.

I wish I had.

But, instead, I felt inexorably drawn by that half-opened door. Maybe by curiosity, or righteous anger. Maybe by something I couldn't explain. All I knew was that I had to find out who—or what—was on the other side of that door. Inside my office.

I quietly pushed the door all the way open and stepped into the suite's waiting room, empty but for the deep onyx shades of night. Even so, I could tell it was just as it had been when I last left the office. Not a thing out of place.

Then, one measured step at a time, I went through the con-
necting door into my consulting room. Barely able to breathe,
I squinted into a darkness threaded only by faint moon glow.

Again, everything seemed the same. My desk, the walls—

Then I saw it. Saw *him*.

Shrouded in shadow. Sitting in the leather chair that my
patients use. The one opposite my own.

I was facing the back of the chair, so at first all I saw was the
top of his head, above the seat back.

Heart banging in my chest, I slowly moved in an arc around
the two chairs. Until I came to stand before him.

He reminded me of a shy, reluctant patient. Feet crossed at
the ankles. Hands folded on his lap.

The only difference was his head. Tilted up, eyes wide and
bright, leaning against the chair's cushioned back.

It was then that I recognized him, even in the room's feeble
light. It was his hair. Coarse, straggly, parted in the middle and
hanging on either side of his head.

He was the perp identified by his fingerprints at the mining
office as Tommy Ames. The long-haired guy who'd watched over
Gloria Reese and me at the printing factory.

Now watching me again, in my office. Staring, really, with
white, lifeless eyes.

Even as I stared back. At the neat, blood-encrusted bullet
hole in the middle of his forehead.

Chapter Thirty

For the second time in less than a week, my office door was crisscrossed with crime scene tape. It wasn't yet dawn, but with every light in the suite on, including the seldom-used overheads, the rooms were as bright as if bathed in noon sunshine.

I'd spent the last hour sitting in my waiting room, nursing a Styrofoam cup of black coffee that a thoughtful uniform had brought me. Since finding the body and calling it in, I'd been barred from my consulting office, which was soon crowded with uniforms, CSU techs, the ME, and, inevitably, Lieutenant Biegler. Less than twenty minutes later, he was joined by Harry Polk, summoned on his cell from the Spent Cartridge, with his temporary partner, Jerry Banks, who'd been summoned from his bed.

Nobody, it seemed, had so far alerted the FBI.

I'd just drained the last drop of coffee from the cup when the medical examiner—a slim Asian woman to whom I was never introduced—strode out of my office, through the waiting room, and out the hall door. In her wake, a CSU tech pushed a wheeled cart bearing Tommy Ames' remains, zipped into a body bag.

Moments later, Biegler, Polk, and Banks came out of the office, the latter two stripping latex gloves from their hands. The lieutenant had his own manicured hands in his pockets, which was where they'd been when he first entered the room. By my reckoning, that still left two CSU techs in my office, going over every inch of the crime scene.

"Well?" I slowly climbed to my feet.

"Not that it's any of your concern," Biegler said archly, "but the ME says death was instantaneous. A single bullet to the brain. No powder burns, so the shooter was a decent distance away from Ames."

"Must've been a good shot. Probably Max Griffin." I took a step toward Biegler. "And what do you mean, not my concern? I just found a dead guy sitting in my office. Deliberately positioned like a patient might be. Almost a parody of a *new* patient, in fact. Hands folded. Feet crossed at the ankles."

Harry Polk sniffed. "You figure Griffin did that to fuck with you?"

"Who knows? Probably. Though I bet Sykes gave the orders. Griffin doesn't have the imagination."

Biegler frowned. "But why would Sykes do that?"

"My read? Based on meeting him, and the way he's behaved since this whole mess began, I'd say he's a textbook narcissist. Likes to think he's smarter than everyone around him—which he probably is. I could tell from how he questioned me when Reese and I were his captives that he wanted me to be impressed."

Jerry Banks spoke up. "Now it looks like he wants you to be intimidated."

"Well, he sure as hell succeeded."

The kid actually grinned. "One other thing. ME says that there's been blood loss, but none found on the body or anywhere near. She says she'll know for certain after she gets the corpse on her table, but that Ames was probably killed somewhere else and then brought here. Maybe in some kind of bag or rolled-up blanket. Which the perps took with them."

"Even so," Biegler added, "there oughta be forensics in the room. Prints, DNA. Stuff we can use to tie Sykes or Griffin or both to the murder."

Polk let himself collapse onto the waiting room sofa.

"Look, boys and girls, I can understand why they whacked Tommy Ames. Now that they have the ransom money, he was just a loose end. Like Fred Gilroy. I'll even buy the idea that Sykes wanted to mess with Rinaldi's head. Make some kinda half-assed statement about what an evil fuckin' genius he is. But the ME puts the time o' death at about midnight. Only five hours ago."

"So?" Biegler glowered down at him. "What's your point?"

"My point is, why the hell are Sykes and Griffin still here in town? Why aren't they three states away by now?"

I shrugged. "Maybe I wasn't the only one that Sykes felt he had unfinished business with. He does have a big operation here. Covers the tri-state area, according to Agent Reese."

Biegler turned to me. "So you're saying it could be that he needs to settle some accounts. Maybe give some final orders to his men. Get things squared away before he can take off?"

"Then he's takin' a helluva risk," Polk said. "He's got ten million bucks. What else does the bastard need?"

"Control." I gazed at the three police officers. "Look at the kidnapping. Planned with military precision. With Sykes determined to call the shots at every step. All of which blew up in his face when his identity as the kidnapper was revealed. Undoing his feeling of control. Forcing him to improvise."

"What do you mean?"

"Remember, his original plan was to collect the ransom and then kill Lisa Campbell. With no one having the slightest idea who he was. Which meant there'd be no reason to abandon his regular operation. The drugs, the human trafficking. Even his little side business, arranging sex parties for the rich and powerful. Why should he? After all, while the FBI knew about these activities, they had no evidence to use against him. For Ray Sykes, once Lisa was dead and the ransom in hand, it would be back to business as usual. With a nice ten million-dollar pension plan he could count on for a rainy day."

Biegler grunted. "Okay, Rinaldi, let's say you're right. But if this Sykes is as smart as you say he is, he still won't hang around here long. *Nobody's* that conceited."

"For once, Lieutenant, I agree with you. Agent Reese told me that the Bureau's already planning to keep tabs on Sykes' known associates. Wire-taps, hacking their emails. The problem is, I'm sure Sykes has assumed that already."

"Right. So if I were him, I'd grab as much face-time with my people as I could, get all my ducks in a row, and then skip town. Probably what he's spent this whole night doing."

I nodded. "That's the way I see it. He leaves me Tommy Ames' dead body as a parting gift, gives his people their marching orders—at least for the short term, until the heat dies down—and then takes off."

"But how?" Jerry Banks frowned. "The Feds are watching the airports, bus terminals, the cab companies…I mean, how the hell do Sykes and Griffin get through the net?"

Polk rubbed his thick neck. "Plenty o' ways, kid. I bet Sykes already got people on the pad in some o' those places. Even if he don't, he's got the cash to bribe anyone he needs to. Like they say, money talks, bullshit walks."

An awkward silence filled the room.

"I still have a question." I walked over to the suite's hall door. The one I'd found already ajar.

Bending, I peered at the lock. And saw some telltale scratches adjacent to the keyhole.

"Yeah, they picked the lock." It was Polk, calling over from his seat on the sofa. "Not the prettiest work I ever seen, but it got the job done."

I straightened, just as the remaining two CSU techs came out of my office. One held a number of small evidence bags. The other carried a fingerprint kit under his arm.

"Didn't get much, Lieutenant," said the first guy. "Mostly prints, some of which I figure will match Max Griffin or Ray Sykes, or both. The rest will probably turn out to belong to the Doc and his patients. Plus a few hairs and fibers. Maybe stuff the cleaning crew missed on Friday evening."

"Okay, thanks," said Biegler. He waved the two men away.

Jerry Banks peered at his two senior officers.

"Excuse me, sirs…But shouldn't we reach out to the FBI? Since we're working together. I mean, they've got to be informed about Tommy Ames. That's what my uncle would want. Right?"

Biegler and Polk exchanged unreadable looks, though I could guess what they were thinking. Like it or not, Banks was right. He was also the assistant chief's nephew. It was probably a toss-up as to which fact the two men found more irritating.

Finally, Biegler nodded and reached for his cell.

The lieutenant soon left to report personally to Chief Logan, though it was clear from the way he and Polk acted that the murder of Tommy Ames wasn't going to cause anyone to lose sleep. Like Fred Gilroy, Ames was a bit player whose death merely added another name to the list of Max Griffin's victims. If the Pittsburgh Police—and the FBI—were going to utilize their resources to find Sykes and Griffin, it would be for the political payoff of bringing to justice the men who'd kidnapped Lisa Campbell and killed Arthur Drake. As well as Donna Swanson, Charles Harland's longtime personal nurse.

Visibly relieved at Biegler's departure, Harry leaned back against the sofa, hands clasped behind his head. Gave me one of his flat, sardonic looks.

"Better cancel your patients for at least another couple days, Doc. Your office will stay a crime scene till CSU can run all the prints they found. I mean, those that don't belong to you, Sykes, or Griffin. Who knows? Maybe one of your whiny head cases has a record."

I met his gaze. "I doubt it, Harry. Most of my patients are themselves crime victims, as you well know. Unless you plan on hassling already-traumatized people over traffic tickets and unpaid parking fines."

He snorted, but didn't answer. Instead, he turned his attention to Jerry Banks, who was biting a thumbnail. Bored.

"Jerry, grab some uniforms and start canvassing the area. Talk to anyone who might've seen suspicious activity on the streets outside around midnight. Maybe somebody saw two guys luggin' a heavy bag or rolled-up carpet into the building. Even if all anyone saw was a car parked out front, or in that alley in the back. Since Ames was killed elsewhere, Sykes and Griffin hadda get his dead ass here in *some* kinda vehicle."

Jerry Banks didn't look particularly motivated by this assignment, but he nodded and ambled out of the room. Polk looked pretty happy to see *him* exit the scene, too.

Meanwhile, I'd already decided to go along with Harry's suggestion about cancelling my patients for another few days, if for no other reason than to give me time to buy and have a new chair delivered. Frankly, I didn't have the stomach to work with patients who'd be sitting in the same chair in which I'd found Ames' body.

I also planned to have both rooms in the suite thoroughly cleaned and sanitized. Again, for its psychological benefit. To erase, symbolically as well as physically, the lingering traces of what had happened here.

With an exaggerated sigh, Harry Polk levered himself out of the sofa. Then he closed the hallway door, beyond which stood two uniforms, charged with guarding the crime scene.

"Okay, listen up, Rinaldi. I'm gonna take a run at this Julian Hines mook. Like I said, I'm gonna work solo, at least for now. But as soon as Biegler yanks my leash, I'm done playin' the Lone Ranger. You got me?"

I nodded, then gave him the address of a motel in East Liberty where Skip was staying. Charlene had told me that it was only until he got a job and could afford his own apartment. Apparently, she'd offered to let him stay with Noah and her in their living quarters behind the bar, but Skip had declined the offer. The place was too small for all three of them, he'd said, and he didn't want to impose.

After writing down the address, Polk took off, leaving me alone in the waiting room. I smiled at the two uniforms, then gently closed the door again.

Taking Polk's seat on the sofa, I used my cell to check my voicemail. Two patient calls, both relatively urgent. I returned the first and got her answering machine, but was able to speak in person to the second patient. He'd been the recent victim of a mugging, and now suffered frequent panic attacks. Though his anxiety lessened initially, he became alarmed when I told him I had to cancel his upcoming session on Wednesday. Given his level of agitation, I made an appointment to meet with him at his usual time, only at a Starbucks just off-campus.

After hanging up, I called a colleague and asked if he could cover my practice for the next few days. Luckily, he was available. Then I left messages for the remaining patients I was slated to see during the next two days, cancelling the sessions, and leaving my colleague's number in case of emergency.

The last call I made was to Lisa, at the hospital. She answered her cell after two rings.

"I was hoping that was you, Danny."

"How are you doing? Driving the nurses crazy?"

"More like they're driving *me* crazy. Luckily, young Doctor Gorgeous signed off on me getting outta here."

"Have you seen Charles?"

"I'm just going up there now. You won't believe it, but the old bastard made them bring in a couple phones. He's already sitting up and conference-calling with the board of directors. Trying to figure out how to spin his stroke."

"Probably because the investors are nervous."

"Fuck 'em. He's made most of them rich."

That sounded like a dollop of sympathy for Charles. Or at least an appreciation for what he'd accomplished over the years. But then she laughed. "And no, I'm not going soft in the head all of a sudden. My hubby's a prick, no matter how many strokes he has. I just hate to see the goddamn vultures circling. Reminds me of the movie business. Sharks always biting your ass when you're on top, vultures waiting to eat your innards when you're down."

It was good to hear her spirits returning. I said so.

"Yeah, yeah. Meanwhile, that video's still out there. In James' hands. Like a ticking time bomb."

"I've been thinking about that. There's got to be a way to get it back from him. To find out where he's hidden it."

"Forget it, Danny. I'm screwed and you know it. Shit, I got a good mind to go up to Charles' room right now, shove a pillow in his face, and send him to that Great Boardroom in the Sky. Then I'll raid the nurses' station for all the pills they got and follow the old man right off this mortal coil."

"Great plan, Lisa. Except for the murder-suicide part."

"C'mon, Danny, I'm kidding."

"Uh-huh. I think I liked you better when you were sedated. Besides, we have a suicide contract, remember?"

"Of course I remember. Jesus, man, anybody ever tell you you're kinda obsessive?"

We chatted for a few more minutes, then Lisa said she couldn't stall going up to Charles' room any longer. Apparently, print and TV reporters were camped, at a prescribed distance, outside his closed door. All waiting impatiently for the ailing billionaire's loving wife to make her appearance.

"So I gotta get ready to be all over the evening news. Then everybody can talk trash online about how old I look. Now, tell me *again* why this is better than just taking myself out?"

Chapter Thirty-one

Special Agent Anthony Wilson shut off the tape recorder.

"That's the extent of your statement, Dr. Rinaldi?"

"That's it," I said evenly. "Including everything I can remember about finding Tommy Ames' body."

He slid off the edge of his desk and went to the shuttered window. Surprisingly, when I'd shown up at the Federal Building I was immediately ushered into Wilson's office. I assumed I'd be giving my statement to some junior G-man, as before. But it looked like Wilson wanted to hear it from me himself.

Now, lifting the shutters to squint out at the noonday sun, he presented the familiar demeanor of a disappointed law enforcement officer. The stern, puckered face I'd seen many times before in my dealings with the cops—and the Feds.

"Are you sure there aren't some details you're withholding from us?" He turned from the window, taking a seat behind his desk. I was in the sole chair facing it.

"Not consciously. But you know what a tricky devil the *un*conscious is, Agent Wilson. Things slip through the cracks."

"This is no time to be facetious, Doctor. To be candid, I have some concerns for your safety."

"I'm touched. Care to elaborate?"

"The death of Tommy Ames is of no value to this case, except for the one notable assumption it allows us. Namely, that Raymond Sykes feels strongly enough about you to leave Ames' corpse in your office."

"If you recall, I said something to that effect in my statement. In my opinion, Sykes is a classic narcissist."

"I remember quite clearly. But Ames' death also tells us that, as of last night, Sykes hadn't left the tri-state area. In fact, it appears he still hasn't."

"What are you talking about? Biegler believes that Sykes wanted to get his business house in order before skipping the country. Which he's probably done by now. Right?"

"Probably. All I'm suggesting is that it's possible Sykes is personally offended that you've escaped him, Doctor. Twice. And that if, for whatever reason, he's still in the vicinity, and could arrange to do so safely, he'd—"

"Take one final crack at me before he gets out of Dodge."

"I'm not saying it's smart. I'm just saying it's possible." Then, hands folded on the desktop, he smiled. There's something about the way an FBI agent smiles that really bugs me. It always manages to be both self-assured and condescending, even when it's supposed to be conveying concern or sympathy. Yet somehow it stops just short of being smug. I don't know; it must be something they teach at the Academy.

"Okay, Wilson, what the hell are you keeping from me? What's happened?"

Smile fading, he looked off, as though needing a moment to decide something. Then he reached for a file folder tucked under his desk blotter, slid it across to me. I opened it.

I recognized its contents. A pair of preliminary homicide reports, color-coded in a way that distinguished them from those of the Pittsburgh PD. Along with pages of hastily written notes, signed and dated only hours ago by various Bureau field agents, there were two harrowing crime scene photos. Two different men, roughly the same indeterminable age, in two different locations. Each lying in a pool of blood. Each with the backs of their heads sheared off.

"Their names are Burrows and DeNardo. Two higher-ups in Sykes' operation. Both shot execution-style, sometime between midnight and five this morning. Burrows was killed in the backroom of a nightclub he owns in Steubenville, Ohio. The other one, DeNardo, got whacked in the crib of one of the whores he runs for Sykes out of Greensburg. All in all, counting Tommy Ames, a busy night for Sykes and Griffin."

"But what does this mean?" I handed him back the file.

"It means that Sykes wants to send a message to his other lieutenants. To anyone who might be thinking of making a move against his leadership if and when he skips town. Turns out, Biegler was right. Sykes *does* want to get things in order before he disappears. Before he leaves town for an extended vacation in Barbados or the Caymans or whatever. Which means he's going to make his escape on his own timetable. Not ours."

I stroked my beard. "But then if he's still in the area, where the hell is he?"

Wilson carefully tucked the file folder back under the blotter. Whose eyes he was hiding it from was a mystery to me.

"Sykes could be anywhere in the state. Or Ohio or West Virginia, for that matter. Given the size of his operation, his contacts, he has a hundred different holes he could hide in. Remember, there's a reason he's eluded arrest all these years, despite the circumstantial evidence the Bureau's compiled. He's smart, thorough, and knows how to hide in plain sight."

I suddenly remembered Biegler's reluctance to inform the FBI about the discovery of Ames' body.

"I assume you've sent copies of that murder file to the cops. Biegler. Chief Logan."

A noncommittal shrug. "When we've put together a more formal, more complete set of evidentiary material, then of course we'll share it with Pittsburgh PD. For the present, my understanding is that the director has contacted Chief Logan and the mayor to let them know that Sykes is probably still in the vicinity. Whereabouts as yet unknown."

"That means the Department will have every uniform and detective hitting the streets again. Rousting their informers. Looking for Sykes. Doing *your* legwork."

"Just as we've stepped up our surveillance of his known associates. The ones who still have a pulse, that is. Though my guess is, after what happened to Burrows and DeNardo, Sykes' remaining under-bosses will get the message and crawl under their respective rocks until the heat dies down."

"And when will that be?"

"Well, if I were to take a guess, I'd say Sykes would stay around at least long enough to kill *you*."

I took a breath. "I have to admit, I agree with you. Sykes wants me dead. Everything he *is* demands it. But not just because of his fragile ego, his blatant narcissism. And not because of the two times I escaped from him."

"What are you getting at?"

"When he failed to kill Agent Reese and myself, thus allowing us to be able to identify him to the authorities, we forced his hand. Now Sykes has to go into hiding, and for a considerable time, if not permanently. Plus he has to deal with ambitious men in his organization. Making sure his authority is unchallenged. Which entails the huge risk of hanging around here, when he'd certainly rather be long gone."

I paused, as another thought occurred to me.

"There's something else. According to what Gloria told me, Ray Sykes has been this successful by keeping his operation contained. Local. No threat to the big families or the Russians. Who's to say, once he's out of the country, that one or the other won't swoop in and take over Sykes' little slice of the criminal pie? See what I mean? Instead of Lisa Campbell's kidnapping being a one-off source of big money, a crime of opportunity whose perpetrators were never to be known, it's led to the dismantling of his whole world. And all because *I* was involved in it."

Wilson nodded. "When you put it that way, I can see why Sykes might want revenge. On you *and* on Agent Reese."

"Then I trust you'll provide her with protection. At least in the short term."

"Don't worry, I'll detail a fellow agent to be with her at all times. And outside her place when she's home."

"Good. I know she'll probably bitch about it, and say that she can take care of herself, but—"

"This is the FBI, Doctor. There's a clear chain of command. If I give Agent Reese an order, she'll obey it. Unfortunately, that isn't the case where you're concerned."

"Are you suggesting I have protection, too?"

"I can't force you, of course. Though perhaps, since you're a police consultant, Lieutenant Biegler might have more luck getting you to comply."

"I doubt it. For one thing, though I'm paid for my services to the Department, I'm still a civilian. Besides, I've had police protection before. On another case. Let's just say, it didn't exactly work out. But I'm not as stubborn as you think, Agent Wilson. I'll at least consider it."

"Good idea. I just hope you come to the right decision before Sykes has Max Griffin put a bullet in *your* head, too."

There it was again. That goddamn smile.

"It's just a theory, Danny." Agent Reese was unhappy.

"I agree. Maybe I'm wrong about Sykes, and he isn't looking for revenge. I'm a psychologist, Gloria, not a mind reader."

We were in her office, a spacious room with a southern exposure, the mid-day sun gleaming off the modern lines of her functional furnishings. The only personal touches were a couple of Matisse prints on the walls, a Pittsburgh Pirates beer mug on top of a file cabinet, and an authentic-looking artificial banzai tree on her desk. Next to it was the standard government-issue computer-fax-printer combo.

Opposite her desk were two plush armchairs, another out-of-place concession to human comfort in the sterile, no-nonsense environment of the Federal Building. I sat in one of them, while Gloria paced.

She'd caught my eye as I was leaving Wilson's office, and casually called me into hers. Closing the door, she asked what he and I had discussed. It was when I replayed the conversation for her that she started pacing.

"I'm not saying it isn't a *good* theory," she went on. "I think your take on Sykes' personality is probably correct. The problem is, I'm afraid Wilson will use his so-called concern about my safety as an excuse to keep me under wraps. Away from the action. I already feel frozen out. I mean, it's subtle. I'm officially still on the case. But I can feel it. If he gives me a full-time babysitter, it'll only make things worse."

She stopped pacing long enough to stare down at me. "And yet, *you* get to refuse protection. Pisses me off."

"I didn't refuse. I said I'd think about it."

This hardly mollified her. But at least she stopped pacing, choosing instead to go around to her chair behind the desk.

"Anyway," I said, "I'm glad we bumped into each other. I was going to call and ask for a favor."

"Another favor? Sure, why not? I've got nothing else to do at the moment."

"Great, thanks. There's a guy I wanted you to run a check on. A Marine vet named Skip Hines. Real name's Julian Hines."

She started. "*Julian*…? Really…?"

"Hey, maybe it means something, maybe not. Could you see what's in the database?"

"It wouldn't be in ours. I'd have to check the Marines. Or the DOD database. Could take a while."

"This might help—Skip was injured in Afghanistan. Lost a leg. He wears a prosthetic one now."

She nodded and began typing. Really fast. I suspected that an official FBI computer search was practically an "open sesame" for most government databases.

I was right. In moments, she looked up from the keyboard. "When was Hines discharged?"

I told her the date he'd arrived stateside. When Charlene and I had talked, she said she'd never forget that day. Nor how happy she'd been when Skip called her from his hospital bed at Bethesda. Missing a leg, in poor health generally and poorer spirits, but back on American soil. "At long last," Charlene had said, her eyes growing moist at the memory.

"Found him." Gloria squinted at the computer screen. "Hines did two tours in Afghanistan. About eighteen months apart."

"He lost his left leg on his second tour. An IED."

"Know anything about his first time in action?"

I shook my head. "Could you check?"

Another rapid-fire series of keystrokes. Then, suddenly, the staccato tapping stopped.

"You better take a look at this, Danny."

I got up and went around to her side of the desk. Peered over her shoulder at the monitor screen.

I felt my pulse quicken. "I'll be damned…"

During Skip Hines' first tour in Afghanistan, he was in a combat unit under the command of Lieutenant Raymond D. Sykes. Also on the twelve-member team was Sergeant Maxwell J. Griffin.

"Julian 'Skip' Hines served with Sykes and Griffin." Gloria nodded slowly. "So all three knew each other."

"Intimately, I suspect. Nothing bonds a group of people like combat. Your fellow soldiers become family."

She leaned into the screen again. "According to their files, everyone in the unit was honorably discharged. With no record of their activities after that. As civilians."

"Well, we know where Skip ended up. Working security at Starr Sentinel. Where he met Mike Payton."

Gloria tapped another succession of keys and another file appeared. This one was bannered with the FBI logo.

"And from our own data, we know what happened to Sykes and Griffin. They decided to go into business together when they came back to the States."

I considered this. "Assuming they met while serving together, they probably saw in each other a kindred spirit."

Gloria smirked. "That's putting it a lot more poetically than I would."

"Granted. But what I mean is, from what I experienced of the two of them, Sykes saw himself as an unquestioned leader. Like he'd been during the war. Yet someone who stayed away from the action. Griffin is his exact opposite. Action is all he understands. He's a weapon himself, but one in need of another's finger on the trigger. A narcissist like Sykes fit the bill."

She regarded me warily. "I appreciate psycho-babble as much as the next person, but how does that help us?"

"Maybe it doesn't. But it helps me understand how the two of them got together. Remember, Sykes comes from money. With an Ivy League education. One of 'the best and the brightest,' as the phrase goes. You yourself said he was the black sheep of his prominent family, who've probably long since disowned him. What better way for a narcissist to get his own back, to rub his family's nose in the dirt, than to become a career criminal?"

"Good point. I've seen that kind of thing before."

"With an eager, probably psychotic second-in-command like Griffin at his side, I bet it didn't take Sykes long to start building his operation."

"It didn't." Again, Gloria checked the monitor screen. "He first showed up on the Bureau's radar less than a year after his discharge. Taking over a local drug dealer's territory. And it went on from there. Not that we have enough evidence to bring to the state attorney. And even if we did, there's no way to know that he doesn't have officials like that in his pocket."

"Makes sense. Probably how he's managed to stay out of a courtroom all these years."

Gloria sat back in her chair. "Even so, what does all this have to do with Julian Hines?"

"I'm not sure. But think about it—after his discharge, Skip goes to work for Starr Sentinel, where he meets Payton. Then, not long after Payton leaves the firm to go work for Charles Harland, Skip re-enlists. Gets sent for a second time overseas, where he loses his leg. Then he comes home again."

"What are you getting at?"

"Once Skip got back, I wonder if he looked up his old buddy from Starr? What if he pays a visit to Mike Payton at his new job, sees all that Harland wealth, and figures why not kidnap the famous wife for big money? But he'd need help, so he brings in his former Marine buddies, Sykes and Griffin."

"But what about Payton? Was he involved, too?"

"Could be. But even if he wasn't, and merely knew or suspected who was behind the kidnapping, he's kept silent about it. Which could explain something I've been thinking about."

"What do you mean?"

I paused, choosing my words carefully. Wanting to share my thoughts without revealing everything I knew about Payton's former relationship with Lisa.

"It seems to me that Payton's been acting pretty guilty since Lisa's kidnapping," I said. "I've thought all along it was because he felt he'd failed the Harlands by not protecting her. By letting her get abducted. But maybe he's feeling that way because he knows—or at least, suspects—who was behind it."

"His friend from the security firm."

"Yes. Remember, Payton would know that Skip's real name is Julian. And he was in Harland's office with the rest of us when the kidnapper called, identifying himself by that name. Payton would have to figure that the caller was Skip Hines."

"Then why hasn't he come forward? Said something?"

I shrugged. "Maybe we should ask him."

Chapter Thirty-two

My Mustang's windows were open, the wind causing Gloria's newly trimmed ponytail to flop around behind her. I'd already driven us across town through heavy midday traffic on our way to Fox Chapel. Once we'd decided to question Mike Payton, I realized it didn't matter where he actually lived. He seemed to reside permanently at the home of his wealthy employer.

Gloria held her palm flat above her eyes, shielding them from a surprisingly bright spring sun.

"By the way, where's Skip Hines now?"

"Sergeant Polk is tailing him. Off the books, until we know more. For one thing, we don't want to spook Hines into making an escape. For another, in case I'm wrong about all this, I owe it to him and his sister Charlene to make sure things stop here."

"I have no trouble keeping it from Biegler and Wilson. I think they're both sexist jerks. Plus, if we give them Skip Hines as a prime suspect, they'd each trip over themselves bringing it upstairs to *their* bosses. I know for a fact that Wilson's getting a lot of pressure from the director."

"Just as I'm sure Biegler is feeling the heat from Chief Logan. Who's no doubt feeling it from the people above *him*. Even though Lisa's been returned safely, bagging the guys responsible would still be quite a feather in the Department's cap."

"Don't even go there, Danny. The Bureau hasn't gotten over the *last* feather that Pittsburgh PD picked up."

I smiled. "Yeah, I'm getting that vibe."

She shouted over the wind. "Watch it, Doc! The Bureau's higher-ups may be brown-nosing, envious little creeps, but they're *my* brown-nosing, envious little creeps. Got it?"

"Loud and clear. Especially the 'loud' part."

The large, multilevel homes and manicured lawns of Fox Chapel were arrayed on either side of us as we wended our way toward the Harland residence. I was just about to turn onto the billionaire's private access road when another car pulled out at the intersection. I recognized it immediately as one of the company's SUVs. I also recognized the driver.

"Hey!" Gloria was pointing. "Isn't that Payton?"

It was, indeed, barreling past us without a glance in our direction. Wherever he was going, he was in a pretty big hurry to get there. Without consulting Gloria, I made a U-turn and followed him.

When I did glance in her direction, she spread her hands.

"Why not? Let's see where he's going."

As it turned out, Payton's destination was only a ten-minute drive from the Harland house. Keeping a safe distance, I watched as he pulled into a small though stylish shopping mall just outside the Borough. He parked, then walked into a quaint restaurant fronted by ivy-laced trellises. An upscale sidewalk cafe, appropriate to the sensibilities of tony Fox Chapel.

I slid into a parking space two cars over from his SUV. Before we got out of the car, I remembered to check my voicemail, in case that one distressed patient had called again. Luckily, there were no urgent messages.

Unfortunately, checking my voicemail was the only thing I *did* remember. It wouldn't occur to me until much later that, at the same time as Gloria and I were walking through the front entrance of the café, I was supposed to be having lunch with Sam Weiss down at the Strip.

How differently things would have gone if I had…

Having little choice, Mike Payton smiled uncomfortably as he asked us to join him at his corner table. The well-appointed dining area was only half-filled with customers, adding to the café's hushed feeling of intimacy. Reminding me of an after-hours coffee bar in some European capital. One in particular, in fact, in Rome, where my late wife Barbara and I had honeymooned.

Payton recommended the cappuccinos, indicating the half-drunk, generous mug before him. Gloria and I ordered our own from a passing waitress, after which I turned to Payton.

"Agent Reese and I were just on our way to see you, Mike. I was surprised to find you leaving the residence."

"I know, but I really needed a break from the place. With Charles and Lisa both still at the hospital, the only people in the house are cops and a few Federal techs, mopping up from the kidnapping case. Interviewing the staff, dusting for stray prints, that kind of thing. Leaving me alone in that big house with James. Drunk on his ass, as usual. Barking orders to the maids. Being his typical charming self."

Gloria indicated our posh surroundings. "Nice place. This your regular caffeine watering hole?"

He smiled. "And wine bar, when the mood hits. When I've had enough of the Harlands. Which can happen, believe me, even for a dedicated head of security like myself."

"Speaking of which," I said, "I understand you worked at Starr Sentinel with someone I know. A guy named Skip Hines."

His eyes widened. "Skip? Sure, I know him. He'd just come home from the war and went to work for Starr. I sort of showed him the ropes. We became good friends. Why do you ask?"

"Well, as I'm sure you know, soon after you left the firm, Skip re-enlisted and got sent back into action."

"I'd heard that, yes."

"Then, after he was wounded, he returned home. Here in Pittsburgh. Kind of at loose ends, from what I understand. I wonder, Mike, did he ever try to get in touch with you? Maybe looking for work?"

Just then, the waitress returned with our drinks. After she left, I watched Payton mindlessly stirring a spoon in his mug.

"Well, Mr. Payton?" Gloria's voice was firm. "Did Hines contact you or not?"

Payton sighed heavily. "Yeah, he did. He looked me up at Starr Sentinel, where they told him I'd left to work for Charles Harland. So he called and made an appointment to come by. I gave him the tour, then we went back to my office in the residence."

"How did he seem at the time?"

A sad frown. "Impressed, I'd guess you'd say. With the house, the celebrity of the Harlands. With how lucky I was to have landed such a cushy job. I could practically see all of that on his face."

"How did *you* feel?" I asked.

"I felt bad for the guy. Especially after I saw that he'd lost a leg. He hadn't told me about it on the phone, so it came as a surprise when he showed up with that prosthetic. Part of me thought he hadn't told me on purpose, so he could shock me with it. Spring it on me, if you know what I mean."

"Did he strike you as that kind of guy?"

"Not before, when we worked at Starr. But maybe getting wounded changed him. He sure seemed bitter and unhappy when he visited me at the residence. Not the best face to show someone when you're asking for a job."

"So he *did* ask for work there?" said Gloria.

"Yeah. But I told him there wasn't an open position at the time. Which was the truth. What I *didn't* tell him was that there was no way I could hire him anyway. Not with that one leg. Half of what's involved in personal security is appearance. The perception that you're a kick-ass dude who shouldn't be messed with. No matter how tough Skip was—and I know he was damned good and tough—I also knew I couldn't hire him. I mean, Harland would've killed me if I had."

"How did Skip take it?"

"Not real well, to be honest. So then I suggested he should look up some old Marine buddies. See if maybe any of them could help him out. But he *hated* that idea. Got angry as hell. Then he just gets up and leaves. I haven't seen him since."

I sipped my smooth, milky drink.

"When you two worked together at Starr, after Skip's first tour of duty, did he ever talk about his old unit?"

"Never. I asked him about it a couple times, but he said he didn't want to talk about it. I figured I had to respect that."

Gloria tapped her fingernail against her untouched mug.

"Would it surprise you to know that Skip's unit commander the first time he was deployed in Afghanistan was Raymond Sykes? And that Max Griffin was also part of the unit?"

Payton stopped stirring his coffee.

"Sykes? And Griffin? Skip *knew* those guys?"

"From the war, yes," I said. "They all served together, before Skip came home and went to work at Starr."

Gloria leaned in to Payton. "And you're *sure* he never mentioned his time with them?"

"I told you, he refused to discuss his experience over there. Said he wanted to put that part of his life behind him."

"Yet he re-enlisted later," I said. "He quit Starr soon after you did and went back into the service. Any idea why?"

Payton lay down his spoon very quietly. Voice softening. "The only thing I can think of is that Skip hated civilian life. Even on a tactical team with me at Starr, with all its military-like aspects, we were still civilians. People with homes, families, pets, who had to buy groceries and pay bills and deal with noisy neighbors. He hated every bit of it. He always seemed...I don't know...lost. Overwhelmed. Not that he even liked the work at Starr much, either."

"What do you mean?" Gloria asked.

"We offered protection to CEOs, movie stars, all kinds of big shots. Skip thought most of our clients were assholes—which they were, of course. Plus there really wasn't much field action. It was mostly babysitting, setting up security systems, doing paperwork. That's why *I* left, tell you the truth. So I wasn't surprised when I heard that Skip did, too. Though I thought he was crazy to re-up. Go back to that hellhole in the Middle East. The land of sand and shit."

I met his gaze. "But civilian life works for you?"

"Hell, yeah. I like it stateside. Modern plumbing, girls in bikinis, all the beer you can drink. I like it fine."

I noticed Gloria finally taking a sip of her drink. We still had one big question for Payton that needed an answer. Since she was the one with the badge, I assumed Gloria would be the right person to ask it.

I guessed right. Putting down her mug, she narrowed her gaze at Mike Payton.

"I'd like to ask one more question, Mr. Payton."

"Okay, but make it quick. I can't be away from the house too long. I've still got my duties to perform."

"I understand. But you were in Harland's office, as were Dr. Rinaldi and myself, when the kidnapper called to make his ransom demand. Though his voice was electronically altered on the phone, he told us his name was Julian."

"Yes. Like he just picked it out of the air."

"That's what he implied, yes. But I have to assume you knew that Skip Hines' given name was Julian. Did you?"

He paused before replying. "Yeah, I did. Though I never called him that. Never heard *anybody* call him Julian. And he always introduced himself as Skip."

I interjected here. "But you *knew* that was his real name?"

"I already said I did."

Gloria's features darkened. "And yet you never suspected that maybe this 'Julian' on the phone, the kidnapper of your employer's wife, was the same Skip Hines you knew from Starr Sentinel?"

Payton pulled nervously on his lower lip.

"Answer the question, Mr. Payton," Gloria said. "Or we can continue this conversation at the Federal Building…"

"No…There's no need for that."

"Well," I said sharply, "did you think it was Skip who was behind the kidnapping? That it was *his* voice on the phone?"

"Not at the time. But later, yes, it occurred to me that maybe…I mean, it seemed crazy…I thought it *couldn't* be Skip.

It had to be a coincidence that the kidnapper used the name 'Julian.' It just *had* to be…"

"Even so, why didn't you inform the police about it? Lisa Campbell was missing, possibly injured…and you kept silent. Why, Payton? Why not at least raise it as a possibility?"

"Because I knew the answer. I knew that it couldn't have been Skip."

"How did you know?" Gloria pressed him.

"Because when I had a few moments alone, not long after the kidnapper hung up, I got in touch with Skip. He'd left me his cell number when he came to the house to ask for a job. I called Skip and asked him, point-blank, if it was *his* voice on the phone. If he was behind Lisa's kidnapping. And he denied it."

"And you believed him?"

"Absolutely. He told me he had an alibi for the time of the kidnapping. And of the phone call to Harland's office. Both times he was at the bar where his sister works. And if I thought her word couldn't be trusted, he said there was a room full of customers who could confirm it."

"But that doesn't mean he wasn't involved in some way."

"It did to me, Agent Reese. He swore on the lives of his fallen comrades in Afghanistan. No way he'd do that if he was lying. In fact, he was offended that I'd even suspect him. And that as far as he was concerned, we were no longer friends."

Payton pushed his mug away from him. Face grim.

"I'm telling you, Skip Hines was not involved in Lisa's kidnapping. And you know why you can believe me?"

"Why?" I asked.

"Because if I thought he was, I'd kill him. Dead."

Chapter Thirty-three

Mike Payton was right about the cappuccinos—they were delicious. Unfortunately, neither Gloria nor I got to finish ours. Because all of a sudden her cell rang.

She picked up, listened for a moment, said, "Right, on my way," and clicked off. Then she gave me an urgent look.

We left Payton to finish his drink—and, at his insistence, pay the check when it came—and went out to my car. Soon we were driving back the same way we'd come, beneath an expanse of clear azure sky, headed for the Federal Building.

"They've just called a special briefing," Gloria explained. "A joint Pittsburgh PD and FBI meeting to get everybody up to speed on the manhunt for Sykes and Griffin."

"Why the sudden urgency?"

"Apparently, Charles Harland's well enough to make phone calls from his hospital bed. One was to the governor, wanting to know if we'd caught the bastards who kidnapped his wife yet."

"I guess his memory's returning. Or else Lisa told him about it when she went to visit him in his room."

"Whatever. But the governor started making a few phone calls himself, as you can imagine. To the director, your mayor. He's screaming for results."

"Sure. Harland's a potentially huge campaign donor."

Coming into view up ahead were the clean silver lines of the Federal Building. I pulled around to the front entrance and stopped at the curb. Gloria climbed out, then leaned her head back in the passenger side window. Smiled.

"Hey, in case Wilson's right about Sykes, keep your head down. That's an order, Dr. Rinaldi."

"You do the same, Agent Reese."

She winked, then hurried into the building.

◇◇◇

I'd just rolled back into the flow of midday traffic when my own cell rang. Harry Polk. I switched on the hands-free app.

"Listen, Rinaldi, I got a call a minute ago about some bullshit briefing at the Feds. Attendance is mandatory."

"Yeah, I heard."

"That means I gotta get my butt over there ASAP."

"Where are you now?"

"Same place I've been for the past two hours. I followed Skip Hines from his fleabag motel in East Liberty to this pool hall a couple blocks away. Near the old fire station."

"I think I know it, yeah."

"Well, I'm parked across the street, but I got a good view into the place through the front window. I've had Hines in sight the whole time."

"What's he been doing?"

"Ya mean, besides gettin' his ass kicked playin' pool? Nothin'. Waitress comes over with a beer every twenty minutes, but he ain't budged. I mean, not even to take a leak. Unless he's pissin' into that fake leg o' his."

"Jesus, Harry…"

"Anyway, other than jawin' with the other players, he hasn't been approached by anybody. Nobody suspicious, if ya know what I mean. Plus he hasn't called out on his cell, or answered a call from nobody. Not that I could see."

"So what do you think?"

"Who the fuck knows? Maybe he's just layin' low. Actin' normal 'til Sykes contacts him. Or maybe they're meetin' later."

"That's possible, too."

Over the phone, I heard Polk start his car.

"Look, Doc, I gotta book outta here. If I don't show up at that goddamn meeting, Biegler'll hang me out to dry."

"I get it, Harry. Thanks."

"For what? We got nothin' on Hines, other than he's good at gettin' hustled at pool. See ya later…"

Polk clicked off, leaving me to stare distractedly at the back of a semi chugging to a stop in front of me. The intersecting lines of cars, buses, and trucks had grown, slowing traffic to a crawl. Angry horns beeped, frustrated drivers cursed. A cool but dazzling sunlight glared from windshields, glazed the edges of steel-and-glass buildings. Threaded the thin haze of billowing diesel smoke and bus exhaust.

None of which had its normal irritating impact, as I thought about Skip Hines. *Was* he involved in any of this? Maybe Polk was right, and he was merely going on about his business until he was contacted by Sykes. Purposefully acting like any other aimless guy on the block. Hanging out. Killing time.

On the other hand, maybe he was exactly what he seemed to be—a wounded vet at loose ends, one of many living casualties of that war, struggling to come to terms with a civilian world into which he no longer fit.

Suddenly, I needed to know for sure. I figured I owed it to him. I knew damned well I owed it to Charlene.

Glancing to my right, I spotted a rarely traveled side street. A narrow tributary adjacent to this clogged, sluggish river of traffic. Spinning the wheel beneath my hands, I whipped the Mustang out of my place in the line of cars and headed straight for it.

Ernie's Billiard Hall was less like a hall and more like a head-banger's basement. Dark, low-ceilinged, air thick with the smell of cigarette smoke mingled with the pungent aroma of weed. Its chiaroscuro ambience due to a combination of sunlight coming through the smudged front window and the hazy glow from a half-dozen frosted-glass wall lamps.

Three guys who looked like refugees from a biker movie, all in sleeveless leather jackets to show off their tats and 'roided-up biceps, lounged at the bar. Behind which a single waitress—slim and barely legal, with nose and lip rings—stood looking vacantly at her purple nails. Her name tag read "Penny."

When I came in, there were only two other guys—fraternity brothers of the solid citizens at the bar—playing pool. The other tables stood unused. One of the pool players looked up as I passed, so I nodded. He merely stared.

At first, there was no sign of Skip Hines. Then I heard a toilet flush, and a worn wooden door at the back of the room opened. It was Skip, zipping up his pants as he shuffled toward the bar. Despite what Polk said, Skip had finally needed to make use of the facilities.

It wasn't until I joined him, pulling up the stool next to his, that Skip acknowledged my presence. Then he broke into a broad though uneasy grin.

"Hey, my man Danny!" He stuck out his hand. I took it.

One of the guys in leather jackets dropped his cigarette butt in his beer mug and slid off his stool. The other two reflexively followed suit, but not without giving Skip and me a menacing, suspicious look.

Suddenly, the first guy leaned across the bar, put his forearm around Penny's neck, and drew her to him. Though she struggled, he gave the waitress a long, deep, angry kiss. Then he shoved her away. She staggered, blood dotting her lip.

I'd gotten up from my own stool by then, but the girl shot me a beseeching look. *Please don't do anything, mister.*

When I turned back to the creep who'd kissed her, he was holding the business end of a switchblade about six inches from my sternum.

I planted my feet, muscles tensed. Then heard Skip from behind me.

"Not worth it, Danny. Bad-ass motherfuckers, these guys."

The guy with the knife nodded.

"Listen to your friend…*friend*." Giving me a tight smile.

Out of the corner of my eye, I saw the two guys who'd been playing pool gently lay down their cue sticks. Though looking the part, neither apparently wanted anything to do with what was currently going down in Ernie's Billiard Hall. Instead, they quickly and quietly went out the front door.

As they fled, Penny spoke to the guy with the knife.

"Get outta here too, Joe. *Please?*" She pointed across the bar, at the door. "No charge for the beers. Okay?"

I was still gauging my chances, eyes never leaving the tip of that knife as it made lazy little circles at my chest. Even as I realized my chances weren't good.

"You gonna back down, hero? Or are ya gonna get cut?"

"*C'mon*, Joey!" pleaded Penny, voice rising. "Give the guy a break. He didn't *mean* nothin'!"

Joe stared at me.

"Is that true, hero? You didn't mean nothin'?"

I didn't budge. Instead, I let my gaze drift up from the knife to Joe's hard, resolute face.

"Put that goddamn knife away, pal. Before I *take* it away."

Empty bravado, I assure you. Stupid. Dangerous. Where it comes from in me, from what well of pain and rage and grief, I'll never know. But there it is. As though bred in the bone.

I felt Skip's hand on my shoulder.

"Christ, Danny. Chill."

Joe kept staring at me.

"Again, I'd listen to your friend…"

But I could tell that some of the sting had gone out of his words. Joe was starting to look bored.

"Aw, fuck it," he said at last.

Giving Penny a boozy leer, he backed up, flicking the blade in and out of its handle. His two companions flanked him, glaring back at me. Until, without exchanging a word to each other, all three ambled out of the pool hall.

At that point, I remembered to breathe. Which I did, deeply. Then I let myself sit back down on the stool. Skip's hand still gripped my shoulder, which now felt rigid as stone.

"Told ya, man. But I gotta admit, it took guts. First round's on me."

Meanwhile, Penny had taken a cigarette from her blouse pocket and was lighting up. Eyes boring into mine through the rising smoke.

"Do me a favor, okay, mister? Next time, mind your own fuckin' business. Joe's my boy's daddy, and it don't do me any good to have some stranger in here pissin' him off. He don't give me enough money for the lousy kid as it is."

"Hey, girlie." Skip frowned at her. "Is that any way to talk? Now get me and my buddy Dan a couple beers."

She blew a sizeable smoke ring. "Get 'em yourself, asshole. I'm on my break."

With that, she sauntered down to the end of the bar and disappeared out a rear exit door. Skip turned to me.

"Cool place, eh?"

Cool or not, it was obvious we suddenly had the place to ourselves. For how long, I didn't know. Or care. I figured I wouldn't need much time.

I grabbed two cold Rolling Rocks from behind the bar and brought them over to the pool hall's sole booth, wedged in a corner next to the bathroom. Skip had already made his way there and slid into a seat. I sat opposite and handed him his beer. We touched bottles.

"To my long-sufferin' sister," Skip said. "I don't know how the hell she lives with that lunatic."

"I think she and Noah are actually good for each other." I sipped my beer. "I mean, true, Charlene does most of the heavy lifting, sanity-wise. But he loves her and she knows he loves her. He may be crazy, but he knows what love is."

"If you say so, Danny. As long as he treats her right."

"No need to worry about that, Skip."

Skip guzzled half his beer, then carefully placed the bottle on the table. Turned it slowly with his fingers.

"This isn't a social call, is it, Doc? I'm guessin' Ernie's is not the kinda place you normally hang out."

"Tell you the truth, Skip, I do have some questions I wanted to ask you. About your first deployment in Afghanistan. Your unit commander. Raymond Sykes."

He stopped turning the bottle, fingers frozen in place.

"How'd you know that?"

"Did some research. I was surprised to learn that you served with Sykes. And with Max Griffin."

Skip sat back, face tightening. Then, hand still gripping the bottle, he put it to his lips and drained it.

"Skip…"

He shook his head. "No way, Danny. I'm not talkin' about that shit. I wanna forget all about it."

"I understand. But, believe me, the best way to come to some kind of peace with it is to talk about it. It's not a cure. It doesn't make it like it never happened. Hell, it doesn't even mean it'll hurt any less. But you'll be able to put it in perspective. Give it its rightful place in your memory, in the history of your life. Or else it fucking *owns* you. Know what I mean, Skip? *It owns you.*"

He seemed startled by the vehemence in my voice. Frankly, so was I. Though I meant every word I said.

For a long moment, we just looked at each other. Two proud, stubborn men. Staring, as though neither would give an inch.

Then, finally, Skip let out a low, heavy sigh.

"I'm gonna need another beer," he said quietly.

I got up to get it for him.

Chapter Thirty-four

"My unit was dug in outside Kandahar. About two months. Started with twelve guys, ended up with eight. Lotta ground fighting. Sometimes goin' house to house, in some shit-hole of a village, depending on what intel came down. But mostly exposed field. Nothin' but sand for miles around. Back roads, insurgent supply routes. So you're lookin' at snipers, spider holes, land mines. Real fun stuff.

"I think I hated Lieutenant Sykes on sight, but maybe it took a couple days. Listenin' to his bullshit. His big-shot Ivy League way o' talkin'. Thought he was better than everybody else. No 'Band of Brothers' stuff with this guy. Used to walk around with these highbrow books in his pocket. Sit off by himself, readin'. Philosophy and that shit. He loved this one guy, Shopen-somethin'...Always quoted stuff this dude wrote about how fucked-up life was..."

"You mean, Arthur Schopenhauer?"

"Yeah, that's him. Typical for Sykes. He loved showin' off how smart he was. Pissed the rest of us off. Even Max Griffin, who was pretty tight with Sykes, used to make fun of him about it. Not to his face, but..."

He paused, took a slug of beer. Maybe his third since I'd shown up. No way to know how many before that. But Skip's eyes had already turned glassy.

"Anyway," he went on, "every other day, Sykes gets intel from HQ, sends us on search-and-destroy missions. Rootin' out snipers, mostly. Out in the middle of nowhere. Half-blind from the goddamn sand and sun. Gettin' our asses shot at by some towel-head with a Kalashnikov, or maybe takin' a mortar shell in the gut. Yet Griffin…man, that macho jerk loved it. Always took point. Like he dared the bastards to try to waste him."

"What about Sykes?"

"Big surprise, he always stayed behind. Well back from the advance line. Sat on his ass in the Humvee, nice and safe. Probably jerkin' off to one of his bullshit books. Meanwhile, there were a couple times the unit took some heavy fire out in the field. By the end of the first month, we'd lost two guys. Third was shot up pretty bad and got choppered out. By the end of the second month, another guy—some Okie kid, good buddy o' mine—got his damn fool head blown off."

Then Skip glanced over his shoulder. I'd seen her, too. Penny, the young waitress from earlier, now sidling back behind the bar. Watching us with a feigned lack of interest.

Moments later, a pair of lowlife guys in denim and cowboy boots strolled in. The taller of the two threw some bills on a vacant pool table and started racking up the balls. His partner, who also wore a cowboy hat, went over to the bar and ordered some beers. Then something he said made Penny laugh, though it was more like a cynical snort.

"Maybe we oughta go somewhere else," Skip said.

I gave him what I hoped was a reassuring look.

"We'll be fine here, Skip. Just go on. What happened after your friend got killed?"

After another nervous glance across the room, he lowered his voice to reply.

"I guess I did somethin' stupid. When we got back, I went over to Sykes, in front of the whole unit, and accused him of bein' a coward. Of not givin' a shit about his men. I mean, I just lost it with that cocksucker. Called him out on all the crap he pulled since we got there. The way he talked down to us, treated us. Couple of the other guys tried to restrain me, get me to calm down. But I practically spit in Sykes' face."

"How did he take it?"

"He just smiled at me, the smug bastard. The next thing I know, Griffin has me in a choke hold. Draggin' me away. Some of the guys have to restrain *him*. Then Sykes orders everybody to stand down, or he'll put us all on report. So I finally manage to chill out. Just start walkin' it off, ya know? By myself. But the next couple days, me and Sykes stay the fuck away from each other. No eye contact, nothin'. Which is fine with me."

"Was that the end of it?"

Skip finished his beer. Looked at the bottle in his hand.

"I wish. Two days later, we move further in-country. Intel says there's significant activity. Which is command-speak for there's a bunch o' sand-rats waitin' to frag your sorry asses. So Sykes gets the coordinates sent down from HQ and orders us to scour the perimeter. Which we do. Me, Griffin, and the rest of the unit."

"And Sykes stays behind again?"

He nodded. Slowly and deliberately. As though steeling himself for what he was to say next.

"Anyway, a couple hours in, the patrol finds itself in a firefight. Bullets, smoke, guys screamin' and yellin'. Our guys, their guys, who the fuck knows? Then, somehow, I get separated from the unit. Maybe twenty clicks away. I freak out, and start runnin' back to where I think my guys are. But there's so much smoke and swirlin' dust, I can't really tell. All of a sudden, my foot slips on somethin' and I hit the ground. At the same time, a bullet flies past my head. I swear, I could hear and feel that sucker whizzin' by. Missed me by an inch. If I hadn't stumbled when I did…"

Another long pause. I waited.

"The thing is, Danny…when I turn around, I see Griffin. About ten clicks away, half-hidden behind a dead olive tree. M-16 in his hands. And he's just smilin' at me. Doesn't move for a couple seconds. Like he *wants* me to see it was him."

"Jesus…"

"Then he runs off. And I'm still shakin' like a leaf, with a mouthful of sand and a leg cramp from fallin'. My *left* leg, in case you're wonderin'."

"The left leg…?"

"Nice irony, eh? Same leg I'm gonna kiss good-bye a couple years later, when I'm back in that godforsaken country. Don't tell me God doesn't have a screwed-up sense of humor."

His sudden smile was a rictus of pain.

"Skip, what happened when you met up with your unit again? Did you confront Griffin?"

"Sure did, once we got back to safety. I accused him in front of everybody. Includin' Sykes. But Griffin just denied it. Said why would he waste a bullet on a shit-stain like me in the middle of a firefight? But I saw the look that passed between him and Sykes. And I knew. For certain."

"Knew what?"

"That Sykes had ordered Griffin to take me out. So it'd look like I got killed in action. All them bullets flyin'…"

I rubbed my chin. "Even if somebody took the trouble of matching the bullet to Griffin's gun, it could still be chalked up to accidental death in combat. Friendly fire."

He laughed shortly. "Goddamn *un*friendly, ya ask me."

"I believe you about Sykes, by the way. Given who he is, how he's built psychologically, he couldn't tolerate being confronted by you earlier. He'd have to make sure that you were punished for it."

Skip shrugged. "Like they say, payback's a bitch."

"Any other incidents like that?"

"Nah. The unit got called back to Kandahar base soon after. By then, my tour was almost up. So I just kept my head down 'til I could catch the next plane stateside. Damn shame, too, since I loved the service. Loved being part o' somethin' important."

"Is that why you re-enlisted? After working at Starr Sentinel for a while?"

"What, you got a private eye checkin' up on me?"

"No, I have your sister, who gave me the details. Who wished you'd never gone back. Who loves you very much."

"Yeah, I know."

Then he reached under the table, rapped his knuckles on his prosthetic leg. A dull, dead sound.

"Guess I wish I'd never gone back, too."

◇◇◇

"You want anything to eat, Skip? I saw a place down the block. Didn't look too bad."

"Nah. Maybe just another beer."

He signaled for Penny, who sullenly shuffled over. Skip asked the waitress for two more Rolling Rocks.

"Not 'til you guys pay for the beers you drunk already. Includin' the ones you stole from the bar while I was takin' my break. Sneaky bastards."

I looked up at her. "Of course we'll pay for them, too. We always intended to."

"Yeah, like I believe you. See, Ernie don't just count the cash in the register every night, he counts the bottles. If the numbers don't add up, it comes outta my pay."

"Your boss sounds like a total dick." Skip smiled at her.

"Takes one to know one." She held out her hand, palm up. "That'll be thirty-two bucks, even. You want any more beers, I'll have to start you a new tab."

Skip reached behind him for his wallet, but I beat him to it. Handed her two twenties.

"Keep the change. And, yeah, bring us a couple more Rocks. Then we'll get out of your hair."

She pocketed the bills and scowled. "Won't be soon enough for me. You two shit-heads are bad for business."

Skip and I sat in silence until she came back with our beers, and then departed again. As Skip took a pull from his bottle, I noticed Penny sauntering over to the two cowboys playing pool. Something the shorter one said made her laugh again, though more invitingly this time. Flirting.

When I turned back to Skip, I saw that he'd been watching the girl, too. He sipped his beer reflectively.

"Jesus, Danny, I ain't been laid in, like, forever. I mean, I love my beer as much as the next guy, but I love me some pussy more. But it's been damn slow since I got back."

I smiled. "Who knows? Play your cards right and you might get lucky with our girl here. I think she's warming up to you."

"Yeah, right."

Then, abruptly, a guarded look crossed his face.

"Tell me somethin', okay? How come you asked me about Sykes, anyway? Is somethin' goin' on I oughta know about?"

I took my time before answering.

"The fact is, Skip, you already know about it. And you're one of the few people outside law enforcement who does. Because Mike Payton told you."

"What are you talkin' about?"

"I spoke with Payton earlier today. He said he called you a few days ago and asked if you were involved in the kidnapping of Lisa Campbell. Because the guy who abducted her called himself Julian, which is your real name. As Mike Payton knew."

Skip flushed, then slammed his beer down on the table. One of the two cowboys looked up from his pool game, cue stick in hand, irritated. At the bar, Penny peered anxiously in our direction, too.

"Listen, Danny, I'll tell you the same thing I told Mike. I had nothin' to do with any kidnapping. Shit, I didn't know what the fuck he was talkin' about. I mean, I never saw nothin' about it on the news, or—"

"That's because it was kept out of the media. The story still hasn't broken, even though Lisa's been returned safely. Her husband, a rich businessman named Harland, paid a ten million dollar ransom to get her back."

The ransom amount leached some of the color from his face. Though he was still plainly angry.

"And this guy who kidnapped her…Payton told me the prick said his name was Julian. Like mine. That's why Mike called to see if it was me. Which really pissed me off."

"Yeah, he told me how you reacted."

"Did Mike also tell you that I got an alibi? He gave me the time line, and I was at Noah's bar the afternoon this lady was snatched. And I was still there that night when the kidnapper called. So I'm sorry to disappoint you two, but I'm not your guy. I didn't snatch nobody. And I *hate* this fucker for usin' my name. I mean, who the hell *is* he, anyway?"

I took a breath. "Okay, here's where it gets a little weird. You should know that the FBI has been keeping tabs on Ray Sykes and Max Griffin since they came back from the war."

"What? Why?"

"Sykes has become a pretty high-profile criminal, involved in drugs, human trafficking, that kind of stuff. Apparently, he's known as 'Splinter' Sykes, because he's unnaturally thin. Almost emaciated."

"Tell me about it. He was already startin' to look like hell back in Kandahar. Rumor was, he'd contracted some kinda bug, like that flesh-eatin' shit, then tried treatin' it with black market drugs. Only made him sicker. Almost killed him, I heard. It didn't, which sucks. But it left him lookin' like a pipe cleaner. Couldn't happen to a nicer guy."

"I agree. But it didn't stop him from building up quite a criminal operation. And Max Griffin's working with him."

"I'll be damned. I mean, I can't say I'm surprised. Sykes and that psycho Griffin…Makes sense they'd end up together, after what they tried to do to me over there."

I watched him drain the rest of his beer.

"That's not everything, Skip. That kidnapping we were talking about? The man behind it was Sykes. When he called with his ransom demand, his voice was altered so it couldn't be recognized. But he said to call him 'Julian.'"

He gaped at me. "*Sykes* was the guy who used my name…?"

"Yes. I don't know why, not for sure. Maybe to implicate you, in case things went sideways. But I don't think that's it."

"Me, neither. Knowin' that arrogant piece o' shit, he just did it for the hell of it. For kicks."

"It fits my assessment of him, of his personality. Sykes probably saw using your name as some kind of private joke. His own sick, self-titillating revenge on you for having survived the murder attempt in Afghanistan. For having gotten away with insulting him in front of his men. Not only that. Once he was safely away with the ransom money, he could revel in the thought that the authorities would always believe that Lisa's kidnapper was someone called Julian."

Skip glowered down at the empty beer bottle, now gripped with both hands. I was afraid he'd shatter the glass.

"I know this is a lot to absorb," I said evenly.

"Yeah, you could say that."

Then he looked up, past my shoulder. Peering at the world outside the pool hall's grime-streaked window.

"I don't wanna talk about this crap anymore. I mean, I'm done talkin' about anything. Period."

And he was.

Chapter Thirty-five

Lisa Campbell jumped up from her chair at her husband's bed-side and took hold of my forearm. She was wearing brand-new sweats and spotless Nikes, clothes obviously brought in to her from home. She looked like someone had also done her hair.

"Danny! I'll be damned, I was just gonna call you. Charles wanted to see you in person. To thank you."

The old man lay in his hospital bed, amid a tangle of tubes, with his bony wrist connected to an IV drip. The private room was as spacious as I'd expected, though with the jarring addition of a laptop and a bank of phones on a wheeled table beside the bed.

I'd left Skip Hines at the pool hall, after he'd refused my offer to drive him back to his motel. He explained that since it was just a few blocks away, he'd rather walk. After which he again rapped his knuckles against his prosthesis. "Still breakin' her in," he said.

I battled Monday rush-hour traffic all the way across town to Pittsburgh Memorial, my radio tuned to the news channel. I'd thought that the joint police-FBI briefing that took place this afternoon might result in some kind of press statement regarding the murders of Donna Swanson and Arthur Drake. Because both victims were employed by Charles Harland, and their deaths happened so close together, local media had been hounding the police about the progress of the two investigations. Accusations of cover-ups, political manipulation, and corporate conspiracies were rampant, especially online.

Meanwhile, the ostensibly "sexier" story, the kidnapping of Harland's wife—a homegrown, former Hollywood starlet—remained undisclosed. Prime red meat for a media feeding frenzy, yet remarkably nowhere on the menu.

I pulled into the hospital parking lot, but stayed for a few minutes in the car. Replaying the conversations I'd had with Mike Payton and Skip Hines. Wondering if there was something I should've asked each of them but didn't. Wondering if there was something I'd missed.

The sun was still bright against a cloudless sky, though the steadily rising wind chased away whatever warmth it might provide. And the weather report claimed that the coming night would be even cooler than the previous ones, accompanied by increased winds. *Great,* I thought. I climbed out of my car.

When I arrived outside Harland's hospital room, I saw two nondescript guys standing on either side of the door. Private security, probably brought in by Mike Payton to ensure his boss' privacy. It worked. There wasn't a reporter or camera in sight.

Now, as Lisa brought me to her husband's bedside, the old man awkwardly raised himself from his pillows. Then he gave me his version of a welcoming smile.

"Doctor…" His voice a dry, raspy croak. "My wife…told me that it was you who rescued her…from those sick bastards. I… words can't express my gratitude."

"I got lucky, Mr. Harland. Lisa and I both did."

His thin lips trembled, as he struggled to reply. Taking deep, gasping breaths.

"No, Doctor," he said at last. "When a man does something for me, I don't forget my…my obligation to him…There will be a reward…Money…"

I shook my head. "Not necessary. Really."

If possible, Charles Harland looked worse than the last time I'd seen him. Skin more sallow, cheeks sunken. Even those glittering, penetrating eyes had lost much of their vigor, their ego-directed fervor. Every word he uttered seemed to cost him air, energy. As though it was an act of will to keep breathing. Speaking. Living.

A dead man talking.

Lisa, at my side, leaned over her husband and none-too-gently lay his head back against the pillows.

"Charles needs his rest. He's been through a helluva lot. The stroke...and then learning about what happened to me." She darted her eyes up at me. "I also told him about poor Arthur."

Here the old man's eyes regained some life. He stared up at me with sudden urgency.

"Yes...I know about Drake. Good man...Been with me for years...I was unhappy to hear he'd been...been killed."

I nodded. "I'm sorry about him, too."

"But not as sorry as I am..." Voice rising. "Now I have to find another goddamn lawyer I can trust...And the good ones... they don't grow on trees, as my father used to say...They—"

He sputtered, and it turned into a harsh cough. Wracking his whole shell of a body beneath the covers. Without a word, Lisa took a glass of water from the nightstand, put it to the old man's lips.

As he sipped his drink, Lisa glanced up at me again. Gave me a cool, disgusted look. *Welcome to my world, Doc.*

I got the message. Harland's brush with death obviously hadn't mellowed him. The only thing Arthur Drake's murder meant to him was the loss of a valued asset. He probably felt the same way about the killing of his longtime nurse, Donna Swanson. Both deaths were merely annoying, troublesome. Inconvenient.

People were possessions to him. Prized for their utility. For what they could do for him, or for what they represented.

Lisa Campbell, as she well knew, was Harland's most valued possession. But perhaps, I thought, not merely as the stereotypical "trophy wife." Or as a much-younger woman who restored some image of himself as still youthful, vital. Someone whose Hollywood past gave their marriage a glamour the old man craved.

Instead, it was possible that what he valued most about Lisa was simply how he felt when he was with her. That the miracle was that he could still feel anything at all. Maybe, in his mind,

this meant that he did indeed love her. At least more than anything else he owned...

Some of the water dribbled from Harland's lips, so Lisa
returned the glass to the table. Carefully wiped his mouth with
a Kleenex.

I looked down at his pale, hollow face.

"Lisa's right, Mr. Harland. You need your rest. I'm sorry if I
disturbed you."

"No, no...I wanted to see you. Besides, I'm feeling better ...
much better. In fact...I just told my doctor...that I'll be going
home tomorrow..."

"He agreed to that?"

"He...He doesn't have a choice...He works for me...There's
no reason he can't...attend to my needs...at the residence."

Lisa gave me a half-hearted look of consternation.

"My stubborn, pain-in-the-ass husband is having a hospital
bed, monitors, everything the doctor might need, brought to
the house. Including round-the-clock nursing care."

"A necessity..." Harland forced the words out. "I can't...
conduct business from here...I want to be home...In my own
study...With my own people..."

He tried to get up on his elbows again, but Lisa restrained
him with a hand on his shoulder. He blinked up at me.

"See, Doctor...it's important that I be released from the
hospital...as soon as possible. My board says it's better...if I'm
seen as on the mend...Even my worthless son James agrees...
He says it sends a positive message...to the stockholders."

Her hand still on his shoulder, she patted it.

"Maybe so, Charles, but I think it will be goddamn hard
enough recuperating at home. You don't need any extra stress."

Harland offered me a weak smile.

"She means the anniversary gala...next month...Lisa wants
me to...to cancel it..."

"Damn right I want to cancel it," Lisa said. "In your condition, no way you should be hosting a fucking party. And you
know it, Charles."

"We've held the gala every year…since our wedding…and I'm not going to stop now…Besides, as James said, it'll signal that everything's…back to normal…That it's business as usual …for the Harland brand."

I frowned. "*James* said?…"

"Yes…though he…he probably just wants to make sure… our stock prices stay up…Greedy little shit…"

Lisa leaned closer to her husband.

"But your health is more important than anything. I still think we should cancel. Believe me, people would understand."

"*I said no!…*" Wheezing now. Trembling. "I said…we're going to have the gala…same as always…*So we will!…*"

He suddenly began coughing again, at the same time waving Lisa away from the bed with a bony hand.

"Charles!" Lisa said. "Calm down…"

I turned to her. "I think you should call his doctor."

Nodding, she reached for the signal button on the wall.

Outside Harland's room, far enough down the hall to be out of earshot of the two security guards, Lisa and I met with her husband's personal physician.

A small, gray-bearded man with wire-rim glasses, he assured her that Charles was stable, and that the best thing for him was rest. He also repeated to her his reluctance to release Harland to home care, but that his hands were tied. His contract with his patient was apparently quite specific when it came to things like this.

After he'd gone back down the hall to once more check on Harland, Lisa let out a gale-like sigh.

"Could that guy be more of a pussy? Christ!"

"He seems competent enough."

"Maybe. But, shit, I was looking forward to having the house to myself. Just me and the maids and the cooks and the drivers. But no Charles."

Her grin was forced. As though even she was aware she was trying to use humor to keep her hysteria at bay.

"I know what you're thinking, Lisa. And feeling. If the anniversary gala takes place…"

Her face fell. "James gets to present his little horror show. And then I'm…I know it sounds melodramatic as hell…but then I'm destroyed. Finished."

Lisa's tone hardened. "And I told you, Danny. I won't let that happen. Or at least I won't be around when it does."

"Lisa, listen—"

"Don't worry, Doc. I didn't forget our deal. I'll call you before I do it. If nothing else, I'll want to say thanks…and good-bye."

She turned to go, but I grabbed her wrist.

"Dammit, I can have you put under suicide watch. Right here in the hospital."

"You wouldn't fucking dare."

"Try me. Involuntary commitment for at least forty-eight hours. I can do it, Lisa. Comes with the license."

"And here I thought you were my friend."

"I'm your therapist, first and foremost. And I don't want you to do this."

She smirked. "Fine. Put me in a goddamn padded cell for two days. Then my lawyers'll get me out and I can do what I want."

"Please, Lisa. That's not how I want this to go."

"Well, then, do something about it. Help me get the flash-drive back from that louse James."

"I would if I could. Any idea where he might be hiding it?"

She glanced nervously up and down the corridor.

"Fuck if I know. I've searched his bedroom, his office at the residence. I even stole his keys once, snuck into the garage and checked his car. Nada. Zip."

I paused. "I'm tempted to beat it out of him."

She chuckled. "Yeah, right. Though thanks for saying it. Probably the most therapeutic thing you've ever done for me."

Now I smiled. "Thanks…I think."

"But, seriously, Danny. We gotta find that goddamn thing. Or I *will* take my final exit…" Another pained sigh. "Hell, it'd be a relief, anyway…And pure Hollywood, to boot. The perfect tabloid end to my tabloid life."

"Now you *are* being melodramatic, Lisa. But my instincts say you don't even believe your own words. Maybe I'm wrong, but I think the terrified, half-starved woman who tried to escape her kidnappers wanted to live. And still does."

For once, she seemed at a loss for words. Instead, she crossed her arms and slumped back against the wall. Pouting.

"Besides," I said quickly, "there's a month before the anniversary gala. A lot can happen between now and then."

She shrugged, then peered past my shoulder at a calendar on the wall opposite. I turned, followed her gaze.

"Actually, we've got less than three weeks," she said. "Man, time flies when you've been kidnapped…"

I walked Lisa across the hospital parking lot to her car, a silver BMW newly leased for her through her husband's company. She was heading back to the residence, to supervise the clean-up once the few remaining cops and FBI techs finished their work.

She told me that Payton had called right before I'd arrived at Harland's room, saying it looked like they were nearly done.

As she drove off, I realized this meant that, true to his word, Payton had left the sidewalk café soon after Gloria and I did. And that he'd returned to his duties at the residence.

By now, the sun had dipped, its cool rays fanning out from behind the serrated urban skyline. Coating with a suffused white glaze the planes of the new downtown high-rises, while sending the buildings opposite into deep shadow. The entire cityscape funneled by a rising, oblivious wind.

I crossed the lot and found my own car. I'd just climbed behind the wheel and turned the ignition key when my cell rang. I looked at the display. It was Charlene.

"Danny! Thank God you picked up!"

She was breathless, panicked.

"Charlene, what is it?"

"It's Skip. He was supposed to be here at the bar an hour ago. But he never showed, and I can't get a hold of him. I called his cell, the room number at his motel. Even the pool hall where he's started hanging out."

"Yeah, I know the place. I was with him there earlier."

"They said he left hours ago. I tried the VA, and this one other friend of his I know. Another vet. But the guy said he hasn't seen Skip in weeks."

"Did you call the motel front desk? Maybe the manager can go knock on Skip's door."

"I keep trying, but all I get is a busy signal. Maybe the phone's off the hook, or broken or something. I don't know. Skip's been drinking so much lately, I'm afraid he's passed out on the street somewhere, or—"

"Don't worry, we just have to—"

"But that's not all. Noah's gone, too."

"What?"

"He saw how upset I was and suddenly decided he'd go pound on Skip's door at the motel. He said Skip was probably sleeping off a drunk and doesn't hear the phone. It's room 103."

"Jesus, Charlene, you should've stopped him…"

"I tried, but you know how Noah's been acting lately."

"Yes. Erratic. And aggressive. I'm sorry, I didn't mean to blame you. I called Nancy Mendors about adjusting his meds…."

"I know. She's supposed to come by tonight and check him out. Oh God, what am I gonna do? Now both Noah *and* my brother are gone."

I'd already pulled out of the lot and was heading across town, back toward East Liberty again. With traffic thickening, it'd take me at least thirty minutes to get to Skip's motel.

"I'll find them, Charlene. How long since Noah took off?"

"Just a few minutes ago. He grabbed the keys to the old pickup and ran out the door. Danny, please! I'm going out of my mind! You know what a bad driver he is, and—"

"I'm on my way. Just hang in there."

Chapter Thirty-six

The Three Rivers Motel was a squat, ugly, single-floored string of rooms forming a U around a gravel lot. The peak-roofed registration office, curtains closed, was located at the far end. As I pulled into the lot, it occurred to me that it was awfully early in the day for the windows to be covered.

My Mustang was only one of a half-dozen vehicles parked in the lot. Thankfully, this included Noah's dented, paint-flecked pickup. It was parked at an angle across two spaces, nose aimed at room 103.

I jumped out of my car and headed for the door. When I reached it, I saw that its lock was broken.

The door swayed open at my touch.

My breath tightened like a fist in my chest. Fighting the impulse to call out to Noah, I went inside.

No lamps were on, and the single shuttered window blocked whatever fading sunlight might've shone in. It was a fairly large room, but the walls were dingy, dirt-streaked. Furniture old, musty. The bed, set back about two feet from the far wall, was bare except for a tangle of sheets, some of which spilled to the threadbare green carpet.

Something was moving under the cascade of linen on the floor. A figure wedged between the bed and the wall.

I hurried around the end of the bed and pulled back the sheets. It was Noah Frye, facedown on the floor. Slowly, awkwardly moving his arms and legs. Like a big, rangy crab trying to get purchase on the thin carpet weave.

"Noah!"

I bent down, took hold of both hands, and helped him get to his feet. Though he almost toppled over again.

I knew I'd have better luck wrangling a bear, so I pivoted and guided him down to a sitting position on the bed. His shaggy head fell to his chest, and I quickly tilted it up from under his chin. His eyes were dull, clouded. Mouth slack.

"Noah, are you okay?"

He mumbled something, then reached with one big hand to rub the back of his neck. It was then that I noticed the familiar, painful-looking lump on his head. It was just like the one I'd received from Max Griffin, back at my office that day.

"Noah…?"

"I'm all right, dammit," he growled, blinking up at me. "Some chicken-shit bastard clobbered me from behind, that's all. I've had worse done to me on the streets. Lots worse."

I sat next to him on the bed.

"Jesus, Noah, Charlene's worried sick. I'm going to call her in a minute. But first, tell me what happened."

"Not much to tell. I got here, saw that the lock was busted, and came in. Prick musta been hiding behind the door, 'cause all of a sudden I feel a helluva pain in the back of my head and everything goes black. Next thing I know, you was helpin' me up off the floor. Christ, Danny, if this is the kinda shit that goes on in reality, gimme back my hallucinations. At least when Satan and I mix it up, my goddamn head don't hurt so much after."

I went into the bathroom and, after a moment, brought him back a glass of water. While he gratefully gulped it down, I called Charlene on my cell. She answered at the first ring.

"Danny, is Noah—?"

"He's fine, Char. I'm sitting right next to him. But he's gonna have a nasty headache for the next day or two."

"Thank God. Just bring him back home to me, so I can give him a big hug and kiss. Right before I beat the hell outta him."

"I know. He has the same effect on me."

Then her tone became grave.

"What is it you're *not* telling me, Danny? About Skip…"

"I'm afraid he isn't here. But that's all I know. Maybe he never came back to the room."

Now Noah was looking at me. An oddly lucid, pensive stare.

"Let me get Noah home, okay?" I said into the phone. "Then we can alert the police. Get some real help in finding Skip."

I'd tried to put more confidence into my voice than I felt. But I don't think Charlene was fooled.

After I hung up, and despite Noah's grumbled protests, I did a rudimentary check for signs of a concussion.

"I think you're okay," I told him afterwards. "But when Dr. Mendors comes by the bar tonight, make sure she does a more thorough exam."

Then I clicked on my cell and called for a cab. Luckily, the dispatcher said there was one only a few minutes away.

More protests from Noah. "Hey, what about my truck? We can't just leave it here. In *this* fuckin' neighborhood."

"Don't worry, it won't get stolen. Trust me, nobody's that hurting for wheels."

"Nice. Ya know, you got a real mean streak, Danny. Anybody ever tell you that?"

"I'll add it to the growing list of complaints. Now let's get going."

My arm around his shoulder, I walked us both awkwardly out of the room. At the same time, a city cab rolled onto the lot. I put Noah in the backseat. He squinted up at me.

"Why can't *you* drive me back?"

"I have a few things I need to do. But I'll check in with you later. Okay?"

He shrugged, and settled himself comfortably back against the cab's seat. While I was giving the cabbie some cash and the bar's address, Noah spoke up again.

"By the way, Danny, I like to tip big."

To which the cabbie responded with a widening grin. I took some more bills from my wallet and handed them over.

I watched as the cab pulled away, then went back into the motel room. And sat down once more on the bed. My eyes riveted to the cell phone I held in my lap.

Waiting.

I hadn't been entirely honest with either Noah or Charlene. Skip had in fact come back to his room. I knew this for certain because of what I saw in the bathroom when I went to get Noah a glass of water.

It had been thrown casually to the tile floor, angled against a corner. One of its straps torn loose.

Skip's prosthetic leg.

My guess was, Griffin had broken into the room, assaulted Skip, and removed it. Maybe purely as an act of cruelty, maybe to ensure that his victim was hobbled.

Then, after subduing him, Griffin must've heard poor Noah approaching. Probably calling out for Skip as he headed for the room. So Griffin hid behind the opened door and hit him from behind as he entered.

Which left me wondering how they'd found Skip so quickly. Maybe one of Sykes' under-bosses had people scouring the streets looking for him. Or maybe, now that I gave it some thought, one of those three biker dudes at the pool hall knew someone in Sykes' operation. Followed Skip when he left the place and went back to his motel. Then made a couple calls.

I'd probably never know for sure. Not that it mattered. All that mattered was that Skip was gone, and that Sykes had him.

As the grayness of dusk filled the room, I considered—for perhaps the tenth time—calling the cops. But I knew in my heart that I wouldn't.

Skip's life depended on my playing my part in this final act exactly as Raymond Sykes planned it.

Which meant waiting, cell in hand, for him to call.

I didn't have long to wait.

◇◇◇

To my surprise, it was a video. Streaming live.

Given my cell's small screen, the images weren't very distinct. But there was no question about what I was watching.

It was Skip, mouth sealed with duct tape, bound to a chair with thick rope. One of his trouser legs, the left, hung limp.

Drawing a hard breath, I looked closer. Skip's eyes were open wide, white with fear. Staring straight at the camera.

Then I saw what I was supposed to see. Squared packets held against his chest by leather straps. When Sykes finally spoke, his face unseen off-camera, the first thing he did was tell me what they were. Though I'd already guessed.

"As you may have surmised, Dr. Rinaldi, Skip here has a number of C-4 packs strapped to his chest. Connected wirelessly to the trigger I'm holding in my hand."

The camera moved slightly, and I got a quick look at a portion of wall behind where Skip was positioned. I saw a couple life rafts hanging from hooks. A crescent of glass that was probably a porthole. He was on a boat of some kind.

Then, abruptly, the camera moved again, and I was staring at the face of Raymond Sykes. His smile a thin curl of disdain.

"I'll be succinct, Doctor. So please do not interrupt me. As you've also no doubt guessed, before I disappear for a well-earned sabbatical, I need to tie up some loose ends. One of which involves Mr. Hines. He and I go way back to Afghanistan, where some unpleasantness occurred that I'm only now having the opportunity to redress.

"But then there's *you*. Because of your interference, and, to my mind, unholy luck, I have to leave the country. Perhaps indefinitely. Putting my whole operation at risk. Obviously, this total disruption of my various business ventures needs to be punished. Which I intend to do. In fact, I refuse to leave for warmer climes until I have done so.

"So I propose a trade. You, in exchange for Julian Hines. Or 'Skip,' as he childishly refers to himself. Despite his discourtesy when under my command overseas, I'm willing to let bygones be bygones. Once you've taken his place, he can crawl out of here to safety. Back to the hollowness of his miserable life. Are you willing to make that trade, Doctor?"

The camera lens quickly returned to Skip's listless form, head now bowed. The explosives rising and falling on his chest with every forlorn breath.

"Or do Mr. Griffin and myself vacate the premises, making sure we're at a safe distance, after which I press the button and blow Mr. Hines into a hundred little pieces?"

I'd barely breathed myself during Sykes' monologue, its narcissistic self-justification wedded to sadistic malice. I knew I couldn't take his word for it that he'd release Skip if I agreed to the exchange. But I also didn't see any choice.

"All right, Sykes. I'll take the deal—me for Skip. Where and when?"

"Here and now. Simple enough, right? Now, tiresome as it is to have to keep repeating myself, I'll expect you to come alone. No cops or Feds. Just you. Are we clear? Because you and your colleagues seem to have a hard time following instructions."

"We're clear. Now where the hell are you?"

Chapter Thirty-seven

The lights along Allegheny River Boulevard were just coming on. At this stretch of road, ten miles past Oakmont, there was a mix of homes, apartment buildings, and block-long industrial supply stores. Lumber, concrete, marine equipment.

I squinted in the thickening darkness for the turnoff that Sykes described. With every mile, there were fewer and fewer lights. More empty road between streetlamps and buildings, commercial or otherwise. The only things moving were the tops of trees, bending before the stiff wind coming off the river.

Finally I found the turnoff and swung the Mustang onto the gravel access road. Narrow, curving, and barely visible in the dark, it meandered down to what looked like an abandoned wharf. Though given its small size and lack of a service building, it was more like a dock. Reaching out into the black waters of the Allegheny, its wooden platform weathered and tar-patched.

I shut off the engine and peered at the boat tied to the end of the dock. It was an old tugboat, obviously long out of service. Creaking mournfully as it lolled in the water.

I got out of my car and made my way slowly down the length of the dock. The splintered planks moaned and buckled under my every step. My eyes now accustomed to the gloom, I spotted a lone sedan in the nearby weeds. Sykes and Griffin had obviously ditched their van for the car, which was probably stolen.

Standing at the dock's end, I peered up at the shadowed frame of the tugboat. The small pilot house was caked with dirt, windows blackened. Even in the unremitting darkness, the hull showed the ravages of long years spent moored in the river. Oil-streaked, dotted with bird droppings. A relic of a time when tugs numbered in the dozens, hauling heavy barges laden with coal down this venerable river. Past the Point, and on to the Ohio River, and then to harbors east, south, and west.

I found myself taking short, uneasy breaths, but not against the stinging river smell. It was the unmistakable sign of my rising anxiety. Almost a panic. The reality of what I was about to do hitting me hard, like a sudden jab to the face.

I knew Skip's life was at stake. I knew that his only hope was to let Sykes exchange him for me. And that I was going to let him do it.

I also knew something else. I was afraid.

Yet there was nothing to do but acknowledge it. *Own* it. Swallowing a mouthful of rank air, I stepped onto the boat.

I found them in the main hold, below deck. A low-roofed rectangular space thick with river musk and the dust of years. A generator in a far corner fed electricity to three sets of lights positioned around the room. Meaning the retired tug had probably been used by Sykes as a safe house for a long time. Just as he'd converted the abandoned printing factory into a clandestine sex-and-drugs retreat for his wealthy clients.

In the middle of the room was Skip Hines, bound and gagged, explosives still strapped to his chest. His eyes were hooded, his head lolled. He was either drugged or wearily resigned to his fate. Or just hungover.

Facing him was a video camera on a tripod, similar to the one I'd seen at the printing factory.

I registered all this in a few brief moments, while I tried to adjust to the tug's steady lift and roll. Keep my balance. Then I heard a familiar voice behind me. Griffin.

He was leaning against a bulkhead. As before, a measured distance away from me. An automatic pistol was in his hand.

"Welcome aboard, asshole." He grinned that easy grin.

Behind him, stepping like a wraith from the shadows, was Raymond Sykes. In a clean, newly pressed white shirt and tie. His civilian uniform, I thought. The shirt plumed about him, as did his voluminous trousers, like a sail caught by a breeze. His visible wrists, hands, and face grotesquely thin.

"I'm glad to see you're a man of your word, Dr. Rinaldi. If you'd taken much longer to get here, Mr. Hines would have been suddenly and rudely disarticulated."

I met his gaze. Fear turning unexpectedly to anger.

"Spare me the fancy bullshit and release Skip. Now. Then you can verbally bore me to death."

I smiled over at Griffin.

"Really, Max, I don't know how the hell you stand it."

His jaw tightened. "Shut the fuck up, Rinaldi. I mean it."

Sykes took another few steps toward me. The smile beneath his thin mustache was bemused.

"I'd hoped you'd present us with something entertaining. The defiant, wisecracking hero. Good choice, Doctor. I'm glad you went with it."

"Whatever. Now, come on, Sykes. I kept my end of the bargain. I'm here. Let Skip Hines go."

Sykes put his hands in his loose pockets.

"To be candid, I'm still considering my options. There's yet some time before an associate arrives to pick up Griffin and me. A seaplane, landing on the river at night. A real sight, they tell me. Few pilots can do it. Luckily, my gifted associate is one of them."

"You'll never make it. Air traffic controllers log every plane. Private and commercial. And they're on alert for you."

"As I assumed they would be. Which is why the flight plan has been filed with someone in my employ. As is the dock captain at the Boston seaport who'll expedite our passage on a merchant ship bound for distant shores."

"Let me guess. You're taking the same route, with the help of the same corrupt bastards, that your human trafficking setup uses? A small operation, like Gloria Reese said. Profitable, yet not so extensive, or financially successful, that it threatens or entices the big boys. At least not while you're around. What happens after you go into hiding is another matter."

Griffin, still keeping a safe distance from me, growled.

"C'mon, Sykes. Let me take the fucker out. Right now."

Sykes shrugged, hands still in his pockets. "A tempting thought, Max, but I'm wondering if there's anything else Dr. Rinaldi can tell us. About the Four Horsemen, for instance."

"You're in luck, Sykes. I've finally found out what you were talking about. And who the Four Horsemen are."

"I doubt that. They all wore ski masks when they enjoyed the company of Lisa Campbell."

"Three of them did, before James Harland put on his own mask. But even so, he was stupid and cocky enough to introduce them by name to Lisa. Big-name VIPs, whose identities are now known. Should be fun watching the news the next couple days."

"I don't believe you. Lisa was in no state to remember."

"I guess we'll have to wait and see."

"Besides, why would she come forward with the names? She's going to be ruined when James shows the video at that ludicrous anniversary gala."

"If she's going to be ruined anyway, why not name names? Tell the world who the sick bastards were that assaulted her? She'll have nothing to lose, right?"

Sykes finally lifted a hand from his pocket. Rubbed his narrow chin thoughtfully.

"I must concede your point there, Doctor. And I know Jimmy Harland well enough to know that he's champing at the bit to show that video. It's his chance to destroy both his despised stepmother and his equally despised father."

"So you and James are best bros, eh?"

He chuckled. "Hardly. Client and provider, at best. He and his fancy friends needed an inconspicuous arena for their sexual explorations. And I provided it. Though, yes, after a while we became intimate enough for him to tell me his plans for that video. However, it's not my concern what a client chooses to do once they've made a record of their escapades."

"Though you usually keep a copy, like you said. Except not this time. James had a computer whiz buddy download it to an encrypted flash-drive. One that can't be copied, and can only be opened with a pass key. And only James has it."

"Yes. Damned clever of him. Apparently he has more brains than I gave him credit for."

Griffin angrily cleared his throat.

"We gotta get goin', Sykes. C'mon, let's wrap this up."

Sykes glowered at him.

"Do you hear the sound of an approaching seaplane? Because *I* don't. Nonetheless, I agree I've spent enough time exchanging pleasantries with Dr. Rinaldi."

He turned back to me.

"Though it is a shame, really. I have so few people I enjoy talking with."

I smiled. "You could always let me live. Hell, I'll talk your ear off."

He spread his bony hands. "See what I mean? Where can one find amusing banter anymore? I so regret having to kill you. I mean that sincerely. But if I don't, your interference in my business will go unpunished. Which sets a terrible precedent among my associates. I trust you understand?"

"Completely. But let me ask two questions, if you don't mind."

"Not at all."

"You knew about James Harland's plans for the video, which means you knew how much Charles Harland valued his wife. Not to mention the extent of the old man's fortune."

"That's right. He's obscenely rich."

"So I understand why you decided to kidnap Lisa. I even think I understand why you called yourself 'Julian' when you made your ransom demands."

"I admit, I was allowing myself a bit of fun. Plus anything that could possibly misdirect the authorities was certainly an added benefit."

"So my first question is this: Did James have anything to do with the kidnapping? Did he help you hack into the house's security system, for example? Or let you know about Lisa's comings and goings?"

Sykes laughed again. "Good Lord, James had nothing to do with kidnapping Lisa Campbell, I promise you. As to helping me get into and manipulate the security system, you can't be serious. He spends so much time inside a bottle he can barely help himself to the bathroom. You know, I'd heard rumors that old man Harland had nothing but disdain for James. Believe me, it's no surprise why."

"So then how did you know to send Griffin to snatch her at my office? How did you know about our appointment?"

Instead of replying, Sykes nodded over at Griffin.

"How did we know, Max?"

Griffin gave me a sardonic look. "I waited outside the house and followed her to your office. Easy as pussy."

Inwardly, I almost groaned. Just as Gloria had guessed, the kidnappers had been keeping tabs on Lisa, waiting for the right moment to strike. When she was alone, unsuspecting. Away from any security detail.

Suddenly, before another word was exchanged, I heard the distant sound of an engine. Coming closer. Out over the river.

Sykes and Griffin heard it, too.

"And that sound means our time is up, Doctor. The seaplane is about to arrive."

"I still have my second question."

Griffin growled. "Jesus fucking Christ…!"

But Sykes, enjoying himself, sighed indulgently. "Make it a quick one, Dr. Rinaldi."

"Sure thing. Did you ever intend to release Skip Hines after I showed up?"

"Not for one moment. Sorry to say, I lied."

"So what's the plan?"

"Quite simple, really. I promised Max here he could shoot you, though I'm sure he wishes he had the time to make your death a lingering, exceedingly painful one. Instead, I suppose it'll have to be the traditional execution-style bullet to the head. Bang, and then you're gone."

Again, Sykes glanced at his partner. "Sorry, Max. I swear, I'll make it up to you."

Griffin gave me a dark smile. "I can live with fast and dirty. No goddamn fun, but efficient as hell."

"After which," Sykes continued, "Max and I will take the tug's dingy over to where the seaplane has landed and climb aboard. Once safely in the air, I'll press the trigger button and Skip Hines—along with this old tub—will be scattered in pieces to the night wind. Two useless relics disposed of, for the price of one. Not bad, eh?"

I was barely aware of his words now, my ears pricked for the rising whine of the seaplane as it neared. Echoing over the river, not far beyond the tug's walls. Then I heard it cut its engines, which meant it was getting ready to make its approach.

As if on impulse, I glanced back at Skip. His head had lifted, eyes once more wide and awake. I don't know how much he'd heard of my conversation with Sykes, but I could tell he knew the sound of that plane's arrival wasn't good news. For either of us.

"Well, Doctor…" Sykes' voice brought my head around again. "I'm afraid this is good-bye. At such a moment, I suspect you'd have to agree with Schopenhauer. He maintained that life is something that should not have been. Kind of a Gloomy Gus, I'll grant you. But not entirely wrong. No, sir, not entirely."

Then he nodded at Griffin, who raised his gun. I knew I was too far from him to try anything. And he was too good a shot.

Two-handing it, Griffin pointed the automatic at the space between my eyes.

For some reason, I didn't close them. Instead, I returned his narrowed gaze with my own unblinking stare.

"Go ahead, you son of a bitch. Do it!"

Suddenly, I heard a gun go off.

But it wasn't his.

Chapter Thirty-eight

Max Griffin uttered a short, startled howl of pain and clutched his left shoulder. Blood oozed from his fingers. His body jolted by the bullet's impact, the revolver flew from his other hand. Skittered across the oil-stained floor.

"Freeze, Griffin! FBI!"

Sykes and I were both caught off guard. Too stunned to move. Even after I'd recognized the voice. Young. Female.

Then, at almost the same time, we each saw Griffin's revolver on the floor and dove for it. Sykes was closer than I and quickly scooped it up. But before he could bring it to bear, I was on him.

My arms outstretched, I tackled him at the waist and brought us both crashing down to the floor. I landed on top and managed to grab his hand holding the gun. With a fierce cry, I slammed his thin wrist against the grimy floorboards, knocking the gun free. I heard the bones of his wrist snap. Break.

I didn't know what was happening behind me. All I heard was Griffin cursing, and Gloria's footsteps coming into the room.

But my eyes were riveted on Sykes. My fists clutching the loose folds of his shirt collar, I was aware of the freakish insubstantiality of the body beneath mine. Shifting position to steady myself, I heard the brittle bones of his ribs splinter under me. It was as if I'd wrestled a skeleton to the ground.

Instinctively, I rolled off his splayed, emaciated body. Keeping one hand firmly clasped at his throat, I felt revulsion as he smiled up at me. His teeth small and unnaturally white beneath that crease of a mustache.

I turned and looked up. Gloria Reese, armed with a Glock, had Griffin backed up against a bulkhead. The big man glowered at her, his huge hands held up, shoulder high, palms out.

Gloria kept her feet wide apart to maintain her balance against the sway of the boat. Her service weapon was gripped in both hands, arms out straight. Her breath coming in quick bursts. Every instinct I had told me that Griffin was going to make some kind of move. The moment he saw one.

Without taking her eyes off him, Gloria called over to me. "You okay, Danny?"

My fingers still gripping Sykes' collar, I didn't answer, nodded instead across the room at Skip Hines. Straining against his ropes, he stared at us in disbelief, as though silently screaming for one of us to untie him.

"They've rigged Skip with C-4," I said. "We've got to—"

I almost missed it. With the barest whisper of movement, Sykes' hand snaked down to his pants pocket. Slipped inside.

I knew what he was reaching for. What had been in that pocket the whole time. The trigger. To detonate the explosives strapped to Skip's chest. To finish his victim, and himself, and everyone else.

Without thinking, I grabbed his hand through the pocket's fabric and squeezed with all my might. He cried out, a harsh, guttural scream, as the bones in his hand cracked. But I didn't care. Savagely, I yanked his hand out of the pocket, his gnarled fingers still clutching the transmitter.

It was no bigger than a penknife, with a recessed plunger at the top. His thumb rested on the button, and he was straining mightily to press it. To will his fingers to obey his mind's command. But his fingers were now only so much crushed bone and cartilage. Useless.

Eyes wide, sweat sheening his narrow brow, Sykes could only watch in horror as I peeled back his thumb and snatched the transmitter from his grasp. A hoarse gasp rose from his throat. A sputtering, inarticulate keening of frustration and rage.

"Jesus Christ," Gloria said in a hushed tone, as she glanced involuntarily at Sykes. Letting her gaze shift from Max Griffin for only a moment.

But that was all the time he needed. With surprising quickness for a man of his size, he lunged at her. Still on my haunches next to Sykes, I was too far away to stop him.

"Gloria!" I shouted.

Griffin crossed the distance in two long strides. Backlit by one of the racks of lights, his immense shadow literally engulfed her. As he reached for her with those powerful hands—

Startled, Gloria stumbled backwards, but kept her two-handed grip on her gun. And started firing.

I watched as she pumped the entire clip into Griffin's chest. At first, his forward momentum—or maybe his inchoate rage—kept him on his feet. Staggering, but coming closer and closer…

And then he was falling forward, arms flailing. Dead, but still moving. Collapsing on top of her.

Gloria rolled away as Griffin sprawled face-first onto the floorboards, which groaned in protest. She'd barely managed to get out from under him, though she took some of his considerable weight on her shoulder as he hit the floor.

Still clutching the transmitter, I hauled Sykes to his feet. He almost instantly buckled and doubled over, like a marionette whose strings had been cut. In my hand, he felt like a thin wrapper of flesh over a twisted scaffolding of bone and soft, stringy muscle.

With Gloria's help, I maneuvered Sykes into a second chair by the bulkhead. After popping another clip into her weapon, she pointed it at his head. But it was obvious from his dulled eyes and constant grimace of pain that most of the fight had gone out of him. His fingers curled like desiccated claws on his lap.

I hurried over to the porthole and tossed the transmitter into the river. As I did, I could see in the haze of moonlight the outlines of a compact seaplane, engine idling, propellers lazily spinning. Black water lapped at the plane's pontoons. But I couldn't make out the pilot's face, an indistinguishable blur in the dim light of the cockpit.

I called to Gloria. "The plane's arrived."

This brought some life into Sykes' drawn features, despite his obvious agony. Gloria smiled down at him.

"Darn, looks like you're going to miss your ride."

He glared at her, as though too affronted by his present circumstances to lower himself to reply. I felt as if I could actually see his rattled self-regard re-constituting itself. The protective, narcissistic shell forming once again around his fragile ego.

Quickly, I crossed the hold and gently removed the duct tape from Skip's mouth. He let out a throaty sigh of relief.

"Thanks, man. I thought I was fucked sideways."

"Don't thank *me*, thank Agent Reese."

I began carefully loosening the straps holding the C-4 packets against his chest.

"There oughta be a receiver wire in there somewhere." Skip's words were punctuated by a series of deep breaths. "For the signal from the transmitter."

"Got it." I slid the wire out of the lead packet. Then I hurriedly untied him. He was hardly free of the ropes before he started shaking the stiffness out of his arms.

I took another look out the porthole. The plane was still idling. Bobbing expectantly in the water.

Gloria said, "Time to bring in the cavalry," and took out her cell. Following protocol, she called the police first, then her superiors at the Federal Building.

I leaned down to Skip. "And time to get *you* out of here."

He blanched. "Look, I don't wanna be carried outta here like some goddamn cripple—"

"Don't worry. I brought what you need with me. It's in my car."

Skip smiled, and held up his hand to clasp mine.

"Like I told Charlene, Danny, you're all right."

I bent and picked up Griffin's revolver, still laying where Sykes and I had struggled. I handed it to Skip.

"Do me a favor, okay? Keep it pointed at Sykes while Agent Reese is on the phone. If he moves, shoot him."

"Hell, yeah..!"

Then, with a nod at Gloria, I went out to my car to get Skip his leg.

◇◇◇

Before the cops and the Feds could arrive at the scene, the seaplane had lifted off. I guess the pilot finally figured out that something had gone wrong, and didn't want to stick around to find out what it was.

Meanwhile, Skip had reattached his prosthetic, using the strip of duct tape as a makeshift replacement for the torn strap. Then he'd insisted on tying Sykes to the same chair to which he'd been bound. Now, grinning, he stood over him, Griffin's revolver still in his hand.

"I got this." Skip indicated Sykes, who seethed in silence. Refusing to let us see his obvious discomfort. Roughly bound to the chair, his crushed ribs and fingers must have been shot through with pain.

"Go on, you two," Skip said casually to Gloria and me. "Go out and wait for the good guys."

I regarded him warily.

"Now that Sykes is safely tied up, can I have your word you're not going to accidentally shoot him?"

"Man, you're a real buzz-kill. But yeah, okay."

Outside, Gloria and I sat on the edge of the dock. The starred night was cold, clear. A stiff wind buffeted the old tug moored behind us, its hull scraping the dock's rough timbers.

"So." I looked at her profile in the scant moonlight. "How the hell did you know where I was?"

"Easy. I bugged your car."

"What? When?"

"When we were both in it earlier, on our way to talk to Payton. I knew you were right. For Sykes, it was intolerable that you'd get away alive after having messed up his plans. Forcing him to flee the country. So I put a GPS tracking device under your dashboard when you weren't looking."

"Does Wilson know you did that? And that you followed me here, alone and without backup?"

She shrugged. "He'll know soon enough. He and Biegler are probably drag-racing right now to see who gets here first. So, no, he didn't know. Nobody on my team at the Bureau knew."

"You went rogue, eh?"

"Don't be so dramatic. I figured if Sergeant Polk could work solo, based on a hunch, then so could I. Serves Wilson right, anyway. The way he and the rest of the brass were freezing me out. Treating me like somebody's kid sister."

I thought about it. "You'll catch shit, Gloria. But you'll also get a medal."

"Yeah. But probably not in that order."

She gave me a shy smile.

"In case you're wondering, I started tracking you right after the briefing ended this afternoon. I was just about to pull into the Three Rivers Motel when I saw you driving out."

"You spotted Skip's room. The broken lock on his door."

"I put two-and-two together, yeah."

"Did you happen to ask at the registration office? Skip's sister had tried calling earlier, but kept getting a busy signal. Then, when I showed up looking for Skip, the office seemed like it was closed. In the middle of the day."

"Yeah, I checked it out. ID'd myself and pounded on the door 'til the desk clerk opened it. Turns out, the curtains were drawn and the phone was off the hook so the guy and the motel's maid wouldn't be disturbed. Apparently, they'd spent most of the afternoon banging each other's brains out. Though it was all very romantic. The girl swore they were in love and begged me not to tell the management."

"You won't, of course."

"Hell, no. Who am I to stand in the way of true love? At least until the poor girl finds out there's no such thing."

I glanced up then at the wail of approaching sirens, the undulating cascade of flashing lights. Squad cars and unmarked sedans barreling down the curved gravel road toward us.

I helped Gloria to her feet and we climbed back aboard the tug. Sykes was pretty much the way we'd left him, bound and trembling silently in pain. Skip was now leaning against the bulkhead, a new fatigue etched on his face. The adrenaline surge of his capture and eventual release having drained away, he was left weary, shaken, and, doubtless, still hungover.

As Gloria took the revolver from him, turning to train it on her prisoner, I peered down at Max Griffin. Pools of blood had formed a lake around the island of his lifeless body.

"Funny," I said aloud. "Somehow I thought it'd come down to him and me. At the end."

Gloria's smile was indulgent.

"Only in the movies, Doc. Instead it was a skinny chick with a gun. Disappointed?"

To be honest, I didn't know how I felt.

So I said nothing.

Chapter Thirty-nine

I stood on the gravel next to the dock, in a cordoned-off area broad enough to encompass the sedan parked in the nearby weeds. Presumed to be stolen, and used by Sykes and Griffin to get here, it was being given a cursory inspection by a couple of CSU techs. Soon, I knew, it would be towed to the Department impound for a more thorough, detailed examination.

Ringed by a dozen cars, both the dock and the old tugboat were illuminated by a kaleidoscopic combination of front grille high beams and flashing roof lights. Beyond, out on the water, a Pittsburgh River Patrol boat swept its magnesium searchlight back and forth across the scene, like an all-seeing eye. I felt uncomfortably exposed every time its steady arc brought that blind gaze past me on the river's bank.

Turning away from the water, I watched as police and FBI personnel went through their practiced paces, securing the crime scene, scouring for bullet casings and footprints, gathering whatever evidence could be identified. Then, squinting in the flickering play of dark and light, I suddenly made out Special Agent Anthony Wilson conferring with Gloria Reese. Though that was a polite term for what appeared to be going on. Seques-tered near some trees just inside the perimeter, yet too far away to be heard, Wilson's stern face and animated gestures revealed quite clearly that Gloria was being given a severe reprimand.

God, what an asshole, I thought. Whatever else he was, Wilson was a classic government bureaucrat. Never mind that Gloria had risked her life to save mine, as well as Skip's. Never mind that she helped capture a wanted criminal before he could make his escape. She hadn't followed FBI procedure. Hadn't alerted her superiors, nor gotten the authority to put a GPS tracker in my car. And, as I'd feared, was catching hell for it.

Just then, a rush of movement on the dock competed for my attention. Two coroner's attendants were wheeling Griffin's corpse out of the tugboat, zipped up in the ubiquitous body bag. The medical examiner herself—the same unnamed woman I'd seen earlier in my office—was apparently still inside the tug, attending to Raymond Sykes' injuries.

As I watched Griffin being loaded into the morgue wagon, Sergeant Polk crunched across the gravel, muttering to himself. Before launching into one of his by-now familiar rants.

"Another goddamn crime scene, Rinaldi? How the hell do ya keep windin' up in the middle of stuff like this?"

"Beats me, Harry. All I was trying to do was keep an eye on Skip Hines. *Somebody* had to."

"Hey, don't blame *me*. That bullshit briefing went on for hours. I couldn't get outta there."

"Because that's where you were *supposed* to be, Sergeant."

It was Lieutenant Biegler, stepping gingerly over a patch of weeds sprouting up among the gravel. His petulant features shone starkly in the headlights of a nearby unmarked.

Facing me, he put his fists on his hips. "If you understood chain of command, Rinaldi, you'd know what I mean."

"Oh, I understand it. I'm just lucky enough not to be one of the links in that chain."

He grunted unpleasantly. "Which doesn't mean I still can't arrest you for interfering in an official investigation."

"Been there, done that, Stu. What else you got?"

I was rescued from this sorry banter by the arrival of Detective Jerry Banks, who'd trotted over from the car in the weeds. Wearing a name-brand overcoat and an untroubled smile.

"Just ran a check on the VIN number. Sedan's stolen, Lieutenant, like we figured."

Biegler nodded. "Now what about this Julian Hines? We'll be needing his statement."

"Dr. Yang, the ME, has him waiting in the ambulance. She says he looks okay, but wants to check him out anyway when she's through with Sykes."

Polk nodded in my direction.

"Word is, you busted Sykes up pretty good, Doc."

"Hell, all I did was fall on him. His chronic illness did the rest."

"Yeah." Biegler clucked his tongue. "Agent Wilson told me all about it. According to their intel, Sykes picked up some kind of horrible disease in Afghanistan. Like that flesh-eating stuff. Plus he had something wrong with his bones."

"Probably *osteogenesis imperfecta*. A very rare, genetic predisposition to brittle bones. I thought as much."

"Speak o' the devil…"

Harry had turned his back against the wind to light up a Camel unfiltered. Now he pointed with its glowing tip at the entrance to the tug.

With Dr. Yang following behind, Sykes was being carried out on a stretcher by those same two attendants. As the procession arrived at the foot of the dock, and the rear doors of the ambulance opened from inside, I strode over to meet it.

Ignoring Yang's disapproving stare, I leaned down over the stretcher. Not ten inches from Sykes impassive face.

He stared back. "I thought our business had concluded, Dr. Rinaldi. Though, regrettably, not as I'd hoped."

His words were slurred, his cadence deliberate. The ME had obviously pumped him full of painkillers.

"Save it for your prison memoirs, Sykes. But there's one more thing I need to know."

He managed an insolent smile. "Only one?"

"What happened to Donna Swanson, Harland's nurse? Why did she have to die? Was she involved, or—"

"That's between me and my lawyer. Who would no doubt advise me to stop talking to you. And I—"

He'd tried to lift his head and suddenly winced in pain. With a groan, he let it fall back.

"That's enough!" Dr. Yang spoke like someone used to being obeyed. And probably feared. She nodded at her assistants. "Put Mr. Sykes in the ambulance. *Now*." Then her steely eyes found mine. "As for you, Mister…uh…"

"*Doctor* Rinaldi. And I was just going."

I back-stepped, giving the attendants room to maneuver the stretcher into the back of the ambulance. After lifting Sykes carefully into the medical bay, one of the attendants went around front to climb into the driver's seat. Then, with a quick wave of her hand, Yang motioned for the doors to be closed.

Before they did, I caught a glimpse of Skip Hines, sitting inside on a cushioned wheel hub. Busily adjusting the makeshift strap on his prosthetic leg, he didn't see me.

As the ambulance slowly pulled away, I extended my hand to the ME, giving the slim, officious woman my best smile.

"I'm sorry, Doctor. We haven't been properly introduced."

Her returning smile was icy.

"That's right, we haven't."

After which, she turned on her heel and walked off. Then I heard a soft peal of laughter behind me.

It was Gloria Reese, watching Dr. Yang's departing form. She was still chuckling when she came over to me.

"I see you haven't lost your touch with the ladies."

"I have my moments," I said. "Unfortunately, this wasn't one of them."

As if reading each other's thoughts, we drifted away from the chaos of the crime scene. Near a bank of trees.

"You going to be okay?" I asked at last.

"I'm still with the Bureau, if that's what you mean. Wilson was pissed as hell, but there's only so much crap he can dump on me. I *did* collar the bad guy."

"Damn right."

"With some help, of course. I'll be sure to mention you in my report, Danny."

"Do you have to? I get enough grief from the Department. I don't want to be on *another* outfit's shit-list."

"Okay, but it'll cost you. Dinner, maybe?"

I hesitated. She searched my face, the color quickly fading from her own. As though she'd misstepped.

"I'd like to, Gloria…but I'm kind of with someone."

A pause. "Kind of?"

"It's complicated. There's a triangle thing going on."

"Yeah? Who's the other guy, some combination of Muhammad Ali and Freud?"

"Actually, it's a woman."

She gave a slow, thoughtful nod.

"Well, Danny, if *you're* involved, I guess it *has* to be complicated, right? Though, Christ, for a smart guy, you're really a jerk."

"It sure seems that way sometimes."

Suddenly, a loud, authoritative voice boomed.

"Agent Reese!"

Agent Wilson was striding purposefully toward us. Once he'd joined us, he just as purposefully ignored me.

"Leave your car, Agent Reese. I'll have it picked up. You're riding with me."

"Where to, sir?"

"Downtown. With Raymond Sykes in custody, there's a real possibility one of his under-bosses will make a play. Start something that gets out of control. This could be an opportunity for us to bring down a big chunk of the operation."

She straightened, as if at attention. "I agree, sir."

Then she offered me a brief, collegial smile. "I'm sure we'll run into each other again, Dr. Rinaldi."

Gloria held out her hand. I took it.

"I'm sure we will, Agent Reese."

Wilson finally deigned to glance once in my direction, offering a brief, meaningless smile of his own before heading over to the parked cars.

Gloria Reese hurried to catch up with him.

At Lieutenant Biegler's insistence, I followed Harry Polk's unmarked back to the Old County Building. I parked my Mustang in the lot, nodded at the desk sergeant in the lobby, and went up to the detectives' floor. Once again, I was being required to give a statement about my involvement in a police matter. Or, as Polk put it, to explain what the hell I was doing on a goddamn tugboat with an FBI most-wanted criminal and a one-legged guy with explosives strapped to his chest.

A fair question, I thought.

I found Harry waiting for me in one of the venerable building's windowless interview rooms. Maybe even one I'd been in before. Leaning back in his chair, Polk waved a meaty hand at the tape recorder on the table between us.

"Let's make this quick, okay, Doc? I wouldn't mind gettin' to bed before the sun comes up. For once."

"Where's your partner, Jerry the Boy Wonder?"

"Biegler poached him to be his go-fer. Run errands, get coffee, that shit. Just 'til they wrap things up at the crime scene. Fine with me."

"I'm surprised Biegler isn't tucked in bed himself by now."

"Usually he would be. But he wants to be in on the call when Agent Wilson tells the governor about the Sykes bust. Just like Wilson'll wanna be cheek-to-cheek with Biegler when *he* informs Chief Logan and the mayor."

"So much for inter-agency cooperation."

"Whatever." He switched on the tape recorder. "Okay, you know the drill. Start at the beginning and keep the damn time line straight. And do us both a favor, will ya, Rinaldi? Stick to the facts, leave out the wise-ass remarks, and skip all the therapy mumbo-jumbo."

I smiled. "Hell, then this won't take long at all."

It didn't.

The steel girders of the Liberty Bridge had a somber, melancholy cast in the pre-dawn gloom. With morning commuter traffic still a couple hours away, the scant number of cars made the drive across the wind-dimpled Monongahela River almost restful. Meditative.

Tired, my joints and muscles aching, and woefully sleep-deprived, I was glad to be heading home. Since I didn't have to return to work until tomorrow, I could allow myself the luxury of a full day's R and R.

Or so I thought.

My cell rang as I was winding slowly up the hill to Mt. Washington. To my surprise, it was Mike Payton. Calling from the Harland residence.

"We just heard the news from Chief Logan, Doc. They got the bastards. Both of 'em."

"That's right. Griffin is dead and Sykes is in custody."

He chuckled. "Well, one outta two ain't bad. Man, I'd love to get my hands on that Sykes asshole. He's a disgrace to the military. To the guys who were under his command."

"Like Skip Hines."

"Yeah. He's okay, though, right?"

"He's fine. Truth is, we all got lucky. It could've gone the other way."

"Maybe. You've been in this thing up to your neck since it started, and you really came through. And I appreciate it. But like I've said all along, it shoulda been me."

"Happy to trade places with you next time, Mike."

There was a long, strained silence on the phone.

"Listen, Doc," he said finally. "There's something I've been meaning to talk to you about. Something important. At least I think it is."

"What is it?"

"Not on the phone. Besides, it'll keep for now. I'd rather talk about it in person, anyway."

"Well, I promised to pay a call on Charles Harland and Lisa later today. To see how they're both doing."

"Okay, great. We can grab a few minutes alone then."

◇◇◇

Before taking a longed-for hot shower, I'd put enough ground Columbian in the coffee-maker to fill a whole pot. So when I finally came out of the bathroom, dressed in fresh jeans and a Steelers sweatshirt, the welcome aroma of brewed coffee wafted throughout the house.

Taking a steaming mug into the front room, I collapsed on the sofa and clicked on the TV news. And saw what I'd expected—footage of the abandoned tugboat, as well as the surrounding area, accompanied a report about the arrest of Ray Sykes. With no mention of the Harland family or Lisa's ordeal, the story focused on Sykes' alleged criminal activities in the tri-state area. How the police and the FBI had been gathering evidence against him and his associates for years. Then the on-scene reporter, microphone in hand, stepped in front of the camera. With appropriate gravity, she said that during a brief gun-battle with an unnamed FBI agent, another suspect, Max Griffin, had been shot and killed.

When the report returned to the station's news desk, the anchor added, "Though unconfirmed, sources at the scene believe that another man, identity unknown, was in the boat, and had been held prisoner by Sykes and Griffin. Naturally, we'll keep following this story as it develops…"

I lowered the set's volume and gingerly sipped my coffee. The Harland money and influence may have succeeded in keeping Lisa's kidnapping out of the story, but it wouldn't for long. It would all eventually come out at Sykes' trial.

Though I doubted that Skip Hines would be able to maintain his own anonymity until then. Given the media's relentless probing, his identity was bound to be disclosed much sooner.

I hoped he'd be able to handle it. Regardless, I was prepared to help.

If he'd let me.

Chapter Forty

It felt strange, driving across town on a regular Tuesday afternoon, when normally I'd be in my Oakland office, seeing patients. Whatever solace I'd hoped to derive from my day off hadn't materialized, perhaps due to some questions still nagging me about the Sykes case. I couldn't tell. All I knew was that I was vaguely, irritatingly uneasy.

The wind had finally abated somewhat, and the weather report promised that calmer days were ahead for the Steel City. Which meant the return of those big, white, shoulder-pad clouds that often hunched over the county, along with the possibility of rain they usually augured.

I'd turned onto Second Avenue and was stopped at a light when my cell rang. This call surprised me even more than the one from Mike Payton.

"Danny? Dave Parnelli here. How's it hanging?"

I'd gotten acquainted with Assistant District Attorney Dave Parnelli last summer, in connection with that bank robbery case, before meeting up again during the Jessup investigation. Since then, we'd bumped into each other from time to time, usually at Noah's Ark. To the dismay of Noah, I'd introduced the brash, opinionated, heavy-drinking attorney to his bar, at which he was now a more or less regular customer.

For some reason, Dave Parnelli considered us good friends. *Paisans*, since we were both Italian-Americans. Brothers under the skin.

"What's up, Dave?" The light had turned green, so I switched to the hands-free app. I was in the middle of a phalanx of cars, buses, and smoke-belching semis.

"I just came from my initial sit-down with Sykes' lawyer. Real slick bastard, this one. Lotta prick potential."

"Well, Sykes can afford the best."

"I don't care if his lawyer's Clarence-fucking-Darrow, Sykes is toast. We've got him on kidnapping, attempted murder, conspiracy to commit murder. Not to mention the trafficking charges, if the FBI gets off its ass and hands over their files. You know what those clowns are like. Stiffs in cheap suits."

"I've had the pleasure, yeah."

"Anyway, we got enough to put Sykes away for a couple lifetimes. He might even get the needle, if we can tie him to Griffin's acts. The DA wants that sucker on Death Row."

"Maybe he can have the cell next to the Handyman."

"Don't even *say* something like that. The voting public's furious that that sick bastard keeps dodging his death sentence with appeals. If Sykes' lawyer pulls the same shit…"

"You know he will, Dave. But why are you calling?"

"Can't a buddy just call to say hello?"

"Not when a high-profile case like this is gearing up."

"When you're right, you're right. But I wanted to give you a heads-up. Sykes is gonna sue you for excessive force."

"He's *what*?…"

"He claims unnecessary bodily harm when you tackled him on the boat. His lawyer's got the ME's report on his injuries, as well as that of his attending doctor at Pittsburgh Memorial. That's where they got Sykes now. Under guard, of course."

"But I'm not a cop. How can he sue for excessive force?"

"I've seen it before, Danny. They'll argue that, as a paid consultant, you were acting in the capacity of an agent of the Department. Under its direction."

"That's bullshit and you know it."

"Sure I know it. But I can think of a few dickless judges who'll see the merits."

"So what do I do now?"

"Nothing. Until Sykes' lawyer goes ahead and files the papers. Then *you* better get yourself a good lawyer, too. Call me when the time comes and I'll give you some referrals."

Then Parnelli got another call on his line and had to hang up. Leaving me stuck in rush-hour traffic, with what felt like a coil of barbed wire twisting in my gut.

Happy Hour at Noah's Ark was even happier than usual, since the drinks were on the house. Charlene's way of celebrating the safe return of her brother Skip. Though when I showed up and took a stool at the crowded bar next to him, I didn't know how much detail he'd gone into with his sister about his ordeal.

So I asked him.

"I tried to keep most of it to myself," he said, "but Charlene saw the news. Took her two seconds to figure out that *I* was the poor bastard rumored to be on the boat. Then I got a zillion questions about what happened to me, who this Sykes creep was, how I escaped. I told her it was you and some girl FBI agent. But mostly it was the girl."

This last was said with a boozy grin. I could tell he'd already had more than a few.

"Well, you're right about Agent Reese. She's the real hero. But how are you doing? Any the worse for wear?"

"Nah. Dr. Yang checked me out and released me. She also saw me checkin' *her* out. Nice ass on that woman."

"Christ, I hope you didn't come on to her."

"Sure did. We're havin' dinner later tonight. Someplace nice. I just gotta hit Charlene up for a loan."

I laughed, and motioned for Noah to come down to our end of the bar. He did, but wasn't too quick about it. And didn't look real happy.

"Look," he said, "we're busy as hell, so I don't got time to chew the fat with you two jerks. What'll you have, Danny?"

"Whatever's on tap, Noah. But there's no rush."

Skip held up his empty beer mug. "Same for me, okay, man?"

Noah glared at him. "You've had enough, Skip. It's still day-light. How much fuckin' celebratin' are you gonna do?"

"Shit, man. I'm just gettin' started."

But I was peering carefully at the glint in Noah's eyes.

Then I turned to Skip. "Why don't you go ask Charlene to fix you something to eat? You can't keep drinking like that on an empty stomach."

"Yeah? Just watch me…"

"Come on, Skip. Humor me, okay?"

"Okay. But only since you helped save my ass."

His grumbled assent was only half in jest. Despite what had happened to him the night before, Skip was still, to my mind, on a potentially self-destructive path. One that—when and if he ever sobered up enough to talk to—I intended to try to steer him away from. With Charlene's help.

After Skip left to find his sister in the noisy sea of tables, I crooked my finger at Noah. Had him lean in closely.

"You still feeling a bit wiggy, Noah? I can't tell."

He scowled. "Yeah, well, Dr. Nancy can. She showed up last night and read me the riot act."

"Did she change your medication? Or the dosage?"

"Nah. Just reamed me out for skippin' the pills sometimes."

"You're not taking your meds regularly? Dammit, Noah, you know better than that. I ought to clobber you."

"Shit, man, I'm still hurtin' from Dr. Mendors bitch-slappin' me. But I'm back on the straight and narrow, Danny. Scout's honor."

"Like you were ever a Boy Scout."

"Hey, you don't know everything about me, man. You oughta see me tie a knot. Charlene thinks I'm real good at it, if ya know what I mean."

His leering wink was a disconcerting addition to the glazed, intense look in his eyes. I knew that, even if he did return to taking his meds daily, it would be a while before they took effect.

Which was when it occurred to me that I'd probably be worry-ing about Noah for the rest of his life. Or mine.

And that that was okay with me.

◇◇◇

The decibel level at the bar rose significantly as more customers flowed in. Dusk had fallen, a damp gray mist over the river visible through the portholes at the back of the room.

I'd made my way to a rear corner and stood, beer in hand, near the swinging doors leading to the kitchen. As I'd hoped, Charlene soon came pushing through them, carrying a large tray laden with sandwiches and fries. She gave me a wink, promised she'd be back in a minute, and headed out to the crowded floor.

When she returned, she threw her arms around me and gave me a fierce hug. She was a big woman, and her embrace almost lifted me off my feet. The sweet tang of her sweat mixed with perfume filled my nostrils.

Finally, she released me, though she held me at out arms' length, her grip strong on my shoulders.

"My God, Danny, I don't know how I can ever thank you. My idiot brother got himself into a mountain of trouble and you got him out."

"Forget it, Charlene. I'm just glad he's all right. At least physically. But you and I have to talk at some point."

Her arms fell, hands finding pockets. "I know, he's all screwed up. The war, and his leg. Our old man was an alcoholic, so I know the signs. I've gotta get him to see it."

"It won't be easy. Once the story about what happened to him last night comes out, his connection to that high-profile arrest…Trust me, Skip will be under intense media scrutiny. Which means huge stress. Not easy for anybody to handle."

She nodded. Then her moist eyes found mine.

"But you'll help me, right, Danny? I mean, I love Noah, but with stuff like this…Hell, he's practically useless. It's hard enough for him to keep *himself* from goin' off the deep end."

I assured her I'd do what I could. Then we hugged again.

"You gonna stay and eat? I can put together a table for the four of us, for later. Noah, me, you, and Skip."

"I'd love to, but I promised someone I'd check in on her tonight. She's been through quite an ordeal herself."

Charlene gave me a sad grin. "No rest for the weary, eh?"

"Something like that."

"You and me both, Danny."

Sighing heavily, she swept the sweat from her brow with a forearm. Then, hips-first, she pushed through the swinging doors, back into the kitchen.

Poor Charlene. Now she had both Noah *and* her brother to deal with. I didn't envy her the task.

Heading out the front door, I saw Noah engaged in what looked like a heated discussion with Skip at the bar. Meanwhile, impatient customers on either side of them were calling out drink orders. And, on the raised stage in another corner of the room, a quartet of musicians was tuning up. Loudly.

It was going to be a long, raucous night at Noah's Ark.

The sun's last rays had vanished as I drove toward Fox Chapel Borough, leaving an indigo tinge to the sky.

I realized that I probably should have taken Charlene up on her offer of a meal, because I was suddenly ravenous. No big mystery there, since I couldn't remember the last time I'd eaten. But I didn't like the idea of joining the Harlands for dinner, assuming they'd even ask me. If for no other reason that I didn't plan on staying long.

So I pulled into a drive-through place and got a couple over-cooked burgers and another cup of coffee. Just what I needed— more caffeine. Then I found an empty space in the restaurant's spacious lot and parked.

Two bites into the first burger, my cell rang.

"Danny? Sam Weiss here. Your favorite reporter."

"Let me guess. You want an interview."

"Sure do. And because of our long and intimate friendship, I expect it to be an exclusive. No selling your story to the *Enquirer* or Fox News."

"Jesus, Sam, give me a little credit."

"Just messing with you, man. But seriously, I hope I can count on an interview. This Sykes story is steamrolling, and I'm hearing a lot about how involved *you* are. I'd like to say I'm surprised, but given your weird track record with this kind of thing…"

"My involvement is probably being overblown, like it usually is. Which is why I've got to pass on the interview."

"Come on, Danny. You've done it before, remember?"

"Yeah, and I still have mixed feelings about it. The last thing I want to do is sign up for that circus again."

He grew silent for a moment.

"Okay, tell you what, Danny. You give me an exclusive interview, and I give you some inside dope that you might find interesting. Very inside, and very interesting. How does *that* sound, Mr. High and Mighty?"

"Sounds like bullshit, is how it sounds."

"Then let me whet your appetite. I have a source down at the district attorney's office. Real inside guy. I happen to have something on the poor *schmuck*—you don't need to know what—so he's always happy to give me stuff. Our deal is, he gives me enough good stuff and that messy thing I got hanging over him goes away."

"That really sucks, Sam."

"That's journalism in the big city, Danny. Besides, this is not some nice, upright citizen. By rights, given what he's done, he oughta be in jail. But he's so well connected downtown, he's of more service to the community as a snitch for me than as an inmate. Especially since the stories I do usually end up helping to bring bad guys to justice."

"Sounds like a rationalization to me."

"Of course it's a rationalization. But it's one I can live with. Now do you wanna hear what I've got or not?"

I threw the remains of my meal into the trash can beside my car, then peeled the lid off the scalding black coffee.

"Okay, I'm listening. What's it about, and why would I be interested?"

"Because it's about Ray Sykes. The guy you helped bring down. My inside guy says that Sykes' lawyer approached the DA to try to make a deal."

"A deal? No way Leland Sinclair would let Sykes take a lesser plea. Besides, what would he have to trade?"

"That's the beauty part. Sykes claims that he wasn't the one behind Donna Swanson's murder. And that neither was his trigger man, Max Griffin."

"Then who was?"

Sam chuckled. "Like Mr. Sykes, I expect to get something for my information. That prick wants his sentence reduced, plus the death penalty taken off the table. All *I* want is for my good friend the psychologist to give me an exclusive interview."

I was still struggling to take in what Sam had said.

"I can't believe Sinclair would go for it."

"Believe it, Danny boy. They're already talking to a judge about an arrest warrant. My guy says they still need to confirm a few details in Sykes' story, but…"

I took a long swallow of the burnt, bitter coffee. Making him wait a few more seconds for my answer. Though I already knew what it was going to be.

"Okay, Sam. You've got your exclusive. Now tell me what Sykes said…"

Chapter Forty-one

Trevor, Harland Industries' taciturn driver, followed my movements with suspicious eyes as I went up the broad steps to the front door of the residence. My knock was answered by Mike Payton, whose demeanor was more relaxed than I'd ever seen.

No wonder, I thought. Lisa Campbell had been safely returned, and Charles Harland was back at home, on his way to recovering from a stroke. Two crises averted, though he must have seen the same thing I had at the hospital. That his aged employer's days were numbered.

We shook hands at the door and he ushered me inside.

"Good to see you, Doc. They've got Mr. Harland all fitted up in his study. You wouldn't believe it. It's like a regular hospital room."

As he led me across the foyer and toward Harland's study, I noticed that nothing had changed in the house. Except for the comings and goings of a couple maids, plus some stiff-necked guy who looked like Hollywood's version of a butler. My guess was that, soon after their wedding, Lisa had selected him.

So, now that the kidnapping had come to an end, Payton had allowed the house to return to its usual workings. Staff going about their duties. I even heard Muzak piped into the hallways. Though my knowledge of classical music is pretty limited, it sounded like Vivaldi.

When we arrived at Harland's spacious study, I found that Payton hadn't been exaggerating. Much of the oversized, ornate furnishings had been removed from the room, to be replaced by a hospital bed and a range of beeping, multi-screened monitors. There were also IV stands, small tables laden with pill bottles, syringes, and other medical supplies, and in a far corner, what appeared to be a generator. Just in case, I supposed, the power to the house went out for some reason.

It was impressive, all right. I would've expected no less from Charles Harland. Though the whole setup made the lurid movie posters from Lisa's acting days, still hanging from the walls, seem even more incongruous.

"It's Dr. Rinaldi," Payton announced, taking a place near the wall-length glass window that opened onto the porch. "I answered the door myself."

"Why?" James Harland was lounging on a sofa that had been shoved into a corner. Wearing jeans, another designer-label sweater, and loafers without socks. "Are we expecting another kidnapper to show up?"

Payton ignored him, as did I. Instead, I headed across the room to greet Charles Harland. And Lisa.

Looking only a shade less cadaverous than he'd looked in the hospital, Harland lay under freshly pressed white sheets on the bed. In stark contrast, Lisa, in a chair beside him, was pink-cheeked and vibrant. Hair and makeup perfectly done, she wore her own designer-label outfit and low heels. Presenting the quintessential picture of a mature though still beautiful, always fashionable, wife of a very rich, very important man.

When I approached, the old man's hollow-eyed gaze shifted from the middle-aged nurse fussing with his IV drip to me.

"That's enough…" he murmured to the nurse. A flutter of his hand. "Now…go…away."

Embarrassed, the nurse ducked her head and scooted past me, even as Lisa rose to quickly clasp my hands in both of hers.

"Danny! Jesus, it's good to see your face. Charles and I were just talking about you."

Another hand-flutter from the sick man. "I told you…the reward, Doctor…Remember…we talked about a reward…"

"*You* talked about it, Mr. Harland. And again, it's not necessary."

He blinked a couple times, cracked lips slowly forming the words. "I…I decide what is necessary…and what is not…"

James laughed from across the room.

"See, Rinaldi? Same old stubborn bastard. I mean, you didn't think a little thing like a stroke would change him…?"

Lisa cut her eyes at Harland's son.

"C'mon, for once in your fucking life, play nice. Your father's still recuperating, for Christ's sake."

James hooked his thumb in the gold chain around his neck. Idly played with it.

"Another thing I'm getting sick of, Lisa. You and your gutter mouth. Is that something you picked up in Hollywood? Along with the clap, and Chlamydia, and God knows what?"

Standing next to Lisa, I felt the anger boil up in my throat. But before I could do or say anything, Payton strode over from the picture window to confront him.

"Listen, James, you lazy, good-for-nothing…"

Face flushed, James got to his feet and glared back at the family's head of security.

"Who the hell do you think you're talking to, Payton? No goddamn employee talks to a Harland that way."

But Payton stood his ground.

"And *you* don't get to talk to Lisa that way. If I could, I'd like to—"

"You'd like to *what*, Payton? I don't care how long you've worked here, you can be replaced. Shit, if Arthur Drake can be replaced, so can you!"

I'd heard enough from James. And had enough.

"Speaking of lawyers, *Jimmy*, you're going to be needing one of your own."

Lisa gave me a quizzical look as I began slowly moving around the foot of the bed and toward James.

His glance shifting from Payton to me, James said, "I don't know what you're talking about."

"By now, the DA's probably gotten a warrant for your arrest. Which means the cops ought to be here any minute."

The old man gasped, struggled to get up on his elbows. Hampered by the tangle of tubes going in and out.

"The police…? Here again…? Why?"

I answered by taking another step toward James.

"Because Ray Sykes just made a deal with the DA. I don't know all the details, but it looks like they're going to shave a lot of years off his sentence in exchange for his testimony—against you."

"For what?" Payton's anger subsiding into curiosity.

"For the murder of Donna Swanson. According to Sykes, James told him that she was blackmailing him. That she knew—"

Charles Harland struggled for the words. "Knew…what…?"

I turned to him. "James did something terrible to Lisa. Something he knew would hurt you. But somehow Donna found out about it. And saw her chance to make a lot of money…"

James laughed. "Donna was a dried-up, greedy old cow. She didn't care about Lisa *or* my old man. All she cared about was the money. So that she could live the rest of her life in ease, as she put it."

"That's when she threatened to tell your father what you'd done," I said. "And what you planned to do, at the anniversary gala. Unless you paid up."

Payton frowned. "What's this all about?"

But James looked right past him, eyes focused on me. "Donna wasn't stupid, I'll give her that. Turns out, she'd overheard me talking with Lisa in the library. Telling her about the surprise I planned for the gala. I guess that's when the light bulb went off in Donna's head."

Lisa and I exchanged looks. So that's how Donna Swanson had learned about the video. She'd eavesdropped on James and Lisa's conversation that morning after the assault.

James still glared at me. "And like I said, Donna wasn't stupid. She knew that if my old man found out what I was about to do, he'd put a stop to it. More important, he'd cut me off. Permanently. Vacate the trusts. Leave me out of the will. I'd have nothing. *Nothing!* Do you understand?"

Harland stirred, wincing in pain. "Donna…she did that?… she…blackmailed you…?"

"Yeah, Dad. Your loving, devoted nurse put the squeeze on me. I guess she was tired of dressing you and wiping your ass and listening to you bitch all day long. She wanted out."

I pressed him. "But there was no way you'd let her blackmail you. Be under her thumb for the rest of your life."

James leaned against the wall, his head just below one of Lisa's movie posters. Struggling to regain his composure.

"If you say so, Rinaldi…"

"Not me, James. Ray Sykes. He's going to testify that you showed up at the printing factory the day of Donna's death. That you told him you'd arranged for her to meet you there to discuss terms. Settle on the money."

Payton pulled reflectively on his lower lip. "So *that's* where she went that morning. When she left the residence without telling anyone where she was going."

"Yes," I said. "It was to meet secretly with James and seal the deal. At least, that's what *she* thought was going to happen. Right, James? You might as well tell us everything, because it looks like Sykes is going to. He'll have no trouble throwing you under the bus if it'll take a few years off his sentence."

James didn't respond, but instead glanced knowingly at each of us in turn around the room. Then gave a brief smile.

"What's so goddamn funny?" Lisa demanded.

"I just remembered where my passport is. Sounds like I'm gonna need it. Especially if the cops are on their way."

"Don't be a fool…" Harland croaked. "It's only…this Sykes person's word…against yours. Drake's firm…they have criminal lawyers, too…One of them can…"

"Shut up, you piece of shit!" James scowled. "Christ, why haven't you died yet? Do the world a big fucking favor…"

"How…how *dare* you?…Why, if Chuck were here…"

"Well, he isn't, is he? He OD'd, remember? Your Golden Boy shot garbage into his veins and—"

Lisa gasped. "For God's sake, James—!"

Payton whirled to face me. "Where the hell are the cops?"

"On their way. Paperwork takes time. And the DA is no fool. He knows he'd better have a damn good case if he's going to arrest a Harland for murder."

"It wasn't murder!" James bristled with sudden rage. "It was self-preservation. Get it? Donna was unreasonable. The way she talked, I knew she'd have her hooks in me forever."

Again, his gaze flitted from one of us to the other. But whatever he saw in our eyes only fueled his rising anger.

"Okay, you wanna know what happened? 'Cause there's not much to tell. When Donna got to the old factory, I took her into Sykes' office in the back. Griffin was there, too. Soon as we show up, Donna freaks out. Wanting to know who these guys were. I said, these are the guys who're gonna get me outta this jam. The guys that are gonna kill you."

I smiled coolly. "But I'm guessing Sykes hadn't gotten the memo. He refused."

"That lousy prick! After all the business I brought his way. All the high-rollers—"

"Like you and the three other Horsemen…"

"Hell, *dozens* of guys like that. The top one-percent of the one-percent. But that smug asshole Sykes wouldn't help me out. Said he didn't see the upside of him killing some old bitch he didn't even know."

James pointed his forefinger at me. His florid indignation fed by alcohol and hate.

"I screamed at him. Told him to order Griffin to shoot her. But Sykes wouldn't budge. So then *I* ordered the big creep to do it. Griffin just laughed at me. He said not unless his boss told him to."

I stepped closer to him. "That's when you took matters into your own hands—literally. According to Ray Sykes, you grabbed Griffin's gun out of his back pocket…"

"Yeah, I did. And I shot the bitch. One shot, back of her ugly head. Like in the movies. Now Sykes *had* to help me. Had to deal with her. She was bleeding all over his goddamn floor."

"Fucking hell…" Lisa's voice was a choked whisper.

Charles Harland stared at his son. "I…I can't believe what I'm hearing…You…you monster…"

James stared back. "Ha! Coming from *you*, that's hilarious. Truth is, Dad, I'm more like you than your precious Chuck ever was. He'd never have had the guts to do what I did."

"No," Payton said, "he was too much of a man. A real one."

"How would *you* know what a real man is, Payton?" James gave him a sardonic wink. "After letting poor Lisa get kidnapped on your watch?"

With a muttered curse, Payton suddenly lunged at him, fists coming up. But James was surprisingly quick, reaching smoothly for his side pocket. And pulling out a gun.

"Stay where you are, Payton. I mean it!"

I don't know much about guns, but it looked like a .38. Whatever it was, it was enough to stop Payton in his tracks.

I, too, froze where I stood. With his back still flush with the wall, James was too far away for me to risk some kind of move. Not any that I could see.

I vaguely remember the sound of Lisa crying out, as well as the staccato wheezing of her bedridden husband. But I was unwilling to look, to take my eyes off James Harland. Or his gun, pointed at us. Held in his smooth, manicured hand. Another incongruity in this large, incongruous room.

Recovering her poise, Lisa spoke sharply behind me. Her voice laced with bitter humor.

"I'll be damned. A trust fund kid holding a gun on his rich, rotten family. Fucking perfect. If *this* doesn't get me back in the tabloids, I don't know what will."

Chapter Forty-two

Taking a long, slow breath, I struggled to keep calm. And keep thinking.

"Well, James," I said evenly, "I guess once you'd shot Donna, you developed a taste for playing with guns."

He shrugged. "A guy can't be too careful nowadays. But you're right. After what happened at Sykes' place, I figured I oughta get one of my own. For personal protection."

I nodded. "Speaking of guns, the police have Griffin's piece from the tugboat. It'll have his prints on it, of course. Probably Agent Reese's, too. And Skip Hines'. And mine. But it wouldn't surprise me if at least a partial print of yours turns up. Nothing like forensic evidence to back up Sykes' eyewitness account."

James shook his head. "I'm not an idiot, Rinaldi. No way they can separate out all those prints. Not enough to make a match, anyway. I've seen *Law and Order*. I know how it works."

Again, that placid smile. "Besides, I don't plan on being around when they go to court."

"I figured that. After you mentioned your passport…"

"Lots of places for a man like me to settle down. To enjoy my usual pursuits, my simple…pleasures. With all the sun and sand a guy could want, and no extradition treaty with the U.S."

"Sounds like the same kind of plan Sykes had. I guess it's true, great minds think alike."

His brow darkened. "Don't lump me in with that common criminal. I don't give a damn that his family goes back to the

Mayflower, or how fancy he liked to talk. He was nothing but a lousy crook with delusions of grandeur."

"If you say so."

Abruptly, Mike Payton spoke up. The head of security's features once again calm, alert. Professional. As was his tone.

"But you never finished your story, James. What happened after you shot Donna?"

"Tell you the truth, Payton, I have no fucking idea. And I could care less. I just tossed Griffin's gun on a table and got the hell out of there. The last thing I heard was Sykes yelling to Max to get a big tarp or blanket to wrap up the body. Like I said, now she was Sykes' problem."

"That's what I don't get," Payton said. "How did Donna end up in that shack at the observatory? And why?"

"For what it's worth," I replied, "I've been thinking about that. And I have a theory."

James laughed, casually indicating me with the gun.

"Hear that, everybody? The Doc here has a theory. Love to hear it, Rinaldi. But make it short. I feel an urge to flee the country, and you know what that's like. When you gotta go, you gotta go."

"Don't worry, I'll keep it simple." I paused. "I could be wrong, but a man with Sykes' intellect usually sees a problem as a potential opportunity. Which is how I think he saw Donna's dead body. There it was, now wrapped in a canvas bag. All he had to do was tell Griffin to dispose of it. Throw it into a dumpster, or drive out to the woods somewhere and bury it. But that's not what he did."

"Why not?" said Payton.

"Because Sykes was about to have Griffin kidnap Lisa, after which he'd call Charles Harland and warn him against notifying the police. Then, when we were all here in the study, and he picked me to deliver the ransom, he gave explicit instructions that I was to come alone. No cops, no Feds."

"So?"

"Mike, you know as well as I do that the police usually ignore those instructions from kidnappers. They put a wire on the person delivering the ransom, or else have people watching the exchange from a safe distance. Ready to move in at a moment's notice."

"And you figure Sykes knew that?"

"I'm sure he at least suspected it. And he wanted to be ready. Plus he probably realized that if he was right, it gave him an opportunity to get even more money out of Charles Harland. Another five million.

"So he had Griffin take Donna's body, still wrapped in the canvas bag, up to that shack at the observatory. Sykes even pre-recorded a message, expressing his anger at the fact that the police had ignored his command to stay out of it. And demanding that, as a result of their actions, he'd now need another five million dollars in exchange for Lisa's freedom."

Payton grimaced. "A promise he never intended to honor."

"I'm afraid not."

I turned back to James Harland, who'd listened to me with a kind of bored bemusement.

"See, James? By killing Donna Swanson, you gave Sykes the chance to double his money. To turn Lisa's kidnapping into an even bigger score."

"That's me, Rinaldi. Always glad to help out."

Lisa hissed at him. "You don't have to be so goddamn cheery, you sick bastard. I mean, shit, don't let us keep you. Why don't you take your little gun and get the hell outta here?"

He smirked. "I have to tell you, Lisa, there's a lotta things I expect to miss when I'm gone. But you're not one of them. Fact is, I'm kinda looking forward to it. Though not as much as I look forward to never seeing my old man again. Never even hearing about him. 'Til I read his fucking obituary."

Charles Harland stirred in his bed, but seemed suddenly too weak, or else too medicated, to speak. Unless it was something else. Because, to my eyes, it looked as though the old man had just given up. Or given in. He lay there, this industrial giant, this lauded billionaire, wheezing helplessly. Blinking up at the ceiling. Defeated.

Lisa must have noticed it, too. She took a plastic cup of water from a bedside table, put it to her husband's lips. But he didn't drink. Or even acknowledge her.

I watched her, wondering what she must be thinking at this moment. And feeling. Her longed-for release from Charles was imminent. Yet she'd just offered him water. A token gesture? I wasn't sure. Maybe she wasn't, either.

Finally, at a loss, she put the drink in Charles' limp hand on the bed. Gently curling his fingers around the cup. So that, if need be, he could bring it to his lips.

Lisa straightened. "I think we should call his doctor."

"Where is he?" I said.

"At dinner in town," Payton answered. "He said Charles was stable, but that we should call him if there was any change. I think we should at least get that nurse back in here. Now."

He started to leave the room, but James stopped him with a look. And the gun, its nose aimed straight at Payton's gut. James' finger lightly tapping the trigger.

"No, no, Payton. You stay where you are."

Then he peered over at Lisa, who stood stiffly at her husband's bedside. James let out an aggrieved sigh.

"Aw, hell, everything's turned to shit. I gotta get going, get on a company jet before the cops alert airport security."

He started moving sideways, back still close to the wall, toward the opened door. Swinging his gun in a waist-high arc, keeping us all at bay.

Then, abruptly, he stopped. And headed back across the room toward Lisa. A smile slowly creasing his face.

"Guess you won't be the main attraction at the gala, after all. Though I would've loved to see the look on the old man's face when he saw that video. Along with all his rich, important friends. Jesus, I've been looking forward to that."

"What video?" Payton looked helplessly at me. "I don't understand…"

James merely chuckled, sidling closer to Lisa. As though he couldn't stop himself. Eyes glittering with malice.

"But don't worry, Lisa. People will see it. *Everyone* will see it. What we did to you. The Four Horsemen. I mean, what the fuck else is the Internet for? Nothing'll go viral faster than a rich bitch getting gang-banged. A Hollywood has-been, naked, screaming, getting it from every direction. Begging for mercy. Being made to…"

By now, James had reached his father's bedside, directly opposite where Lisa stood. He risked a glance at the old man.

"Maybe he'll live to see it, maybe he won't. But, I swear, every other person in the goddamn world is going to. Hell, I bet more guys'll shoot their load watching you get fucked over and over than—"

That's when it happened. Though all so fast, so suddenly—

With a strangled cry of pain, Lisa threw herself across the bed at James. At the same time, I advanced on him from one side, while Payton came rushing toward him from the other.

Startled by Lisa's enraged lunge at him, James stumbled backwards.

That's when the gun went off.

Lisa screamed, grabbing her shoulder, and collapsed on top of her husband's body.

Righting himself, James raised the gun again, pointing it down at her head. His face a mask of murderous fury.

"Fucking cunt!" he shouted.

He fired again, but not before Mike Payton could jump in front of him. Taking two bullets in the stomach.

Payton hit the floor, gasping. Rolling over on his back.

I stood right above him, not more than two feet separating me from James Harland. His gun pointed now at my chest.

"Get back, Rinaldi. Or I swear to Christ—"

Lisa gave a low moan, and slowly heaved herself up from the hospital bed. Gripping the bed rails, she stood on shaking legs. Blood seeped from the wound in her shoulder.

Just then, the nurse came hurrying into the room. "I thought I heard gunshots, and—"

She froze, hands to her mouth. And screamed.

"Shut the fuck up!" James showed her his gun.

The woman took two steps, then fainted. Falling awkwardly to the floor.

Keeping the muzzle pointed at me, James leered at Lisa.

"You know, honey, I don't think I mind if your global embarrassment is posthumous. 'Cause it felt real good shooting you just now. Even better than fucking you on camera. So after I whack Rinaldi here, I'm gonna put another bullet in *you*. In your pretty head, this time."

He turned his attention back to me. Raised his gun.

"So say good-bye to the good doctor, Lisa. Therapy's about to be terminated."

I had no choice. If I was going to go for his gun, it'd have to be now. It'd have to be—

Suddenly, Charles Harland's hand moved on the bed. Fingers still gripping the plastic cup, he raised his arm up, flinging the water at his son. Right into his face.

Caught off guard, James looked away, blinking. Distracted, but only momentarily.

Which was all the time I needed. I crossed the distance between us in two quick strides and delivered one goddamn sweet right cross. Like when I was a kid in Golden Gloves. Only backed by more intent, more justification.

And a helluva lot more rage.

James' head snapped hard to the side, the gun flying out of his hand. And then, already unconscious, he fell backwards. His body thumping as it collapsed on the floor.

I stood there, quivering. Adrenaline surging like rushing lava through every vein.

Soon, I knew, the hand I'd hit him with would start throbbing. Without the protection of training tape and a thick glove, punching someone usually did as much damage to the guy who threw the punch as to the guy who caught it.

From the pulsing I already felt in my hand, I knew I'd probably strained it.

But, Christ, it was worth it.

"Danny…"

Lisa's breathless voice drew my eyes. Standing as before at the side of the bed, holding her bleeding shoulder.

"You all right?" I asked her.

"I'll live. Unfortunately."

"So will I. Thanks to Charles."

I glanced down at the old man, whose thin fingers still clasped the plastic cup. It trembled in his hand.

"Yeah." Despite her pain, Lisa managed a wry smile. "The old bastard came through. Ain't that a kick in the pants?"

If her husband registered anything we'd said, he gave no indication. Merely closed his tired, rheumy eyes.

"But what about Mike?" she asked anxiously.

"I know. The nurse is useless. Get on a phone and call for an ambulance. For you *and* Payton. Then get a hold of Charles' doctor. Dinner break's over."

She nodded and moved slowly but steadily toward a phone on the other side of the room. I bent to tend to Payton, fearing that the only one who'd be riding in an ambulance was Lisa. For Mike, it was probably too late.

The security man was bleeding profusely from his stomach wounds. I peeled off my jacket and pressed the fabric against the insistent ooze of blood, but to little effect.

I shifted position, gazed down at his pain-flecked eyes.

"James…" He struggled to form the word.

"He's down, Mike. We got him."

He blinked rapidly, as though willing himself to understand the meaning of my words.

Suddenly, I heard a low groan behind me. I turned on my haunches. It was James Harland, stirring slightly. A gurgling noise in his throat.

Quickly, I went over to where he lay. Crouched down. He was still unconscious, his movements involuntary. As were his moans. Like a child sleeping fitfully. In many ways, I realized, an unfortunately apt description.

Then I noticed something else.

The loop of gold chain he invariably wore had been flung free, no longer tucked inside his sweater. The pendant whose vague outline I'd seen earlier now lay exposed on his chest.

Except that it wasn't a pendant.

Of course, I thought. No wonder Lisa had been unable to find it, despite rummaging through James' room, his office, even his car. He'd keep something that valuable, that important to him, on his person. Always. He'd never want it out of his sight.

I scooped it up. No, it wasn't a pendant.

It was a flash-drive. Containing the one and only copy of the video made of Lisa's assault.

"Lisa…" I called over to her.

She was just hanging up the phone. Wincing from her wound, she came over and stared flatly down at James.

"Gimme some good news. Did you kill the bastard?"

"No, he's just out. But I do have some good news."

I tossed her the flash-drive. At first, she stared at it in her hand with incomprehension. Then her eyes widened.

"Holy shit, is this…?"

"It sure is. James had it with him the whole time. Now if I were you, I'd destroy that horrible thing. Burn it, smash it, throw it down the mouth of a volcano. Whatever."

"Don't worry, Danny. I'll think of something."

She encircled the flash-drive in her fingers, then held her fist to her chest. Her eyes filled with tears.

I got to my feet, gave her good arm a squeeze, and hurried back over to Payton.

"Ambulance is on the way, Danny," she called after me.

"And I'm available, too."

It was the nurse, rousing herself as she awkwardly rose from the floor. She straightened her clothes and carefully stepped toward Charles Harland's bedside.

"Sorry I fainted, Mrs. Harland," she said to Lisa. Though she didn't look that sorry. Mostly perturbed. "This kind of thing isn't what I'm used to."

Lisa frowned. "Who the fuck is?"

I knelt once more by Payton's side. His face had lost its color. And the light in his eyes was fading.

"Forget Harland, nurse." My voice tight. "We have a man with gunshot wounds here."

She looked ill. "I'm not bonded for anything like that, mister. You need to call a doctor."

Then she turned back to her patient, adjusting the old man's tubes, fussing with his sheets. While Lisa, leaning unsteadily against the bed rails, peered nervously across the room at Payton and me.

Hurriedly, I tried again to staunch the blood spreading across his torso. Folding my jacket into a thick wad.

"Forget it," he said haltingly. "I'm done...."

"Look, Mike, the ambulance is coming and—"

Then, surprisingly, he reached up and gripped the collar of my shirt. Pulled my face down, inches from his.

"Listen, Doc..." He coughed, a spittle of blood dotting his lips. "Remember when I said I wanted to talk with you...that I had something to tell you...?"

"Sure, Mike. I remember. But don't try now to say—"

"I need you to know...about your dossier..."

"My dossier? You mean the one that Lisa asked you to put together, about me?"

He nodded slowly, painfully.

"Look, Mike, we don't have to talk about that now...."

"Yes...we do. You need to get a copy..."

Another cough, threaded with phlegm.

"Everything's in there...including the police report on the mugging...You and your wife Barbara...years ago, when that thief shot her...killed her..."

I felt a dryness in my throat as I strained to hear him. His voice growing weaker by the second.

"What, Mike?" I tried to keep my own voice calm. "What about the mugging?"

He licked his cracked, blood-spattered lips.

"The cops…they missed stuff…it wasn't a mugging…I think your wife…she was the target all along. I think she was murdered…."

"Murdered?" A whisper, almost softer than his own.

But there was no answer. His mouth had gone slack.

"Mike? Mike?" I leaned lower, my ear to his lips.

I no longer felt breath.

My mind was a chaotic jumble of thoughts and feelings, a roiling cauldron of emotion. As though the floor had opened up beneath me. As if I were falling through a void…tumbling and tumbling…

Forcing myself to focus, I quickly felt for Payton's pulse. Nothing. Checked his breath again. And, again, nothing.

Mike Payton was dead.

Sam Weiss' source in the district attorney's office had been right. I'd no sooner closed Mike Payton's lifeless eyes and slowly risen to my feet than the butler—if that's what the guy was—appeared in the doorway.

After giving the room, and what had obviously gone on inside it, a horrified look, he recovered himself enough to speak to Lisa. As formally as he could muster.

"The police are at the door, Mrs. Harland. They insist on being let in."

"Then let them in, Davis, for Christ's sake."

"Very good, madam."

"And by the way, Davis, where the hell have you been? Any of you? You must have heard the fucking gunshots."

"Yes we did. We all hid in the library, with the door securely locked. It seemed the only prudent thing to do."

She waved him away, and Davis strode quietly from the room.

"Can you *believe* that shit?" she said, coming over to where I stood. "I swear, I'm gonna fire their asses. The whole fucking staff—"

With a horrified gasp, Lisa froze, her hand over her mouth. Looking down at Payton's body.

"Oh, God, no…He isn't…?"

"I'm afraid so, Lisa. I'm sorry."

"He saved my life," she whispered, stricken. "Mike took those bullets meant for me."

I nodded. Then, sensing she was about to falter, I put my arm around her waist. For a brief moment, she let herself lean in against me.

Until, favoring her injured arm, she righted herself again. Though something about my silence, my own stricken look, made her uncomfortable.

"Are *you* okay, Danny?" Her voice choked, thick with tears. "I mean, of course you're not okay, *nothing's* okay…Not with Mike and…everything. But is there something else going on?"

I mutely shook my head.

Then there was a stir of loud, authoritative voices. Men and women coming down the hall just outside the room.

I had to pull myself together. At least for now.

Later, when I could think…

When I could get my hands on a copy of that damned dossier and see for myself if what Payton had said was true…

Then, and only then, I could let myself feel the impact of his words. The urgent last words of a dying man.

But not now.

Giving Lisa a brief, reassuring smile, I turned to the opened door and waited to greet the police.

Chapter Forty-three

There are limits to power and privilege. Even money.

During the next forty-eight hours, pretty much the whole story came out. Lisa's kidnapping by Sykes, the murder of Arthur Drake by Sykes' man Griffin, the death of Mike Payton at the hands of James Harland.

Though subsequent reports also named James as the killer of Donna Swanson, her murder held less fascination for the media. As always, it was the aberrant lifestyles of the rich and famous, and the lurid consequences of those lifestyles, that fascinated a bored, restless public.

Still, as Lisa was only too happy to inform me when we talked by phone on Wednesday evening, no details of her assault by James and his fellow Horsemen would ever emerge.

"God knows, none of those four pricks are going to mention it. And even if James does decide to brag about it, he has no proof. That goddamn video is gone for good."

"You destroyed it? How?"

"I took your advice, Danny. I burned it, crushed it, and threw it down the mouth of a volcano."

I laughed. "Well, whatever you did, sounds like it's finally out of your life. Behind you."

"Yeah. Now the only excuse I have for offing myself is boredom. And cellulite."

I was standing out on my rear deck, Rolling Rock in hand, watching the sun set on the Three Rivers. It had been a long, hard day at the office, seeing a number of vulnerable, deeply troubled patients. Including that one man who'd refused to miss his usual Wednesday appointment. When I saw him today, I congratulated him on his adamant self-care.

After I got home, and fixed a typical single guy's dinner of microwaved meatloaf and a beer, I'd returned a number of calls. One was to Sam Weiss, to arrange a date and time for my promised exclusive interview. Another was to Harry Polk, to arrange a different date and time to give my final statement in the Harland case.

I also talked to ADA Dave Parnelli, who assured me that Sykes' threatened lawsuit against me was a non-starter. In fact, dropping the suit was one of the conditions of his plea deal with the district attorney.

"Wow," I said. "I didn't know the DA cared."

"About *you*? Trust me, Danny, he doesn't. But what he and Chief Logan *do* care about is a lawsuit that might embarrass the Department. They don't want the public to think they sanction the reckless actions of a civilian who's on the police payroll."

Whatever, I thought. Relieved that there was one less thing I had to worry about.

Finally, I checked in with Noah and Charlene.

"Hey, Danny, good to hear from you," he said. "Every time I leave a message for you, I'm always afraid you'll be too dead to call me back. Dead as in fuckin' *dead*, if you get my drift."

"Never fear, I'm still alive and kicking."

"Cool. 'Cause you still have a bar tab that needs lookin' into… Uh, wait a minute. Charlene wants to talk to you."

I heard him grumble as he handed the phone to Charlene.

"How's Noah doing, Char?"

"Gettin' better, I think. Though with him, it's not easy to tell. But at least he's stopped insulting the customers."

"That's a start, anyway."

"Listen, Danny. I wanna thank you again for saving Skip's ass. And I did like we discussed. I started talkin' to him about getting into a program. Like AA or somethin'."

"Good, Charlene. Give him my best, will you?"

"I will. But you'll still hang out with him once in a while, right? I mean, go to a ball game or whatever."

"Least I can do."

◇◇◇

I'd saved the last call for Lisa. Now, having assured me that she'd destroyed the flash-drive, we talked about the upcoming Sykes trial, should there be one. And her concerns about having to testify. Though from what I'd heard through the Department's rumor mill, and from what Sam had said, I doubted if Raymond Sykes would ever set foot inside a courtroom. He would get his deal, DA Leland Sinclair would get his conviction, and all would be right with the world.

Which left Lisa and me free to discuss other matters.

"I have to ask, Lisa. How are you holding up since Mike Payton's death?"

"All right, I guess. I don't think it's really sunk in yet. Not just about what happened to him, but...I mean, I cared about him a lot when we were together. Now I'm starting to think it meant more to him than I thought. More to him...than it did to me. Does that mean I've been right all along, and I really *am* a shitty person?"

"You know better than that. I don't think we choose to fall in love with someone. Just as we don't choose *not* to."

"Easy for you to say, Doc."

"Maybe not. You'd be surprised."

"Anyway, I know I'm gonna feel bad about him for a long time. But maybe that's okay, too."

"It just means you're human, Lisa. Like the rest of us."

Her breath quickened. She was eager to change the subject. "Hey, speaking of surprises, guess who called me? My daughter Gail, out in L.A. She saw the story about my kidnapping on the national news."

"She was probably worried about you."

"Bullshit. She wanted to make sure I'm still well enough to keep sending them checks. But at least she called. Hell, that's something, right?"

Finally, I got around to asking her the one question she'd most wanted to avoid.

"So, Lisa, how's your husband?"

"Not great, but not dead. Which pretty much describes Charles *before* the stroke. They got him pumped full of tranks, but I think he knows that James is under arrest."

"But does he know about the video? Did he hear James talking about it?"

A heavy sigh. "Who the fuck knows? Maybe James'll tell him about it someday. Or it'll come out if there's a trial. Though the lawyer we got from Arthur Drake's firm says there won't even *be* a trial. James will cop a plea, and that'll be that."

"Just like Sykes. Two of a kind, despite what James said."

"Yeah, twin pieces o' shit. Anyway, if James tells his father about the gang-rape, and Charles somehow blames me for it, I guess I'll be shown the door. But I can live with that. *I* can get lawyers, too. Probably end up with *some* kinda settlement, right? I mean, if there's one thing Charles Harland hates, it's bad publicity. And nothing says 'bad publicity' like a messy divorce."

"I noticed you said you could live with it, Lisa. And I don't think you're just referring to a divorce. Right?"

"What are you implying, Dr. Rinaldi?"

"I'm suggesting that maybe your suicidal impulses have lessened. That you've found that, in spite of everything that's happened to you, you have the inner resources to handle life. That you can cope."

She made her voice breathy, a little girl's. "Gosh, Doctor, do you really think so?"

"Come on, give me a break. And think about what I said."

"If you mean that you and I still have a verbal contract, and that I can't kill myself without calling you first, then I agree. But that's as far as I'll go."

"We still have an appointment on the books, right?"

"I'll have to check my calendar. Unless I'm getting a mani-pedi, I guess I can make it."

"Great. See you then."

And I did. In fact, I still do.

◇◇◇

The city below me was cloaked with a heavy, opulent darkness. As predicted, the wind had ceased, and gray edifices of clouds had begun to form in the sky.

I sat on the sofa in my front room, the only illumination coming from my tableside lamp. I was on my second Jack Daniels, facing a thick stack of folders on my lap. All held together by a three-ring binder.

It was a copy of the dossier that Mike Payton had prepared on me. I'd called Harry Polk earlier that day, and, in exchange for the promise of a steak dinner on me, got him to send Jerry Banks over to Payton's office. As a murder victim, his personal and professional effects were of interest to the police.

CSU techs were swarming all over the room when Banks got there, but he was able to cajole or threaten one of them into making a Xerox of the dossier. They'd found it in a steel file cabinet, along with numerous files relating to the Harlands.

Now, sipping my whiskey, I found myself unable to open it. The weighty stack of college diplomas, police reports, birth certificates and other documents asserting that I'd had a life—and that a good part of it had been shared with the former Barbara Camden, PhD—seemed suddenly too intimidating to examine. Too laden with memories, both good and bad.

And, if Mike Payton was right, too fraught with stunning, unbelievable revelations.

I swallowed the rest of my drink and reached for the bottle beside me. Refilled the glass. I was just about to taste it when I paused. Then carefully lay the glass on the table beside me.

Positioning the dossier more firmly on my lap, I turned to the first page and began to read…

To receive a free catalog of Poisoned Pen Press titles, please contact us in one of the following ways:

Phone: 1-800-421-3976
Facsimile: 1-480-949-1707
Email: info@poisonedpenpress.com
Website: www.poisonedpenpress.com

Poisoned Pen Press
6962 E. First Ave. Ste 103
Scottsdale, AZ 85251